This well-researched, well-documented, and timely book SHOULD STIR PARENTS AND HONEST EDUCATORS to put a stop to a VERY DISTURBING TREND in public school curricula. It gives A GOOD ANALYSIS AND PRACTICAL ADVICE to parents who don't want the minds of their children to be molded by liberal and New Age social engineers.

> —Phyllis Schlafly
> President of Eagle Forum

The work of John Ankerberg, John Weldon, and Craig Branch is OUTSTANDING. I highly recommend their *Thieves of Innocence* FOR ALL PARENTS concerned with the INFLUENCE of the NEW AGE MOVEMENT and related subjects IN OUR SCHOOLS.

> —Paul C. Vitz, Ph.D.
> Professor of Psychology
> New York University

If ever a HANDBOOK FOR PARENTS was a TIMELY IDEA, *Thieves of Innocence* would be at the top of the list. This WAKE-UP CALL against the insidious influence of the New Age Movement upon our children in the classrooms of America should be A WEAPON in the MORAL ARSENAL of every home.

> —D. James Kennedy, Ph.D.
> Senior Minister
> Coral Ridge Presbyterian
> Church

Thieves of Innocence

This book ably and FRIGHTENINGLY DEMON-STRATES that the CURE that our educational establishment has prescribed for the WOES of our SCHOOLS is WORSE than the disease. I firmly believe that *Thieves of Innocence* is MUST READING for every parent, teacher, and taxpayer. NO LONGER CAN IT BE SAID THAT IGNORANCE IS BLISS.

—George Grant
Well-known author, social commentator and popular speaker

PARENTS will find this EYE-OPENING book to be an extremely VALUABLE resource. It is the MOST INFORMATIVE book I have seen on the subject of New Age incursions into public schools.

—William Kilpatrick, Ph.D.
Associate Professor, Boston College
Author, *Why Johnny Can't Tell Right from Wrong* and *Psychological Seduction*

Thieves of Innocence

Thieves of Innocence

JOHN ANKERBERG
WITH JOHN WELDON
& CRAIG BRANCH

HARVEST HOUSE PUBLISHERS
Eugene, Oregon 97402

Chapter 12 was excerpted from *SCP Journal*, Fall 1992.

Chapter 14 was excerpted from *SCP Journal*, Fall 1992.

Chapter 15 was excerpted from Dr. William Coulson's article in *Adolescent Counselor* (Sep. 1991).

THIEVES OF INNOCENCE

Copyright © 1993 by John Ankerberg, Craig Branch,
   and John Weldon
Published by Harvest House Publishers
Eugene, Oregon 97402

Library of Congress Cataloging-in-Publication Data

Ankerberg, John, 1945–
     Thieves of innocence / John Ankerberg, Craig Branch, John Weldon.
     ISBN 1-56507-116-6
     1. Occultism—Controversial literature. 2. New Age movement—Controversial literature. 3. Education—United States—Curricula. I. Branch, Craig. II. Weldon, John. III. Title.
BF1042.A548   1993
375'.00973—dc20   92-44140
                                                      CIP

CONTENTS

PART 3
Important Articles

AN IMPORTANT WORD
TO THE READER

A 1992 U.S. Department of Education press release observed the following: "In spite of the increased investment in education spending by all levels of government in recent years, there has been no corresponding improvement in student achievement."[1] For example, in 1960 we spent $16 billion per year on education and our schools were the envy of the world. In 1990 we spent $200 billion and our schools are among the worst of the industrialized nations. Throwing more money at schools clearly doesn't seem to be the solution. But something has certainly changed the quality of children's education in the last 30 years.

What has changed? In *The Devaluing of America*, former Secretary of Education William J. Bennett argues that the inferiority of American public school education is partly a result of our modern scorn for the public expression of religious values and our abandonment of morality. In the last 30 years we have turned our schools into secularist institutions which have demeaned the very principles which work in society's best interests. Thus today,

> The extreme to which educators go to deny the place of religion in American life is mind-boggling. ... [Yet] we cannot deny in our public schools that from the Judeo-Christian tradition come our values, our principles, and the spirit of our institutions. That tradition and the American traditions are wedded. When we have disdain for our religious tradition, we have disdain for ourselves.[2]

But to abandon the values and principles of the past is to leave empty that which was once occupied. What has replaced traditional American principles? Almost anything, and in large measure this explains the direction (and problem) of education in our nation today. This also explains why many parents are surprised when they discover what their children are being exposed to in public schools. This information might have to do with an explicit sex education that assumes children will be sexually active, the teaching of decision-making skills based on false premises, the teaching of origins in a lopsided manner, New Age practices and premises in certain programs or curricula, and a variety of other issues.

In the end, classroom education will often reflect the values of the culture simply because it can do little else.

This is why it is important for parents to be reminded that they are responsible for the education of their children. They may elect to delegate part of that educational process to others, such as the public school system, but parents must not abdicate that responsibility. Statistics reveal that 90 percent of all children from Christian homes are still attending public schools. Therefore, we feel that it is time for widespread attention to how these concerned parents can make a difference in the education of their children.

This book takes a critical look at certain trends in education as they relate to particular religious, psychological, moral, or scientific issues. Our basic concern is to evaluate two key trends which may be termed the *transpersonal* ("beyond the person") and *humanistic* approaches to education. The transpersonal method is also known as New Age education and employs various Eastern/occult beliefs and techniques to allegedly help children develop their "full potential." The humanistic trend incorporates a secular and/or psychological approach which stresses 1) values clarification (or an allegedly morally neutral approach toward helping children develop their own values independently), 2) the importance of fostering a child's self-esteem, and 3) the use of various psychotherapeutic techniques (such as those incorporated in affective education) or hypnotic methods.

But the fact that transpersonal education is religious and humanistic education is secular does not at all mean these approaches operate independently of one another. What we find is a significant degree of overlap so that transpersonal and humanistic approaches are often used together (see chapter 5). The question is whether or not either approach is in the best interests of our children.

We recognize that some people will disagree with our perspective. Different worldviews will, of course, lead to different conclusions. For example, many parents and schools have enjoyed positive results (or at least what seem to be positive results), with programs like Pumsy, DUSO (Developing Understanding of Self and Others), Quest International, DARE (Drug Abuse Resistance Education), and various affective, "values clarification" approaches. Other schools believe that visualization, self-esteem, and meditation practices have also been helpful to their students.

Schools, in general, and teachers, in particular, want the best for their students. So do we. We have no quarrel with any educational method established to be both effective and safe (free from unexpected consequences which may harm a child emotionally or in other ways). But we are not at all certain that initially positive reports answer all the questions that can be raised over what, in many cases, can only be labeled as experimental programs. A student may indeed be helped by a particular aspect of a particular program. But are we looking at only temporary results and ignoring the larger issues that should also be examined? This is why we think it important to offer this preliminary critique which attempts to raise additional issues and examine a larger perspective.

For example, by opening children to certain New Age methods, beliefs, and techniques, what else are we teaching them about how to live their lives? How do we best evaluate these "new" methods? Practices like meditation and imagery may be good or bad depending on a number of factors, including the premises, content, context, and goals of the program. Altered states of consciousness may be mild, moderate, or severe and may have different outcomes depending on the degree of mental change produced. The worldview and purpose of the teacher are also relevant to the end results of a given program. Thus, whatever programs are looked at critically must also be looked at carefully to be certain that, to the best of our ability, we are accurately addressing the real issues. In the area of nontraditional education (what are called humanistic and transpersonal approaches), we grant that this may sometimes be problematic. Nevertheless, our basic concern is that programs and methods which may not be in the student's best interest be examined critically by all concerned. And if we have not answered all the questions, we hope we have at least raised issues that should be considered.

9

For parents, it is important to remember that effective influence begins with accurate information. Concerned parents should make every effort to become informed about what is really going on in public schools. This may necessitate active participation in the PTA, attending school board meetings that are open to the public, and remaining aware of your child's experience and activity in school through perusal of his textbooks, homework assignments, and the general character and content of the classroom presentation and discussion. It may also be important to become acquainted with those who are members of the board of education and get to know your child's teachers and principal. What are their qualifications? What are their backgrounds? Have they made statements that would indicate what their personal philosophies are? What do they see as the role and function of education?

Further, what is the history and worldview/mind-set of the school system itself? What about other unconventional educational methods that may comprise unadvertised aspects of a school's philosophy? For example, the Montessori method or the occult-oriented Waldorf schools have a unique set of educational presuppositions and methods that radically condition their educational approach (see appendixes A and B).

Introduce yourself to school board members, teachers, and the principal. Let them know who you are. Acquaint them with your concerns. Do everything you can to establish good rapport. For example, unless relevant, don't approach secular school officials on religious grounds; evaluate each controversial curriculum on its own merits. Don't harshly confront school officials. Generally, they are also seeking the best interest of your child and deserve the respect and appreciation due them. A quiet, reasoned approach that is nonconfrontational is best. When those in the school system get to know you personally and witness your continuing concerns and active involvement, that will not only extend your influence, but will also be a personal encouragement to them. Thus, always approach school officials with the attitude that this is a cooperative effort between parents and school administrators to improve the quality of the school and of children's education. Indeed, there is nothing as refreshing as an informed, concerned parent who has something of substance to offer when a school or board is facing a challenge.

Finally, where you do find programs, teachers, resources, or other features of the educational system which are good, be certain to express your approval. This can be done in many ways from writing letters of commendation or thank-you letters to all involved. In essence, your best support for the school system should include a continuing active interest in your child's daily education.[3]

Note: Before beginning this book, readers may wish to familiarize themselves with the terms in the glossary (page 311) for future reference.

P A R T

The Issues

O N E

AN INTRODUCTION TO THE ISSUES

> A generation in love with Tolkien's fantasy and
> Castaneda's sorcery are ready for magic in them-
> selves and in their young children.
>
> —Marilyn Ferguson,
> *The Aquarian Conspiracy*

> You can only have a new society... if you change
> the education of the younger people.
>
> —Marilyn Ferguson,
> *The Aquarian Conspiracy*

"What did you do in school today?" used to be asked
without fear. But today many parents are surprised to find out
what is going on in both public and many private schools.

Parents who aren't hearing unusual answers should not
necessarily feel secure, because some children are told not to
tell their parents what they are doing.[1]

In November of 1988 we received a letter from a couple
involved in researching a program used in elementary schools
in Florida and other states. This program utilized tapes called
"Quieting Reflex and Success Imagery." A mother had told
this couple that her little girl had contacted an inner guide
through the hypnotic techniques used in this program. The
daughter commented, "My 'wise person' told me not to pray
in the name of Jesus anymore." Further, this "wise person"
was not the guide that the little girl had chosen for herself but

rather someone that had appeared unexpectedly and spontaneously in her consciousness. It claimed that it resided in the corner of a "safe place" in her mind. But it proceeded to command her to do "mean and nasty things." The mother was distraught and had no idea what to do.

Perhaps you saw the "Oprah Winfrey Show" when she had Shirley MacLaine as her guest, explaining her spiritual journey into the New Age Movement and Eastern mysticism. Oprah asked Shirley, "What question were you asking yourself, that needed answers?"

Shirley responded with, "Who am I, where am I going, what is life all about, where do I go when I die?"

Oprah urged on, "And when you asked the questions, how did the answers come?"

Shirley smiled and said, "Well, first I had to learn how to meditate. I had to be very quiet, to be still—and then *boom*, the answers would come to me." And the answers are coming to little schoolchildren as well.

Standard induction techniques of meditation or hypnosis, commonly called progressive relaxation and guided imagery or visualization, are being imposed on our young children all over the country. Why does it matter? In this book we will tell you why.

According to Melton's *New Age Encyclopedia* some 300 colleges and educational institutions (over 75 are accredited or state-approved) now offer programs or even degrees on New Age topics.[2] This has influenced many educators who have proceeded to introduce these topics into their schools.

Brooks Alexander, noted authority on New Age philosophy, observes why the New Age has targeted education:

> In the ideological contest for cultural supremacy, public education is *the* prime target; it influences the most people in the most pervasive way at the most impressionable age. No other social institution has anything close to the same potential for mass indoctrination.[3]

Children especially are targeted because most New Agers (such as prominent educator Jack Canfield) believe that the innate innocence and sensitivity of children render them much closer to the influences of the spiritual world—such as the spirits who reside there. These are the very spirits who seek to help direct the course of human evolution into a New Age of peace and prosperity. By reaching children *before* they have been "corrupted" by Western culture and Christian values, New Agers hope they can educate an entire generation to the spiritual values of New Age philosophy. In other words, if children can be indoctrinated in New Age techniques and beliefs, as adults they will become powerful agents of change, helping to move society toward a new era of global harmony.

How did those of a New Age or transpersonal perspective manage to slip their ideas into the public school curricula? In part, they have been effective because they have often arranged their beliefs under the disguise of neutral, academic, psychological, or scientific-sounding terminology. If parents want to protect their children in the public schools, they should become familiar with the new terminology used by these educators. For example, "transpersonal psychology" sounds pretty impressive. So does adjusting one's "left brain/right brain" equilibrium. What could be wrong with such a harmless-sounding concept as "guided imagery" or "centering"? And who would think that "human potential" or imaginary "inner guides" might be capable of leading to a more sinister reality?

In some ways transpersonal and humanistic education are still in their infancy, but their influence is growing. The reason is simple. We now live in a culture in which tens of millions of people have rejected traditional Judeo-Christian principles and have opened the doors to exploration of occult phenomena. This has not only influenced education, but many other aspects of modern culture.

Although unconventional educators believe that by endorsing these disciplines they are truly helping students and society at large, there are legitimate reasons to question this assumption. Because of underlying philosophies and potential dangers (whether physical, psychological, or spiritual), these practices and techniques are not promoting the best interest of our nation or its children.

Yoga and Eastern meditation may indeed calm a nervous student; visualization, guided imagery, and fantasy practices might eventually help improve his grades or creativity; teaching principles of psychic development may enhance his self-esteem and increase his sense of power. Occult techniques and philosophy are effective; they do work as pagan and occult history demonstrates. But what is the ultimate cost of exposing our children to the occult? Those enamored with a child's "human potential" usually reject any concept of demonic activity, but this does not change the facts. Those persons integrating Eastern and occult methods and ideas into school curricula will exact a great cost and lay a heavy burden on our children and future generations.

Again, many of these people truly do have good motives, and they really do care for children and educational excellence, but they really may not understand all that is involved in occult practice. Let us illustrate.

It is important to realize that in visualization, guided imagery, and hypnosis we are not merely dealing with the natural or even innocent use of the imagination. In normal use of the imagination, we find a discriminating use of internal thoughts. The person is in control of how he uses these thoughts whether it is visualizing winning a race or what it would be like to marry another person. This natural use of the imagination is not what we find in New Age visualization, guided imagery, or hypnosis.

In essence, it is the particular characteristics of visualization, guided imagery, and hypnosis which distinguish them from a normal use of imagination. These may include: the use of relaxation, suggestion, the creation of a new reality, an altered state of consciousness, being directed by another person so that the participant is not ultimately in control, and having to be brought out of the internal condition into which one has been placed. Further, visualization, guided imagery, and hypnosis can all be powerful methods for introducing children to the occult, something not true of a person's own unaided imagination.

New Age visualization attempts to use the mind to actually control reality outside oneself. For example, it might use the mind in an attempt to influence events, objects, or even people through a supposed psychic power of the mind that "travels" outside the mind to have an influence.

Guided imagery and hypnosis are identical (or almost identical). Here we also find the use of relaxation and psychological suggestions in order to produce a new reality. For example, when a child reaches a suggestible state of mind (without discrimination and where he is not in control of his inner environment), and he starts to do, remember, or believe things that ultimately aren't real, and then he has to be brought out of that state of mind by another person, this is guided imagery or hypnosis. But there may be hidden psychological and spiritual consequences to these methods (see chapter 7).

Consider another example of how new educational methods can be counterproductive: values clarification. Eric Buehrer recalls how he initially failed in his role as a teacher to instruct his inner-city students that it was wrong to steal. Why? Because he had adopted a values clarification approach. During his first year of teaching, he told his students that he was going to help them grow in the decision-making process through values clarification. He asked his class how many felt that stealing was okay. Half the class felt it was fine. So he attempted to "clarify those values." What he found was that the kids clarified for *him* what their values were—and they had endless justifications for their belief that stealing was right. Buehrer discovered that in values clarification it is impossible for a teacher to bring his or her own value judgment into the educational process. All a teacher can do is affirm to students that it is okay to believe whatever they *want* to believe. He further became convinced that values clarification was a terrible thing to teach impressionable youngsters. He concluded that not only *should* we teach students absolute values, but that we *must* teach them absolute values.

> If we don't, then we can write off all these other issues, whether it's abortion or euthanasia or promiscuity or drug abuse—it doesn't matter. If at the root of it, the child believes that whatever he chooses is right simply because he *chooses* it—then we've lost the battle.[4]

We have prepared this manual to assist parents, teachers, and school administrators in the quest to safeguard the quality of children's education in America.

In chapter 1 we will begin by showing what the New Age Movement (NAM) is and why it is religious. We will do this because if, in various forms, its practices and beliefs are being introduced in public schools, then parents have a right to know what their children are being taught in the name of modern education.

Chapter 1

■

WHAT IS THE
NEW AGE
MOVEMENT?

Why hat is the New Age Movement? Is it religious or not? Is the New Age Movement an occult-oriented religious movement? Many educators and parents are uncertain.

Some parents around the country have protested the promotion of New Age beliefs and practices in the schools. Educators have often countered with questionable statements such as, "I don't know much about the New Age Movement, but our program is not New Age." Or they may reply with, "The New Age is not a religion, and it is certainly not anything occult."

In this chapter we will respond to such objections and answer the questions, What is the New Age Movement? Is it religious? Is it occultic?

What Is the New Age Movement?

The New Age Movement (NAM) is a title that refers to a worldview or a philosophy of life in which many people believe. It is a particular way of defining reality and living. In large measure the NAM is basically a synthesis in varying degrees of many religious traditions and practices, including Hinduism, Buddhism, Taoism, spiritism, shamanism, witchcraft, and other forms of classical occult practice and philosophy. The New Age Movement is indeed a religious philosophy because it is based on religious views; for example, New Agers hold to pantheism—a belief that everything is part of God. That is, God is all, and all is God. They believe that every person is part of God, even though people outside the New Age might not realize it.

Through mystical experiences, or while participating in techniques which alter their state of consciousness, people are powerfully persuaded that the religious worldview of the New Age Movement is true.

But for some people, the religious nature of the NAM may not be well understood because America's perception of religion is biased toward our majority practice of Christianity and Judaism.

In other words, many Americans equate *religion* with belief in a specific supernatural being—the personal God of the Bible—as well as the normal accompanying worship practices attending Protestant, Catholic, and Jewish faiths. But religious faith and practice in America have changed.

America is becoming more and more of a melting pot as the religions of the Far East have become increasingly prominent in our culture. As *Harper's Encyclopedia of Mystical and Paranormal Experiences* points out, "Asian immigrants, some of whom have come to America specifically to spread Eastern religions, have found receptive audiences, especially since the 1960's."[1] For example, by 1990, 10 to 20 million people were following Eastern religions of one kind or another. The Hindu practice of Transcendental Meditation alone—a method frequently encouraged by transpersonal educators—has initiated some four million people.

Another reason New Age premises and practices may not be readily discernible is because New Age educators have sometimes camouflaged them for easier incorporation into public schools. For example, meditation practices having religious premises and goals may simply be termed "centering." (Until it was declared illegal, the Hindu practice of Transcendental Meditation itself was found in many school systems under the euphemism "The Science of Creative Intelligence.") Yogic breathing and postures that are ultimately related to religious goals may be offered merely as physical calisthenics. A practice called "Arica psychocalisthenics" has also been used in some schools under the banner of normal physical education, even though its ultimate purpose is clearly religious, as demonstrated by the occult background and books of its founder, Oscar Ichazo.

Regardless, the specific philosophy of the NAM gives its own unique religious definition to the nature of God, man, the material and immaterial universe, and the future of humanity.

Let us examine the phrase *New Age Movement* itself to better enable us to see this. In its context, the term *New Age* suggests a millennial expectation, that our world is about to move into a whole new form of existence, a utopian bliss of spiritual harmony and peace. This is not only seen as a oneness of each person with others, but a oneness with the entire planet and universe itself.

The term *movement* can be described as a broad and diverse cultural trend united by a common worldview. As New Age religion expert Robert Burrows, formerly of the Spiritual Counterfeits Project in Berkeley, California, comments,

> The NAM is thus a multi-faceted, multi-focused trend. It does not refer to any one group or even primarily to a collection of groups. It is fundamentally a mindset, a way of viewing reality that has implications for all of life.[2]

An authority on new religious movements also observes,

> The movement does possess an identifiable ideological framework, and members do share a common set of beliefs. The distinctiveness of New Age beliefs, in contrast to doctrines held within the more dominant Christian ideological framework, is apparent in their function within the movement and the manner in which they are held.[3]

NAM Religious Tenets

Although diversity of belief and practice among New Agers is great, a common religious philosophy can be found.

J. Gordon Melton, founder of the Institute for the Study of American Religion, is a nationally recognized authority on religion and a visiting scholar at the University of California. He is described by the *Los Angeles Times* as a "leading chronicler of religious movements in the United States."

Melton writes,

> While the New Age Movement is a social movement, it is also an inherently religious one, though many New Agers might prefer the label "spiritual," as the word religion carries negative connotations for some. In any case, the movement is centered upon the experience of a personal spiritual-psychological transformation that is identical to what is generally termed "a religious experience."[4]

Below we present a brief synopsis of NAM religious views:

- *God*—an impersonal, all-pervading energy.

- *Jesus Christ*—a New Age teacher who personally illustrated the proper attitudes and practices of an individual who recognizes his own inner divinity.

- *man*—inwardly good and divine.

- *salvation*—the attainment of "higher" consciousness or realization of one's own inward divinity through the practice of New Age techniques, such as altered states of consciousness and meditation.

- *death*—the moment one hopes to experience a merging with "ultimate reality," the omnipresent energy of the universe. However, this happens only if the individual has attained "enlightenment" in this life; otherwise the "soul" will be reincarnated into another body.

- *heaven and hell*—positive or negative states of consciousness in this life.

Publisher's Weekly also noted the religious nature of the NAM and even its increasing outreach to children. They write,

> The essence of the New Age has always been an exploration of the spiritual side of humankind. . . .

Domestic trends indicate that New Age values and principles are finding their way into mainstream concerns. Almost every New Age catalog offers titles directed to the expanding children's market. ... Immense opportunity exists in the future for the flow of inwardly directed, transformative material, whether it is called metaphysical, esoteric, occult, mystical, holistic, human potential, or New Age.[5]

But it is important to realize that New Age practices and philosophy have also become increasingly "secularized" as proponents seek to find converts in the secular marketplace. And this has caused some problems. For example, the inundation with programs based on New Age philosophy has led to hundreds of employee complaints. As a result, Equal Employment Opportunities Commission attorneys and commission officials drafted regulations titled "Main Programs Conflicting with Employees Religious Beliefs" under the Civil Rights Act of 1964—Title VII.

This resolution pointed out that "Employers are increasingly making use of training programs designed to improve employee motivation, cooperation, or productivity through the use of various so-called 'New Age' techniques."[6] Thus, it directs the employer to either excuse employees or provide alternatives for them if the program is in conflict with an employee's religious beliefs.

To be able to understand and recognize the intrusion of the NAM into our schools and elsewhere, a person needs to further understand the religious philosophy of this movement. Therefore, it is also necessary to help the reader understand the term *occult*.

What Is the Occult?

Our word *occult* is derived from the Latin *occultus*, which means "to cover up, hide, or conceal." Perhaps most Americans are accustomed to defining the occult as Satanism, black magic, voodoo, and witchcraft exclusively. But it is much more than this.

While these are forms of the occult, a consultation with dictionaries would reveal that *occultism* really involves the acquisition of hidden wisdom, knowledge, or power by the use of various acts or techniques—particularly consciousness-altering ones. Standard definitions of the word include the following:

The *Oxford American Dictionary* defines *occult* as:

> 1. Secret, hidden except from those with more than ordinary knowledge; 2. Involving the supernatural, occult powers. The occult [involves] the world of the supernatural, mystical, or magical.[7]

Webster's Third International Dictionary Unabridged defines *occult* as that which is

> deliberately kept hidden... of, relating to, or dealing in matters regarded as involving the action or influence of supernatural agencies or some secret knowledge of them.[8]

The *Encyclopedia Britannica* defines *occult* as:

> A general designation for various theories, practices, and rituals based on esoteric knowledge, especially alleged knowledge about the world of spirits and unknown forces of the universe. Devotees of occultism strive to understand and explore these worlds, often by developing the higher powers of the mind.[9]

By the above definitions we can see that the term *occult* is not strictly limited to Satanism, black magic, or witchcraft. Any religion, practice, or technique which promotes the goals and worldview of the occult may be properly labeled *occult*. For example, yoga and much meditation is not characteristically thought of as something occult; nevertheless, the methods, philosophy, and goals of yoga and meditation are classically those of the occult (see chapter 7).

Is the NAM occultic? What Are Its Goals?

In Melton's *Encyclopedic Handbook of Cults* he describes the goal of the NAM—a goal which is synonymous with the goals of the occult:

> The central vision of the New Age is one of radical mystical transformation on an individual level. It involves an awakening to such new realities as a discovery of psychic abilities, the experience of physical or psychological healing, the emergence of new potentials within oneself . . . the acceptance of a new picture of the universe. The essence of the New Age is the imposition of that personal vision onto society and the world. Thus, the New Age is ultimately a vision of a world transformed, a heaven on earth, a society in which the problems of today are overcome and a new existence emerges.[10]

It is precisely within the framework of this description that the NAM has affected our educational system.

Melton goes on to observe that the NAM "has become visible in every major metropolitan complex in the United States," and he supplies the reason for its success: "Insofar as the New Age Movement represents an updating of the long-standing occult and metaphysical tradition in American life, it has a bright future."[11]

But as a religious philosophy the NAM is decidedly anti-Christian. For example, it denies the Christian belief of a personal, all-knowing, all-powerful God who is separate from and rules over His creation.

Instead, the NAM affirms there exists only one ultimate divine reality (monism), and in its true nature everything that exists is part of that reality. This one reality is cataloged under various pantheistic terms such as *the divine essence, universal energy,* and *all-pervasive consciousness.*

In other words, all humans are inherently divine or part of God—even if they don't yet realize it. While they are smaller manifestations of the divine essence, they have tremendous power available to them (within their divine nature) if they will just turn inward and unleash its powers.

According to New Age thinking, man's basic problem is that he perceives himself incorrectly—as a finite and limited being. According to the NAM, all men and women must realize that their perception of finiteness is an illusion from which they must be delivered. (In *advaita* Hinduism, the illusion is referred to as *maya*.)

New Age groups characteristically offer the techniques and practices which they feel will better enable us to individually and collectively evolve spiritually—to inwardly unveil awareness of our true divinity through a state of occult enlightenment. This so-called enlightened state is referred to as "self-realization," contacting the "higher self," achieving "God" or "Christ" consciousness, etc. This is where New Agers say we can find secret power and wisdom to solve all our problems.

Although the terms and techniques vary, almost all New Age groups employ various forms of meditation in the attempt to produce altered states of consciousness which they believe will permit people to get in touch with their true self, the essence of God. Some of the other common techniques employed in the search for inner divinity include using talismans (such as amulets or crystals) in order to allegedly enhance or amplify psychic energy, the use of spirit guides (as in channeling/mediumship), and the practice of yoga (see chapter 7).

Most New Agers admit that it doesn't really matter which of the techniques a person uses; the real goal is to get in touch with your higher self/intuitive self. Again, New Agers believe this will help them create their own reality and discover the alleged divinity that lies within.[12]

The logical derivative of this teaching is that if someone is inwardly divine, then he does not need to look to any source outside himself to find God, truth, or morality—he determines his own God, truth, and morality through occult practice and self-realization.

Thus the goal of New Age practice is "in the production of a mystical consciousness or awareness, frequently called by such names as higher consciousness, self-realization.... To have a consciousness that transcends mundane reality is to be aware of the universal energy [God] that strengthens existence."[13]

This is why New Agers "place a renewed emphasis on self-knowledge, inner exploration, and participation in a continual transformative process.... The Power to bring about the transformation of individuals comes from universal energy . . . a basic energy that is different from the more recognized forms of energy."[14]

But this energy is nothing new. It is described in classical occult or pantheistic terms such as *universal energy, chi, prana,* and *mana.* These transformative energies can be found in scores of New Age practices such as psychic healing, dreamwork, shamanism, meditation, yoga, and contacting spirit guides.[15]

In conclusion, to say that the NAM is not religious is incorrect. Nor it is fair to permit NAM practices and philosophy in our schools while prohibiting Christian belief and practices. If teachers cannot promote Christianity in the schools, neither should they be permitted to promote the practices of occultism.

In a significant court case related to this issue (*Malnak v. Yogi*), a broader definition of religion has emerged. On February 2, 1979, the U.S. Court of Appeals, Third District, affirmed the earlier decision of a federal district court that declared Transcendental Meditation was religious in nature and therefore could not be employed in public schools.

Why is this important? Because Judge Adams wrote a concurring opinion entitled "The Modern Definition of Religion." He observed the current growth of Eastern and other nontraditional religious movements, and the need for the courts to broaden the traditional theistic definition of religion.

In his definition of religion, he suggested three specific elements: 1) Does the nature of the ideas in question relate to matters of ultimate concern, such as the sum of one's basic attitudes to the problems of human existence? 2) evaluation of the comprehensiveness of the ideas in question—do they constitute a systematic series of answers that might begin to resemble a religion? and 3) what are the formal and structural elements of the particular group or activity and are there external or surface signs that may be analogized to those of the accepted religions?[16]

In light of this we should ask a question: In education today, is the essence of religious philosophy increasingly an issue to be dealt with? The answer is yes.

In his article "Transpersonal Communication in the Classroom," educator Barry K. Weinhold claims that one purpose of the teacher is to enable students to recognize that all life is an essential divine unity:

> Transpersonal communication involves the use of skills and understanding to help individuals reach and maintain a *conscious experience* of their essential unity and connectiveness with all life energy. It is based upon the belief that unity, not separateness or aloneness, is the basic human condition. . . . The main goal of transpersonal communication is the *realization and maintenance* of higher states of consciousness.[17]

For Weinhold, transpersonal communication "is designed to expand all human abilities" to enable students to reach "higher levels of awareness and functioning" and to "establish and maintain contact with 'a student's' inner core, where unity with all life energy occurs."[18]

In *Transpersonal Education: A Curriculum for Feeling and Being*, the following subjects are given as appropriate "educational possibilities" for opening up transpersonal vistas in the classroom:[19] 1) The work of the Russian occultist Gurdjieff, 2) the work of Sufi Idries Shah, and 3) Buddhist educational methods.[20] For example, in "The Education of the Buddhist Child," Buddhist teacher Giyu Kennet observes that in Eastern nations "the average child is taught to meditate as soon as it is possible for it to sit upright; i.e., around one or two years old."[21] Further, the whole point of Buddhist education involves an *uneducating*:

> The child . . . must never be thought of as something that is *needing* to be educated rather as that which has within itself all the knowledge that matters, that ever was. . . . [Unfortunately today] we educate ourselves out of our original oneness of mind into a duality which, at a later date, we have to transcend if we are to be able to do anything whatsoever to overcome the spiritual illnesses our education has generated.[22]

In other words, the premise of Buddhist education is that from infancy the child has the omniscient Buddha nature within and that conventional education only functions to destroy this primal connection to ultimate reality. The child is potentially omniscient since in his inner nature he is already divine. Thus, "the Buddhist teacher, if he is a real teacher, says, 'This child knows all, as indeed I know all, but he cannot yet express it.'"[23] Thus "even the stupidest child is fully accepted as having the Buddha Nature; it is embraced within the Buddha Mind." And,

> My advice to those who educate anyone is, "Remember, there is no difference between you and the pupil other than that of age. Neither of you possesses more than the other; there is only the illusion of knowledge. Unless you understand that mental knowledge is an illusion in the religious sense, you will never be able to impart anything whatsoever of real value."[24]

Consider the following statement by well-known educational theoretician Barbara Clark. She is a professor and educator of teachers in the area of gifted education. In her popular textbook *Growing Up Gifted* she writes,

> Lifestyles and belief systems change, dichotomies no longer exist, and time and space have another dimension. Reality is seen as an outward projection of internal thoughts, feelings, and expectations. Energy is the connector... Western pragmatists will soon join Eastern mystics.... We are all part of this great hologram called Creation which is everybody else's Self—you create your own reality.[25]

Further,

> We must first give up the need for dichotomies. ... Even our classrooms are places of the integration of polarities of knowing. Without a need for right/wrong, true/false, we are free to examine a few of these bigger, more wonderfully outrageous ideas, and those who ask us to entertain them.[26]

For some educators one of those "outrageous ideas" is contacting the spirit world in order to allegedly receive their wisdom and insight into many different educational subjects and philosophies. Spiritism in the classroom? Are we serious?

But perhaps we should not be all that surprised. Spiritism— or, as it is popularly called in the New Age Movement, "channeling"—is now a 100- to 150-million-dollar-per-year business in the United States.[27]

While spiritism in the classroom is still relatively infrequent, it is no longer rare. Some school districts have already been exposed to an incipient spiritism. The *Mission SOAR* (Set Objectives, Achieve Results) program was recently rejected, at least by the Los Angeles Unified School District, when it was shown to be occult in nature, introducing children to both living and dead people as potential spirit guides.

Although the program is now temporarily halted in Los Angeles, the program director continues to promote it in other states.[28] The SOAR program utilizes relaxation techniques to contact two spirit helpers and/or the dead, who are stated to be *not* necessarily imaginary beings. They are contacted as a means to foster the self-esteem of children. In its approach the program follows the book *Beyond Hypnosis: A Program for Developing Your Psychic and Healing Power*.

In his critique of New Age education, noted writer Tal Brooke, president of Spiritual Counterfeits Project in Berkeley, California, discussed the late prominent educator Beverly Galyean's visualization-directed approach to education. He observes,

> First graders were introduced to spirit guides through the Galyean approach. Although, as she remarked at a plenary session of the conference entitled "Education in the 80's," "Of course, we don't call them that in the public schools, we call them imaginary guides."[29]

Perhaps spiritism in education is not really surprising for another reason. The basic philosophy and practices of the NAM are the basic philosophy and practices advocated by the spirit world, as Dr. Ankerberg and Dr. Weldon have already documented.[30]

This presents a unique problem for educators who, whether innocently or deliberately, use various New Age methods with children. Many New Age practices, such as developing altered states of consciousness, meditation, visualization, yoga, and progressive relaxation make it easier for the mind to interact with the spirit world. Whether or not this is the intent of educators (and usually it is not), how do we know that by using these methods we are not conditioning our children for the same possibility of contact with the spirit world? (See chapter 7.)

During the 1989 school year, Craig Branch of Watchman Fellowship represented some parents of the Huntsville, Alabama, city schools before the school administration, concerning parental objections to a newly developed curriculum called *Peace, Harmony and Awareness.*

Mr. Branch expressed his concern over the illegality of using these progressive relaxation techniques for conflict resolution and personal guidance. From the perspective of occult tradition, he was concerned the curriculum's encouragement to contact a "white rabbit," as innocent as it might seem, could, under the proper circumstances, also be using meditation induction techniques to potentially contact a spirit guide. One administrator disagreed, saying that the white rabbit wasn't a spirit guide but merely an exercise in imagination or a symbol of the child's higher or intuitive self.

But how can administrators know that such techniques will never involve spiritism? Spiritists themselves frequently contact their own spirit guides in the form of an animal who supplies them with the guidance and counsel they request. For example, in shamanistic traditions (e.g., Native American) the spirit guide classically appears in the form of a "power animal," who provides the needed power/information to the shaman.

Further, when little children are taught to use progressive relaxation techniques for entering other states of consciousness, can administrators be certain people won't seek to use these same techniques *outside* the classroom, perhaps for more blatantly occult purposes? Again, what might we be conditioning these children to accept later in life?

Nor are these techniques always harmless. For example, consider the experience of most spiritists. Once they have opened their minds to the spirit world through progressive relaxation, visualization, meditation, or other methods, even these spiritists may find it difficult or impossible to distinguish the normal workings of their own mind from the influence of their personal spirit guides.[31] If the spirits can operate so invisibly, how does anyone know what might or might not be happening in a classroom setting that offers children New Age instruction and practice?

Granted, in many cases the specific conditions under which an otherwise innocuous procedure becomes potentially occult can be difficult to ascertain. Much depends on the required environment, goals, and methods necessary to produce an occult influence. But we do know that, given these requirements, even children may be exposed to genuine occult powers.

Again, this may not necessarily occur in the classroom itself. But the mere fact of exposing children to various New Age methods, however introductory, means that children may be more open to these methods—and what they lead to—outside the classroom.

This demonstrates the ignorance that may exist today in the educational establishment because, by and large, rationalistic educators are unfamiliar with the history and practices of the occult, not to mention the dynamics of spiritual warfare undertaken by spiritistic powers (Ephesians 6:11,12).

Regardless, we have seen that the NAM is clearly a religious philosophy and, as such, does not belong in the public school curriculum.

But even if secular educators do not accept the supernatural, they are left with the compounded problem that the child is being taught that the answers to his questions lie within himself. This militates against any outside authority— parents, church, school, or state. This ultimately produces anarchy.

Chapter 2

New Age and Psychotherapeutic Influence in Education

I n this chapter we will provide specific examples of how New Age and/or questionable psychotherapeutic materials are finding their way into educational curricula around the country.

At "The John Ankerberg Show" and Watchman Fellowship in Birmingham, Alabama, we have had an interesting response to publication of this book in its earlier form. Many people, some of them quite irate, wrote us complaining that we were engaged in a witch-hunt and that we were simply wrong because there was no occultism or psychotherapy being practiced in public school curricula.

In order to respond to such charges, we have cited more examples than we normally would. If the material becomes redundant, you may wish to skip to the next chapter. The fact is, these things are happening. To refuse to see the direction that education is heading underscores part of the real problem.

That these practices are not necessarily isolated can be seen from public testimony given before the U.S. Department of Education in 1984. Immediately preceding the Protection of Pupil Rights Amendment, a number of parents revealed that their children had been exposed to such practices as meditation, yoga, astral projection, ESP and other forms of psychic experience, hypnosis, astrology, questionable relaxation techniques, occultic games, and even spirit guides.[1]

The more than 30 illustrations we cite below are from Alabama, California, Colorado, Florida, Kansas, Maryland, Michigan, Mississippi, Missouri, New Hampshire, New Mexico, New York, North Carolina, Oklahoma, Oregon, and Texas; however, similar ones could be supplied from most other states. One of the coauthors of this book, Craig Branch, has been involved in researching this subject for many years. Because of his wide experience, we shall emphasize a number of illustrations that he has researched personally.

Example 1: In the fall of 1988 the city of Birmingham, Alabama, and the board of education published their Community School Course Listing. Perusing the actual course titles is instructive.

Among the classes taught are those on the following subjects:

- Spirit Journeying
- Psychic Development
- Astral Travel
- Astrology and Metaphysics
- Trance Channeling and Experiences with Spirit Beings
- Accessing Universal Energy
- Mandalas
- Crystal Healing
- Taoist Philosophy[2]

When questioned about these classes, the director of the Southside and Avondale schools, Sara Roseman, asserted that these topics were not in conflict with school board policy, admitting that a course cannot promote the ideology or practice of religion. Roseman was queried as to whether or not she realized that these courses were promoting the ideology and practices of the religions of Hinduism, Buddhism, Taoism, and occultism; she replied she was unaware of any connection. But after raising the issue with the school board president of whether or not these practices involved religious aspects, these courses were immediately terminated.[3]

Example 2: Los Angeles Times religious editor Russell Chandler has discussed the issue of New Age education in his *Understanding the New Age*. He observes that some children in the Los Angeles city school system have been taught to imagine that they are one with the rays of the sun and that, in so doing, to realize that they are part of God.[4] He also refers to the late transpersonal educator Beverly Galyean, who developed three federally funded educational programs for Los Angeles public schools using meditation and guided imagery. As part of her educational philosophy, she described her religious convictions as well,

> Once we begin to see that we are all God, that we have the attributes of God, then I think the whole purpose of human life is to re-own the God-likeness within us; the perfect love, the perfect wisdom, perfect understanding, perfect intelligence. When we do that, we create back to that old, essential oneness which is consciousness.[5]

Chandler also observes that the Citrus Community College provides academic credit to its students for classes that incorporate such things as parapsychology, self-hypnosis, psychic development and interpreting auras, out-of-body experiences, and telepathy.[6]

Example 3: The New York Times Magazine referred to the influence of New Age practices in Colorado education when it discussed the concern of parents over second and third graders being led in visualization techniques. The article confessed that "meditational techniques have become common fare in the state's public and private schools."[7] The article observes that noncredit courses for both adults and children include psychic channeling taught by "a conscious voice channel who allows an entity of light to speak through her" and a "crystal workshop" which promotes a hands-on introduction to the alleged healing energies in crystals and other stones.

The article also revealed that until her resignation was forced by concerned individuals, Sylvia A. Falconer, a Unitarian Universalist minister who supports witchcraft and goddess

worship, was appointed chairman of Colorado's Youth Suicide
Prevention Task Force.

Nevertheless, the article pointed out the basic approach of
those who seek to integrate New Age practices into the educational curricula of today:

> Many Colorado schools, public and private, uti-
> lize practices adapted from Eastern meditation under
> the rubrics of "centering," "stress reduction," or
> "guided visualization," usually with the aim of
> enhancing students' self-esteem and creativity, or
> presenting an alternative to alcohol and drugs.[8]

Example 4: In fall 1990 the Mobile city schools in Alabama
contracted with the Mobile Mental Health Center in order to
fulfill the state board of education mandate to help students
deal with self-esteem and other problems. The Center wrote a
letter telling parents that it would help students cope with
stress through a program sponsored by the Office of Substance Abuse Prevention in Washington, D.C. Among the
objectives noted were the following: "The students will learn
about... breathing exercises, relaxation exercises, visual imagery, yoga, massage, pressure points, biofeedback."[9]

Example 5: One popular elementary school curriculum in
Huntsville, Alabama, is titled *Visual Thinking: A "Scamper" Tool
for Useful Imaging.* The foreword to this curriculum confesses
that the exercises are intended to encourage "right brain visual
imagery and creative fantasy." Children are admittedly instructed into entering altered states of consciousness. For
example, they are taught "how to rub the genie and gain
entrance into our pre-conscious storehouse of information.
The process is one of intentionally willing oneself into an
altered state of consciousness."[10]

After instructing children in a meditative "flight plan," the
teacher conducts the children through progressive stages of
guided imagery exercises. Among these are exercises in meeting special "friends" along their inner journey toward accepting the "world of the weird," processes designed to help the
mind to "go with the flow," and meeting an internal "wise

person" who can answer all their questions and give them direction.[11]

The alcohol education *Get Set* program in Topeka, Kansas, also encourages children to contact a "wise person" within them and to ask its assistance and listen to its instructions.

Example 6: In 1992 Picayune, Mississippi, began implementing SALTT programs in the elementary schools (SALTT [also SALT] stands for Suggestive Accelerative Learning and Teaching Techniques). SALTT was developed by Georgi Lozanov, a Bulgarian hypnotist and psychotherapist. This program contains instructions on hypnosis/meditation and a New Age technique called "mind mapping."[12]

Appropriately, the National Academy of Sciences has recently criticized the SALTT approach, observing that,

> After ten years of informal research there is little scientific support even for the mild claims.... There are few independent evaluations of accelerated learning and these do not support claims that SALTT substantially enhances performance of normal students.[13]

Example 7: In 1989 the Birmingham office of Watchman Fellowship was asked to review a program titled *Peace, Harmony and Awareness*, part of the APPLE (*A Positive Program of Life's Experiences*) curriculum used in Alabama's Huntsville elementary school program. The child is instructed to contact a white rabbit (which some administrators have told us is part of the child's higher self or intuitive self). The practice of meditation is used to access this so-called higher self in order to provide the child with special guidance. In fact, this rabbit is supposedly all-wise and the child may ask it any question at all. Children are taught to *expect* the rabbit to answer their questions.[14]

Example 8: A health program is funded by the U.S. Department of Health and Human Services and the Public Health Service and used in grades 9-12 throughout Alabama. In "Handling Stress," activity 5 of *Teenage Health Teaching Modules* (THTM), we find a reliance upon "affective" approaches which include progressive relaxation (hypnosis/meditation), deep breathing incorporating a mantra, autogenics, and a form of yogic alternate nostril breathing. Proponents claim such methods are properly used as a means to deal with conflict or stress by escaping inward into an altered state of consciousness.[15]

But it is not merely the New Age influence here that is of concern. THTM's "Violence Prevention" module tells seventh to twelfth graders that some of the healthy ways to express anger include having sex, locking yourself in your room, slamming doors, biting nails, screaming, eating, meditating, and throwing things that can be broken.[16]

In the module dealing with drinking, smoking, and drugs students are taught a nondirective approach wherein they are to make "a responsible choice about drinking that is right for them."[17]

Example 9: In Birmingham, Alabama, the last issue of the Mountain Brook High School newspaper for the year 1988 (May 12) contained an editorial written by a student. It advised fellow students of the merits of New Age visualization, affirmations, and crystal work to attune them to the higher self and access information to pass exams mystically rather than by traditional approaches. Not surprisingly, the parent of this young girl had been an occasional speaker in various classes in the junior high and high school, leading students through progressive relaxation (meditation/hypnosis) and visualization exercises.

Craig Branch was in attendance at the Mountain Brook teachers' meeting where this same parent was the invited speaker on the subject of coping with stress. She led the teachers through the same exercises urging them to "create their own reality" and to tap into the "energy of nature."

Example 10: In Decatur, Alabama, a high school literature course, "Elements of Literature," studies the novel *A Wizard of Earthsea*. Its theme is that people can learn the use of magic to demonstrate the alleged link between the worlds of fantasy and reality.

The teacher's guide actually instructs the student in Taoist religion—a powerful form of occult philosophy and/or practice. For example, Taoism teaches that the dualities of life (such as male/female; good/evil; inner/outer) are ultimately illusions and thus seeks to help people realize that all reality, in whatever form it seems to be appearing, is one divine essence.

The teacher's guide thus directs the students in "reteaching alternatives" to help the student see that in order to be a complete person, he/she must learn to adopt Taoist attitudes. There is also a guided imagery exercise where students are mentally taken into an internal psychological environment to experience wizardry or sorcery.[18]

Example 11: The *Birmingham News* for January 5, 1990, reported that the private Redmont School had begun a Waldorf curriculum for three- to five-year-olds. Waldorf education was founded by spiritist Rudolf Steiner and is based on the occult principles of the religion he founded, known as Anthroposophy (see appendix A). The children begin their day in a candle-lit room sitting in a circle holding hands while chanting a "blessing."

Example 12: The New York Commissioner of Education is now ruling on a petition by parents challenging the legitimacy of group psychological treatment, progressive relaxation techniques, and the appropriateness of eliciting confidential information from students' families as encouraged in such programs as Quest, *Developing Understanding of Self and Others* (DUSO), and TAD (Toward Affective Development).[19]

Example 13: Quest Skills for Growing has been rejected for use by the Tiffin County School System in Ohio after a one-year pilot program. The school noted a lack of scientific data to support effectiveness of the encounter group/affective approach of Quest, as well as the damaging findings by researchers at Heidelberg College who found no positive impact when compared to control groups.[20]

In July 1990 the school board of Lawrence, Kansas, also dropped Quest due to the work of a parents' rights group. The objections given were that 1) values clarification is inappropriate for students, 2) Quest was not ultimately an effective drug prevention program, and 3) Quest is primarily psychological in nature rather than academic.[21]

Example 14: A well-organized parents' group in Northville, Michigan, recently challenged the *Michigan Model* education program which uses progressive relaxation techniques, non-directive decision-making, and self-esteem enhancement methods. The major objections cited were 1) it changes children's and family values through values clarification problem-solving methods, 2) it encourages the "responsible" use of sex and drugs, 3) it has an antifamily bias, 4) it offers a use of techniques that could produce altered states of consciousness, and 5) it may invade family privacy.

(This parents' group has produced a booklet documenting these objections which might serve as a prototype for other groups around the country.[22] Also see appendix D.)

Example 15: Birmingham Southern College recently conducted its annual dean's forum on the subject of witchcraft and a coven called Ravenwood in Atlanta. Dr. Campbell, a professor at the college, spent four and one-half months of her sabbatical with the coven.[23]

Example 16: Parents in Lee's Summit, Missouri, challenged their school's use of group counseling sessions in Pumsy and DUSO (programs employing unscientific therapeutic and self-hypnosis/meditation techniques) without prior parental approval. Their objection underscored the necessity of the school to comply with the Federal Pupil Rights Amendment (see chapter 9).[24]

Example 17: In the spring of 1990, a community school program for Wade County public school system of Raleigh, North Carolina, offered a course on kundalini yoga for both high school students and adults.[25] But kundalini yoga is inherently religious as well as extremely dangerous, as we document in chapter 7.

Example 18: The October 1989 newsletter of *Concerned Women of America* discussed how parents in Oklahoma and Maryland discovered an array of New Age courses in public schools intended to promote "the attainment of higher levels of consciousness . . . [and] even encouraging children to go home and try their Ouija boards."[26]

Example 19: A sixth-grade health textbook used in Missouri, *Understanding Health*, teaches children "to relax by meditation," and includes instruction on Transcendental Meditation and yoga.[27]

Example 20: DUSO has been removed from the Jefferson City, Missouri, school district. The superintendent conceded that DUSO could be dangerous if misused stating, "DUSO has more of a tendency to get you into the psychiatric area."[28]

In late 1987 the New Mexico state senate passed a memorial/ resolution which called for the elimination of psychological or mind-altering techniques in schools. The resolution, approved by the state board of education, was sent to all school districts. The resolution stated psychological counseling "can involve such techniques as Transcendental Meditation, altered states of consciousness, or the occult." The resolution resulted from concerned parents who discovered that the DUSO program was frightening their children. In addition to DUSO counseling, New Mexico schools were found to be using the game "Dungeons and Dragons" and a companion book entitled *Wizards*, replete with occult instructions for fantasy purposes.[29]

Example 21: In Florida's Pinellas and Pasco counties, a program called *Quieting Reflex and Success Imagery* was implemented. This program includes teaching children to deal with stress through meditation/hypnosis techniques and guided imagery. Like many other programs, the imagery leads children to contact a "wise person" in their minds for guidance and counsel. In addition, many forms of occultism are promoted, including parapsychology, ESP, yoga, and psychic healing.[30] When made fully aware of the potential dangers of this program and the board's liability, many schools have dropped these methods.

Example 22: Project Self-Esteem provoked debate and a lawsuit in San Juan Capistrano, California. In 1986 fourth graders were led in hypnosis/meditation exercises to enhance self-esteem, and 50 parents withdrew their children.[31]

Example 23: The same year *Coping with Kids* caused a furor in Oregon. The program included 28 stress control and taped relaxation exercises. The district review committee suspended the curriculum because it was "borderline religious . . . questionable . . . [and] inappropriate."[32]

Example 24: The September 17, 1990, issue of Focus on the Family's *Citizen* magazine reveals that "thousands of public and private school children, first through sixth grades, will be taught how to cast spells." It also mentioned that themes of despair, mutilation, occultism, and witchcraft weaved their way through an educational series called *Impressions*, which is marketed in all 50 states and is designed to teach language arts from reading to vocabulary.[33]

Example 25: Watchman Fellowship recently received a letter from a parent in Columbia, Missouri, informing them of the experience of her daughter in the second grade. She had been subjected countless times to progressive relaxation techniques and guided imagery. She began to experience frightening episodes of being taken by an old man (her inner guide) downward into a locked room, which resulted in her experiencing nightmares.

Example 26: In the spring of 1987 a speaker from University of Alabama at Birmingham came to Birmingham's Mountain Brook High School for a demonstration of the martial art known as T'ai Chi and led the students through a meditation exercise on the gym floor. This same teacher had also taught a 1990 T'ai Chi course offered through the Birmingham Board of Education, describing it as "meditation in motion . . . the tranquilizer of the East . . . [which] works on the play of opposites—Yin and Yang." Her course was also offered as an elective at the Birmingham campus, where it is described as "an ancient system of movement-meditation practiced by Buddhist monks."[34]

Since T'ai Chi attempts to harmonize the body's inner polarities of yin/yang and bring them into proper alignment with the Tao, or ultimate reality ("God"), the essence of T'ai Chi can only be described as religious. In *The Martial Arts of the Orient* the underlying principles of T'ai Chi are cited as involving:

> two of the ideas about man and the universe which are part of the Chinese way of life . . . that life is maintained by a balance or harmony between two opposite forces: yin and yang. . . . In addition to the nervous and circulatory systems . . . there exists another palpable system of "meridians" which carries

vital energy to different organs and parts of the body.... [In] T'ai Chi movement the forces of the yin and yang are harmonized not only in the nervous and circulatory systems, but in the finer systems of meridians.[35]

Example 27: The University of Alabama at Birmingham and Auburn University at Montgomery regularly offer elective classes in the dangerous practice of hatha yoga, as do many colleges and universities. People are usually given the impression that hatha yoga is merely a physical exercise. But in a standard text, *Hatha Yoga*, Swami Radha writes,

When most people in the West think of yoga, they think of yoga *asanas* or postures. They think of them as a form of exercise . . . without understanding their real nature and purpose. Asanas are a *devotional* practice which, like all spiritual practices, brings us closer to an understanding of the truth.

Thus, "each asana affords certain physical, physiological and psychological benefits. Beyond this there also lies a mystical or spiritual meaning. Each asana creates a certain meditative state of mind."[36] In other words, "Hatha yoga places an important part in the development of the human being . . . to bring the seeker into closer contact with the Higher Self."[37] The University of Alabama at Birmingham has also recently offered "The Art of Meditation," "Polarity-Theory and Body-work," "Creative Visualization," "Exploring Your ESP Potential," and other classes. Many of these are regular courses.

Example 28: In Birmingham, Alabama, a large number of parents from the Mountain Brook Elementary School challenged the use of progressive relaxation (hypnosis/meditation) and guided imagery exercises for second graders in the *Pumsy the Dragon* curriculum. The parents' goal of an official policy banning the use of Eastern mystical techniques from school curricula and exercises was successfully implemented.

In consideration of this policy, a school counselor/creative writing teacher was introduced and given the opportunity to defend her use of meditation in the classroom. The teacher offered material which taught that the value of meditation was to "move into a state . . . where higher intellectual facilities are suspended." For example, "A sure guide in our deep knowing is a *non-thinking level*." The material she cited also explained how to enter an altered state of consciousness and "experience . . . your omniscience, your full access to complete understanding."[38]

Example 29: Jefferson State Junior College and the University of North Alabama recently required an orientation course using the text *Becoming a Master Student* by David Ellis of College Survival, Inc. In the acknowledgments, Ellis thanks a variety of New Age leaders for their trainings, writings, and assistance, including Werner Erhard, originator of est/the Forum; Ken Keys, author of *Handbook to Higher Consciousness*; and transpersonal educator Virginia Satir.

Ellis' book employs various meditation exercises to help enhance the lessons offered. It cites New Age occultist Krishnamurti and psychologist Abraham Maslow as helping to focus students on their "self-actualization" and "self-transcendence."

The book's Power Process No. 5, "You Created All," emphasizes the est/occult philosophy that

> nothing in the world exists at all except what you create in your head. You create everything . . . your textbooks, instructors, classmates, classrooms, campus town . . . the weather, wars, world hunger, the planets—you create those too.

In chapter 9 on health, meditation is used to assist students to locate "your center, your inner wisdom." New Age medicine is also offered, including macrobiotic diets (longevity through a diet balanced in accordance with Eastern philosophy), acupressure, reflexology, rolfing, acupuncture, iridology, and psychic healing.[39]

Example 30: In October 1992 parents objected to DUSO and Pumsy being used at the San Angelo, Texas, elementary schools. Although the superintendent agreed to eliminate the fantasy trip and guided imagery, a review committee voted to retain the programs. The parents are currently gathering documentation for an appeal to the school board.[40]

In November 1990 the Hartselle, Alabama, board of education told a meeting of concerned parents that the controversial portions of DUSO (progressive relaxation and guided imagery) had been eliminated, and that a committee was reviewing the programs to determine whether other portions should be removed.[41]

In December 1991 a review committee of the school district in Colorado Springs, Colorado, studied complaints from parents for six weeks and concluded that the "self-esteem program Pumsy would be dropped." The same action was taken in school district 20.[42]

In August 1992, after several months of lengthy debate between parents and educators, especially guidance counselors, the Clay County School Board of Jacksonville, Florida, voted 4–1 to drop Pumsy and DUSO. Predictably, some educators charged censorship. A board member responded that censorship was not the issue because the school board has the authority to remove inappropriate programs.[43]

In Putnam, Oklahoma, in 1991, parents objected to both Pumsy and DUSO. Upon review of relevant research, even with great resistance from the educational establishment, the board voted to remove both programs.[44]

Example 31: The program called *I Am Power* teaches children animism—that they no longer need to be lonely when their parents are away at work because trees, rocks, and water all have spirits within them which can be contacted for comfort.[45]

Example 32: Finally, astrology in education and especially in our culture at large also plays a part in the promotion of New Age teaching in the schools. The late Beverly Galyean advocated astrology in her confluent education curriculum. Also, a number of astrologers are active in children's education, child psychology, helping children who have a learning disability, and treating children's emotional disorders.[46] "Professional astrologers find that work on children's charts forms a large part of their regular business."[47] Numerous texts exist today on how to use astrology with children, such as Dodie and

Allan Edmands' *Child Signs: Understanding a Child Through Astrology*, Rosicrucian Max Heindel's book *Your Child's Horoscope*, and Gloria Star's *Optimum Child: Developing Your Child's Fullest Potential Through Astrology*.

Rearing a child astrologically, whether in school or the home, is raising him to accept an occult worldview that may carry lifelong consequences. At the least, astrology conditions a child to accept the occult, and at worst, it may even introduce him to spirit guides.[48]

Unfortunately, the astrological diagnosis/education of a child may force parents or teachers to make important decisions based on false astrological assumptions about their "true" personality and destiny. For example, a child with a Neptune influence is allegedly "drawn into the inner realms more easily" and may seem "rather removed much of the time." This child will find it easy to spend hours "in a world of inner visions. Parents should not discourage this but aid the child in focusing his visions and finding ways to direct them. A good affirmation for this child is 'my guardian angel is my good friend.'"[49]

Children influenced by Pluto should realize that their power comes from their "higher self," and parents should realize that the child should not be taught to look to the church or its teachings concerning basic principles for living.[50]

And so it goes. All these programs have been developed by educators who have become enamored with various aspects of New Age philosophy and practice and have sought to incorporate what they have felt are beneficial methods into the educational curriculum.

With hundreds or thousands of educators encouraging similar explorations for children, it is not surprising that even health and economics books may contain these themes. When author Craig Branch appeared to testify before the Alabama textbook committee hearings in 1990, in reviewing six proposed texts he discovered that four health books and two home economic books contain the same pattern of promoting Eastern religious practices and psychotherapeutic techniques. Among these were progressive relaxation, visualization, guided imagery, meditation, yoga, and autogenics, a form of self-hypnosis.[51] Almost 20 pages in the popular textbook *Health: Choosing Wellness* are devoted to promoting a number of techniques such as yoga, hypnosis, biofeedback, and the deep breathing, progressive relaxation, meditation sequence.[52]

From our brief survey, it should be clear that there are a number of programs around the country which utilize either nondirective affective approaches, inappropriate experimental techniques or, to varying degrees, Eastern mystical religious premises and practices. But there are many more:

- Michigan Model for Comprehensive Health Education
- Coping with Kids
- Flights of Fantasy
- Dungeons and Dragons
- Impressions
- Here's Looking at You
- Bridges
- DARE (Drug Abuse Resistance Education)
- Discovery Skills for Life
- Life Education Centre
- Free the Horses (Active Parenting)
- Flexing Your Test Muscles
- Letting Go of Stress
- Get Set
- Growing Healthy
- Heart to Heart
- Tactics for Thinking
- Self Concept
- SOS (Strengthening of Skills)
- TAD (Toward Affective Development)
- Whole Mind Learning
- Workshop Way
- Yoga programs
- Visual Thinking: A Scamper Tool
- Integrated Thematic Instruction
- Project Aware
- Project Strain
- PALS

We stress that the degree of utilization of questionable methods varies considerably and that parents should not necessarily assume that the subjects we have discussed are equally represented in the programs we have listed.

Chapter 3

■

QUEST, DUSO, PUMSY, AND DARE

One opponent to traditional family values is the liberal People for the American Way (PFAW). They publish an annual report entitled *Attacks on the Freedom to Learn*, in which they list the results of their annual survey concerning alleged "censorship and other challenges to public education."[1]

PFAW states that in 1991-92, 44 states reported 376 formal objections. Roughly one-half of those challenges were controversial library books, usually having themes involving the occult and witchcraft, profanity, sexually explicit material, or pro-homosexual content.

But the other half were *school* curricula—self-esteem, sex education, and drug/alcohol prevention/abuse programs. In all, PFAW begrudgingly reported that 41 percent of these challenges succeeded. The report lists Pumsy, Impressions, Quest, Positive Action, and *Developing Understanding of Self and Others* (DUSO) as the most frequently challenged materials for 1991-92. They also accurately conclude that most challenges were unreported. *Tactics for Thinking* and the *Michigan Model for Comprehensive School Health Education* were also listed as being among the most frequent challenges for the period between 1982-92.

This is certainly not a new issue. But it is an issue to which parents are slow in responding—and unfortunately, one for which they are not well-prepared.

Four of the most influential and widely used of these programs include *Quest International, Pumsy, DUSO*, and *Drug*

Abuse Resistance Education (DARE), which are employed in thousands of school systems.[2] These programs are characteristically used in the attempt to help students deal with such issues as self-esteem, alcohol and drug use, and other social issues. Unfortunately, the programs may employ either various hypnotic and meditation techniques and/or questionable or scientifically discredited psychotherapeutic methods. Also, critics claim they may work to undermine parental authority and traditional values.

For example, according to James Dobson's "Focus on the Family" publication *The Arkansas Citizen*,

> The DUSO and Pumsy programs are by far the most prevalent New Age curricula as of yet uncovered in Arkansas. . . . Both DUSO and Pumsy have been removed from schools in other states for "their religious" nature. . . . School administrators fail to see the Hinduistic traits in these [programs'] relaxation techniques. [But] any encyclopedia of Hinduism will show the uncanny resemblance Hatha yoga steps have to the relaxation exercises in DUSO and Pumsy. Tensing and relaxing of muscles, deep breathing, meditation, and even the lotus and cobra positions are all identical.[3]

Next, we will examine Quest, DUSO, Pumsy, and DARE.

Quest*

Quest International has marketed three programs: *Skills for Growing* for elementary children, *Skills for Adolescence* for middle schools, and *Skills for Living*** for high school students. As these programs have been increasingly influential, they have come under criticism by some professionals who have

---

*See Appendix E prior to reading this section.

** Quest International ceased to publish *Skills for Living* in 1990 with no admission of controversy over affective education. However, no recall has been made to the many school districts where it is or has been in use. According to Quest literature, the *Skills for Living* program has been installed in "more than 2000 school systems and seven countries."[4]

investigated them. For example, the earlier *Skills for Adolescence* program has been shown to have the potential to actually increase drug use and also has had its philosophy and methodology criticized.[5]

In *Quest: Review and Analysis* (1987), Gary and Janice Beeker, who were with the Citizens for Excellence in Education, State Board of Ohio, documented that parts of the Quest curricula are based upon or utilize such things as "values clarification, positive mental attitude, Eastern mysticism, New Age philosophy and other religious concepts."[6]

Interested parents should especially take a look at Unit 11 in *Skills for Living*. This program presents students with a smorgasbord of alternate "life choices" in the attempt to help them clarify their own values.

Chart 11b of Session 2 discusses the eight basic ways to live a life. The options given are 1) living only for pleasure, 2) the philosophy of nihilism or meaninglessness and despair, 3) meaning derived from one's family, 4) working for social change to bring out the potential of mankind, 5) the search for individual enlightenment, 6) development of a personal relationship with God, 7) meaning through art, and 8) personal growth and self-transformation through psychology, parapsychology, metaphysics, and meditation.[7]

Then Unit 11, Session 3 tells the teacher to close this part of the session by having students:

> combine the best parts of any of the "Ways to Live" statements and add any words of their own to it and come up with a way to live statement that comes as close as possible to reflecting their own philosophy of life at this time. . . .[8]

In Unit 11 the authors teach, "We believe that by considering such issues as life and death, the meaning of life and the nature of the cosmos, each of us gains insight, even wisdom, which may enable us to better direct our daily lives." Students are given lessons to explore their beliefs and challenged to form their own views as to the meaning of life. But they may also be exposed to New Age concepts such as reincarnation and human potentialism.[9]

In Unit 11, Session 2, under "Procedure" the teacher is told the following:

> Explain to the class that, in this unit on philosophy, they will be dealing with such subjects as life and death, the meaning of life, the nature of the universe, and the place of humans in the larger scheme of things. Based on different life philosophies, people choose to live their lives in many different ways. Pass out or have them open their journals to the "Ways to Live Life" worksheet (chart 11b). Give the following instructions:
>
>> You have been given a set of ways to live which different persons, at different times, have advocated and followed. I'm not saying that one way is as good as another, but that all these ways do reflect how different people live. You are to write numbers next to each description to indicate how much you like or dislike each of these ways to live. Do them in order, one after the other." Further, "Remember, we are not considering what kind of life you are now leading, or the kind of life you think is prudent to live in our society, or the kind of life you think would be good for others to live, but rather the kind of life you personally would like to live.[10]

From reading these program materials, one almost gets the idea that, in the end, it really doesn't matter *which* "way of life" students choose, because the choice is ultimately up to them. Further, by broadening their horizons and exposing students to the variety of ways in which people live their lives, the teacher supposedly is attempting to help the students ascertain that which is best for them. But can children really do this all on their own, merely by looking inward? Inward to *what*?

The problem is that this approach is flawed. In any classroom, students are taught both directly and indirectly. If they are not taught positive values and morals, but left floundering to choose whatever they think at a tender age is "right for them," or what they feel subjected to through peer pressure or the surrounding culture, they may indeed choose what is *not* "right for them."

Nevertheless, visualization and even meditation techniques are interspersed throughout the curriculum. For example, in Unit 2, Session 1, a deep relaxation, visualization, and meditation technique is used in a discussion of success:

> In imagining, we can make something "almost like real" and learn from that imaginary experience, just as we can learn from our real experiences. But, in order to imagine well, it is important our bodies be relaxed. . . . Help students relax by guiding them through a short exercise such as the one that follows: give the instructions very slowly, taking long pauses between each phrase or sentence. "Become conscious of your breathing . . . take 10 deep, slow, and regular breaths . . . survey your body to see if there are tense spots. . . . Now, as you breathe in, picture your breath going all the way to these tense places. As you exhale, your breath is going to draw the tensions out with it. . . . Breathe to each tense spot. As you exhale, let all the tensions in that spot flow out of your body with your breath." Let them breathe in this relaxed way for 30 seconds or so.[11]

Another example in Unit 11 is given under "Additional Activities." Objective B, Activity 2 is called the "Energizer." The purpose is "to create an environment in which students may recall significant incidents or events from their lives, reinforcing the concept that we are the sum total of our past experiences." The directions are given as follows:

> This energizer [i.e., a specific method to help bring "energy" to the process of values clarification] is called "Elevator." Establish a quiet, meditative atmosphere within your class. Say to the students, "You are in an elevator. . . . Notice the

buttons at the side, for the different floors. . . . Each
button is marked with a number, and each number
represents different ages of your life. . . . Now, reach
the button marked "five" . . . see the doors close
. . . feel the elevator descending . . . feel it stop. . . .
The doors open and you are looking out on a scene
from your fifth year of life. . . . Notice everything
that is there . . . who is there . . . how it smells. . . .
Now say goodbye to that scene, and reach and push
the button marked eleven. . . . The doors are closing . . . etc. At each stop encourage them to recall
one or two specific memories. Make several stops
that aren't age-oriented, such as a button marked
"happy experience," "happy birthday," "very important person," "the future."[12]

In the same section, Objective D is stated to further "help
students to clarify their own philosophy of life." Activity 4
encourages them to think about questions such as:

1. If you became absolutely convinced that there were
   other realities, or that extrasensory perception or spiritual phenomena were truly possible, what would that
   do to your view of the universe and how would you
   live your life any differently?

2. If you became convinced that there was another intelligent life similar to ours on one or more planets in
   outer space, what would that do to your view of the
   universe and how would it make you live your life any
   differently?

All this indicates that students are being taught certain
things; it is not traditional education. They are taught how to
develop whatever beliefs they choose to through exposure to a
variety of possibilities and mental exercises designed to empower those possibilities.

In Unit 2, Session 10, under "Procedure," we find another
visualization:

Have them close their eyes, take deep breaths,
and relax, as you had them do in the first session of

this unit. Then, ask them to "visualize" what it would be like if they achieved this goal. Have them try to visualize very specific mental images.

One of the things they may choose to visualize is, "My name is _____ and I can get an A in English." After "opening their eyes and returning to the present," they are given further opportunities for discussion.[13] The student handbook by Jim Fadiman asserts the following about visualization: "What you are doing is training your mind to have the kind of experience you want. By imagining positive experiences, you can cause them to come true."[14]

Finally, in Unit 1, Session 3, under "Procedure," we find discussed the IALAC method, an acronym standing for I Am Lovable and Capable. Although the segment is too long to quote here, one "lesson" is that it may be a person's family members and those in authority who tend to restrict and hold back the child's potential. In the chapter by Jim Fadiman, "You Are Somebody Special," he teaches that the limitations we have are derived from our parents and family. Supposedly, when we are born all things are possible. Therefore, the way to be free of limitations is to believe in the unlimited power of ourselves and our minds.[15]

For example, children are taught to make decisions subjectively on the basis of things that are right for them or how they feel about something. Decisions are to be made primarily within oneself rather than seeking counsel primarily from parents, society, or any standards outside of an individual. The impression a student may get is that what is really important is the process of decision-making, not the final decision. Students may be presented with some of the negative consequences of certain behaviors, but the bottom line is that students must come to decisions that they personally feel comfortable with. But by telling young children that ultimate decisions and values in life are primarily found within themselves, how are we helping to guide them into making right decisions?

The basic conclusion that someone could expect students to arrive at from this program is that *everything is relative* and, in the end, it really doesn't matter.

For example, Objective C of Unit 11 states its purpose as, "To have students recognize that different people have different philosophies of life, and that one's philosophy might change at different points in one's life." Objective E of Unit 11, Activities 5 and 6, attempts to have students view both themselves and their place in the universe from differing perspectives through a process of visualization where students "use their imaginations to go on two voyages to outerspace and innerspace."[16]

In Unit 7, Session 4, "Marriage: For and Against," students are encouraged to look at the pros and cons of getting married. After a values clarification approach, students are asked whether or not it has changed their views (values) in any way.[17] Again, this is more like an indoctrination in relativism than a straightforward education in learning academic facts.

Finally, in the *Skills for Living* curriculum, students may even be encouraged to accept the idea of psychic abilities or development as a latent potential within themselves.

> It is clear from this research that *some* people have exceptional abilities [e.g., ESP] *some* of the time. What is useful for us to realize is that *most* people (the rest of us!) have some of those abilities some of the time. Also, it turns out that some of these abilities can be trained (and improved) in the same way we might learn to play a musical instrument.[18]

Quest, Humanism, and Values Clarification

The Beekers also point out that the *Skills for Adolescence* portion of Quest introduces 10- to 14-year-old children to some of the basic tenets of humanism, such as 1) the child has complete control of his own life, and 2) by using the supposedly "unlimited" power of his mind, he can achieve whatever he wants and even create his own reality. Further, by the use of written journals and visualization techniques students are encouraged to reveal intimate details about their lives and feelings. Finally, these programs may begin a process that can open students to additional New Age ideas and humanistic philosophy.[19]

The Beekers understand that Quest International officially denies that it is teaching a system of values clarification: "Quest programs do not teach 'values clarification' but guide young people to choose a healthy, drug-free lifestyle. . . . In addition, the classes make a point of not asking students to choose values that may conflict with those of their families."[20]

But to say that Quest does not use values clarification is wrong. One of the authors of the *Skills for Living* portion of the program is Howard Kirschenbaum, Director of the National Humanistic Education Center in Saratoga Springs, New York. One of the books he has coauthored is *Values Clarification: A Handbook of Practical Strategies for Teachers and Students*. In fact, the annotated bibliography and resource list at the end of Unit 1 of *Skills for Living* lists Kirschenbaum's *Values Clarification* book and specifically identifies it as the source for the "group interview," "rank ordering," "voting continuum," and "other activities used throughout this course."[21]

Again, values clarification basically teaches students to develop the set of values that is "right" for them and encourages them with the idea that they should be able to choose those values freely, without the potential "encumbrances" of adult values.[22]

Of course, Quest does not directly teach students that they must choose beliefs that are contrary to those of their own family's values. But that is not the point. It does present students with a large variety of values from which to choose in the attempt to enable them to select their own philosophy of life. For example, in Unit 11, Session 2, titled "The Meaning of Life," the *Skills for Living* curriculum defines its objectives, in part, as 1) "to help students recognize and understand many different orientations toward the meaning of life" and 2) "to help students begin to formulate their own viewpoint on the meaning of life."

As noted above, Unit 11, Session 3, discusses various "ways to live." This unit asks students a number of questions about the "ways to live" that are given. For example, "Do you know anyone whose life follows fairly closely one of these 'Ways to Live'? . . . Do they seem to have meaning, love, career satisfaction, close relationships, and psychological security in their lives?" Or, "Are any of these 'Ways to Live' harder or easier than others to follow?" Or, "Do you have any heroes or heroines (perhaps the one you are reporting on)? Which 'Way to Live' would they be most likely to choose and why?"

What is clear is that even very young students who are still forming their values *are* in effect being instructed to determine *for themselves* their own philosophy of life. This is basic values clarification. This is why the Beekers observe that both *Skills for Adolescence* and *Skills for Living* are "filled with values clarification techniques" and therefore do not constitute responsible education and "have no place in public education." Why? Because, in essence, values clarification is instruction in a form of situation ethics. There is no right or wrong, there are no moral absolutes, and personal ethics are individually acquired, depending on the situation itself or how one feels. Thus, what is right or wrong for a child may change based on his own situations or feelings. In other words, morals are entirely relative. This, of course, is a basic tenet of secular humanism.

In addition, there are seven basic steps to values clarification (again, also called nondirective decision-making) that "are used throughout" these curricula. The seven steps are:

1. choose freely, that is, free from parental or religious influence;

2. choose from a list of alternatives;

3. choose after carefully considering all the consequences of each alternative;

4. prize or cherish your choice;

5. publicly affirm your choice;

6. act upon your choice;

7. act upon your choice regularly[23]

Unfortunately, if and when children are taught to make their choices apart from parental, religious, or social authority, the child becomes his own supreme authority over what is right or wrong and what he will or will not do.

Even the National Education Association (NEA) supports this method in their publication *Values, Concepts and Techniques*:

Social psychologists underscore the importance of developing a firm set of values since they see our values as the prime determinants of our behavior. To be fully "in charge" each individual [student] needs to know the determinants of behavior and since the external world offers few consistent models [parents, religion, etc.], each needs to look at other sources, namely internal sources. The role of the teacher becomes one of helping students discover and clarify their own values [values clarification] rather than one of teaching a prescribed set of values.[24]

The Beekers present a number of objections to values clarification, noting that besides promoting secular humanism, it restricts academic excellence. Whereas quality education measures what students have learned, values clarification has nothing to measure since it is impossible to evaluate a subjective process of determining individual beliefs.

They point out there are five basic problems with values clarification:

1. Values clarification is negligent. It defines few particular values. It offers a list of alternatives with no absolute standards.

2. Values clarification is restrictive. It requires individuals or groups to create their own values without reference to outside authority or mature guidance. For a child this could lead to confusion, rebellion and chaos.

3. Values clarification is intolerant. It accepts only individuals or groups as sources of real values. It rejects tradition or divine revelation as possible sources of real values. Traditional family values are called old fashioned and out of date. Divine revelation such as the Bible is called narrow in its view and no longer needed.

4. Values clarification is inadequate. It defines few particular learning goals for students. Responsible education helps students define their learning goals.

5. Values clarification is vague. It does not evaluate students on the values they learn. Because there are no moral absolutes in values clarification, evaluation is impossible.[25]

In other words, it is impossible to clarify values until you first determine what your values are. Without this, our values can only be based on emotion and experience.

Again, much of the Quest program may be incorporated under the heading of affective or nondirective education. A former leader in the field, Dr. William Coulson, is now convinced that his allegiance to this method was a serious error. Besides ignoring the traditional method of teaching whereby information is passed from teacher to student, nondirective education leaves major decisions up to children and, in effect, makes them the teacher. Everything is left up to the student to decide; the student is the god of his own world. Again, it emphasizes emotions, feelings, and experience over facts and assumes a relative approach to ethics, implying there is no right or wrong way or belief.

All this is why Coulson is against the Quest program and now lectures around the country to warn parents and encourage their opposition. He believes that Quest programs are "fundamentally flawed, requiring a completely new foundation."[26]

If the parents' instinct tells them that there is something wrong with Quest, I want them to come away more confident in their instinct. I want them to feel like they are parents with common sense, not book burners, sensors and fanatics.[27] (See chapter 15.)

Because of its content, parents' groups have challenged the Quest program and, as we have seen, had it removed from a number of school districts in New Hampshire, Ohio, Kansas, and elsewhere. Quest's *Skills for Adolescence* was initially removed from the entire state of North Carolina by the state board of education which observed of Unit 6 on drugs and alcohol,

"Although revisions have been made to this material, the revisions still do not meet state requirements or standards."[28]

Quest subsequently complied and was reinstated. It has thus been responding to parents' and professionals' concerns and in some cases has made revisions that make the program less affective and more directive. *Skills for Adolescence* has recently added a four-page insert which quotes the Federal Drug-Free Schools and Communities Acts (see pp. 174-76) and complies with it by stating a no-use message.

But Quest continues to try to mix decision-making exercises with a no-use stance toward drugs and remains essentially an affective-based program.

Dr. William Kilpatrick notes in his book, *Why Johnny Can't Tell Right from Wrong*, that Quest "still operates on the dubious assumption that morality is a by-product of 'feeling good about yourself.'"[29]

DUSO

The author of Developing Understanding of Self and Others (DUSO), Don Dinkmeyer, accepts the idea that there are no absolute values and therefore all things are relative. He also thinks it is important for children to know this. Parents who teach their children absolute right and wrong make them "misdirected," and as a result these children need to experience "reorientation."[30] "During Reorientation, the counselor helps the counselee consider alternative attitudes, beliefs and actions."[31]

DUSO programs have been in use since 1970 among guidance counselors and elementary schoolteachers. When revised versions (DUSO-1R and DUSO-2R) began incorporating various "fantasy trips," which employed meditative and hypnotic-like procedures, parents and others began to investigate the appropriateness as well as effectiveness of DUSO. Besides self-hypnosis/meditation techniques, DUSO also uses affective and values clarification approaches, as well as experimental group counseling. But the scientific research on many of these programs, including DUSO, has been ambiguous at best, but generally has demonstrated their ineffectiveness.[32]

DUSO has also been challenged throughout the country and it, too, has been modified or removed in many cities. For example, one challenge in New Mexico led to adopting Senate Memorial 45, a resolution stating that

> the teaching of or counseling by certain mind altering psychological techniques be entirely eliminated in New Mexico public schools.... These psychological methodologies can involve such teachings as Transcendental Meditation, altered states of consciousness or the occult.[33]

Other states are beginning to follow suit. For example, on July 1, 1990, a new law went into effect in Colorado. It mandated that every state school board adopt a policy concerning "all educational programs and courses of instruction which expose pupils to any psychiatric or psychological methods or procedures."[34] This law requires adequate review and input from parents and other concerned members of the public. Such legislation was the result of a citizens' campaign that began when a parent discovered his seventh-grade child was being subjected to hypnosis techniques as a stress-reduction method in his health class.

Despite a significant degree of success in combating programs that are suspect either because they are unsubstantiated scientifically or because they promote religion, it is easy for parents to meet resistance. For example, in the spring of 1990 in Cullman, Alabama, a school superintendent refused to meet with a parents' group who wished to discuss their objections to the DUSO program. It is felt that he illegally blocked their access to either use or rent the school auditorium for an informational meeting. He further denied parents the right to withdraw their children from participation in the counseling program without an excused absence. Nevertheless, over 600 parents attended a meeting to examine their school's curriculum. Their concerns produced two results: 1) removal of sections dealing with progressive relaxation, guided imagery, fantasy, etc., and 2) the parents' option to remove their children from the program was reinstated.

Pumsy

In similar fashion, parents' groups have also protested the Pumsy programs such as *Bright Beginnings* (kindergarten–first grade); *Pumsy: In Pursuit of Excellence* (ages 6–9); and *Thinking, Changing, Rearranging* (ages 9–17).

Parents have protested this material for its incorporation of methods which are now illegal according to the Hatch Amendment, such as hypnosis and meditation techniques and unscientific therapeutic methods (see chapter 9). Concerned parents' groups have resulted in the Pumsy curriculum being dropped or significantly modified in Arkansas, Florida, Colorado, Texas, Alabama, South Carolina, and other states.[35]

The following is a statement of the Dallas Baptist Association, November 26, 1990:

> Pumsy and Friend utilize mind control techniques normally associated with hypnotism and other psychologically based treatments. Unless written consent has been received from informed parents authorizing their child's participation in the program, this appears to be a violation of the Code of Federal Regulations, 98:4. Pumsy and Friend as a curriculum embraces and promotes philosophies associated with the New Age Movement. . . . It is our sincere belief that public educators should not be promoting the beliefs which are characteristic of New Age philosophy, lest they find themselves involved in the promotion of religion, and in violation of the directives of the law of the land. Finally, the ethical base upon which the Pumsy curriculum is founded is that of a Situational Approach, i.e., there are neither absolute rights or absolute wrongs. Students are encouraged to decide ethical issues based on the "givens" of a situation. The situational ethic is a base doctrine of the secular humanist movement. . . .
>
> The clear findings of researchers indicate the healthy child is developed in a setting with clearly stated right and wrongs on issues of significant ethical import. . . . It is our request that the utilization of this curriculum be discontinued at the earliest possible moment.[36]

Let's take a moment to examine one aspect of Pumsy, which according to promotional literature is in over 40 percent (16,000) of our nation's elementary schools.

After several teaching sessions designed to help the child learn to base his self-esteem on internal processes rather than external realities, there is a session called "Painting Mind Pictures" (recently changed to "Let's Imagine"). "Let's Imagine" is a relaxation guided imagery exercise designed to internalize the particular lesson being taught to the child.

The following is to be read slowly by the teacher: "Relax and get comfortable with both feet on the floor. Let your shoulders relax, and let your arms and hands rest in a comfortable way. Let your head relax. You can let it fall forward a little if it helps you relax. Let your whole body work like it was in slow motion. Close your eyes, but not tight. Take slow, deep breaths. When you breathe out, you might feel like you could sink into the chair."

The counselor or teacher then guides them in a visualization, meeting "Friend" and "Pumsy the dragon," two characters upon whose back the children experience flying. The emphasis is on feeling "very, very safe" and strong and powerful. Long pauses are taken during the narration—including time to communicate with "Friend" and "Pumsy."[37]

If the child experiences a negative external conflict, the message is that this technique can be used to help the child progress from a "muddy" confused or stressful mind into a "sparkle" creative or secure mind. To cite an illustration, Craig Branch of Watchman Fellowship received a call from a distraught mother in Atlanta, Georgia. She had just experienced a disturbing episode with her daughter.

The mother was making the routine drive to school with her second-grade daughter and older son. The son, just as routinely, was picking on his younger sister. But the daughter was unusually quiet. This prompted the mother to call out her daughter's name. The mother called louder when she received no response. Still there was no reply, which caused the mother to turn around where she observed her daughter, eyes closed and head nodded forward as if asleep.

A bit alarmed, the mother stopped the car and loudly called her daughter's name, shaking her arm. The daughter seemed to awaken, a little startled. The mother asked, "What's wrong? You wouldn't answer when I called." The daughter responded, "Oh, don't worry, Mom; I was with my friend Pumsy."

Upon further inquiry the mother discovered that her daughter's class had been learning this meditation technique from the school's guidance counselor. This was the first time she had ever heard of Pumsy or that a guidance counselor was regularly conducting visualization sessions in the classroom. She was concerned. Why was her daughter learning to meditate at school? Was this an innocent exercise in imagination? Or was it a technique that might possibly mentally condition her daughter toward something unhealthy? And who was Pumsy, and why was the guidance counselor teaching her to make it a friend? What was Pumsy teaching her daughter? The mother wanted answers and had none.

If a school administrator, school board members, or anyone else does not see the connection between hypnotherapy, Eastern practices, and such techniques used in certain school curricula, you might have them compare the following four verbatim excerpts. One is a standard induction technique from a book on *hypnosis*, one is a *yoga* exercise, and two are *school* curricula. Can you tell which is which? And if not, what does this tell you?

1. Sit in a chair or lie on the floor on your back with your arms extended on the floor about six inches from your body and your palms facing the ceiling. Keep your legs flat and turned slightly apart. Move around a little until you are comfortable, then be still.

Take slow, full breaths through your nose and feel the rise and fall of your stomach as you breathe. Try breathing without any pauses or jerks between your inhalation and exhalation. Imagine that with every breath you take, you're becoming more and more relaxed. Pay attention to nothing but the rhythmic movement of your breath as you inhale and exhale.

Find a comfortable position. Close your eyes. Focus your attention on the place between your eyebrows. Relax that area. Relax the muscles around your eyes. Relax your cheeks. Relax your mouth and jaw. Relax your tongue letting it rest comfortably on the base of your mouth. If you feel tension anywhere in your face and head, focus your attention on that spot and let go of the tension.

Let that wave of relaxation flow into your neck. Relax your shoulders—your upper arms—your lower arms—your hands—and your fingers. Feel your arms getting warm and pleasantly heavy.

Relax your chest—your abdomen—and your pelvic area. Let that wave of relaxation flow down into your legs. Relax your thighs—your knees—your calves—your ankles. Relax your feet—and your toes.

Feel your whole body getting warm and pleasantly heavy. Allow yourself to be supported by the chair or the floor. If you feel tense anywhere in your body, focus your attention on that spot and let go of the tension.[38]

2. Make sure you are completely comfortable. Stretch your legs, your arms. And now begin to relax. Close your eyes and take a deep breath . . . and exhale . . . and relax. Completely relax. Relax your legs, lower back, relax your shoulders. Relax your shoulders, your arms, your neck, your face. Relax your whole body, just relax. Take another deep breath . . . and exhale . . . let go, and relax. Become aware of the rhythm of your breathing, and as you inhale, relax your breathing and begin to feel your body drift and float into relaxation. The sounds around you are unimportant, let them go, and relax. Let every muscle in your body completely relax from the top of your head to the tips of your toes. As you inhale gently, relax. As you exhale, release any tension, any stress from any part of your body, mind and thoughts.[39]

3. Lie on the floor with legs slightly apart, arms loosely at sides, palms turned slightly upwards, fingers gently, but slightly curled, eyes closed. Tense and relax the following body parts separately.

   - Tense toes on right foot and hold for 5 seconds and release;
   - Tense entire right foot for 5 seconds and release;

- Tense lower leg for 5 seconds and release;
- Repeat with upper right leg, then right buttock;
- Then repeat with other leg;
- Repeat with abdomen, chest, shoulders, right upper arm, lower arm, upper arm, neck, lower face, upper face, skull.

Lie in this relaxed state for 3–4 minutes, while you concentrate on your breathing, not thinking of anything else.[40]

4. Lying on your back with arms at sides, adjust the body into its most comfortable position.

We want to become aware of each area of the body to determine if it is truly relaxed (limp). Begin by directing full attention to the feet. If tensed in any way, relax them.

Next, focus attention on the calves and knees. "Feel" them, and remove all tension by making the necessary adjustments. Slowly draw the consciousness into the lower abdomen, upper abdomen, chest. If you detect even the slightest muscular contraction, relax it.

Now become aware of the fingers, forearms, upper arms, and shoulders. "Feel" the condition of each of these, and withdraw all support so that it becomes limp. Adjust the neck as necessary, and relax jaw and all facial muscles.

Finally, direct your attention to your breathing. Have it become slow and rhythmic. This will minimize the thoughts that can enter and divert the mind.

You are now in a state of profound relaxation. Remain this way for several minutes with the attention fully focused on your breathing.[41]

From where are these techniques derived? They just didn't happen spontaneously. The similarity to psychological methods or Eastern techniques is obvious. But if what we are giving our children in school is difficult to distinguish from hypnosis and yoga methods, what exactly do we expect our children to learn? Perhaps this is why even many professionals have expressed their concern.

Brian Newman, director of inpatient services at the Minirth Meier Clinic in Richardson, Texas, comments, "I have reviewed the [Pumsy] material from a professional standpoint, as have two psychologists at our clinic; and each of us has expressed feelings of concern in regard to using this within the school system."[42]

Dr. Majel Braden, a curriculum expert in Arkansas, noted the following points in his detailed analysis of the Pumsy curriculum.[43] Dr. Braden holds a doctorate in education/counseling with a specialty in curriculum development and has had eight years teaching experience and four years counseling experience.

1. The concept is not based on sound learning theory;

2. It offers a distortion of normal child development and promotes a form of indoctrination by attempting to restructure the way a child thinks;

3. It ignores a variety of different variables within a child's environment;

4. It fails to address the needs of special children;

5. It offers a false assumption that all feelings must be judged as either good or bad and that the "clear positive mind" is the only thing of value;

6. By concentrating on unseen factors such as one's attitude and emotions, the primary base of measurement is a reinforcement/reward model which is easily subject to abuse;

7. Pumsy invades the privacy of the pupil and his parents.[44]

Physician observed of Pumsy and similar programs,

No need for such broad-based, unselected intervention counseling has ever been scientifically established. In fact, government studies have shown that 87 percent of children *do not need* the emotional and behavioral "help" that programs like Pumsy claimed to provide. The net effect, therefore, is potentially very harmful to a majority of elementary students.[45]

Dr. Martin Orne of the University of Pennsylvania Medical School, author of the article on hypnosis for the *Encyclopedia Britannica*, has also critiqued the progressive relaxation and guided imagery methods, specifically using Pumsy and DUSO as examples.[46]

We recognize that there are many people, Christians included, who see nothing wrong with the use of Quest, Pumsy, DUSO, and DARE in the public school system. They do not feel that these programs are New Age, religious, or psychological in nature.

For example, Jill Anderson is the developer of Pumsy. In response to critics, both she and Timberline Press (the publisher) have distributed a fact sheet and other material which attempt to answer parents' objections to this program. Unfortunately, their facts are often not accurate.[47] Anderson and Timberline Press claim that the Hatch Amendment deals with religion and therefore Pumsy is not a violation of the Hatch Amendment. But the Hatch Amendment refers to programs which are not directly related to academic instruction and are psychological in nature, designed to impact behavioral, emotional, and attitudinal characteristics. In fact, Jill Anderson attributes her theories as originating with substantial "reliance upon the theories found in R.E.T.—Rational Emotive Therapy," developed by atheistic psychotherapist Dr. Albert Ellis.[48] Therefore, Pumsy does violate the Hatch Amendment.

They also claim that Pumsy does not involve the use of meditation or hypnosis, yet again it does. They claim that Pumsy has nothing to do with the New Age Movement, and yet it does. Jill Anderson herself should certainly be familiar with New Age philosophy since she studied process theology (a form of panentheism) in seminary. So, in essence, the response of Timberline Press and Jill Anderson is not credible.

As more and more news and information concerning Pumsy has circulated around the country, parent groups have mobilized effective challenges in their school districts. The more that school boards are taking the time to examine the issues and documentation presented by the parents, the more they are restricting or eliminating Pumsy.

The following are some additional school districts which have modified or dropped Pumsy in addition to those on page 65: Bristol, Tennessee; Coffee County, Oklahoma; Mountain Brook, Dothan, and Decatur, Alabama; Carollton, Texas; Pettsylvania County, Virginia.*

What About DARE?

DARE (Drug Abuse Resistance Education) is the most widely implemented drug education program in the United States and arguably the one most recognized by the public. Not only is it in all 50 states (and several foreign countries), it is also being taught as part of core curricula and has been expanded to all grades, K-12.

DARE is a very popular program and certainly offers a number of positive features, such as the use of police officers as role models. Further, DARE does not employ visualization, meditation, guided imagery, or anything New Age.

The problem with DARE is not with the motives behind the program and certainly not with those who implement it, but in its methodology. For example, it is modeled upon a values clarification approach and frequently incorporates humanistic premises.

Unfortunately, police officers are trained in law enforcement not psychology. Thus, with the best of intentions, they are employing psychological methods which have yet to establish their effectiveness and may be harmful.

Some of the problems involved in the DARE program include certain faulty assumptions and methods. For example:

— The DARE manual itself confesses the following, "A basic precept of the DARE program is that elementary school children lack sufficient societal skills to resist peer pressure and say no to drugs"[49]

— The assumption that fostering self-esteem will prevent drug abuse (see chapter 9)

---

* Newspaper accounts and superintendent's letters on file with Watchman Fellowship, Birmingham, Alabama.

— The role of the police officer as more of a buddy, without reaffirming a healthy fear and respect for law enforcement

— Psychological methods such as role playing, psychodrama, and values clarification

— "risk assessment"—delving into a student's personal home life which may violate the privacy of the home and, in a few cases, has ended up pitting students against their parents.

In affective education systems, parents are usually not cited as role models for a number of reasons. First, in values clarification approaches, children are taught to make their own judgments without pressure from anyone, including parents, who naturally tend to put pressure on their children to make value judgments similar to theirs. Second, parents may actually be seen as "negative" role models because of the rules they impose on children. Third, because of peer pressure or other reasons, children may not look to parents as role models; hence, in DARE police officers provide the adult role models for children.[50]

Overall, perhaps the greatest concern is the values clarification approach of DARE. Values clarification may be taught under such names as "decision-making skills," "critical thinking," and "personal choice"—terms which make the program sound better than it really is. Unfortunately, to the extent the DARE program is based on values clarification it will not be successful. In fact, it will probably be harmful to the best interests of children.

The problems of values clarification approaches were noted in the *Wall Street Journal* over a decade ago:

> By affirming the complete relativity of all values, they, in effect, equate values with personal tastes and preferences. If parents object to their children using pot or engaging in pre-marital sex, the theory behind Values Clarification makes it appropriate for the child to respond, "but that's just *your* value judgment. Don't force it on me."

Furthermore, Values Clarification indoctrinates students in ethical relativism. . . . Sidney Simon, Howard Kirschenbaum and other Values Clarification authors repeatedly belittle teachers of traditional values. Such teachers, they claim, "moralize," "preach," "manipulate," and "whip the child into line." Their positions are "rigid" and they rely on "religion and other cultural truisms."[51]

William J. Bennett himself, the former chief of the U.S. Enforcement Agency and former U.S. Secretary of Education, emphasized that "values clarification programs in today's classrooms range from the inadequate and impoverished to the intolerable and detestable."[52]

The real problem with values clarification is not merely that it makes the child his or her own final authority, but as we noted earlier, it is ultimately an indoctrination in situation ethics. For example, values clarification may work for moral values in an area the child is convinced is wrong (such as drug abuse), but work against moral values in an area the child thinks is right (such as premarital sex). Thus, teaching children to independently develop their own values cuts both ways. A child may resist the pressure of a drug pusher in one instance, but then turn around and resist parental pressure for sexual abstinence. Once children are convinced that their own choices are the absolute standard of what is good and right, then on what basis do they find any authority outside of themselves as legitimate? In part, what the child is being taught in values clarification is to resist anything with which he personally disagrees, regardless of its source. Could this emphasis explain why the DARE program has apparently been so secretive? For example, why are interested researchers forbidden to have copies of the DARE program materials? Why are DARE officers forbidden to release the curriculum to parents, teachers, and school administrators until the program has ended? Why aren't parents' meetings held until at least six weeks into the program? And why are officers forbidden to release the instructors' guides to anyone—including parents, teachers, and school administrators—except drug coordinators?

Paradoxically, some DARE officers have opposed bills which

contain key provisions that would result in appropriate revision of DARE. These bills reject values clarification approaches and mandate that students be taught that use of drugs and underage use of alcohol is wrong, harmful, and illegal. These bills assert that public schoolchildren should not be taught that they have a legitimate right to decide on their own whether or not to use drugs.

For example, Sergeant Charles Thompson, president of the DARE Officers Association of Alabama, recently wrote to all county sheriffs in the state asking them to protest two sections of Law SB72 (sections 3 and 4) because, "These Two Sections, as referenced, would effectively remove *decision making skills* and *critical thinking* [values clarification] as prevention techniques from all currently practiced curriculums."[53]

Finally, a number of studies have indicated that the DARE program is far less effective than its proponents claim. Given its values clarification approach, this is not necessarily surprising. These studies have been published by the Research Council on Ethnopsychology in Comptche, California, and by researchers at the University of Illinois, the University of Kentucky, and elsewhere.[54] These studies indicate that the DARE program has either little or no effect or has actually increased drug use among program students.[55]

Although the DARE program has had some success with one drug (cocaine), for other drugs such as LSD, amphetamines, depressants, heroine, PCP, and inhalants, the *DARE Evaluation Report for 1985–1989* submitted by the Evaluation and Training Institute of Los Angeles concluded that reduction levels were "not statistically significant."[56]

This may explain why M. Amos Clifford wrote in the *California Prevention Network* that "every expert prevention specialist" he knew who had independently and critically evaluated the DARE program "believes that DARE should be ranked somewhere between a sham and mediocrity."[57]

In light of all this, we should remember that a new law which took effect October 1, 1990, mandates that a drug education course is illegal if it involves students in values clarification decision-making approaches where they decide for themselves whether or not drug use is right for them. The U.S. Department of Education now claims that all public school districts have certified that they are in compliance with the new law. That, of course, is not necessarily the case, and it is up to concerned parents or other individuals to find out if the schools really are in compliance. For example, if through its values clarification approach DARE is actually teaching students to decide for themselves whether drugs should be taken, rather than actively teaching them (in accordance with law) that illegal drug use is wrong and harmful, then DARE itself would be in violation of the law.

The above materials prove that education across the country is not what it used to be. Increasingly, we are finding encroachments of various aspects of New Age religion and practice, unsubstantiated psychotherapeutic techniques, and other questionable methods. The programs we have mentioned in this chapter are far from exhaustive. Merely because a particular school district is not using one of these programs does not permit the conclusion that similar methods are not being utilized. In fact, it might be safe to say that in the entire country there are relatively few school districts that are not touched in some way by the flood of these types of programs currently on the market.

This is why it is important for parents and educators to become aware of the issues involved and why these programs may actually be harmful to the educational and psychological development of children. We understand that educators are concerned about children, and we do not question their motives. But we maintain that before programs are implemented at the local school level, let alone nationally, that they be subject to appropriate criteria for determining both effectiveness and safety.

In an area as important as medical treatment, the nation expects proof of safety and efficacy before powerful drugs, treatments, or surgical techniques are permitted. The nation also has the right to expect that safety and effectiveness be demonstrated in the field of education before questionable techniques are widely used upon our children.

Chapter 4

∎

TRANSPERSONAL EDUCATION: THE HIDDEN AGENDA

One of the most disturbing aspects of transpersonal education is the apparent legerdemain or subterfuge of some of these educators who seem to have their own agenda, regardless of parents' wishes.

Most New Age theorists and curriculum developers acknowledge problems of implementation because of resistance from parents. New Age educator Gay Hendricks and Northern Illinois University educator Thomas B. Roberts write, "Often, schools that are ready to adopt new ways of teaching hesitate because they expect the parents will not understand what is going on."[1] These educators do acknowledge that there may be some resistance to the implementation of their philosophy and techniques. But they don't really like it. In *Spinning Inward*, Maureen Murdock encourages teachers with, "You may receive resistance from some family members, but don't be deterred."[2]

After heaping praise on the "heroes" in New Age education who are pioneering their methods, Marilyn Ferguson quotes Mario Fantini, former Ford consultant on education, now at the State University of New York, as saying, "The psychology of becoming [i.e., enlightenment] has *to be smuggled into* the schools."[3]

Deborah Rozman's *Meditating with Children* is a good example of such smuggling. This book was distributed to all California

77

public school teachers, many of whom began to implement its occult techniques in their classrooms. Rozman even describes how she hides the real nature of her Eastern/occult meditation: "Due to fear of parent criticism, I call it centering and concentrating our energies. . . . I tell the parents and my classroom's volunteers that centering was a relaxation exercise for increasing the children's concentration."[4] Thus,

> The process of integrating these meditations into a classroom has been left to the teacher. This is intentional because so many changes are now occurring in classroom policy. . . . If you don't see how you can possibly integrate them into your particular situation, pick out the elements you feel you can use.[5]

In a question-and-answer section of *Growing Up Gifted*, Barbara Clark rhetorically asks, "Can we really use altered states of consciousness in the classroom? What will the parents say?" This is a good question. How does she answer? She counsels, "The phrase altered states of consciousness may sound too strange so you need to use other terminology that better communicates what you intend to do."[6]

To be sure, these educators don't often use potentially emotive or controversial terms like *meditation*, *hypnosis*, or *spirit guides*. As Jack Canfield comments, "If you're teaching in public school, don't call it meditation, call it 'centering'"[7]

In *How to Help Your Child Have a Spiritual Life: A Parent's Guide to Inner Development*, psychiatrist Annette Hollander observes that a *secular* approach to New Age practices has proven useful for implementation of these methods:

> A revolution is happening in education. . . . Transpersonal educators believe we can learn to experience the divine within ourselves. In practice, this usually means teaching children how to alter their consciousness in order to be able to relax and "center" at will, and to contact inner wisdom. . . . Transpersonal educators have found *secular ways* of teaching children to work on their inner lives.[8]

Thus, she points out that although altered states of consciousness and occult rituals used to be taught only in religions, "Now there are secular disciplines, nonreligious 'trainings' to reach those [same] goals."[9] As an illustration in the purely psychological realm she observes,

> When Chogyam Trungpa, Rinpoche, set up a preschool for his Buddhist community in Boulder, Colorado, there were no Buddhist "teachings." The spirit of Buddhism was conveyed by the psychological state of the people who worked with the children.[10]

Consider a standard text on transpersonal education: *Transpersonal Education: A Curriculum for Feeling and Being*. It begins by noting that "transpersonal education *is* for the whole person, and views the school as a place where this wholeness can be supported and encouraged."[11] This "wholeness" involves an essentially *religious* view; in other words, transpersonal education seeks to employ the classroom in the promotion of religion. Further, it has entered the classroom because its religious practices have been "stripped of their jargon":

> [Transpersonal educators] are incorporating practices from a dozen fields into the teaching/learning situation. Insights gained from the upsurge of interest and meditation, biofeedback, martial arts, Eastern thought, and altered states of consciousness are finding their way into the classroom. *Stripped of their jargon*, these fields of study are accelerating and improving conventional learning, as well as bringing new and more personal areas of learning into the classroom.[12]

In other words, taking out the religious jargon supposedly means that these practices are no longer religious and can be used in public schools. Unfortunately, in Eastern/occult practices, merely removing religious terms and replacing them with secular counterparts does not affect the essence or outcome of the practice at all. As Shakespeare observed, "A rose by any other name would smell as sweet." For example, the Hindu practice of Transcendental Meditation may be termed the "Science of Creative Intelligence," the religious practice of yoga may be called "psychophysiological exercise," or meditation may be called "centering," and visualizing spirit guides may be called contacting one's "higher self." Nevertheless, the essence remains the same and has similar results no matter what you call it. And regardless, exposing children to religious methods without the religious words is certainly a preconditioning for those practices when they are encountered in a full-blown religious context.

Transpersonal educators do indeed see occult methods as "a source of powerful new tools and possibilities for the classroom,"[13] and we should not think that teachers who are members of religious groups, enthusiastic graduates of New Age seminars, spiritists, parapsychologists, or followers of Eastern gurus are never going to influence children positively in the direction of the premises of their own worldviews.

In *The Humanist* John Dunphy observes what everyone knows—that in many ways the battle for the future is a battle for the minds of children. He is one of the few who is perfectly clear about his particular agenda: Christianity and humanism are in a war to the finish:

> I am convinced that the battle for humankind's future must be waged and won in the public school classrooms by teachers who correctly perceive their role as the proselytizers of a new faith. . . . [One that recognizes] Divinity in every human being. . . . The classroom must and will become an arena of conflict between the old and new—the rotting corpse of Christianity, together with all its adjacent evils and misery, and the new faith.[14]

An article in the *Rocky Mountain News* (June 3, 1992) by economist Thomas Sowell of the prestigious Hoover Institute, illustrates the bias of some modern educators and the consequences it has brought to schoolchildren. Although strongly worded, the assessment by Sowell is not incorrect; he underscores what many parents and educators seem unwilling to concede:

No small part of the reason why American school children fall so far behind their contemporaries in other countries is that Japanese and other youngsters are studying math, science and other solid subjects while our children are being brainwashed with the latest ideological fashions—whether about homosexuality, environmentalism, multi-culturalism, or a thousand other non-academic distractions....

We are not sending our children to school to have their values and psyches remolded to suit ideological zealots on world-saving crusades. Few parents or citizens realize the pervasiveness of classroom brainwashing, or the utter dishonesty with which it is smuggled into the schools under misleading labels....

By what right do other people usurp the responsibilities of parents and use the schools to carry on guerrilla warfare against the values that parents have taught their children?...

The zealots know what they are doing, and are well aware of its illegitimacy. One teacher's manual for a widely used program includes instructions on how to evade complaints and how to deal with students who don't go along. A mother who complains individually is almost certain to be told that she is the only one who has ever objected. There may be controversies raging from coast to coast, and even law suits filed over the program, but you will still be told that you are the only one who has complained. Complain in a group and they will cry, "censorship."...

The glib gurus who set the trends are at war with all the fundamental values of this country. You would have to know these people, or read their writings, to understand the venom in their hatred. To such people, our children's education is a small sacrifice on the altar of their vision.[15]

The flood of new curricula did not occur overnight. It resulted from an incremental process over the past three decades.

Initially, these programs surfaced in rather blatant forms in receptive pockets of the country such as California, but now they are widespread due, in part, to their cleverly disguised nature.

In fact, this strategy has been articulated by New Age leader Dick Sutphen as he writes,

> One of the biggest advantages we have as New Agers is, once the occult, metaphysical and New Age terminology is removed, we have concepts and techniques that are very acceptable to the general public. So we can change the names and demonstrate the power. In so doing, we open the New Age door to millions who would not be receptive.[16]

In our next chapter, we will see examples of where we are headed.

Chapter 5

WHERE TRANSPERSONAL EDUCATION IS HEADED

Many people do not believe that there is a definite under-lying occult New Age educational philosophy or direction in certain areas of public education. Many think that these occurrences are only sporadic or incidental and not increasingly widespread.

The philosophy of transpersonal education is characterized by viewing schools and other learning environments as places to develop "spiritual potential." Spiritual potential is defined as an extremely broad set of philosophies and practices that include Eastern religion, the occult, and spiritism. In fact, most aspects of the occult can be incorporated under the transpersonal umbrella.

One definition of transpersonal education is given by Gay Hendricks and James Fadiman, editors of *Transpersonal Education: A Curriculum for Feeling and Being*: "Transpersonal education is an approach that aims at the concurrent development of the logical and the mystical, the analytical and intuitive."[1] Examining the chapters in their book is illustrative of this approach.

For example, in "Transpersonal Psychology and Education" educators Thomas B. Roberts and Francis V. Clark concede that the domain of transpersonal education involves a new image of man and a new worldview incorporating such things as altered states of consciousness, meditation, self-realization, parapsychology and psychic phenomena, other cultures and their psychologies, especially Eastern psychologies, and "newly discovered forms of energy" (such as occult energy).[2]

We are told that exploring altered states of consciousness can become a natural alternative to the student's desire to use illegal drugs:

> Open discussion of altered states of conscious-
> ness can throw some light on this mysterious topic
> and inform students that there are effective non-
> drug ways of exploring and controlling conscious-
> ness. A complete drug education program should
> recognize the natural human desire for exploring
> consciousness and should provide acceptable alter-
> native routes.[3]

Dreamwork, which in many quarters is used for spirit contact, is also advocated:

> Dreaming is an altered state that is being used
> successfully by teachers both as technique and as
> content. From a transpersonal point of view, dreams
> are important because they give us messages from
> the unconscious, and they afford easy access to a
> different reality. Dreaming is one door to our inner
> selves.[4] (See Glossary.)

Thus, Roberts and Clark believe, "No education of man can be complete which leaves these potential forms of consciousness undeveloped."[5] They observe that centering exercises provide a good introduction to meditation and the inner flow of psychic energy:

> In many Eastern traditions, including the Japa-
> nese martial arts, the center of physical energy is
> located in the belly, about two inches below the
> navel, and two inches in front of the spine. Focusing
> attention on this center while noticing the move-
> ments of breathing in and out is an easy and widely
> used method of centering.[6]

Further,

> Parapsychological topics make excellent class
> reports. Students enjoy learning about parapsy-
> chology and doing their own experiments.... Sub-
> jects which were formerly taboo for "respectable"
> psychologists are opening up, and they provide an
> excellent example of how fields of knowledge change
> with the times.[7]

Significantly, these educators point out that research on
psychic healers indicate they tap into some kind of power or
force and that perhaps biofeedback training or other self-
controlled altered states of consciousness may enable other
people to become psychic healers.[8] But as coauthor Weldon
has demonstrated in *Psychic Healing: An Exposé of an Occult
Phenomenon*, the only power psychic healers tap into is the
power of the spirit world. Spiritism is the lowest common
denominator of virtually all forms of psychic healing.[9]

Nevertheless, many educators have noted why transpersonal education is popular with students: because they enjoy
turning inward. "Teachers are often surprised at how eagerly
students respond to transpersonal teaching techniques. Some
of these approaches seem to awaken the natural desire in each
of us to explore our inner selves."[10]

If this exploration of the inward self for wisdom and power
is the essence of transpersonal education, it is also the essence
of the problem. Turning inward in the ways described is not
only a terribly poor excuse for academic education, it is an
open door for indoctrination into the religion of the occult.

How prevalent are these New Age techniques in the public
schools? Who are some of the contemporary educators promoting them? Consider the following illustrations. According
to Dr. Stewart B. Shapiro and Louise F. Fitzgerald of the
University of California at Santa Barbara, "A transpersonal
orientation to learning was detected in the writings of 89 well-
known representatives of humanistic education."[11]

In testimonials before the U.S. Department of Education in
1984, among the examples of New Age influence in classrooms were how to do horoscopes, conduct seances, use a

Ouija board, meditate, role-play characters such as spiritists and warlocks, cast a witch's circle, and do occult readings.[12] Below we will cite a number of examples from leading educators.

Jack Canfield

Jack Canfield is director of Educational Services for Insight Training Seminars in Santa Monica, California. He is a founder and past director of the Institute for Holistic Education in Amherst, Massachusetts, past president of the Association for Humanistic Education, and has been a consultant to over 150 school systems, universities, and mental health organizations. Canfield is both well-liked and highly influential in the field of education, especially in the popular self-esteem field, which is now a multibillion-dollar industry in America. For example, he is president of Self-Esteem Seminars, which boasts over 400 school districts as clients. He is also chairman of the board of the Foundation for Self-Esteem and sits on the board of the National Council for Self-Esteem. (The former board, interestingly, awarded Jill Anderson and Pumsy the Golden Apple Award.) He is the author of numerous books and articles on education, such as *A Hundred Ways to Enhance Self Concept in the Classroom* and *Self-Esteem in the Classroom*.

According to his 1991-92 self-esteem seminar newsletter, Dr. Canfield has been conducting in-service training to teachers and delivering conference keynote speeches on the topic of self-esteem for over 20 years. He speaks or conducts seminars in 250 public schools a year. He has also practiced psychotherapy for five years.

In one article he and Paula Klimek discuss the importance of transpersonal education. Almost the entire gamut of the occult is endorsed as being applicable to children's education, including dreamwork, mandalas, meditation, Arica psychocalisthenics, yoga, occult "centering," "sacred" dances such as those found at the spiritistic Findhorn community and through anthroposophical eurythmy/sufi dances, teaching children to see their chakras, auras, and healing energies, magic circles, and psychic chanting. He even advocates such books as Robert Masters and Jean Houston's *Mind Games*, which has a section on "raising spirits."

Perhaps not surprisingly, Canfield's *The Inner Classroom: Teaching with Guided Imagery* (1981) and his *Self-Esteem in the Classroom* (1986) teach that the introduction of spirit guides is an important element of self-esteem or other educational programs.[13]

Further, he sees one of the most important aspects of New Age education in general as helping students to contact their own spirit guide:

> One of the most central concepts in New Age education is working with "life purpose." After doing some centering activities, students are asked to review their life in reverse, starting in the present and going backward over time until they come to the time before they were born. Here they meet a guardian spirit whom they ask, "What is my life purpose?" They then review their life in the other direction, coming forward in time and reconsidering the events of their life in the light of their life purpose. We recently conducted this exercise with a group of seventh graders.[14]

In other words, after the softening-up methods of relaxation techniques, the teacher guides the children back through the year, to the previous year, to being a young child prior to entering school, back to being a baby, to the child's birth, back into the mother's womb, and then back to the time *before conception.*

> You are about to meet a special guide, your own special guide. A guide whom you may ask what the purpose of your life is.... Feel your guide's unconditional love, and strength and beauty.... Let whatever happens, happen.... Communicate with your guide.... Listen to your guide.[15]

The authors also write,

> In a growing number of classrooms throughout the world, education is beginning to move into a

new dimension. More and more teachers are exposing children to ways of contacting their inner wisdom
and their higher selves.... New Age education has
arrived.... An influx of spiritual teachings from
the East, combined with a new psychological perspective in the West has resulted in a fresh look at
the learning process.[16]

Part of this "new psychological perspective" utilizes the
occult psychology of Roberto Assagioli as can be seen in Canfield's 1980 paper *Psychosynthesis in Education: Theory and Applications*. Assagioli was the Italian psychiatrist who developed
psychosynthesis and who was a prominent student of New
Age medium Alice Bailey. He even directed her Lucis Trust
organization in Italy for two years.[17] Bailey was the author of
Education in the New Age and 21 other occult books. Actually,
almost all her books were received by inspiration from her
spirit guide, "Djwhal Khul" ("The Tibetan").[18] In essence,
Bailey's spirit guides influenced Assagioli who, in turn, influenced Canfield. Canfield's educational approach then, is fundamentally based on Alice Bailey's material filtered through
Roberto Assagioli. Canfield's interest in spiritism is hardly
surprising if his educational theories are heavily influenced by
revelations from the spirit world.

Nevertheless, Canfield and Klimek go on,

Our work began in the mid-60's with the emergence of the field of "humanistic education" ...
within the past five years we have also witnessed
the birth of "transpersonal education," the acknowl-
edgement of one's inner and spiritual dimensions,
through working with such forms as dreams, meditation, guided imagery, centering, mandalas and so
forth.[19]

They explain that "learning how to center one's self is one of
the most important processes of all the New Age educational
tools."[20] Next, they describe how this "centering" is to be
accomplished—through progressive relaxation techniques
and guided imagery, for which they recommend Hendrick's

and Roberts' *The Centering Book* and *Second Centering Book.*
Canfield comments that, "When students are participating in
a guided imagery experience, they are in an altered state of
consciousness."[21]

Also described is the theory behind using guided imagery
which intends to prove to children their spiritual nature through
exposure to psychic energies. (Dr. Canfield is himself the
author of the handbook *The Inner Classroom: Teaching with
Guided Imagery*): "It becomes very important to validate the
spiritual essence of children to help them discover their own
unique inner qualities . . . [e.g.,] a special inflow of super conscious energy which can be tapped into—indeed must be
tapped into if New Age children are to be fully educated."[22]

Dr. Canfield may indeed be a leader in the field of modern
education, but he is teaching anything but a traditional approach.

Stewart Shapiro

Dr. Stewart Shapiro is a noted educator with the University
of California. In the 1989 *Educational and Psychological Measurement* journal, he observed that "according to the transpersonal
approach, schools and other learning environments should be
used for the development of spiritual potential as well as
academic, vocational and socio-personal learning."[23]

Shapiro describes this transpersonal philosophy as "spiri-
tual/mystical," as "being based on transpersonal psychology
which is concerned with those ultimate human capacities and
potentialities."[24] He believes that in this philosophy, "Intuitive and receptive modes of consciousness are equal in
importance to cognitive, rational, logical and active modes."[25]

But how does Dr. Shapiro see these "intuitive and receptive
modes of consciousness" (that have *equal* importance to cognitive and logical modes of thinking) as being produced? He
describes them as being produced by the "use of various
psychological techniques [fantasy, guided imagery] . . . relaxation techniques" and other methods which "at times border
on the occult."[26]

Shapiro initially sought to objectively measure the alleged
effectiveness of transpersonal methods of learning because of

their growing impact. He felt these approaches were so wide-spread that controversy has arisen and, therefore, there needed to be scientific evidence demonstrating their utility.

> Since various practices in the public schools, ranging from the so-called religion of secular humanism on the one hand, and to meditation, the use of fantasy and imagery, and references to magic, the occult, or witchcraft on the other, have become so controversial of late . . . that an objective, reliable and valid measure . . . was considered both practically and theoretically timely.[27]

Dr. Shapiro also recommends we look into children and youth in schools who have been "taught how to induce altered states of consciousness in themselves, such as those states in psychic healing, parapsychological phenomena, yoga, biofeedback, and meditation."[28] He calls our attention to "twenty-five well-known representative writers in transpersonal/humanistic psychology and education,"[29] especially Thomas B. Roberts. (Among them are leading New Agers, occultists, and psychologists such as Marilyn Ferguson, Ken Wilber, Roberto Assagioli, William James, Gay Hendricks, J. Krishnamurti, Ken Keyes, and Michael Murphy.)[30]

Thomas Roberts

Dr. Roberts is a graduate of Stanford University who now teaches development and special education at Northern Illinois University. He gained prominence in education circles in 1977 when he coauthored *The Second Centering Book* with Gay Hendricks. (Dr. Hendricks had coauthored the original *The Centering Book* in 1975.)

In the preface to *The Second Centering Book*, Roberts and Hendricks discuss the value that New Age education has for them: "We see transpersonal education as part of a larger progression that society is going through. . . . [Those who are] explorers of consciousness, or 'inner space,' indicate that our ideas of human nature are vastly wrong."[31]

What the authors suggest is that our true nature is not limited and human but infinitely knowledgeable, powerful, and perfect (godlike). Our higher self, or divine intuitive self can supposedly be accessed through these Eastern mystical religious techniques.

Again we see the common theme that we must bypass the logical, rational, cognitive mind and move into an alternate state of consciousness if we are to "properly" understand ourselves, to know things correctly—and to enhance our individual performance and spiritual growth.

Roberts continues to explain,

> The consciousness revolution is permeating education, too. This book is part of it. Teachers, administrators, and parents who are concerned with optimum learning are introducing transpersonal techniques into the classroom.... It expands our knowledge of not only where we are, but when we are, what we know and who we are.[32]

For example, in another professional education journal article titled "States of Consciousness: A New Intellectual Direction, A New Teacher Education Direction," he writes, "New principles of learning based on the research on states of consciousness offer opportunities for teacher educators to restructure curriculum, to modify content, and to revise instructional methods."[33]

In other words:

> An enormous amount of curriculum development stands waiting to be accomplished at all educational levels. In terms of methods, teachers continue to use consciousness methods ... that increase student learning of existing content and at the same time give practice in using advanced mental abilities. In terms of professional standards, there is strong evidence that biofeedback, meditation, yoga and similar exercises result in enhanced mental development, physical health, and social responsibility.
>
> From a state of consciousness perspective, the

future of education is wide open. It concludes the intelligent use of all states and their resident abilities.[34]

Barbara Clark

Dr. Clark is a professor of education at California State University, Los Angeles. She is a well-known teacher of those who teach the gifted and author of the graduate school text *Growing Up Gifted: Developing the Potential of Children at Home and at School*. Here, Clark also advocates a variety of Eastern/occultic methods for the educational curriculum.

For example, her concept of "integrative education" is intended to create what she calls "transpersonal learning." She suggests that students learn to find the "hidden teacher/artist" within them and that the philosophies of East and West merge. "Guided fantasies and dreams, recognition and use of altered states of consciousness, and centering activities will develop more of our intuitive [psychic] abilities.... All of this and more lie ahead as we seek to bring all of our knowledge, feelings, talents, and creativity into the classroom in the service of actualizing and transcending."[35]

In discussing psychic energies and parapsychology in general, including out-of-body experiences and healing energies, she says that current research into such subjects contains "valuable content for the education of human beings."[36]

She proceeds to suggest that an Eastern monistic view of reality is beneficial for educational advancement:

> Reality is seen as an outward projection of internal thoughts, feelings, and expectations. Energy is the connector, the center.... Western pragmatists will join Eastern mystics, and all humans will benefit. Human potential, as yet unknown, will have a chance to develop....It may be, as Bentov said, that "we are all part of this great hologram called Creation which is everybody else's SELF....You create your own reality. It's all a cosmic play, there is nothing but you!"[37]

This is, of course, not merely a form of *advita* Vedanta Hinduism. It is also the teachings of innumerable spirits such as "Seth."[38]

Barbara Clark also encourages the exploration of the mystical/ spiritistic energies associated with occult traditions throughout history such as *mana*, *chi*, *kaa*, and *prana*. She believes that we need to tap into or "balance" this psychic energy. In part this is because, "The ebb and flow of human energy has been central to many belief systems—the Yin/Yang of ancient China, the Ka of the ancient Egyptians, the Chi of the Eastern Indians, the Kaa of the American Indians."[39] Thus, she comments, "We are all affected by the differing amounts of energy available in our lives and by what inhibits or facilitates our energy supply."[40] But unfortunately, as we have documented in *Can You Trust Your Doctor?* (chapters 5 and 6), this so-called "universal energy" is fundamentally occultic and frequently indistinguishable from spiritistic energy itself.[41] To encourage children to tap into it is irresponsible.

If we consider what Clark advocates, we can see how easily Eastern/occultic ideas and practices might be incorporated into educational curricula. Clark asserts that Eastern and Western philosophies are merging together today in a climate of acceptance. She views creativity in the classroom as helping to serve students in the process of self-actualization and transcendence. The more we discover through an integration of the East and West, "the more we can validate the ancient wisdom that has come to us from the Chinese, Hindu, Egyptian and other age old teaching."[42]

Among the things advocated in Clark's text *Growing Up Gifted* are parapsychology and psychic abilities, Eastern forms of alleged enlightenment, channeling psychic energy, the use of fantasy, progressive relaxation, autogenic training, centering, guided imagery, and visualization.[43] Would you believe that this book is widely used as a textbook for those who teach gifted children? For example, it was until very recently the required textbook for teachers at the University of Alabama in order to maintain their certification through continuing credits in the graduate program and remains on the recommended supplemental reading list.[44]

Deborah Rozman

Deborah Rozman is an educational consultant and has taught at workshops and related educational programs throughout the country. She has also taught visualization, transpersonal psychology, centering, and meditation "to all age groups in California Public Schools. Her books have been sponsored by superintendents of several school districts and by church leaders as effective learning tools."[45] Rozman is the author of *Meditating with Children* and *Meditation for Children*, having cumulative sales of almost one-quarter million.

Her *Meditating with Children: The Art of Concentration and Centering*, is described as "a workbook on New Age educational methods using meditation."[46] Rozman believes that her meditative educational methods will lead to an unfolding expansion of awareness for both teacher and child alike.[47] She encourages teachers to remain at least "one step ahead of the children" by researching the subject beforehand "and practicing the meditations and exercises before the class" in order to be more effective.[48] Her personal philosophy is basically New Age/Hinduist; she accepts the idea that we are all part of God. "Meditation takes us back to the Source of all Life. We become one with ALL."[49] She defines ultimate reality as "the Source" or "existence, consciousness, and bliss," the standard designation for Transcendental Meditation's description of the Hindu god Brahman.[50]

Thus it is not surprising that Rozman describes her educational philosophy and goals in characteristic New Age categories and the importance of meditation to further these goals. She emphasizes,

> Education, like religion, is in the process of undergoing radical transformation to accommodate the growing recognition of the need to eliminate outworn forms that are no longer effective in providing for the optimal growth of children. New breakthroughs... are bringing new light into the consciousness of man. This light some have called the dawning of the New Age. It is slowly leading to regeneration in the educational system. ...

> Eastern researchers, who for thousands of years have studied the nature of consciousness . . . have developed [meditative] processes for building bridges in consciousness to close . . . [these educational] gaps.[51]

Nor surprisingly, both of Rozman's books contain complete instruction in meditation, using the typical methods of progressive relaxation and guided imagery. She informs us that the ultimate goal of meditation is to tap into the "Source" or God. By doing so, the child will lose all self-identity as he awakens to his true nature: oneness with the true reality underlying the universe—including a oneness with the true reality of all people, vegetables, animals, and minerals.[52] Of course, this has been the goal of Hinduism, Buddhism, and other Eastern/occult religions from time immemorial.

Thus, "Much of the knowledge from which we draw, in learning to use meditation to get in touch with the great wisdom inside us, comes from Eastern meditators, many Hindu or Buddhist, who have researched deeply into the soul."[53] After a discussion of karma she observes that one purpose of meditation is to permit our real self to emerge— our God self. She tells children that there is "no real separation between ourself and others" and she discusses the fact that children can expect to encounter "miracles, psychic experiences, visions, etc., [which] are all part of the unfoldment."[54] She even encourages children to blasphemously apply specific biblical phrases relating to God, making them personally applicable to themselves. Among the phrases listed are "I and my Father are one," "before Abraham was I am," and "I am that I Am."[55]

Jean Houston

Jean Houston was the keynote speaker at the 1989 conference for the prestigious Association for Supervision and Curriculum Development in Orlando, Florida, where over 6000 educational curriculum developers were present. Here she spoke of how in meditation she contacted the goddess Sarasvati. Robert Caldwell, founder of a different Quest educational program, praises Houston as one of the best work-shop leaders he has ever seen.[56] She has served on faculties of psychology, philosophy, or religion at New York University, the University of California, and Columbia University and is past president of the Association for Humanistic Psychology. In 1985 she was awarded the National Teacher-Educator Association's award as Distinguished Educator of the Year (USA).

Not only is her influence felt by curriculum writers, but it is also felt by school guidance counselors, as she was the featured speaker at the 1982 American Association of Counseling and Development, National Conference. In the brochure's advertisement she is depicted as the premiere presenter in the field of New Age human capacities and altered states.

Houston is also the author or coauthor of many books on the occult, including *Mind Games*, *Life Force*, and *The Possible Human*. The name "Jean Houston" continually surfaces as the prime mover and inspirational force for transpersonal educators. But any parent who takes the time to read Houston's books will discover that what Houston would logically propose for education is nothing less than exposing children (many of whom she views as "natural visualizers")[57] to dangerous occult philosophy and practices.

In *The Possible Human*, she reports that researchers, herself included, are "rediscovering what the early Sanskrit psycho-physical philosophers had always known—that the key to transpersonal realities lay in the expansion of physical awareness."[58] This research, she says, is helping us gather "the momentum for bringing new forms into being . . . evolving the self, and finally, growing God-in-us."[59]

Houston instructs the reader in a progressive relaxation exercise and guided imagery in order to become what she calls a "co-creator" in the evolutionary process. The guided imagery takes the participant down deep into his own body and eventually to a door, behind which "is someone who understands all about you. . . . This wise being . . . can become a powerful ally for you . . . however you must act on the advice given."[60] This, of course, is a spirit guide, something Houston advocates contacting in other books such as *Mind Games*, another of her "educational" endeavors in which she confesses that "trances, ASCs [altered states of consciousness] and hypnoid states should prove relaxing and beneficial."[61]

For example, in *Mind Games*, coauthored with her husband, Robert Masters (of Masters and Johnson sex researchers' fame), she tells people how to contact what she terms "the Group Spirit." She discusses how this spirit is to be raised in classic seance terms. For example,

> We are beginning to go now into trance together. We are going to experience deepening together, and, finally, each of us will contribute to the pool of consciousness out of which the Group Spirit will draw its substance and arise to exist once again.[62]

She proceeds to describe this Group Spirit as a literal spirit entity: "an actual, intelligent being, conscious, and powerful," in which participants are to permit the "spirit to inspire us."[63] The Group Spirit contacted will even continue to be with people after the "seance" has ended. For example,

> The Group Spirit will appear to you in a dream, and you will be able to gain a clear and detailed impression of its appearance, and you may be able to enter into a conversation with it, and various things might be revealed to you.[64]

For those who follow the New Age Movement, this is a common pattern, no matter what area of culture one observes. For instance, a parallel incident will demonstrate why parents should actively express their concerns and put a stop to this occult direction in education.

Bernie Siegel

Dr. Bernie Siegel is a professor at the Yale University Medical School and past president of the American Holistic Medical Association. He is the author of a longtime bestseller, *Love, Medicine and Miracles*.

This book emphasizes the use of self-hypnosis and meditation for treating disease, terminal illness, and promoting optimal health. He discusses and describes relaxation techniques, hypnosis, meditation, and guided imagery or visualization, stating that "they are really all part of the one process, as you'll understand when practicing them."

Dr. Siegel describes these as basic techniques for "contacting the unconscious mind and harnessing its powers" and that this emphasis is a result of "the public fascination with Eastern studies combined with a long-established undercurrent of interest among psychologists."[65]

How did Dr. Siegel arrive at this message?

The answer is both revealing and alarming. Siegel writes, "In June of 1978, my practice of medicine changed as a result of an unexpected experience I had at a teaching seminar." Dr. Siegel was attending a seminar on "Psychological Factors, Stress, and Cancer" conducted by Carl Simonton. Dr. Simonton and his wife are cancer therapists who encourage people to contact "inner guides" for health or other purposes.

Initially, the lecture appeared to be a secular, scientific seminar. But the direction soon changed:

> The Simontons were the first Western practitioners to use imaging techniques against cancer. ... The Simontons taught us how to meditate. At one point, they led us in a directed meditation [guided imagery] to find and meet an inner guide. I approached this exercise with all the skepticism one expects from a mechanistic doctor. *Still I sat down, closed my eyes, and followed directions.* I didn't believe it would work. ... Instead, I met George, a bearded, long-haired young man wearing an immaculate flowing white gown and skullcap. It was an incredible awakening for me, because I hadn't expected anything to happen. The Simontons taught us to communicate with whomever we called up from our unconscious minds.[66]

Siegel then describes the spiritual turn in his life and how the content of *Love, Medicine and Miracles* was subsequently directed by conversations and input from "George." In essence, Dr. Siegel began as a scientist. But through guided meditation and his contact with George, he moved quickly into New Age occultism. For example, in his book he espouses kundalini yoga and Eastern meditation: "With guidance and practice, meditation can lead to breathtaking experiences of cosmic at-oneness and enlightenment."[67]

Later he even degenerates into promoting seances (he calls them "healing circles") where people can conjure the dead and communicate with them. He writes,

> Death is no barrier to this intuitive, spiritual consciousness. It continues after death, and it communicates between the dead and the living. . . . As I have opened myself to my patients' beliefs, I have received many messages from those who have died.[68]

But this is specifically what God warns everyone against: "Let no one be found among you . . . who is a medium or spiritist or who consults the dead. Anyone who does these things is detestable to the Lord" (Deuteronomy 18:10-12).

Maureen Murdock

Maureen Murdock is an educator and therapist who conducts teacher workshops across the United States. She is the author of *Spinning Inward: Using Guided Imagery with Children for Learning, Creativity and Relaxation*. She asks, "How do we learn? How do we expand creativity? How do we know those things which we know intuitively?" She proceeds to describe the development of her own theory after research into the New Age movement: "I began meditating . . . [and] introduced this technique to my own children. . . . Encouraged by their response, I then tried short centering exercises with my kindergarten class."[69]

Murdock writes,

> We used to think of the newborn child as an empty cup waiting to be filled with knowledge by its wise parents and an all-knowing society. That theory no longer holds. . . . Their inherent knowledge is such that they see the present and the future more clearly than we do. . . . For this reason, present learning techniques are inadequate for them.[70]

Nevertheless, she goes on to describe the presuppositions behind her strategy—premises which also refer to contacting one's "inner guide." For example:

> The search for a deeper connection to self helps older adolescents to realize their own inner wisdom and recognize that they have all the answers within if they take the time to center... to find a wise being within who gives guidance and support and who may have answers to personal questions.[71]

The American Personnel and Guidance Association

The American Personnel and Guidance Association is the major professional organization for elementary guidance counselors. One of its subsidiaries is the American School Counselor Association (ASCA). Their professional journal is called *Elementary School Guidance and Counseling*.

This journal devoted an entire issue exclusively to transpersonal approaches to learning. Among the authors of 12 articles were leaders' names we have focused on in this handbook: Thomas B. Roberts, Beverly Galyean, Gay Hendricks, and significantly, Dinkmeyer and Dinkmeyer, the former editors of the journal and originators of DUSO.[72]

These articles further demonstrate that techniques used in education such as affective decision-making, progressive relaxation, and guided imagery/fantasy, are not only linked together but may intentionally be a part of the transpersonal/ New Age strategy.

Guest editor Jon Carlson, professor in the Educational Foundations and Counselor Education Department of the University of Wisconsin, begins this special issue by writing:

> I hope that this special issue of the *Elementary School Guidance and Counseling Journal* jars you from your current role and helps you realize the long term futility of traditional approaches to counseling.
> ... This issue intends to expose the reader to the multitude of approaches available to help counselors

help youngsters grow and move toward developing their true potential.[73]

Among the surprising guidelines Carlson lists as being useful in pursuing optimal development are those that encourage children to "learn to empty your mind on a daily basis through centering, meditation, or relaxation. An empty mind has room for new learning and change."[74]

Dr. Carl Rogers is quoted as saying, "The basis for values will need to be recognized as discoverable within, rather than in [religious] dogmas or the material world . . . [perhaps in] our growing use of psychic forces and psychic energy."[75]

The article by Herbert Otto, president of the National Center for the Exploration of Human Potential, argues,

> There is every indication that children have extra-sensory capacities [psychic abilities] that are progressively extinguished or suppressed as they grow older. . . . The school system and especially the counselor play a crucial and formative role in the development of [this] potential.[76]

Next, Dr. Thomas Roberts presents a systematic attempt to help counselors operate within transcendent states of consciousness. He writes:

> Counseling is entering one of the most exciting stages of its development, that of consciousness counseling. It consists of helping people to develop their full capacities in every state of consciousness. . . . What makes consciousness counseling most distinctive and exciting to me is that it recognizes states of consciousness that have not been recognized by most western psychological theories.[77]

Roberts then goes on to list his mentors and other leaders in the consciousness movement: Timothy Leary of LSD fame, Aldous Huxley, Jean Houston, shamans, and other participants or researchers in the occult. Noting that psychedelic users and cult leaders are also explorers of altered states of consciousness, he warns counselors to encourage the "responsible exploration" of these "inner frontier" areas.[78]

Nonetheless, "imagery, dreams, biofeedback, relaxation, [and] beginning meditation . . . should be studied and practiced before they are used. . . . Hypnosis and advanced meditation should be attempted with oneself and with clients only after specified training in those methods."[79]

Don Dinkmeyer and Don Dinkmeyer, Jr. are the developers of the popular self-esteem drug/alcohol prevention program DUSO. They write:

> Affective education has helped us get more in touch with the child's feelings and attitudes. Education needs to place more emphasis on the affective area and more attention on developing affective curriculum. . . . The move toward positive wellness has been accompanied by a great increase in the interests of relaxation response and the renewed interest in Yoga. It is believed that these two activities may stimulate inner healing power. There are many research studies that indicate the positive effect of meditation on physical health.[80]

Dinkmeyer recommends Deborah Rozman's TM-based *Meditation with Children* as an example of "meditation for teachers and students," as well as Herbert Benson's relaxation response as a "simple meditative technique that unlocks your strengths and assets."[81]

Further,

> If education is to be conducted in a milieu that is growth producing, we must recognize that there is a need for retraining of educators. . . . If children are to become able to cope with stress and tension and to learn how to relax, they must learn the concepts with help from teachers who model positive wellness.[82]

Beverly Galyean, the pioneer of confluent education (the merging of Eastern mystical and Western approaches to education), encouraged guided imagery methods in the classroom because,

On the affective plane they enable students to discover the resources of their inner wisdom, their "higher Self," and to source themselves from within rather than depend on outside persons and events for nurturance.[83]

As James Fadiman of Stanford University and the California Institute of Transpersonal Psychology had remarked in the previous article, "The transpersonal approach encourages children... to consider alternative truths."[84]

Following Galyean we find an article by Dr. Deane Shapiro, dean of academic affairs at the Pacific Graduate School of Psychology, and clinical instructor in the Department of Psychiatry and Behavioral Sciences at Stanford University Medical School. The article begins by quoting the Hindu scripture, the *Bhagavad Gita*, and then asks the rhetorical question, "How does the person of enlightenment gain this discipline? And how, as counselors and educators, can we encourage the pursuit of this discipline in children?"[85] He believes:

A new model, a new vision of our human potential is necessary.... This vision may come from the eastern esoteric and mystical tradition; others may come from our western scientific research laboratories and field experiments. Parents, teachers and educators are in a pivotal position to transmit aspects of this vision to future generations, to offer them a vision of an enlightened life.[86]

Next we find Gay Hendricks, professor in the School of Education at the University of Colorado. He refers to the "quiet, compassionate revolution underway in our schools" as laying "the groundwork for a truly holistic curriculum." He points out that "centering activities" and other affective education materials are now "a trend in which several hundred thousand teachers and counselors participate on a daily basis. ... The activities I advance to accomplish this are largely relaxation activities, communication skills, meditation, movement and fantasy journeys."[87]

Concerning children he writes:

Children take to relaxation, meditation, and other centering activities like proverbial ducks to water. . . . I would like centering and other affective educational activities used on a more regular basis in our schools. . . . What I would most like to see is a curriculum that fully integrates centering, communications, values clarifications and other key affective skills . . . to equip students with the skills of communicating about their inner experience.[88]

Following Hendricks we have an article by the very popular teacher/workshop leaders Jack Canfield and Paula Klimek. They begin with a "message of inner wisdom" written by a seventh-grade student after a guided imagery session:

My [inner] guide was a voice and it still is. Many times I feel like a failure, like report cards, and it (the voice) speaks not with a roar, but with a gentle call, like my grandmother who died one year ago: "Press on. Don't give up. Press on. Don't give up."[89]

Thus,

One of the most exciting aspects of our work has been in the areas of centering, fantasy, imagery, and meditation. . . . Techniques such as eye and ear centering, breath relaxation, chanting, mandala work, meditation, and receptive imaging are particularly useful.[90]

Finally, Marianne DeVoe is an educational consultant for the county schools of Knoxville, Tennessee. She concludes:

For the transpersonal educator, spiritual growth includes discovering an expanded view of man, experiencing altered states of consciousness, developing in terms of self-realization and self-transcendence, accepting subjective experiences, and realizing inner states. Specifically, the transpersonal educator is committed to helping individuals focus internally as well as externally in an effort to effect personal growth and improve learning potential. Relaxation, concentration, guided fantasy, dreams, meditation, centering, biofeedback, and parapsychology (ESP, dream telepathy) are all components of the transpersonal approach. A variety of these techniques are being introduced into the traditional classroom setting and are being pursued by students outside the school environment.[91]

In essence, the contents of this journal issue (published in 1979) are characteristic for the field of transpersonal education. But today this discipline has expanded and "matured." Just as national chain bookstores are now abandoning their New Age sections and incorporating this material into the appropriate conventional disciplines (psychology, sociology, biology, etc.), so the educational establishment is now in the process of integrating these New Age education methods into conventional curricula.

Herbert Benson

A name that frequently appears not only in transpersonal education literature, but also in some current and popular curricula as well, is Herbert Benson. Benson's work and books, *The Relaxation Response* and *Beyond the Relaxation Response*, are cited to justify and give some sort of scientific credibility to the use of progressive relaxation techniques in the classroom. Examples can be found in various *Elementary School Guidance and Counseling* journals, major health textbooks, and school health curricula.

Some educators have objected to the accusation that Benson's model of progressive relaxation is hypnosis or promotes Eastern religious meditation. This defense is totally without merit.

For example, some of Benson's professional colleagues, members of the National Academy of Sciences, Committee on Techniques for the Enhancement of Human Performance, make the following observation on Benson after a discussion of the claims of autogenics and progressive relaxation to reduce stress and enhance performance:

These approaches are in many ways similar to Eastern practices of meditation. Of considerable interest in the 1970's was the work of Benson, a Harvard professor of medicine who developed what he called "the relaxation response," which was really a *westernized version of Transcendental Meditation*.[92]

To clear any doubt of the fact that Benson's "relaxation response" is based on the beliefs and practices of Eastern religious meditation, let Benson speak for himself. Benson writes in his seminal book, *The Relaxation Response,*

This book brings together and synthesizes recent scientific data with age-old Eastern and Western writings that establish the existence of an innate human capability: *The Relaxation Response.* . . . It has been evoked in the religions of both East and West for most of recorded history.[93]

He repeatedly reveals the source of his technique in comments like,

From the collected writings of the East and West, we have devised a simplified method of eliciting the Relaxation Response. . . . The altered state of consciousness associated with the Relaxation Response has been routinely experienced in Eastern and Western cultures throughout all ages.[94]

Other Novel Approaches

With transpersonal educators calling for a merging between East and West, the influence of other Eastern/occult philosophies on educational theory should not be neglected. Scientology, psychosynthesis, Theosophy, the educational philosophies of Krishnamurti and Sri Aurobindo, as well as many other similar influences have impacted segments of today's education. A brief sampling is offered below.

Sri Aurobindo's "Integral Education"

Sri Aurobindo was a noted Hindu occultist/spiritist and developer of what is termed "Integral Yoga." His Eastern/occult philosophy is an essential part of his educational method. For example, altered states of consciousness "are of key importance in Aurobindo's system. They relate essentially to the growth of the soul, or the unveiling of the inner center, and of developing its union with Being [Brahman]."[95]

Thus, Sri Aurobindo's "Integral Education" holds that "the first principle of true teaching is that nothing can be taught" because the teacher is merely a facilitator who helps draw out the student's own divine potential from within. Students learn by themselves and the role of a teacher is "not to impose knowledge but rather to guide, suggest, and demonstrate by the example and influence of their own being."[96]

Krishnamurti

Krishnamurti was a novel Hindu "guru" whom Annie Besant, then president of the Theosophical Society, had groomed to become a new Christ. Krishnamurti rejected this role and began his own path. On education he comments, "Another function of education is to create new values. Merely to implant existing values in the mind of the child, to make him conform to ideals, is to condition him without awakening his intelligence."[97] Like Aurobindo, Krishnamurti believed that "nothing can be taught and that true education is a process of mutual exploration."[98] From his viewpoint, the individual student is "already whole and everything is already integrated [therefore] education is [merely] coming to realize the situation."[99]

Maria Montessori

Maria Montessori (see appendix B) felt that education could be used as a vehicle to bring about a true human unity and worldwide peace. Like Aurobindo and Krishnamurti, she saw the teacher more as a guide or facilitator, not as an authority or dispenser of knowledge. Given the proper environmental atmosphere, children would learn on their own. "Like Aurobindo and Krishnamurti, Montessori held the ideal of developing whole people who function at full capacity, with all aspects of their nature."[100] Further, "She experimented with bringing meditative techniques into the classroom, first through encouraging concentration on desired objects and, then, through the use of silence exercises."[101] From the ages of 6 to 12, children were to be given "a vision of the whole, the unity of the universe and the unity of life."[102]

Rudolf Steiner's Waldorf Schools

Rudolf Steiner was a noted occultist who left Theosophy to begin his own religion. Although students at the school are not taught the religion directly, Steiner's educational philosophy is based on the occult system of anthroposophy (see appendix A). Nevertheless, like Aurobindo, Krishnamurti, and Montessori, he saw the purpose of a holistic approach to education as the education of the whole child.

Edgar Cayce

Edgar Cayce, like Rudolf Steiner, was a spiritist and not a formal educator. Nevertheless, the spirits who spoke through him encouraged children to be educated in typical New Age fashion. The psychic readings of Cayce outlined several key aspects to children's education, among them dreamwork to explore the inner self, regular use of the imagination, and presleep hypnotic or other suggestions to stimulate the child's higher self during the night. Not surprisingly,

> The Edgar Cayce Readings suggest a relationship between the faculties of intuition, imagination and psychic ability, as they play a part in the [spiritual] awakening of the soul . . . [this] increases the importance of the parent or teacher providing the child with . . . particular periods for exposure to creative imagination.[103]

In conclusion, what was once strange and even bizarre is now becoming part of accepted educational procedure. If we wait another 20 years the battle for quality education may be lost. This is why concerned parents and educators must begin to work now to retain both the integrity and credibility of our children's learning.

Evaluation

Consider what you have just read. How far have we progressed with this supposed enlightenment of education? We have retreated backward into ancient and pagan beliefs. What was considered a lunatic fringe just ten years ago has now moved into mainstream culture, involving some medical school professors and even our own children's educators.

All this underscores the fact that our country is in the midst of a crisis. At the heart of this crisis is a battle of values, ethics, and philosophy. Someone once said, "Actions or behaviors are the blossoms of ideas." What someone believes about good and bad, right and wrong, self, family, marriage, other people, culture, religion, God, the world, and the nature of reality will affect the way(s) he/she responds to life and its situations.

In the United States the above categories had until recently been shaped by Judeo-Christian values. But our nation is now experiencing repercussions from the dominance of secular humanism and, increasingly, the occult.

During the 1992 presidential and congressional race the family values and respected religious traditions were made a campaign issue. The 1992 Republican platform stated,

> The culture of our nation has traditionally supported those pillars on which civilized society is built: personal responsibility, morality, and the family. Today, however, these pillars are under assault. Elements within the media, the entertainment industry, academia . . . are waging a guerrilla war against American values. . . . Children, the members of our society most vulnerable to cultural influences, are barraged with violence and promiscuity, encouraging reckless and irresponsible behavior. This undermines the authority of the parents, the ones most responsible for passing on to their offspring a sense of right and wrong.[104]

The common perception in our country is that the quality of education is significantly deteriorating. College SAT and ACT scores are falling, illiteracy is rising, and other indicators all reflect an ongoing decline. Many educators, especially the National Education Association, have put the blame on parents, on children's low self-esteem, and on behavioral problems generated from the growing number of dysfunctional homes.

On the other hand, it is our belief that too many educators have been promoting what might be termed an "experimental mysticism" and psychotherapy in the classrooms. We think this also reflects a serious problem and that it, too, is responsible for the decline in education.

Parents' Rights

Parents and educators must become informed about these issues. It is their own children's education and future that are at stake. Everyone has the right to be concerned about what his/her children are taught. Happily, many parents' groups supporting traditional family values have begun to emerge across the country to respond to these issues. And just as happily, some school boards and administrators have reacted in a receptive and responsible manner and have either deleted the objectionable material or, more importantly, have adopted policies to prevent new occurrences.

But many if not most school systems have either not addressed such issues or have reacted defensively—continuing to expose students to some potentially harmful curricula.

The courts have held that parents have the primary right of education for their children.[105] Schools should be academic institutions, as they have been traditionally.

> Families and communities err when by neglect or design, they transfer to the school, responsibilities that belong in the home and in the community. Schools were created to help and strengthen families, not to undermine or substitute for them.[106]

Conclusion

Parents and educators need to be responsive, but in an informed and intelligent manner. By way of summary and .

introduction to the remainder of this book, we offer the following conclusions and observations.

1. The New Age Movement is a spiritual and sociological phenomenon in our country. Its beliefs and practices are establishing themselves in many areas of our culture.

2. It can be demonstrated that there are many educators and curriculum developers who are either personally involved in the New Age perspective or have accepted the practices, techniques, and theories without knowledge of their source.

3. It can be demonstrated that the adoption of New Age/ occultic ideology and practices is not just sporadic and random, but that there is an underlying philosophical current in place, ready to produce a flood of these curricula into the public schools across America.

4. It has been our experience that these beliefs tend to enter through counseling; self-esteem, stress reduction, health, and gifted programs; creative writing classes; some global education courses; and some literature curricula.

5. The usual form these programs take is in deep breathing relaxation or progressive relaxation exercises, guided imagery, and visualization. These are sometimes associated with inappropriate and ineffective value-free or affective learning programs.

6. The techniques and the presuppositions on which such programs are based are intrinsic to Eastern and other mystical religious traditions and practices (such as Hinduism and meditation). Further, they are frequently synonymous with the techniques of hypnosis and trance induction. Unfortunately, often these techniques are disguised to project a secular appearance.

7. Religious practice in the schools constitutes a violation of the establishment clause of the first amendment since public schools cannot promote the practice or ideology of religion.

8. Even if administrators refuse to acknowledge this connection to occult religion, there is the further problem of

using hypnosis and dissociative techniques, or other psychotherapeutic methods. Using psychological techniques without the informed consent of parents constitutes a violation of the Hatch Amendment and is illegal.

9. It can be established that there are genuine risks and liabilities for both school and children if unlicensed teachers are involved in administering speculative or unproven therapeutic techniques so that resulting psychiatric problems occur. This may be considered malpractice.

10. Many self-esteem-oriented, drug or alcohol prevention, and sex education curricula utilize a nondirective decision-making process without empirical justification. In fact, evidence suggests these methods have actually produced a rise in such activities.

11. The content of many of these materials is likely a violation of students' and parents' consitutional right to privacy.

12. Parents should not only be well-informed but closely involved with their children and teachers to make sure such practices are not occurring in the classroom.

13. Because of the frequency of incidents, we are recommending that state or local school boards adopt official policy prohibiting the use of these techniques. This would prevent the costly political, emotional, educational, and financial consequences of litigation.

Chapter 6

∎

Affective Education and Psychotherapy in the Classroom

In this chapter we will examine affective education, its use of psychotherapy in the classroom, and how our current situation came about.

The Affective Approach

Briefly defined, the affective decision-making approach involves a psychological method designed to influence the emotional content of a child's learning process—usually internally and without outside influence. This will supposedly lead children to greater self-esteem, self-determination, and appropriate self-centeredness in personal decisions.

Thus many of the curricula using this approach teach that learning the correct *process* of making a decision is as important as the decision itself. For example, the "Directions" program is part of PALS, a substance abuse curriculum for schools sponsored by the North Central Alabama Mental Health Board. It teaches the following: "*How you decide* is often just as important as *what* you do—maybe even more so."[1] Thus, junior high students are taught to go through the process of considering positive and negative consequences of behavior and to "list any alternative, no matter how wild it may be."[2] Along with many other programs concerning alcohol, the PALS instruction is that "drinking is a personal matter and a decision that only each of us can make."[3]

Another example is found in an Illinois program called *Life Education Centre*, a curriculum for elementary school children. It teaches, "You can trust your parents, teachers and real friends, but *most of all* you should trust your *own feelings* about the best way to act in confusing situations."[4] These programs usually begin with the worldview that the child is basically good (or even perfect) and that all values are relative. Thus, the programs assume no absolute truth exists as an authority. Many of these programs encourage a child to look inward for answers and power. The child's decisions are seen as experiential and autonomous. But it should be noted that the extent to which subjective processes hold sway, they work to undermine the more objective authority of family, church, and law.

Having read some of the New Age/transpersonal theories in the earlier chapters, it should become easier to see how the above teachings might lead to the idea of becoming personally "empowered" through entering the inner "intuitive" realm where real power and wisdom supposedly reside. Indeed, this is the emphasis of New Age education: Teach children to trust feelings and experience over rationality and objective values.

Parents aren't the only ones who are rising up to protest these directions in education. The business community is gaining closer ties with the educational community because they have a vested interest in the quality of young people being turned out into the workforce.

Dr. Thomas Sowell, according to the *Wall Street Journal*, is one of America's premier economists. Dr. Sowell, a black and senior economist at the Hoover Institute, has written a new book titled *Inside American Education*.

In reviewing the book, the writer in the *Wall Street Journal* notes, "Avid consumers of educational fads, teachers affords a ready market for curricular programs and techniques aimed at the psychological adjustment of students. Tucked under the benign banners of self-esteem, decision-making, drug prevention, sex education, or enrichment for the gifted and talented, these programs are all designed to reshape students' attitudes.

"These programs, among other things, elevate feelings over thought, undermine accepted moral and cultural standards, and attack the authority of parents. The techniques that are imported into the classroom are so manipulative that Mr. Sowell refers to them as 'classroom brainwashing.'"[5]

Dr. Sowell has written a recent article published in *Forbes* magazine where he makes an observation on the substance of the issues being raised and on the tactics of those on the left. He writes,

> It is much the same story in the media today, as editorials warn that "the religious right" is "taking over" school boards. Alarms are being raised that conservative or religious indoctrination will be imposed in the public schools.
>
> Where have the media been all these years, while the most blatant, deliberate and pervasive indoctrination by the political left has been taking place in public schools all across the country?...
>
> These are not isolated idiosyncrasies of particular teachers. They are products of numerous books and other "educational" material in programs packaged by organizations that sell such curricula to administrators and teach the techniques to teachers. Some packages even include instructions on how to deal with parents or others who object.... Many parents who have been appalled to discover what has been going on in the schools have fought lonely and frustrating battles against the education establishment. Eventually some have begun to organize, which at least deprives the school bureaucrats their favorite line: "You're the only one who has complained."
>
> That line will be used, even when controversies and lawsuits are raging all across the country over a particular brainwashing program. Parents are also likely to be told that all the educational experts support the program. What they are unlikely to be told is that these "experts" are often the ideological gurus who pushed these programs in the first place, or consultants who profit from them.
>
> When the futility of individual protest leads to organized activity, that is when the cry of "censorship" goes up from the educational establishment

and the media rush to the rescue, invoking the specter of "the religious right." What has caught their attention is someone trying to fight back.[6]

Newsweek, commenting on the affective approach in education, ran as their cover story "The Abuse of Self-Esteem— What's Wrong with the Feel-Good Movement," in the February 17, 1992 issue.

They write," Nowhere has the concept taken root as firmly as in education. Toddlers are encouraged to 'reach their full potential' in self-esteem day-care centers. High school drug and alcohol programs now emphasize self-esteem, on the theory according to New Hampshire school administrator, James Weiss, that 'if youngsters feel good about themselves, those temptations won't be so strong.'"[7]

The article goes on to comment, "Of course, there are still a few kinks to work out." For instance, as the article reports that American school children now rank far ahead of students in countries like Japan, Taiwan and China in self-confidence [self-esteem] about their academic abilities, but in fact, the American children were far behind those countries in actual performance.

As noted, the essence of affective/values clarification approaches—which are taught extensively throughout the country— is to teach children to make decisions on the basis of how they *feel* subjectively rather than on the basis of what is *right* objectively. Thus, for years we have been teaching our children to be governed by a system of emotions rather than a system of morality. But the whole point of teaching *values* should be to teach children how to fight harmful feelings or emotions rather than give in to them. If the mind does not rule the heart, students learn to become victims of pleasure, emotions, or circumstance. Perhaps this explains why some informal surveys have revealed that most kids would rather save their dog from drowning than a human being who happens to be a stranger: They make decisions emotionally, not rationally and morally.

How far can this go? Consider the reply of a junior high school administrator in Fredricktown, Ohio, to a group of parents. He actually told them it would be *immoral* to tell a child under his care not to commit suicide if the child had already decided this was in his best interest! Have we become so enamored with the autonomy of a child's decision-making process that this approach itself has become the final authority, and will we even refuse to do what is right in order to uphold it?

Of course our concern is not with helping a child to understand that he doesn't have to be influenced by negative situations outside himself. Children should be taught, for example, to resist peer pressure to take drugs. Our concern is who determines the nature of a negative influence and how instruction in relativism tends to undermine the very concepts of right and wrong. Again we are hardly against teaching students how to analyze their decisions and learn to take responsibility for them. We just wonder how well this can be accomplished with a subjective approach which is fundamentally amoral.

For example, the Teenage Health Teaching Modules (THTM) are used throughout the country in grades 7–12. One of the objectives is to help children "make a responsible choice about drinking that is right for them."[8] The teacher is instructed

> not to begin negatively with admonishments about the dangers of drinking. It is a fact that many people use alcohol responsibly. . . . If you present all of these options as legitimate ones, defending everyone's right to choose, you will set for your students an important model of tolerance.[9]

Of course tolerance is fine, but should seventh graders be exposed to this philosophy years before the legal drinking age, especially if these programs may actually encourage them to drink? Certainly there is nothing wrong with defending everyone's right to choose, but just as certainly, not all choices are equally wise. Underage drinking is illegal, period.

As Dr. Kathleen Gow observes,

> There is a fundamental difference between the stance that all opinions are equally valid with regard to things like art, music, sports (nonmoral issues)

and identical treatment of questions concerning basic moral precepts.[10]

But in the *Life Education Centre* program, the same message is taught about drugs:

> Decisions . . . are best discussed in a non-threatening, non-judgmental way. . . . An educator . . . should not tell a child what to do or what to think concerning drugs. . . . Whether or not to *abuse* drugs is one of the most important decisions a child can make.[11]

Unfortunately, even extremely popular programs such as Quest, DUSO, and DARE are all based upon this or similar approaches. The tragedy is that rather than being effective, these approaches may actually be increasing the activities they are attempting to prevent. Further, the child's identity is reshaped as he becomes the subjective center of his own decisions as he lives in his own world. Again, this may tend to work against traditional values and parental authority.

We will later discuss the problems of self-esteem approaches in the schools. But no one can deny the tremendous influence these approaches now exert in many programs. For example, interviews conducted at 20 educational schools across the country revealed, "self-esteem is a dominant educational theory."[12] But an article addressing self-esteem in *U.S. News & World Report* concluded that this approach was fraught with problems and a "terrible idea" because no research evidence exists that these programs work and because they hinder the growing movement to "revive the schools academically." The article concluded that "obsession with self-esteem ultimately undermines real education"[13] (see chapter 9).

But how did we ever arrive at our current situation? Why are educators now using psychotherapy in the classroom in place of traditional learning methods? In part it is because the educational establishment has abandoned long-held Judeo-Christian premises about education for humanistic and now, increasingly, transpersonal ones.

The values and traditions of our country are rooted in the

belief system of Christianity. But today we are living in a post-Christian culture. Our Judeo-Christian base deteriorated and has been replaced by a secular humanistic approach to life which actually opposes moral absolutes. For example, a common idea today is that "you can't legislate morality," but this is absurd. Law is inevitably based on some moral code. The question is, whose moral code?

A common depiction of humanism is seen in the idea that man is the measure of all things. In other words, within man's experience and intellect reside the ultimate standards by which the issues of life are to be measured. This is often referred to as secular humanism, which is classically a non-theistic approach to life. The humanist believes that there is no God and, therefore, man is left to himself to devise his own beliefs and values.

Unfortunately, it can be documented that this has logically led to the breakdown of culture. Our society has never before experienced such demise. Drug abuse, abortion, alcoholism, divorce, homosexuality, violent crime, pornography, child abuse rates, and much else that is not good are at an all-time high. Because most of America has rejected the biblical God and with this, moral absolutes, everyone is doing what is right in his/her own eyes. This is just as it was in the days of the biblical judges (Judges 17:6), and the results are similar: social chaos and tragedy.

At "The John Ankerberg Show" we have talked with many Christian teachers in the public schools who have actually been *forbidden* to teach moral values in the classroom—on threat of dismissal. This is quite a commentary on our times when those whose primary concern is upholding of personal values—values that all civilized cultures have deemed important—are threatened with punitive action or labeled as "far-right bigots."

But one thing that both secular humanists and Christians do agree on is that our children are growing up in a very difficult world. Parents want the best for their children, yet where do they go for answers? Educators want the best for children, yet every day they see the residue of broken homes, abuse, and neglect. They want to help, but where do they go for answers?

Many people have turned to the secular humanists of the intellectual elite who include experts in science, philosophy, human behavior, and education.

But in turning to humanism, to what are we really turning? The principles of humanism are laid out for us in documents known as the *Humanist Manifestos* (I and II).

For example, John Dewey, the father of modern education, was a signer of *Humanist Manifesto I*. Dr. Paul Kurtz, a prominent leader in modern American humanism, explains the background of the manifesto as follows:

> In 1933 a group of thirty-four liberal humanists in the United States defined and enunciated the philosophical and religious principles that seemed to them fundamental. . . . It was concerned with expressing a general religious and philosophical outlook that rejected orthodox and dogmatic positions, and provided meaning and direction, unity and purpose to human life. It was committed to reason, science, and democracy.[14]

Both manifestos declare that Christianity constitutes a disservice to humanity. They forcefully reject biblical teaching and argue that because man is basically a free moral agent, determining his own destiny, he must be allowed to evolve naturally through the benefits of science and reason toward whatever cultural heights his powers can take him.

One of the main sources for this humanistic approach to science and reason came through the newly emerging field of psychology. Not surprisingly, the psychology which has had the most influence in shaping humanistic education today is known as humanistic psychology. Its major leaders included Carl Rogers and Abraham Maslow, men who saw man's nature as inherently good and full of great potential and almost infinite possibility.

From this historically naive presupposition, Dr. Rogers, who finally endorsed spiritism, developed what is called "client-centered therapy," a nonjudgmental, nondirective approach to personal counseling. Rogers believed that the solution to each individual's problem resided within that person and that, if all outside influences were removed, the individual would solve his own problems and determine what was comfortable and right for him.

How is all this related to modern education?

Dr. William Coulson, a former coworker and colleague of Rogers and Maslow, has published ample documentation to prove that the teaching methods used in most elementary and secondary behavioral programs have evolved from Rogers' own nondirective therapy and values clarification methods.[15]

Further, some of Maslow's concepts, such as his "hierarchy of needs" and "self-actualization" theories, are a standard source for the underlying methodology in much of today's school curricula.

Consider educator Louis E. Raths. Raths was influenced by John Dewey and through his own study of how the role of values and thinking work out in education. His work has served as the impetus for the "empowerment" movement in childhood education today.[16] Raths believed that "certain maladaptive behaviors resulted from a lack of clear values or purposefulness in one's life."[17] In other words, he believed that children who are unable to discover meaning in life developed "compensatory maladaptive behaviors." In order to help these children he developed strategies designed to allegedly empower them toward more healthy lifestyles.[18]

Raths believed the solution was to help children realize that they are important, lovable, and acceptable (Maslow's "self-actualization"). So far, so good. But then Raths, like Rogers before him, believed that to be empowered, students must learn to choose their own values subjectively. They must learn to evaluate "what's important to them."[19] This takes up squarely into the current affective, nondirective, values clarification approach to education and the problems it has created.

But as our culture has continued its moral decline, another shift is now occurring. Secular humanism is slowly giving way to cosmic humanism, or the philosophy of the New Age Movement. This shift has been felt in psychology (transpersonal psychology) and, in turn, education (transpersonal education). It is this ongoing transition that currently blurs some of the distinctions between the religion of humanism and the religion of Eastern mysticism.

A key figure in this transition was Abraham Maslow. In the preface to *Toward a Psychology of Being* he wrote,

> I should also say that I consider humanistic Third Force Psychology to be transitional—a preparation for a still "higher" Fourth Force Psychology [that is] transpersonal, trans-human, centered in the cosmos rather than in human needs and interests, going beyond humanness, identity, self-actualization, and the like.[20]

Other psychologists who have been pioneers in the emergence of transpersonal psychology include such famous men as William James, Carl Jung, and Aldous Huxley. (Perhaps it is significant that when Marilyn Ferguson surveyed New Age leaders to discover who most influenced their thinking, four of the top five individuals named were these very psychologists: Jung, Maslow, Rogers, and Huxley.)[21]

Regardless, C.S. Lewis astutely observed why there is a logical transition from a humanistic to a New Age philosophy when he wrote:

> Pantheism is congenial to our minds, not because it is a final stage in a slow process of enlightenment but because it is almost as old as we are. It may even be the most primitive of all religions. . . . It is immemorial in India. The Greeks rose above it only at their peak. . . . Their successors relapsed into the great Pantheistic system of the Stoics. Modern Europe escaped it only while she remained predominantly Christian; with Giordano Bruno and Spinoza it returned. With Hegel it became almost the agreed philosophy of highly educated people. . . . So far from being the final religious refinement, Pantheism is, in fact, the permanent level below which man sometimes sinks, but above which his own unaided efforts can never raise him for very long. It is the attitude into which the human mind automatically falls when left to itself. No wonder we find it congenial. If religion means

> simply what man says about God, and not what
> God does about man, then Pantheism almost is
> religion. And religion in that sense has, in the long
> run, only one really formidable opponent—namely
> Christianity.[22]

Nevertheless, since almost all of the self-esteem, values clarification, and nondirective decision-making programs are explicitly or implicitly based on Maslow, it is important for parents and educators to know that both Maslow (and Rogers) later repudiated the use of their theories with children.

For example, Maslow writes the following:

> In chapter 11 on self-actualization I have removed
> one source of confusion by confining the concept
> very definitely to older people. By the criteria I
> used, self-actualization does not occur in young
> people. In our culture at least, children have not yet
> achieved identity, or autonomy ... nor have they
> generally found their calling. ... Nor have they
> worked out their own system of values; nor have
> they had experience enough (responsibility for
> others, tragedy, failure, achievement, success) to
> shed perfectionistic illusions and become realistic;
> nor have they generally made their peace with
> death; nor have they learned how to be patient; nor
> have they learned enough about evil in themselves
> and others to be compassionate; nor have they had
> time to become post-ambivalent about parents and
> elders, power and authority; nor have they gener-
> ally become knowledgeable and educated enough
> to open the possibility of becoming wise.[23]

All in all, the introduction of psychotherapy into the class-room hasn't worked too well. Chuck Colson, former chief advisor to President Nixon, relates in *Against the Night: Living in the New Dark Ages* that Barbara Walters herself produced a piece for television about the deterioration of American education. She stated, "Today's high school seniors live in a world of misplaced values. They have no sense of discipline, no goals, they care only for themselves. In short, they are becoming a generation of undisciplined cultural barbarians."[24]

Colson proceeds to observe that perhaps this is

> because so-called value neutral education which purports to teach no values, does, in fact, promote a value system of its own. And that system runs counter to the moral restraints essential to character.... This atmosphere of hostile skepticism about the accessibility of truth—or even its very existence— combined with a disdain for traditional moral limits has produced a radically new educational environment.... To assert a dividing line between good and evil, or the superiority of one perspective or truth above another, would be a betrayal of the *most fundamental commitment of liberal education: openness.*[25]

No one denies that education needs drastic reform. But until the proper diagnosis of its problems is first made, any repair work undertaken could produce more problems than we might suspect. In fact, isn't the real betrayal the fact that these forms of education are teaching our children things that are not true and that may harm them?

(As an illustration, we supply in chapter 15 an article by Dr. William Coulson, a former leader in humanistic education who has rejected his earlier approach.)

Chapter 7

■

COMMON PRACTICES OF TRANSPERSONAL EDUCATION

Meditation, altered states of consciousness, visualization, yoga, and hypnosis are some of the common practices advocated in the field of transpersonal education. Most people see nothing wrong with these methods. Indeed, there are thousands of testimonies from satisfied practitioners as to their alleged benefits. They are viewed as profitable techniques that improve human performance, wisdom, self-insight, health, educational ability, etc. So why do we feel these practices should be a concern to educators, parents, and students? Because we believe all these methods may influence the mind in such a manner as to open the doors to occult phenomena such as spirit contact. As we document in *The Coming Darkness* (Harvest House, 1993), there are physical, psychological, and spiritual consequences for such activity. Many times they can be severe.

Further, these practices are closely interrelated and supportive of one another. For example, with the qualified exception of therapist-induced hypnosis, every one of these practices may involve the other four as either necessary or corollary accompaniments. Altered states of consciousness are involved with all four methods. Anyone who practices meditation may also employ visualization, self-hypnosis, and yoga. Visualization programs usually involve meditation and/

or self-hypnosis. Yoga involves meditation by definition and frequently employs visualization or, again, self-hypnosis. Even hypnosis may involve visualization or meditation, especially in the self-induced variety.

What this means is that any one of these methods may open the doors to a broader range of practice and phenomena than might initially be suspected. By such natural associations, there may be increased exposure to 1) related techniques, 2) psycho-spiritual conditioning, or 3) various risk factors.

Below we offer some of the reasons we think these practices should not be encouraged for children and do not belong in public schools.

Meditation

New Age (Eastern/occult) meditation involves the control and regulation of the mind for various physical and spiritual purposes or goals. Almost everyone agrees that meditation is one of the foundations of transpersonal education.

The authority on mysticism, William Johnston, warned in his 1975 text, *Silent Music: The Science of Meditation*, "Anyone with the slightest experience of meditation knows about the uprising of the unconscious and the possible resulting turmoil, to say nothing of the increased psychic power that meditation brings. All this could have the greatest social consequences if meditation becomes widespread."[1]

Indeed, meditation has become widespread. Unfortunately, most people view meditation as simply a form of relaxation: a misperception which has frequently masked its true nature and purpose. The real goal of Eastern/occult meditation is to conform a person's perception of himself and his view of the world with the religious philosophy of the program adopted. Thus, in the end, as far as the meditator is concerned, "It lastingly changes his consciousness, transforming his experience of himself and his universe."[2]

Dr. Roger Walsh, a former editor for the *Journal of Transpersonal Psychology*, and Frances Vaughan, past president for the Association for Transpersonal Psychology, both agree as to the potentially profound effects of meditative practice:

> [Meditation is] a profoundly transformative pro-
> cess, for when practiced intensely, meditation disci-
> plines almost invariably lead into the transpersonal
> [occult] realm of experience. . . . A progressive se-
> quence of altered states of consciousness can occur,
> which may ultimately result in the permanent, rad-
> ical [occult] shift in consciousness known as en-
> lightenment or liberation.[3]

Almost all forms of meditation result in the cultivation of altered states of consciousness and an eventual development of psychic powers. These altered states of consciousness are viewed as supposed "higher" states of consciousness while psychic powers are seen as alleged indications of the divinity emerging within the individual.

New Age meditation is also typically accompanied by frequently dramatic energy manifestations. For example, "I felt a great surge of energy within me or around me."[4] And, "The force went through and through my body . . . it was absolutely wild and intense . . . I felt possessed by the energy."[5] In fact, experiencing a great surge of energy has been the dominant characteristic of the meditative experience in a number of studies. Further, this surge of energy was directly related to the cultivation of altered states of consciousness. But what exactly is this dramatic form of energy?

If we examine its nature and phenomena, there is little doubt it is an occult energy operating independently of the person who is meditating. We think these dramatic energy manifestations are best explained as a result of spiritistic influence or, potentially, even spirit possession.

That meditation produces energy manifestations clearly associated with primitive shamanism, the occult, and Eastern and Western spiritism is undeniable. In fact, the particular meditation-induced energy manifestations experienced are so often associated with spiritism there is little doubt that this energy is not something human; rather it is spiritistic. For example, primitive traditions characteristically attribute this energy to the direct or indirect working of the spirit world. New Age meditators, while not discounting the possibility, frequently view it as an internal manifestation of alleged divine power residing potentially within all men.

One advanced practitioner of meditation writes, "I immediately felt within me a surge of great spiritual force... movements similar to those of an epileptic controlled my body for about an hour. Many strange visions appeared and I felt things opening within me that had never been opened before."[6] Buddhist leader Chogyam Trungpa observes, "I will say that for beginners, it is extremely dangerous to play with [this] energy, but for advanced students such work becomes relevant naturally."[7] One woman felt the supernatural power "entering me and taking over my being... I was completely possessed... [it was] taking me over completely.... there was nothing left of the person I thought to be Marie."[8]

What most people do not realize is that most meditation is occult in nature. The practices (some form of daily meditative discipline), results (altered states of consciousness, psychic powers, kundalini arousal, spirit contact), and goals (some form of "cosmic" consciousness or alleged development of the "higher self") may all be classified within the sphere of the practices, results, and goals of occult practice in general.

For example, parapsychologist Dr. Gertrude Schmeidler, former president of the Parapsychological Association, observes that a state of "trance shows many similarities to meditation."[9] Another study revealed that the "most central and complex factor" of the meditative experience is an altered state of consciousness.[10] In addition, meditation characteristically develops psychic abilities. As Daniel Goleman, an authority on meditation observes, "Every school of meditation acknowledges them [psychic powers] as by-products of advanced states of mastery."[11]

But perhaps the most frightening consequence of meditation is the possibility of spirit possession. Even advanced practitioners of meditation freely confess this. For example, Rolling Thunder, a shaman leader in the Shoshone and Cherokee tribes, confesses, "If it is not done correctly, evil spirits can get into people while they are meditating."[12] Indian-born Douglas Shaw, the grandson of Yogi Ishwar Dayal, also warns that during meditation, "Being taken over by an evil spirit ...is a very real possibility."[13] British scholar Os Guiness observes, "Many... who practice yoga or zen meditation have found that they have opened their minds to blackness and spiritism, seeing themselves as mediums and describing themselves as possessed."[14]

In his spiritual autobiography, the late popular guru Swami Muktananda points out that when he "sat for meditation" his "whole body shook violently" and he acted as if he "were possessed by a god or a bad spirit."[15]

The inherently religious nature of New Age meditative practice is another concern. Dr. Daniel Goleman has studied meditation systems extensively and teaches a course on meditation at Harvard Unversity. He is also a committed Buddhist who follows the teachings of his guru. In *The Varieties of Meditative Experience*, he examines a dozen different meditative systems which are representative of varieties of meditation in general. He shows why most forms of meditation are strikingly similar. In other words, regardless of the system of meditation employed, they attempt to secure a similar end state: a radical occult transformation of the individual, affecting how he perceives himself and the world, which harmonizes with Eastern/occult philosophy.[16]

Finally, a number of articles in the psychiatric literature have stressed that meditation can have harmful physical and psychological consequences, including the possibility of serious psychopathology. Among the things commonly experienced by many meditators are violent shaking, moderate to severe depression, involuntary jerks, out-of-body experiences, hallucinations, violent mood swings, acute anxiety, etc.[17]

In conclusion, the problems with New Age meditation practice in general are: 1) developing altered states of consciousness, 2) developing psychic abilities, 3) the possibility of spirit influence or possession, 4) the religious alteration of an individual's view of himself and the world in conformity with Eastern metaphysics, and 5) the possibility of physical or psychological harm.

It is one thing for adults to engage in such a path for personal religious reasons; it is another thing entirely for adults to encourage schoolchildren in such a practice.

Altered States of Consciousness

Altered states of consciousness (ASCs) involve the deliberate cultivation of unusual or abnormal states of consciousness—

states not normally experienced apart from a specific technique or program to develop them. (We do not include normal ASCs such as sleep, reverie, etc.) Altered states of consciousness are most characteristically found in Eastern religion, occult practices, all varieties of spiritism, certain forms of psychotherapy and, of course, encountered through mind-altering drugs.

Altered states of consciousness involve a large number of subjects—everything from hypnosis and other trance states to possession states (as in mediumism and shamanism) to altered states that are characteristically pathological (as in kundalini arousal and shamanism), to directed visualization and imagery, lucid dreaming, drug-induced states of consciousness, meditation and biofeedback-induced consciousness, and many others.

Our concern over using altered states of consciousness in the classroom is both psychological and religious. Altered states are potentially dangerous to a child's mental development and stability. In addition, they are well known for developing spirit contact. This latter fact explains why altered states undergird virtually all of Eastern and Western occultism: they are typical prerequisites for the spirit contact necessary for success along the given spiritual path. Almost all deliberately cultivated altered states seem to share some degree of common ground—especially in pagan religious contexts—and it is this common ground which is apparently conducive to spirit influence. And today, as historically, paganism is pervasive. The research of sociologist Erika Bourguigon indicated that of 488 societies observed, more than 90 percent had made trance and spirit possession states socially acceptable.[18]

In essence, virtually all methods which attempt to induce sustained altered states have at least the potential to lead to spirit contact or even spirit possession.

In fact, in some situations what was once termed "spirit possession" is now simply described as another altered state of consciousness. Cambridge educated John Ferguson observes in his *An Illustrated Encyclopedia of Mysticism* that "spirit possession . . . is the core of mystical experience."[19]

Consider the consequences of the altered states frequently encouraged by Eastern gurus, and incidentally, not entirely dissimilar to those encountered in transpersonal education. The guru Bhagwan Shree Rajneesh is a case in point. His early experiences on the road to "enlightenment" brought him temporary insanity, possession, and almost killed him. Through intense absorption into various altered states of consciousness, the personality of the old Rajneesh literally and completely disappeared. This, incidentally, is the real goal of most Eastern meditation and yoga: to destroy the individual personality so that the experience of "enlightenment" may emerge. Thus, the personality of Rajneesh was permanently replaced by a new consciousness—in fact, one that was entirely alien. The new personality recalls, "the one who died, died totally; nothing of him has remained . . . not even a shadow. It died totally, utterly. . . . Another being, absolutely new, not connected at all with the old, started to exist." Rajneesh had become possessed by a "new consciousness," a living personality that directed his mind and body from that day forward.[20]

An evaluation of the current literature on New Age consciousness research indicates that this modern exploration of altered states is frequently merely a euphemism for psychic development, the exploration of the occult, and spirit contact. As Bourguignon observes, "In traditional societies—and to a considerable extent in modern societies as well . . . altered states tend to be spoken of in connection with supernatural entities such as 'spirits.'"[21]

But besides the possibility of spiritism, altered states of consciousness pose other dangers as well, including the possibility of losing one's grip on reality and a permanent alienation from ordinary human attachments. As noted, the purpose behind much cultivation of altered states is to finally get rid of the individual personality so that the alleged condition of spiritual enlightenment may emerge.

We don't think it is very wise to attempt such dramatic personality alteration, even for adults. Why some modern educators would encourage it for children is beyond us.

In conclusion, the development of occult altered states of consciousness is *not* a form of "higher consciousness" or true spirituality, as New Age proponents would have us believe. The radical altered worldview generated is characteristically occult and this brings consequences, from encouraging occult practices to adopting occult philosophy. Far too often one encounters abnormal and regressive states of consciousness which are particularly conducive to spiritistic contact and manipulation. This may also bring spirit possession.

Visualization

New Age visualization is the use of mental concentration and directed imagery in the attempt to secure particular goals, whether physical, psychological, vocational, educational, spiritual, etc.

Visualization claims to work in a variety of ways, such as using the mind to contact dormant inner powers or one's "higher Self." However, it is rarely used by itself. The typical accompaniments include 1) relaxation and meditation (which may include yoga-like controlled breathing and postures), 2) the cultivation of willpower, 3) various forms of self-hypnosis, and 4) faith in the process of visualization itself and in the visualization "guide" (whether human or spirit).

Because visualization can adapt to almost any philosophy and become uniquely colored by it, there is no well-defined worldview for visualization practices. Nevertheless, New Age visualization is characteristically Eastern or occult in its outlook. For example, one common teaching is that everything is interconnected by divine energy and that in his true nature man is one essence with God. The "enlightened" mind, therefore, has "infinite" potential and the unconscious mind (supposedly the connecting link to the "infinite") is a repository of great wisdom and ability. Visualization is the principal technique which initiates contact with this great source of power.

Unfortunately, we encounter many of the same problems in visualization that we saw in meditation and altered states of consciousness. For example, visualization may develop psychic abilities. Practicing occultist J.H. Brennan cites visualization methods as an excellent means for developing the capacity for astral projection. He also warns that to mix such things as yoga postures and visualization techniques without extreme care "is asking for psychosis."[22] Buddhist authority H.V. Guenther and leading Tibetan Buddhist guru Chogyam

Trungpa warn in *The Dawn of Tantra*, "Practicing visualization without the proper understanding is extremely destructive. . . . Tantric scriptures abound with warnings about using visualization."[23]

Further, visualization methods are frequently used to establish contact with the spirit world. For example, "The capacity to utilize visual imagination is a regular part of the training for psychics and healers in the Philippine spiritist churches."[24]

Indeed, the spirits themselves often recommend visualization practices as important components for securing New Age goals—as they also recommend meditation, hypnosis, yoga, and altered states of consciousness for the same purpose. The spirit "Seth" teaches, "the real work is done in the mind. . . . [occult] beliefs automatically mobilize your emotional and imaginative powers. . . . Imagination and emotion are your great allies."[25]

Mike Samuels, M.D. is a leading authority on visualization, having coauthored a definitive work on the subject, *Seeing with the Mind's Eye: The History, Techniques and Uses of Visualization.* But in books such as *The Well Body Book* and *Spirit Guides: Access to Inner Worlds* he also shows how visualization can become the means to spirit contact.[26]

In his book on magic ritual, *Magic: An Occult Primer*, David Conway discusses how important visualization is to establish contact with the spirits and demons that will assist the magician in performing the ritual purpose.[27]

In magic ritual we see the full power of visualization: directed imagery, meditation, force of will and faith. Unfortunately, what many people do not realize is that although visualization can be used deliberately in magic ritual for spirit contact and spirit possession, the very same things can be encountered in normal visualization practice or even through purely make-believe fantasy rituals.

The story of "Philip," the "imaginary" spirit, is illustrative. A group of psychic investigators and parapsychologists with the Toronto Society for Psychical Research came together to see if they could, through "collective mental power alone" (imagination and visualization), create the physical phenomena found in a seance and produce a materialized spirit. Before they began they named him "Philip," giving him an imaginary past, a personality, etc. Their goal was to see if "ordinary" people could, by "mental" power alone, reproduce the phenomena found in a mediumistic seance.

They eventually succeeded, well beyond their expectations, and remain puzzled to this day—indeed awed over subsequent events. What entered their parlor was not an imaginary spirit but a genuine, living spirit-being with its own personality and power—and certainly not part of the group's "collective" mind or energy. Even the originators of the experiment were forced to confess that the "imaginary" spirits contacted "act with their own personalities and idiosyncrasies and not as though they were part of your subconscious mind."[28]

In a similar fashion, in Robert Masters and Jean Houston's book *Mind Games: The Guide to Inner Space*, visualization and trance are used to develop psychic awareness, monistic consciousness, and then to raise and contact what they term a "Group Spirit," supposedly a manifestation of the participants' "collective unconscious." Yet this spirit is described as "an entity with an independent existence of its own" and as "an actual, intelligent being, conscious and powerful."[29] It would appear then that the spirit world is ready to respond under whatever conditions it is beckoned. Whether the results are viewed in supernatural or merely psychological categories seems irrelevant.

In conclusion, the problem with visualization techniques is that they are frequently employed for Eastern/occult purposes. Again we see the possibility of leading children into techniques that can produce dangerous altered states of consciousness or even spirit contact.

Yoga

Yoga is the occult use of breathing exercises, physical postures, and meditation for allegedly improving mental functioning, health maintenance, and spiritual "enlightenment."

Today, as is true for meditation, altered states of consciousness, and visualization, yoga is increasingly advocated as a positive practice for children, even young children. Many teachers assume that when students engage in yoga postures and breath control this is solely a physical endeavor and unrelated to anything religious.

Unfortunately, it is difficult, if not impossible, to separate yoga theory (Eastern metaphysics) and practice (postures, breath control, etc.). What this means is that when yoga practices are encountered in the schools, they are frequently religious practices even when teachers attempt to remove religious terms from discussion. Of course, in most transpersonal education the whole point is to use yoga for religious (Eastern/occult) purposes.

Yoga authority Gopi Krishna comments that "all the systems of yoga . . . are designed to bring about those psychosomatic changes in the body which are essential for the metamorphosis of consciousness. A new center—presently dormant in the average man and woman—has to be activated and a more powerful stream of psychic energy must [be awakened]."[30]

The underlying purpose of yoga is for the individual to realize he is one essence with God or "ultimate reality." Swami Ajaya correctly affirms that "the main teaching of yoga is that man's true nature is divine."[31] Swami Rama, an accomplished yogi and founder of the worldwide Himalayan International Institute of Yoga Science and Philosophy, confesses, "There are many different methods of yoga, all leading to the same goal of [occult] Self-Realization."[32]

Thus, we must question whether separating yoga theory and practice is ultimately possible. The very physical postures and breathing exercises adopted in yoga are intended to metaphysically influence both mind and spirit. According to one authority, "Physical yoga, according to its classical definitions, is inherently and functionally incapable of being separated from Eastern religious metaphysics. The Western practitioner who attempts to do so is operating in ignorance and danger."[33]

As is true for most Eastern meditation and altered states of consciousness, the goal of yoga is also to destroy the individual personality since it stands in the way of "enlightenment." As yoga authorities Feuerstein and Miller comment, yoga constitutes "a progressive dismantling of human personality ending in a complete abolition. With every step (anga) of yoga, what we call 'man' is demolished a little more."[34]

Virtually all authoritative texts reveal that yoga is an occult practice. Yoga is designed to awaken occult energies in the body, to lead to an occult transformation, and to secure specific occult goals. For example, yoga texts routinely acknowledge that yoga practice develops psychic powers and other occult abilities. In addition, certain experiences under yoga, especially kundalini yoga, may parallel those found in shaman initiation and ritualistic magic, including experiences of temporary insanity and spirit possession.

Because yoga is an occult system, the physical, mental, and spiritual dangers that accompany occult practices are also found in yoga. U.N. spiritual advisor and spiritist Sri Chinmoy, author of *Yoga and the Spiritual Life*, warns, "To practice *pranayama* [breath control] without real guidance is very dangerous. I know of three persons who have died from it."[35]

Yoga authority Hans-Ulrich Reiker admonishes in *The Yoga of Light*, "Yoga is not a trifling jest if we consider that any misunderstanding in the practice of yoga can mean death and insanity," and that in kundalini yoga, if the breath (prana) is "prematurely exhausted [withdrawn] there is immediate danger of death for the yogi."[36]

A standard authority on hatha yoga, *The Hatha Yoga Pradipika*, warns that unless the breath is regulated with extreme care, "It can kill the practitioner."[37]

Other yoga authorities have warned of "dangerous mediumistic psychisms," "neurotic dissociations of personality," "insanity," "serious or incurable disease," "strange trance states," and cancer from "even the slightest mistake."[38]

Finally, yoga can also lead to spirit possession—usually defined as powerful experiences with great surges of transforming energy. Gopi Krishna describes the following experiences of most yogic, meditative, and mystical practices: "During the ecstasy or trance, consciousness is transformed and the yogi, sufi, or mystic finds himself in direct rapport with an overwhelming Presence. This warm, living, conscious Presence spreads everywhere and occupies the whole mind and thought of the devotee."[39] Further, this energy "is *invariably* experienced by all meditators and yogis as some kind of *supernatural* or divine energy."[40]

Although we have yet to read of a kundalini or yoga practitioner (or theorist) willing to define the energy infusion/

possession as actually demonic, there is often recognition of a possessing god or entity and occasionally references to the demonic. The Taoist master Chao Pi Ch'en observed that "as time passes, demonic states will occur to the practiser [sic]."[41]

Significantly, yogic energy manifestations/possession are sometimes initially sensed by the experiencer as the work of an evil spirit. But this primary impression is "corrected" in accordance with Hindu or occult theory, classifying the phenomena as "a divine process."

Nevertheless, the classical energy manifestations of yoga are far more easily interpreted as a result of something demonic than something divine. As in meditation, the yogic energy encountered, particularly kundalini energy, displays 1) an independent, supernatural nature, 2) personal volition, 3) destructive potential, 4) an amoral or evil nature, and 5) a desire for "lordship" that is the exerting of a personal control over the practitioner, forcing compliance.[42] Yogi Amrit Desai warns that unless the yoga experience is interpreted "properly" for the student, "he will become frightened, thinking it to be mental illness" or "evil spirits."[43] Consider the following typical descriptions:

> Your mind gets influenced spiritually as if some spirit has taken possession of your body and under that influence different postures of yoga are involuntarily performed without the pain or fatigue.[44]

> It seemed that I was being controlled by some power which made me do all these things. I no longer had a will of my own.[45]

In conclusion, yoga involves far more than mere physical exercise; at its core it is an occult practice having occult goals. To encourage children to become practitioners of yoga is to encourage them to become practitioners of the occult.

Hypnosis

Hypnosis is a deliberately induced condition of heightened suggestability and trance, producing a highly flexible state of consciousness capable of potentially dramatic manipulation.

What is a hypnotic state? Gerald Jampolsky, M.D. defines the problem when he says, "No agreement has been reached on what constitutes a hypnotic state."[46] Daniel Goleman, who has his doctorate in clinical psychology from Harvard, observes: "After 200 years of use, we still cannot say with certainty what hypnosis is nor exactly how it works."[47]

Although estimates vary, about 10 percent of people do not react at all to hypnosis, 20 percent respond to almost any attempt to hypnotize them, and the remaining 70 percent vary in their degree of susceptibility.[48]

One way we can illustrate our concern with hypnosis is by comparing it to professional racing. For the moment, let us accept the common belief that, competently handled, hypnosis is an effective and relatively safe procedure. For the qualified professional, so is high-speed racing. But even when handled by a professional there are still some risks at every corner. In both racing and hypnosis a significant number of variables enter into play, and these must be carefully weighed.

Obviously, our concern about hypnosis is increased when we consider the nonprofessional, unregulated, unqualified therapists and experimenters that abound in the field. If the ethical and allegedly safe use of hypnosis is subject to some risk, then the amoral and occult use of it is all the more so. And it is this kind of hypnosis which appears to dominate the popular marketplace.

What's worse, even professionals are capable of misusing hypnosis and can be deceived by the power it gives them over people. They, too, may become subject to its occult trappings and other deceptive allurements. More than once we have read of hypnotherapists confessing that it was the "God-like" power that attracted them and "many of their colleagues" into the field.[49]

Hypnosis can produce a wide variety of occult phenomena which it seems may also occur even at relatively light levels of trance.[50] Various hypnotic levels offer a number of parallels to occult states of consciousness produced in the practices of spiritism or Eastern religions such as Hinduism and Buddhism.[51]

In *Hypnosis: Key to Psychic Powers*, Simeon Edmunds concludes, "There is no doubt that hypnosis induced by hypnotists

... often assists the development and functioning of psychic powers."[52] The following are some of the more spectacular phenomena which may occur in hypnotic states: past-life experiences, multiple personalities, speaking in unknown languages, automatic writing and other psychic abilities (astral projection, psychic diagnosis and healing, etc.), committing acts against one's will, seizures and involuntary spirit possession. It is significant that all of these phenomena *also* occur in or through the mediumistic trance state where a person is possessed by spirits. In light of this simple fact alone, some consider it proper to question the advisability of hypnosis.

Hypnosis can also induce channeling or voluntary spirit possession. Here, hypnosis is used as a means to enter the trance state which permits the spirit guide to take over the mind and body. This is one reason the spirits endorse the use of hypnosis—it frequently serves their purposes. For example, the spirit guide of the famous trance medium Arthur Ford, "Fletcher," and the spirit guide of the late Jane Roberts, "Seth," both emphasized the importance of hypnosis.[53]

Even parapsychologists warn about the potential hazards of hypnosis. Shafica Karagulla is a neuropsychiatrist and member of the prestigious Royal College of Physicians in Edinburgh. She is adamantly opposed to hypnosis and warns that it can "open the doors to your mind which can be influenced by other intelligences, some greater than your own. In such a passive state, an entity can get in and obtain control of you."[54]

In fact, cases of spirit possession resulting from hypnosis also occurred historically when the phenomenon was called mesmerism. This is one reason many of the best-known mediums of the nineteenth century first started their careers as mesmeric or hypnotic subjects. Several authorities have even commented that the state of mediumistic trance and the hypnotic state are almost indistinguishable. Psychoanalyst and psychic researcher Dr. Nandor Fodor points out in *An Encyclopedia of Psychic Science*, "The nature of the hypnotic trance is unknown. Its relation to the mediumistic trance is of absorbing interest."[55]

Although the trance states of hypnosis and mediumism are not identical, their parallels are sufficiently established that many find it easy to question the advisability of placing individuals, especially children, into a state that so closely parallels a state of spirit possession.

Merely because hypnosis "works" or helps people is not necessarily a justification for its use. We freely grant there are many positive testimonies. But positive testimonies can be found in almost any activity and these alone do not answer all the issues that may be raised. One leading authority on the occult, Kurt Koch, comments, "If asked for my opinion, I would have to admit that I have heard so many ill effects of hypnotism that I am opposed to it."[56] His opinion is shared by noted Swiss psychiatrist Paul Tournier and many others.[57]

As we consider the modern use of hypnosis, we tend to feel uncomfortable with the number of unanswered questions. If we accept the trance state of hypnosis for solely therapeutic reasons, where do we draw the line in accepting similar methods, such as other altered states of consciousness or the questionable techniques of occult psychologies, for therapeutic reasons?

Why is it that we can deliberately reject cultivating trance states in the world of the occult but accept them in medicine or psychology?

Further, does repeated use of hypnosis increase a person's sensitivity to the psychic world? How do we distinguish the possible spiritual or psychic impact of hypnosis on different populations—the "average" person, the occultist, people marginally interested in the psychic realm or who have recently dabbled in the psychic world, people with occult or psychic activity in their family history, Christians who have former psychic involvement prior to conversion, Christians who are backslidden? In other words, does a person's previous exposure to the occult or spiritual health affect the outcome of hypnosis?

Is the depth of the hypnotic trance proportional to the degree of susceptibility to the psychic realm? If so, can that depth be carefully regulated? Does the worldview and lifestyle of the therapist who hypnotizes his patient affect the outcome of hypnosis?

If occult hypnosis potentially leaves someone open to the influence of the demonic, what is there about the medical and psychotherapeutic forms of hypnosis which prevent this influence? In fact, occult realities can also be encountered in these professional uses of hypnosis.

What about the long-term impact of hypnosis in a person's life?

Finally, the Hebrew words found in the biblical prohibitions against "charming," "casting spells," "enchanting," etc. in Deuteronomy 18:10-12 and elsewhere would seem to indicate a similiarity to hypnosis. If it can be established that such words (*cheber*, *nachash*, etc.) encompass the practice of hypnosis, then hypnosis would be forbidden according to biblical standards and, for Christians at least, the issue of involvement settled.

In essence, we believe that hypnosis is a questionable technique whose use among adults in a culture increasingly turning to the occult is generally ill-advised. For children, this would be even more true.

In conclusion, reflecting upon these five common practices of transpersonal education, we are again constrained to ask, "Are such methods in our children's best interests?"

Legal and Scientific Considerations and Constructive Involvement

Chapter 8

∎

PSYCHIC DEVELOPMENT AND SPIRITISM THROUGH EDUCATION

I n his book *The Original Vision: A Study of the Religious Experience of Childhood*, Edward Robinson selected and arranged significant anecdotes from among 4000 first-person accounts of religious experience in childhood. His study proves what many people have forgotten: Children are innately religious and they can and do have "profound, mature religious experiences."[1] In the words of the Reverend John H. Westerhoff, professor of religious education at Duke University Divinity School, "Religious awareness, the religious imagination, the experience of the holy or sacred, is natural to childhood."[2] Further,

> Children should be affirmed as persons who can and do have significant experiences of the divine which, while only recollected and described later in life, are still mature, mystical, numinous experiences of the holy.[3]

Decades ago children were usually exposed to the Judeo-Christian worldview. But as God has been increasingly taken out of the classroom (and many other aspects of society), children have been stifled in their religious awareness. The "original vision" of children, that is, their innate perception of

God and religious intuition, is something that late twentieth-century education has increasingly obstructed through its secularist orientation.

Major Comeback of Religious Influence in Pagan Form

But today religious influence is making a major comeback in education and throughout society in the form of pagan practices and philosophies which are often, though not exclusively, associated with the New Age Movement.

Sir Alister Hardy, the renowned British scientist and founder of the Religious Experience Research Unit at Manchester College, Oxford, and author of *The Spiritual Nature of Man*, emphasizes that "the most important task for education is not only to preserve this original vision, but to see that it develops."[4] Further,

> It is of cardinal importance that our system of education should be aimed at keeping it alive [awareness of the divine] to endow the later man, or woman, with the imaginative spirit and enthusiasm (*en theos* . . . the god within!) that leads to those adventures in discovery, science, art and, yes, in religion.[5]

Because children are innately religious, they are innately susceptible to religious ideas—any ideas. With traditional religion now effectively removed from the school system, "natural" religion (e.g., pantheism) in all its various forms is ready to emerge. Dr. Hardy believes that the most important thing to stress in the schools today is that the discussion of religious feelings "is no longer to be dominated by conventional ideas of what constitutes religion, or by theological orthodoxies of one kind or another," but rather by observational study.[6] In other words, religious experience itself, of whatever form, is what is important.

Supposedly, occult and mystical experiences of children are valid precisely because they are legitimate experiences worthy of reflection and study.

The problem is not the innate sensitivity of children to God and spirituality. This is a blessing from God which, properly nurtured, works to train a child in the things of God and sensitivity to His will. The problem is the corruption of this natural tendency by New Age mystical experience and Eastern and occult forms of religion. In what direction are we to educate our children? This is something we must decide. Why?

Because given the current bias against considering even the possibility of demonic realities and deception in so lofty an area as "spirituality," the study of "religious experience" in children becomes increasingly tunneled or skewed. "True spirituality" becomes any spiritual experience: mystical, Eastern, occult, New Age, etc. Since these are increasingly nurtured in Western society, many children's experiences now come from these or related categories and are thus becoming interpreted as statistically predominant, hence normal.

But perhaps we shouldn't deceive ourselves. The tens of millions of people who are now part of alternate nonconventional spirituality are to a greater or lesser degree conditioning their children for those same spiritual traditions they have adopted. Children do what Mommy and Daddy do. And if Mommy and Daddy meditate, do yoga, practice visualization, or contact the spirits, children will usually want to emulate them.

Consider books such as Joseph Chilton Pearce's *Magical Child*, James W. Peterson's *The Secret Life of Kids: An Exploration into Their Psychic Senses*, and Samuel H. Young's *Psychic Children*. These books prove that the religious sensibilities of children can be corrupted by exposure to occult philosophy and practice. Some of the consequences are seen in books like Johanna Michaelsen's *Like Lambs to the Slaughter: Your Child and the Occult*. As Michaelsen observes after discussing the influence of New Age religion in modern America,

> The children have by no means been left untouched or ignored by the spiritual "transformation" of their elders. The question of how occultism is affecting the children of this country is no longer one that parents can afford to ignore. The children,

in fact, are the key targets. It is, after all, the little ones who will be the leaders, teachers, politicians, law makers, and parents of tomorrow. What they are taught today as young children about who or what God is and about who they are, what the nature of reality is, what happens to a person after death, and what morality and ethics are based on must necessarily have a tremendous impact on the direction the society of the future will take. It is staggering to realize to what extent the answer they are developing to these crucial questions is firmly entrenched in occult philosophy.[7]

Consider the following citation from New Age leader Marilyn Ferguson in *The Aquarian Conspiracy: Personal and Social Transformation in the 1980s*:

Of the [New Agers] surveyed, more were involved in education than in any other single category of work. They were teachers, administrators, policy makers, educational psychologists. Their consensus: education [must be transformed].... Subtle forces are at work, factors you are not likely to see in banner headlines. For example, tens of thousands of classroom teachers, educational consultants and psychologists, counselors, administrators, researchers, and faculty members in colleges of education have been among the millions engaged in *personal transformation*. They have only recently begun to link regionally and nationally, to share strategies, to conspire for the teaching of all they most value.[8]

Ferguson also points out that *Phi Delta Kappan*, perhaps the most influential journal for school administrators, stated that the field of transpersonal education not only offers tremendous potential for enhancement of learning and for solving the nation's serious social crises, but that it is "perhaps the dominant trend on the educational scene today and presages a momentous revolution."[9]

Because New Age educators are convinced that their techniques are effective and can solve the world's problems, they are convinced that schools must be revolutionized in order to incorporate their methods.

> Because of its power for social healing and awakening, they conspire to bring the philosophy [of transpersonal education] into the classroom, in every grade, in colleges and universities, for job training and adult education. [10]

What Can Happen to Children Exposed to These Ideas?

We don't think that most educators or parents yet understand the ramifications of teaching occultism to children or even introducing it in an offhand manner. As *The Coming Darkness*—Ankerberg and Weldon's forthcoming volume on the dangers of the occult—will document, occult practices are dangerous to adults; therefore, to encourage children in any manner in such a direction is socially irresponsible. Children are impressionable; they want to please their parents and the authority figures around them. They are innately trusting. To precondition or expose them to the psychic realm is simply not in their best interest. Why?

Children who are exposed to the occult become excellent subjects for conversion to the occult. For example, little Dora Kunz "began to meditate from the age of five and has been interested in various forms of meditation all her life. 'My mother,' she laughs, 'did not care what her children ate or whether they ate, as long as they did not skip meditation.'"[11] Today Dora Kunz is a leading spiritist, psychic healer (a co-developer of Therapeutic Touch), and president of the occult Theosophical Society.

Mantak Chia was exposed to Buddhist meditation at the age of six while in grammar school in Hong Kong; he also learned T'ai Chi Chuan, aikido, and hatha yoga. Today he is a practicing occultist specializing in the martial arts and "Taoist esoteric yoga."[12]

In fact, Thomas Armstrong's article "Transpersonal Experience in Childhood" and many other sources prove that children who are exposed to the occult in a systematic manner (including meditation, yoga, and psychic development) are influenced to choose that way of life later. Some of the most powerful and influential occult figures in modern American life were thrust on the occult path by the powerful spiritistic experiences they had as young children. Among examples are Paramahansa Yogananda, founder of the Self-realization Fellowship; Guru Meher Baba, founder of Sufism Reoriented; medium Helena P. Blavatsky, founder of the Theosophical Society; "guru" Jiddu Krishamurti; noted shaman Black Elk; and famous psychic healer Olga Worrall.[13] Some of these individuals actually became spirit-possessed or demonized as young children (such as Ramakrishna and Yogananda).

Unfortunately, in today's transpersonal education, what are essentially spiritistic experiences are redefined by educators in merely psychological or parapsychological terms. For example, Canfield and Klimek use the basic principles of Assagioli's psychosynthesis in helping children contact their "inner guide" or "wise person," which they view as a contact with the higher self or higher nature.

But whether the orientation is Eastern or Western occultism, the emphasis is usually upon the inherent divinity of the child and helping the child to realize he is part of God. For example, Theosophist Hodson observes, "The child, like all human beings, is primarily dual: an immortal spirit being in a mortal material body."[14] Thus the growing field of uncovering the alleged reincarnation experiences of children through hypnosis is seen as one evidence of their previous existence.[15]

> In this view, certain children would qualify as having authentic transpersonal [occult] experience on the basis of having acquired access to transpersonal levels of development in the course of previous lifetimes. Such perspective requires a reconceptionalization of human development to account for the possibility of authentic transpersonal experience in childhood.[16]

Thus, "the recognition of authentic transpersonal experience in childhood promises to provide a whole new dimension to the field of child development, requiring a re-working of traditional development models."[17]

Some Examples of the Trend

Numerous articles in *Gifted Child Quarterly* and other periodicals on the subject of children with creative abilities indicate that psychic powers have often been placed in the category of gifted children's abilities.[18] For example, *Learning: The Magazine for Creative Teaching* has on its cover a child's drawing of their teacher's "aura." The child's words are printed on the cover, "I see white light coming out of your head and fingers. There are bright colors around your face and body." Below that we read, "Is Jessie hallucinating? Or is she one of many children with extrasensory abilities?" The article cites Rudolf Steiner's anthroposophical education noting, "This system serves as a foundation for his remarkable theories of child development, which are parallel to those of Jean Piaget's"[19] (see appendix A).

Professor John Taylor's book *Superminds: An Enquiry into the Paranormal* contains many photos of metal objects bent under controlled scientific testing by the psychic powers of children. Thomas Armstrong's *Radiant Child* is another book discussing the psychic experiences and abilities of children. In *Psychic* magazine the article "Psychic Children" concludes, "In days to come, the psychic child may lead us into a new understanding of the extended nature of man and the universe."[20]

New Age psychiatrist Annette Hollander observes,

> Children with personal "mystical" experience may have less need for what Abraham Maslow calls "the paraphernalia of organized religion." . . . They may develop myths and symbols of profound personal meaning out of their private [occult] revelations.[21]

But even she observes, "I have chosen not to include techniques of encouraging the psychic development of children, because it can be destructive to them. . . . In that realm lies the demonic as well as the angelic."[22]

In Joseph Chilton Pearce's *Magical Child*, we see that under the guise of childhood development some authors are promoting specific steps for psychic development.

> Through a continual suggestion, reassurance, and reaffirming of their [the parent's] power and their ability to lend him [the child] that power, the child's suggestibility receives the idea of healing, and the inner work [of the child] responds. The child learns that mind has dominion over the world. . . . [His] parents have continued to encourage, enhance, and respond to the child's primary [psychic] perceptions. They practice telepathy by using the hypnagogic and anagogic periods right before sleep and on first waking. . . . They exercise this capacity with their child. . . . They practice remote viewing encouraging the child to sense particular target areas.[23]

Teaching Children to Hear the Spirits

Mediums and other channelers or spiritists constantly report how their own spirit guides show concern for the child's education, especially through psychic development. In her book on how to contact and use your own spirit guides, Laeh Garfield observes, "Parenting had been one of the important activities Johannah [the spirit guide] helped me with."[24] She observes that when mothers take their young children to spirit guide workshops, "Newborns and infants who attend these workshops have bubbled and cooed with excitement upon the appearance of their mother's guide."[25]

One reason Garfield actively encourages children to contact their own spirit guides is because "the majority of our celestial friends have worked out their human negativity and have no plans to abuse us in any way."[26] Nevertheless, she also reports the following:

> Young children often encounter their totem animals [spirit guides] in dreams, dreams which are sometimes frightening. The animal may appear

extra-large; it may try to come closer and closer. When a child awakes from a dream like this, the well-meaning parent tends to rush in and provide assurance of ordinary reality. What the child needs, however, is the reassurance that it's natural, when small, to be scared of communicating with the agents that foster one's higher self. Children commonly have such visions between the ages of four and seven, a period of time when their guides are reaffirming the life and work they are to do and the path that they are to take.[27]

In other words, if your child is encountering spirits, let the process continue even if it frightens him! This is why Garfield emphasizes,

Guides are of particular importance to the well-being of children. In many instances your child's imaginary friends are actually his guides, so don't deny their existence or try to send them away. One of the worse things that children go through is being told to give up what they know, especially concerning their connections with the world of spirit. Your child needs his guides as surely as he needs you, and as surely as you need guides of your own.[28]

Not surprisingly, Seth (the spirit guide of the famous medium Jane Roberts) has written a book specifically to encourage children to develop their own psychic powers and to encounter their own spirit guides: *Emir's Education in the Proper Use of Magical Powers*. But Seth is not the only popular spirit who has written books for children—so has "Ramtha." Ramtha requested Douglas James Mahr, who was later converted to Christianity, to write a child's book under his guidance entitled *The Ominous Dragoon of Dothdura* (1986). These are only two of many children's books on the occult (often dictated from the spirit world) that parents can find at their local bookstores or public libraries today.

Consider the following examples of the influence of psychic development and/or spiritism among children.

Example One: Jean Porter

Jean Porter is the author of *Psychic Development*. She initially had her own psychic abilities awakened through the same techniques she describes in her article on how to use psychic development in the classroom. For example,

> Everyone has psychic abilities. Not everyone has explored some of the ways to develop them. . . . The first step involves going inward to find a place which for you is experienced as an inner sanctuary, a retreat, or a place of inner peace. This is a real place in the inner environment of your mind and is to be explored with care, delight, and offensive discovery. You will use the psychic abilities of seeing, hearing, and sensing as well as telepathic communication.[29]

She proceeds to describe how use of the imagination and visualization (active imaging and receptive visualization) can develop children psychically.

But unfortunately there is little difference here between the visualization techniques/experiences when used for psychic or nonpsychic purposes. This indicates that when visualization is used for "educational" reasons, business, or self-help methods, it may be laying the same groundwork that psychics lay in preparation for their own psychic development.

Through visualization, Porter teaches readers how to contact their own spirit guide. After visualizing the proper environment, the participant is approached in his mind by his spirit guide: "You now are aware as to whether this being is masculine in appearance and energy or feminine. . . . In a warm, friendly manner this being approaches you. . . . This being is your guide."[30] She even identifies it specifically as a spirit guide in her explanation to the participant of what has just happened:

> What has happened is that this spirit guide, a non-physical part of yourself but not a product of your imagination, is perceived by your receptive visualization as a form to which you can relate as

you would to a friend. It is the expression of your higher consciousness.[31]

Example Two: Thomas Armstrong

Thomas Armstrong is director of Late Bloomers Educational Consulting Services in Berkeley, California, and has taught undergraduate courses in childhood and adolescent development. In his article "Children As Healers" he discusses his belief that children can be trained to become sensitive to psychic energy and become psychic healers, allegedly because "children have access to healing energies which are not available to the average adult."[32] He believes that children "are healers on many levels" because they have an innate openness to "subtle energies, alternative cultural realities, and developmental shifts of awareness" which permits the process of psychic healing to occur unimpeded by rigid or self-limiting belief systems.[33]

As an example of how to help children become healers, he cites the shamanistic tradition. Here youngsters will receive their "guardian spirit" (often in the form of a power animal) which serves as a guiding principle or "healing factor" in their future role as a shaman. "The youngster then joins the shaman and over a period of years is taught the outward rituals and the inward principles of healing."[34] Armstrong has proposed a Center for the Study of Childhood Consciousness where researchers, parents, and teachers can "gather with children to explore those dimensions" within a child's experience that open them to become psychic healers.[35]

Example Three: Gerald Jampolsky

Gerald Jampolsky is the author of *Children As Teachers of Peace*, a book based upon the spiritistic writings found in *A Course in Miracles*. He also shows how children can become psychically attuned to alleged healing energies.[36]

Example Four: Joseph Chilton Pearce

In "Freeing the Mind of the Magical Child," educator Joseph Chilton Pearce says that one of the false assumptions "particularly damaging to children" is that children must be "civilized" by being taught "adult ideas about the world and reality."[37] In this article he encourages parents and teachers to accept the potential of powerful occult energies which reside within children.

Example Five: Jan Ehrenwald

Writing in the National Education Association Journal, *Today's Education*, psychiatrist Jan Ehrenwald makes the comment that psychic phenomena, spiritism, astrology, yoga, various forms of divination, magic, and parapsychology may hold forth the promise of revitalizing our culture.[38]

Example Six: Georgi Lozanov

Dr. Georgi Lozanov of the Suggestology Institute in Sophia, Bulgaria, developed the educational method known as suggestopedia, which attempts to accelerate learning through relaxation, concentration, and suggestion. This approach, also known as the Lozanov method, has gained attention throughout the world and was popularized in America in Ostrander and Schroeder's book *Super Learning* (1979). The Lozanov method in the United States is referred to as suggestive/accelerated learning and teaching (SALT).[39]

The magazine *New Age* observed that in formulating suggestology, of which suggestopedia is a branch, Lozanov and his coworkers garnered insights from hypnosis, parapsychology, autogenics, and especially yoga: "Suggestology's deepest roots lay in the system of raja yoga."[40] Raja yoga is a yoga method involving altered states of consciousness, visualization training, concentration, and yogic breathing methods, which characteristically work to develop psychic powers or *siddhis*.

What is also significant is that Dr. Lozanov developed his "super learning" techniques in part by studying people with psychic abilities. Then he attempted to select appropriate learning methods from individuals having such occult powers.[41]

In the United States, the University of Iowa in Des Moines is a leading research and development center for the SALT method. SALT illustrates how a program may evolve and how persons concerned about the legitimacy of transpersonal approaches need to carefully evaluate not only a program's origin but also its modification over the years. For example, there are different SALT approaches having different methods, and what is true of one is not necessarily true for another.

Example Seven: James W. Peterson

James W. Peterson's *The Secret Life of Kids: An Exploration into Their Psychic Senses* reveals that, if encouraged to do so, children can become excellent subjects for the development of psychic awareness and psychic abilities. At least 5 to 10 percent of children already have psychic involvement in their family history and are predisposed to psychic capacity or are actively being educated through such techniques as hypnosis, meditation, and visualization, to have such experiences.[42]

Peterson has taught elementary school children for many years in both public and private settings. He has been director of a middle school at Concordia Montessori School in Concord, California, and teaches courses in "Psychic and Spiritual Development in Children" and "New Age Education Movements in America" at the parapsychologically oriented John F. Kennedy University at Orlinda, California.

As already noted, Joseph Chilton Pearce is the author of *The Magical Child*, a book which encourages children to develop psychically. He says in the foreword to Peterson's text,

> Psychic capacities are an integral and early part of a general development which is always by nature spiritual. When we grasp how these early psychic abilities are designed by nature to be integrated into and put to the service of higher realms of intelligence later in life, the mature spiritual intuitions, we are then well on the road to realizing what this divine play of development of consciousness is all about.[43]

In his book on the psychic lives of children, Peterson discusses various psychic senses: telepathy, clairvoyance, spirit playmates, and past-life experiences. He cites noted spiritist Olga Worrall, who has had encounters with spirits from a very young age (three) as an illustration of the potential "abilities" of children. He concludes that such things are either emerging evolutionary advances or the natural products of transpersonal forms of education which have the capacity to bring out children's "human potential."

This is why Peterson says that parents and teachers must help children who are psychically sensitive.

> Since many children seem to be sensitive to hidden dimensions of life [psychic realities], those charged with their care should themselves become more aware of these dimensions. The secret life of kids compels us to see effective child care in new, non-traditional, and even non-physical ways. Learning to cope with the psychic world can be an adventure in itself, in which parents and teachers discover new realms of life as they learn new ways to meet the needs of these children.[44]

But even Peterson is worried at the current trend of encouraging children with a wide variety of New Age practices. He warns parents and teachers in the following terms:

> The child care-giver who nurtures an interest of the psychic life of children is quickly inundated with trendy practices and techniques: guided imagery, visualization, yoga, meditation, breathing exercises, psychic expansion, psychic channeling, chakra awareness, aura balancing, dream research, past life journeys, out-of-body trips, color counseling, music therapy, visionary art, crystal sensitization, and the list goes on. My personal view is that the psychological development of a child, as seen from the spiritual perspective, indicates that many of these "New Age" practices may be less appropriate for children than one might think.[45]

Unfortunately, many are not listening to warnings of this sort and continue to advocate these methods, especially for those advanced or creative children they consider gifted.

Peterson's point is that children are simply not able to handle the powerful psychic realities that they may encounter in many of these practices. As an occultist himself, he believes that these practices are all to the good. But he points out that even occult theory suggests—if not requires—that such occult practices be utilized at the *proper* stage of individual and spiritual development.

> Many teachers who advocate meditation for children will argue that it does work, that children love it, and that it can help keep psychic channels open. From the perspective of the present discussion, these three statements are true. Meditation can "work" for children, but it works completely differently from the way it does for adults. Furthermore, I am suggesting, it is more often than not counterproductive and sometimes even dangerous....
>
> Meditative and spiritual practices for children can encourage the psychic permeability of [their] *chakra* membranes...and interfere with correct development of [psychic] filtering processes. Children can thus be trained to remain open to the psychic world, but is this helpful for them? The astral world is a realm of duality; it contains negative as well as positive influences. A child rendered more open and vulnerable to astral impressions may not be in an enviable position, especially during adolescence. Children are not sufficiently in control of their minds to protect themselves from the powerful, negative currents in the astral. Nightmares, terrifying visions, obsession and possession can be the eventual outcome.[46]

Thus, to think that transpersonal education is innocuous is naive. As more and more children are exposed to the occult and the damage increases, more and more people will become aware of the folly of encouraging children to engage in occult practices. And as transpersonal and other forms of occult education continue to grow in our culture, we may increasingly be forced to deal with the demonic possession of children. Even Peterson confesses, "I have been told that children can be particularly vulnerable to [spirit] possession at the ages of four, five and six."[47] Although stated in an occult and not a Christian context, he proceeds to observe that "incarnate beings" sometimes deliberately attempt to "cause psychic trouble for a child."[48]

This is why he warns:

> Any "spiritual" training children receive which makes their minds blank and passive can, in my view, render them more open and vulnerable to possession. Ouija boards can be particularly dangerous. . . . Furthermore, any training in telepathy or past-life reading, in which children are told to open to inner images, seems to me risky. . . . And once they passively allow outside energies to be consciously channeled through them, possession could be the outcome. I am even suspicious of art training in which the child is taught to leave himself open to his "intuition" before beginning a drawing or painting.
>
> There are schools that attempt to train children in these passive abilities, including a "seminary for psychic children" in Northern California that attempts to open kids up to the astral world. This group also offers seminars for adults on topics such as "how to allow a child to express psychic abilities" and "how to meditate with your child." The view expressed is, "If your child is not already psychic, he ought to be and, with our help, he most certainly will be!"[49]

Peterson proceeds to argue that developing psychic abilities as a child can be contrary to natural growth processes and may "seriously undermine proper intellectual and emotional development." He also believes that psychic development in children can be dangerous for another reason: the possibility of childhood schizophrenia.[50]

He further questions the validity of psychic development at any school age because

> the overwhelming majority of informants found their paranormal experiences confusing and distracting, or even frightening. Another frequent theme is that these experiences interfered with the ability to make friends, to do well in school, and generally to feel happy and comfortable.[51]

We should emphasize that Peterson, despite his concerns and criticisms, does not advocate that children are never to be educated in the psychic realm. To the contrary, he says it must simply be done with regard for the potential dangers and with due concern to prevent problems and thus to make the emerging "spiritual or psychic awareness of the child" a positive life-nurturing process.[52]

Nevertheless, one of his major concerns is over the manner in which many of these techniques are used. For example,

> Guided imagery and visualization techniques are popular these days. Often these techniques are used to take children on bizarre astral journeys, to confront projections of their inner being, "spirit guides," or other astral creatures. Although I do not recommend these exercises for young children, there is no reason visualization activities should be neglected. Modern education is far too reliant on auditory memory, and educators do not take proper advantage of other facets of the child's consciousness.[53]

Finally,

> The recognition of the secret life of children might well be another revolutionary development in child psychology. Although these widespread, atavistic psychic abilities of children reveal a great deal about the natural relationship of children with

inner spiritual realms of existence, one cannot understand them by studying the functioning of corresponding psychic abilities in adults. The mechanism of childhood psychism is unique to children, and it is for this reason that one should not start tampering with and developing additional psychic channels in the child by training them with essentially adult practices of yoga and meditation. Rather, the secret life of kids should be acknowledged in a quiet, relaxed, and natural way.[54]

Example Eight: Frances Vaughan Clark

Frances Vaughan Clark is a transpersonal educator and former president of the Association for Transpersonal Psychology. She defines transpersonal education in the following manner:

> Transpersonal education is concerned primarily with the study and development of consciousness, particularly those states commonly called higher states of consciousness and with the spiritual quest as an essential aspect of human life. . . . [In this quest the belief that] all things are seen as one Reality, remains central to the transpersonal approach. . . .
>
> Transpersonal education challenges the mind to revise outmoded conceptual structures, discarding those belief systems, be they rational or revealed, which do not account for the full range of human potential. . . . The objective of transpersonal education is the realization and maintenance of higher states of consciousness.[55]

When Vaughan refers to human potentialism, she includes a wide range of fields and beliefs, including parapsychology, viewing man as possessing latent divinity, and many forms of psychic practice. She believes that the regular practice of meditation is key to transpersonal education.[56]

She also underscores a point which many people have neglected to fully understand. Transpersonal education rejects

Christian beliefs as innately inferior. In most forms of transpersonal education, the concept of revealed religion—one
which supplies man with absolute truths—is seen as an
extremely rigid, "lower form" of education/knowing. Here,
transpersonal education actually encourages "discarding those
belief systems" that reject the concept of occult philosophy
and human potential.

Thus the educational philosophy of transpersonal approaches
is concerned with the promoting of subjective spiritual experience. For example, Vaughan also states the following:

> Unlike religious education, transpersonal edu-
> cation is not concerned with teaching a particular
> doctrine or inculcating a particular belief system. It
> focuses, rather, on the process of discovery and
> transcendence of self which results from spiritual
> practice, affirming subjective experience as valid
> and even essential for determining the nature of
> reality and the relative validity of revealed truth.
> ... Transpersonal education [is] a process to balance
> knowledge about a subject with direct intuitive
> knowing of particular states of being.... Without
> self-awareness knowledge of facts may be of little
> value.[57]

In other words, children are taught that subjective experiences derived from altered states of consciousness are "essential" not only for allegedly determining the nature of reality,
but also for ascertaining "the relative validity of revealed
truth."

Transpersonal education sees the revealed truth in the Bible
as having only "relative validity" at best. But the experience of
some forms of pantheism, where all things are seen as one
divine reality, is supposedly the "final experience" by which
everything else is to be judged.

Example Nine: Hugh Redmond

Hugh Redmond is a faculty fellow at Johnston College in
Redlands, California, and codeveloper of undergraduate and
graduate programs in transpersonal education. He has taught

courses in parapsychology, altered states of consciousness, and transpersonal psychology. He believes,

> An expanded image of man is evolving out of the literature and work in transpersonal psychology, one which has deep implications for educational philosophy and practice.... Transpersonal education is committed to the expansion of all human abilities.... Experience, intra- and interpersonal, is the major mode of learning.[58]

Thus Professor Redmond espouses the transpersonal education view that experience is an essential, if not *the* essential, form of learning. But what are the experiential techniques to bring about this alleged learning? Professor Redmond identifies them as meditation, biofeedback, psychosynthesis, various spiritual practices, dream studies, guided fantasies, yoga, physical discipline such as the martial arts, and practices from Eastern psychologies such as Buddhism.[59]

But in the transpersonal education programs that he has developed, he also includes altered states of consciousness, Zen, psychic self-regulation, parapsychology, Jungian psychology, Western mysticism, and human energy systems.[60]

In other words, the means by which the core aspect of transpersonal education (essentially learning by mystical experience) is activated is through various forms of New Age/ Eastern/occult practice. Professor Redmond sees the following as goals for transpersonal education: 1) the exploration of altered states of consciousness in education, 2) an educational atmosphere that will stimulate the psychic and creative growth of individuals, 3) the development of a paradigm for higher education that enlarges the awareness of reality and permits the experience of deeper levels of reality, 4) the providing of a forum for the merging of Eastern and Western spiritual traditions, and 5) the encouragement of intuitive and spiritual abilities of people.[61]

All this is further evidence that common New Age philosophies and practices such as psychic development and spiritism may be used in various educational programs and seminars.

Chapter 9

LEGAL ISSUES, MALPRACTICE OPTIONS, AND SCIENTIFIC EVIDENCE

This chapter will discuss the legal problems surrounding the controversies we have mentioned so far. We will see that there are considerations which warrant not only the removal of religious and psychotherapeutic-oriented curricula from the classrooms, but also demonstrate the need for state board regulation (or state government legislation) to provide screening guidelines for curricula selection.

We will also examine the scientific evidence relating to these programs as well as look at the malpractice issues.

To start, it would be helpful to have a basic grasp of the background of the church/state issue as it relates to education.

The Supreme Court has interpreted the establishment clause of the First Amendment to mean that a government agency, or an agency that receives funds from the government, cannot promote the ideology or practice of religion.

Our public schools have encountered problems here because of the expansion of government control over education and the compulsory nature of school attendance. A tension exists between the establishment clause which prohibits the governmental establishment of religion and the free exercise clause which permits the free exercise of religion and prohibits government interference in religion. For example, the courts have had a difficult time distinguishing state involvement with religious symbols and activity on the one hand and the individual right to freedom of expression for students and teachers on the other. This right certainly includes the right of students to not have their own religious beliefs abused or prohibited by the schools.

In the end, our schools and students are left with a seemingly irresolvable dilemma. For example, ethics, morals, or values are ultimately and logically derived from some religious foundation. But if the courts conclude that public education is to be "religionless," they will also make them "valueless," which by nature nurtures a philosophical position hostile to the Judeo-Christian tradition. Neutrality to Judeo-Christian religion almost guarantees neutrality to the values of that religion, and vice versa.

Of course, this has not always been the case. In John Whitehead's *The Rights of Religious Persons in Public Education* he explains the historic logic of our problems today by reminding us that early America had a general acceptance or prevalent value of Christianity, producing a social homogeneity. This is why prayer and Christian-oriented textbooks or readers were commonplace in the schools.[1]

But today "modern society is a collection of races, creeds, and religions not present within early American culture. Contemporary cultural diversity militates against any inculcation of 'common' values."[2] For example, Christians who support the idea of school-sanctioned prayer might consider that success in this regard also opens the doors to all prayer and all *concepts* of prayer, which in today's diversified marketplace includes everything from meditation and chanting to yoga and spirit contact.

As noted, court decisions have been a bit unclear in attempting to resolve the tension between the free exercise and establishment clauses. But increasingly decisions are being left up to individual school boards: "The Supreme Court has recently directed the lower courts to show deference to the judgments of school boards when considering board policies or practices."[3] Nevertheless, even though the trend is toward deference, the Court also stated that deference should be given "absent any suggestion [that a school board's rule] violates a substantive Constitutional guarantee."[4] This means that the courts should not unnecessarily entangle themselves in normal school operations except where there is a substantial violation of the Constitution. Although the courts are also showing an inclination to move away from parental rights, they have clearly made an exception when it comes to a violation of Constitutional law—and this presents problems for the new curricula.

In brief, these and other problems may involve: 1) a violation of the Constitution of the United States, principally but not exclusively the First Amendment (the establishment clause) and the Fourth, Ninth, and Fourteenth Amendments, which have been interpreted as dealing with parental rights and freedom of religious rights and privacy rights; 2) a violation of the Protection of Pupil Rights (or Hatch) Amendment; 3) a violation of the Federal Drug-Free Schools and Communities Act Amendment of 1989; 4) the resulting vulnerability to malpractice lawsuits; and 5) the unfortunate wasting of valuable time and funding on programs with little or no scientific credibility.

For example, if a public school program promotes either the ideology or practice of religion or religious philosophy, it violates the establishment clause prohibiting the governmental teaching of religion. In a similar manner, federally funded courses which are designed to engage a student in psychological treatment or experimentation without his or her parents' informed consent violate the Hatch Amendment.

Programs that seek to affect matters of personal and family privacy, feelings, emotions, attitudes, preferences, and tolerances can be a violation of a student's or family's right to privacy.

Any program or course which is clearly psychotherapeutic in nature and may be psychologically harmful is vulnerable to a malpractice lawsuit. This is especially true when psychotherapeutic methods are performed by teachers who are not licensed mental health professionals and without parents' permission.

Finally, can any school system logically justify spending scarce human resources and funding on unsubstantiated programs which have little or no scientific studies to support their claims, especially when their own objectives are, in many cases, vague and ambiguous?

What would happen if someone, even a reputable scientist, came to a school district announcing he had developed a "smart pill" to make children 50 percent more intelligent and dramatically enhance their performance? What if he claimed the pill was completely safe and would only have to be taken three times a week?

Wouldn't the Federal Drug Administration require appropriate testing to prove such claims? Shouldn't the schools want to see and carefully examine the test results for themselves? As a parent, would you allow your child to take these pills without solid long-term, established research results concerning safety and effectiveness?

Our children's emotional and educational future should not be subject to experimentation. It really is not in their best interest to allow unproven treatments or the usurpation of parental rights and values.

Below we will examine several issues on which we feel parents need to be informed.

The U.S. Constitution

The First, Fourth, and Fourteenth Amendments have been interpreted to provide for basic rights, including the right of parents to be the primary controllers of their child's education, and the right for a person's own freedom of religion to be pursued without interference (U.S. Supreme Court decisions: *Griswold* v. *Connecticut*, 1965; *Pierce* v. *Massachusetts*, 1944; *Abington* v. *Schempp*, 1963; *Wisconsin* v. *Yoder*, 1972; *Stanley* v. *Illinois*, 1972; *Mercer* v. *Michigan*, 1974. Also in *Merriken* v. *Cressman*, 364 F. Supp. 913, the court found that a drug program designed to discover *potential* drug users was a violation of the right to privacy.

For example, in *Griswold* v. *Connecticut*, 381 U.S. 479, 85 S. Ct. 1678, 14 L. Ed. 2nd 510 (1965), the right to privacy is found in the First, Fourth, and Fourteenth amendments.

In *Pierce* v. *Massachusetts*, 1944, we find, "It is cardinal with us that the custody, care and nurture of the child reside first in the parents, whose primary function and freedom include preparation for obligation the state neither supplies nor hinders."[5]

In *Abington* v. *Schempp*, 1963, the U.S. Supreme Court held that if a parent or a child objects to certain practices or materials being taught, it is not the child who is to be removed from the class, since this would violate his constitutional rights. The Court decided that what must be removed is the objectionable material. In this case, the subjects of prayer and religion were involved.[6] However, this precedent can also be applied to sex education and other practices or materials that parents or a child find objectionable. This decision also stated, "No government facility or accommodation may be used to commit inhibitions or hostilities to godly religions" and "Parents remain morally and constitutionally free to choose the academic environment in which they wish their children to be educated."

In *Wisconsin* v. *Yoder*, 1972, the right of parents to supervise their children's overall personal development was further upheld when the justices wrote,

> The history and culture of Western Civilization reflects a strong tradition of parental concern for the nurture and upbringing of their children. This primary role of the parents in the upbringing of their children is now established beyond debate as an enduring American tradition.[7]

In the same year, *Stanley* v. *Illinois* also emphasized that the "nurturing of the child resides first in the parents."[8]

Finally, in *Mercer* v. *Michigan*, 1974, the Supreme Court made the following crucial decision when it wrote, "A teacher does not have a right, constitutional or otherwise, to teach what he sees fit or to overrule the parents' decision as to which courses their children will take."[9]

The following case provides significant legal support for parents seeking to establish policy eliminating a New Age trend for schools.

In *Roberts* v. *Madigan*, Judge Finesilver required that a Christian schoolteacher remove two Christian books from a 237-book classroom library. Further, the teacher had to cease reading his Bible during the class' free reading time. Judge Finesilver reasoned that given the teacher's status as a role model for impressionable fifth graders, he (and thus the school) "must exercise great care so as not to advance a religious view."[10]

Significantly, Finesilver stated the following in rejecting the teacher's argument for academic freedom: "Families entrust public schools with the education of their children, but condition that trust on the understanding that the classroom will not be used to advance religious views that may conflict with the private beliefs of the student and his or her family.... The State must therefore take great care to see that the coercive power which they possess through mandatory attendance and teacher role models does not serve to advance religion."[11]

This case was appealed to the federal Tenth Circuit Court of Appeals and the court upheld Finesilver's decision.[12]

This case was also discussed in an article by Benjamin Sendor, school attorney and professor of public law at the University of North Carolina, in the August 1989 issue of the *American School Board Journal*. The thrust of his article was to encourage school boards to adopt sound policy concerning the school's advancement of religion. Sendor concludes,

> School boards should consider issuing policies about religious issues before disputes arise.... A sound policy on religion in the schools can foster understanding and prevent the costly political, emotional, educational, and financial consequences of litigation.[13]

Even though Christians and others concerned about *reasonable* legal restrictions on religion in schools may not agree with the court's findings, they can utilize this decision to a good end. What's good for the goose is good for the gander. The burden is now on the school to exercise *great* restraint not to promote any religious symbols or activities, and this certainly includes the standard premises and practices of New Age religion in transpersonal education programs.

Thus all the above rulings prove that parents have the legal right to prohibit schools from teaching religious or potentially harmful psychotherapeutic beliefs or practices to their children.

In what other ways are school districts vulnerable to lawsuits? Two legal cases are relevant. In 1988 the Equal Employment Opportunity Commission (EEOC) issued a policy statement. This was intended to guide employers in handling cases where an employee refuses to participate in a training program because it conflicts with his religious beliefs.

Initially, this was part of the Civil Rights Act of 1964, Title VII. But the EEOC and its attorneys deemed it important enough to make it law. Regardless, the explanation of the policy is relevant to current public schools curricula.

The policy begins by noting the following:

> Employers are increasingly making use of training programs designed to improve employee motivation, cooperation, or productivity through the use of various so-called "New Age" techniques.... Most of the nation's major corporations and numerous government agencies have hired some consultants and purveyors of similar inside "personal growth" training programs in recent years. The programs utilize a wide variety of techniques: meditation, guided visualization, self hypnosis, therapeutic touch, biofeedback, yoga, and inducing altered states of consciousness. These programs focused on changing individual employees' attitudes and self concepts by promoting increased self-esteem, assertiveness, independence, and creativity in order to improve overall productivity.[14]

Consider what happens if we substitute the word *schoolchildren* in place of *employees*. We discover it is equally appropriate in this situation as well. This means that legal precedent has been further set to exclude not just employees from practices that conflict with their religion, but children as well.

The second case was mentioned earlier[15] (*Malnak* v. *Yogi*, February 2, 1979, United States Court of Appeals, Third District). Parents had objected to their children being exposed to Transcendental Meditation as part of the regular school curriculum. But the New Jersey school district would not drop the program, requiring parents to resort to litigation. The concepts of TM had been cleverly camouflaged under neutral wording, and the practice itself was given a new name: the "Science of Creative Intelligence" (SCI)—but it was Hinduism, nonetheless.

The judge in the federal district court ruled in favor of the parents, declaring that SCI was a religious practice and therefore in violation of both the separation and establishment clause of the First Amendment. The school board took their case to the U.S. Court of Appeals where the court reaffirmed the earlier decision. Here a significant opinion came from Judge Adams when he discussed the definition of religion as it relates to our legal system.

If we apply Judge Adams' three criteria of religion (discussed in chapter 1) to New Age education, we discover these transpersonal education programs contain all three elements. So here again we find a basis for legal action that parents may wish to pursue.

The Hatch Amendment

The Hatch Amendment is a federal law enacted under the title *Protection of Pupil Rights*, Public Law 95-561, Sec. 1250, Section 439 of the General Education Provisions Act, 20 USC 1232 g, enacted 11/2/78. It requires "prior written consent of the parent" for psychiatric or psychological "examination, testing or treatment." For example, consider Section 439 which we cite verbatim below:

> Sec. 439. "(a) All instructional material—including teachers' manuals, films, tapes, or other supplementary instructional material—which will be used in connection with any research or experimentation program or project shall be available for inspection by the parents or guardians of the children engaged in such program or project, (b) for the purpose of this [section] research or experimentation program or project means any project in any [applicable] program under 98.1 (a) or (b) that is *designed to explore or develop new or unproven teaching methods or techniques*."[16]

Sec. 439. "(b) No student shall be required, as part of any applicable program, to submit to psychiatric examination, testing or treatment, in which the primary purpose is to reveal information concerning:

(1) political affiliations;

(2) mental and psychological problems potentially embarrassing to the student or his family;

(3) sex behavior and attitudes;

(4) illegal, anti-social, self-incriminating and demeaning behavior;

(5) critical appraisals of other individuals with whom respondents have close family relationships;

(6) legally recognized privileged and analogous relationships, such as those of lawyers, physicians, and ministers; or

(7) income (other than that required by law to determine eligibility for participation in a program or for receiving financial assistance under such program), without the prior consent of the student (if the student is an adult or emancipated minor), or in the case of an unemancipated minor, without the prior written consent of the parent."[17]

Legal Definitions

Consider the following official definitions applicable to the Hatch Amendment. (These are included in the Final Regulations to implement Sec. 439 as printed in the *Federal Register*, vol. 49, no. 174, Thursday, Sep. 6, 1984, Rules and Regulations, pp. 35318-21.)

(1) "Psychiatric or psychological examination or test" means a method of obtaining information, including *a group activity, that is not directly related to academic*

instruction and that is designed to elicit information about attitudes, traits, opinions, beliefs or feelings;

and

(2) "Psychiatric or *psychological treatment*" means an activity involving the planned, systematic use of methods or techniques that are not directly related to academic instruction and that is *designed to affect behavioral, emotional, or attitudinal characteristics of an individual or group.*"[18]

Again, these definitions are seen to apply to the specific programs, beliefs, and practices we have been discussing.

The Federal Drug-Free Schools and Communities Act

There are many drug and alcohol school "prevention" programs which employ an affective, nondirective decision-making model. If such methods teach students to decide for themselves whether to take drugs, these programs are also in violation of a new federal law which applies to *all* public schools.

Phyllis Schlafly of Eagle Forum explains why as she discusses this new law in the following extended citation:

A little-noticed new federal law requires every public school receiving federal funds to teach students that "the use of illicit drugs and the unlawful possession and use of alcohol in school is wrong and harmful." This landmark law is the first attempt by the Federal Government to mandate instruction in a specific subject area in order for schools to receive federal funding. This strong message is to be included as part of a "program to prevent the use of illicit drugs and alcohol by students or employees" which every public school district must adopt as a condition of receiving federal funds. *No later than October 1, 1990*, acceptable drug programs must be taught in all grades ("from early childhood level through grade 12") of every federally-assisted school.

In addition to teaching that drug use is "wrong and harmful," the required classroom programs must address the "legal, social and health consequences of drug and alcohol use." The courses must also "provide information about effective techniques for resisting peer pressure to use illicit drugs or alcohol."

The new provisions are contained in Section 5145 of the Drug-Free Schools and Communities Act of 1986, as amended by Public Law 191-226, which President Bush signed into law on December 12, 1989. The new law is classified in the United States Code at Title 20, Section 3224a. It applies to all public schools, since all receive some federal money.

"Drug education" is already commonly taught in public schools but these courses are usually not drug prevention courses. Few if any of these curricula comply with the new law because they are typically non-judgmental and non-directive. They consist of lessons in "decision-making," "self-esteem," or "values clarification." These courses lead the student to believe that he is the final authority and can make his own personal "choices and decisions." These courses teach the student that he can construct his own value system concerning drug use independent of family, religion, the law, or other authority.

Many drug curricula used in public schools confuse the child about drugs as a category that includes everything from aspirin to crack, and some courses do not even mention the fact that use or possession of certain drugs is subject to criminal penalties. Some drug education teaches that only the abuse of drugs is harmful, thus, implying that moderate or occasional use of alcohol, marijuana, or cocaine might be an acceptable option.

In order to comply with the new law, drug courses must clearly teach that the use—not just the abuse—of illegal drugs is "wrong" as well as "harmful."

Some drug curricula do include material that some illegal drugs are harmful, but that is not sufficient to comply with the new law. It is not sufficient to offer the student options or choices in which some harmful consequences of illegal drug use are mentioned. To comply with the law, the curriculum must teach that illegal drugs are wrong—and if they are wrong, then there is no decision or choice for the child to make, since our society and our laws have already made the decision for the child.

The new public disclosure section of this law gives parents and others the right to review all teaching materials used in drug education courses. *The new law requires that every local school district "shall, upon request, make available . . . to the public full information about the elements of its program required by law."*[19]

Malpractice

The use of progressive relaxation, guided imagery/visualization, and other religious or psychotherapeutic methods in the regular classroom presents another legal issue besides the ones already discussed. This relates to malpractice vulnerability.

Despite disclaimers, these methods may constitute a form of hypnotherapy and/or a religious practice of meditation. We elsewhere documented that such approaches are frequently rooted in Eastern religious philosophy. (Even if some school board members disagree, these methods still comprise potentially harmful psychotherapeutic techniques.)

Nevertheless, consulting the professional literature on any of these subjects, in particular hypnosis, autogenics, or meditation, will make the point that progressive relaxation and guided imagery/visualization methods do constitute practice in hypnosis and/or meditation.[20] Such studies prove the words *hypnosis* and *meditation* are frequently interchanged.[21]

If one consults the bibliographic citations to these studies, one consistently encounters treatments such as psychotherapy and behavior modification, which brings guided imagery and visualization under the domain of the Hatch Amendment. In fact, all a parent or educator need do is consult the *Encyclopedia Britannica* for the definition, methodology, and relative appropriateness of hypnosis and related methods.

The Encyclopedia Britannica describes the various methods of hypnotic induction, including those of progressive relaxation and guided imagery. It proceeds to note that the hypnotic subject is one who becomes highly suggestible, whose perceptions are distorted, and whose distinction between reality and fantasy becomes blurred.

The article points out, "The induction of hypnosis requires little training and no particular skill, a tape recording often being sufficient." Thus, it warns that the person leading a hypnosis session should "have the necessary training or skill to treat medical or psychological problems." This is because "improperly used, hypnosis may add to the patients' psychological or medical difficulties."[22]

The author of this article is Dr. Martin Orne of the University of Pennsylvania Medical School, one of the foremost American experts on hypnotherapy. He was recently interviewed for a television report on parents' objections to certain programs in public schools—specifically Pumsy and DUSO. Dr. Orne was very concerned about the extensive use of these fantasy techniques in the classroom. He said,

> You can raise issues that the child is not ready to deal with—guided imagery is just another term for hypnosis. . . . You have to be very careful because an individual who is confused or troubled may require treatment, and hypnosis may not be the treatment of choice—it may encourage different thoughts which are not necessarily helpful.[23]

This seems to indicate that the design and purpose of these methods are psychotherapeutic in nature. Characteristically, they are designed for therapy with troubled children and certainly not proactively!

The Appropriateness of These Methods

These questionable methods are used by guidance counselors, physical education teachers, and teachers in gifted education, even though they are not licensed mental health professionals. But to engage in such shotgun therapy in the classrooms—with our children—would seem to be setting a dangerous precedent, not to mention opening schools to malpractice lawsuits.

Those who desire to reconstruct American education are increasingly convinced that the schools of America are responsible for more than just the traditional academic pursuits. Today many educators feel that schools should carry the burden of responsibilities once relegated to the family. Thus classroom activities and educational curricula around the country extend beyond traditional limits and have incorporated social, psychological, emotional, and even spiritual areas. This allegedly holistic education is based on the premise that old-style education is simply inadequate to prepare students for the many challenges of the twenty-first century. Students must also be educated in subjects that educators believe are in their best interests, such as multicultural understanding, self-esteem, global perspectives, conflict resolution, and even certain religious perspectives and techniques. But school should be primarily a place for academic learning; it is not a substitute for the family, church, psychologist, or the United Nations. Is it really fair to expect this of schools? Isn't this expecting so much of teachers that the primary function of the school can only suffer as a result?

The professional journal of the American Personnel Association recognizes this problem of changing teacher roles and expectations. For example,

> Elementary school counselors have, by tradition and training, been assigned the task of serving the developmental needs of all pupils. . . . In recent years, however, the elementary school counselor has been asked to participate in the resolution of contemporary mental health problems.[24]

We grant that many people believe teachers should be part-time therapists because these programs seem to work in some situations. But Valium also works to calm children and help "solve" their problems. This doesn't mean it is ethical to administer it.

Other people reply that children really enjoy these kinds of programs. Surprise! Children enjoy mind games and fantasy exercises more than learning academics. But what is the purpose of school? And do these programs really accomplish their goals? And do these goals usurp parental rights or values? Finally, do they put children at risk? For example, Dr. Orne is hardly the only professional who warns about the use or misuse of hypnosis in the classroom.

Ross S. Olson, M.D., is a Minneapolis pediatrician who has expressed his own concerns over the use of guided imagery in the classroom. He believes that by turning inward, children may discover a more attractive world than that found in normal reality. Further,

> There is the possibility of psychological injury to participants. . . . I am acquainted with a woman who began to have uncontrollable "out of body" experiences after a similar program. . . . The [program] leaders are inadequately prepared to deal with this possibility. [This is why] physicians using guided imagery for therapy stress that it is a powerful technique requiring proper psychological training. Finally, it is completely consistent with New Age religion and therefore should not be promoted by public schools.[25]

Dr. Olson also expresses concern that some secondary students are actually being taught to visualize diseases away and that these programs may be antieducational, antirational, and dangerous.[26]

Even the professional educational and psychological journals indicate potential problems with using these approaches. An article in *Elementary School Guidance and Counseling Journal* warns,

> There are some situations where use of fantasy may be inappropriate. Children with serious emotional problems that tend to retreat from reality would not benefit and can be harmed by such fantasy exercises. Counselors need to screen students before they begin fantasy activities.[27]

In the same journal, an article describes research findings on the *Magic Circle*, part of the Human Development Program

(HDP). The *Magic Circle* is described as a "comprehensive, sequential, developmentally based, affective education curriculum designed for use with the general classroom population." But the question was asked, "Can psychological education be required of all students if the possibility of detrimental effects is as distinct as these results suggest?"

The study revealed that there was "sufficient general and specific dissatisfaction by students with HDP to question the appropriateness" of the program for students in all cases. Further, the results of this study and that of Gerler and Tupperman (1976) "raised an important philosophical issue as to whether all children should be unquestionably exposed to developmental guidance or psychological education."[28]

Wasting Resources on Unproven or Disproven Programs

The question is often raised whether these programs are cost-effective or whether there may be currently unknown side effects for children. There is a small percentage of parents and educators who are not concerned about the religious or psychotherapeutic aspects of these programs; they are only concerned with alleged results.

But what if scientific testing is demonstrating the ineffectiveness of these methods? What if our children are being used as guinea pigs of sorts for experimental programs?

Particularly damaging to a number of New Age claims about "scientific validation" for their methods is a recent analysis conducted by the National Research Council and published by the National Academy Press.[29] (The National Academy Press was created by the National Academy of Sciences to publish reports of the National Research Council Institute of Medicine. These operate under a charter granted by the United States Congress to the National Academy of Sciences.)

The report was prepared by the Committee of Techniques for the Enhancement of Human Performance and the Commission on Behavioral Social Sciences and Education. It was prompted by the Army Research Institute which asked the National Academy of Sciences to examine the value of certain techniques that had been alleged to enhance human performance.

As a grouping, these techniques were viewed as extraordinary in that they were developed outside the mainstream of the human sciences and yet had been presented with strong claims for high effectiveness.

The value of this report is that it provided a systematic approach to evaluating all studies offered to support the claim that these methods enhance human potential. The range of subjects evaluated included techniques in learning, improving motor skills, altering mental states, stress management, and paranormal phenomena.

Some of the individual topics or programs studied included SALT, suggestology, neurolinguistic programming (NLP), cybervision, hemispheric brain studies in learning theory (right brain/left brain), meditation, and subliminal self-help tapes.

Their final conclusion was that the claim to enhance human performance was greatly exaggerated. Either no real research base existed to support the relationship between a given technique and subsequent performance, or the bodies of research that did exist were too poorly done or too conflicting to make valid scientific claims.[30]

What all this means is that we may be wasting a great deal of time and money in the attempt to help children through the application of experimental programs.

Dr. Charles Heikkinen is Director of Counseling Services at the University of Wisconsin. Although the following excerpt from his article involved a discussion of adult counseling methods, it is these techniques that are now being used on schoolchildren! In the *Journal of Counseling and Development* he points out,

> Counselors increasingly appear to be using visualization, relaxation training, and hypnosis.... I have also seen more people who have gone through these approaches, especially in group formats, and then had hours and even days of unusual mental functioning.

For example:

In my experience, counseling strategies such as visualization, relaxation, meditation and hypnosis almost always induce a qualitatively different type of consciousness, typified by changes in emotion, increases in suggestibility and alterations in logical thought. . . . They can also induce persistent, undesirable aftereffects, including panic and confusion, unless counselors take time to reorient clients after each session. . . . Be extremely careful when using altered states of consciousness experiences with groups whose members you do not know.[31]

Transcendental Meditation

Consider meditation in the schools. Today Transcendental Meditation is by far the most widely practiced form of meditation in the country. Thousands of teachers have become meditators through this system and many have encouraged their students to do TM as well. Although TM has legally been excluded from participation in the classroom (*Malnak* v. *Yogi*), in some school systems its procedures, at least, continue to be taught.

TM proponents claim hundreds of research studies to supposedly validate the alleged benefits of meditation. What they don't say is that these studies have usually not been independently established through rigorous scientific testing. Even though Maharishi Mahesh Yogi's TM enterprise is worth three to four billion dollars and continues to find influence in education, what many teachers are unaware of is that there are dozens of studies showing the harmful effects of meditation. Some of these have been annotated by an organization called the Ex-Transcendental Meditation Members Support Group. They state:

> Suppressed by MIU [Maharishi International University] and the TM movement are many independent research studies with tighter controls which have uncovered the following actual effects from the practice of TM:

1. No specific or broad-scale benefits

2. Impaired mental faculties

3. Depersonalization

4. High percentage of psychological disorders

5. Aggravation of preexisting mental illness

6. The onset of mental illness.[32]

We might also add that in many cases TM has also actually led to outright spirit possession, as Dr. Weldon documented in his 1975 text *The Transcendental Explosion.*

Social scientists Singer and Ofshe express their concerns about

> groups relying more on the use of meditation trance states, and dissociative techniques.... A program relying heavily on meditation trance and dissociation techniques is likely to include elements of emotional arousal devices... [which] can be produced by guided imagery and other trance inducing procedures.... Groups that used prolonged mantra and empty-mind meditation, hyperventilation and chanting appear more likely to have participants who develop relaxation induced anxiety, panic disorders, multidissociative problems and cognitive inefficiencies.[33]

They supplied the example of a man whose condition was diagnosed, paradoxically, as a "relaxation-induced anxiety" which had evolved into panic attacks and atypical dissociative states. He was involved in Transcendental Meditation (TM) for 15 minutes twice a day. But after a few months he began to have bouts of chest pains, fainting spells, palpitations, and lassitude. Ironically, he was introduced to TM in a free lecture advertised as being able to reduce stress in his life!

Regardless, many school programs condition students to deal with stress, conflicts, and problems by employing these kinds of meditative techniques. This means that children could easily begin to practice meditation on a regular basis, and therefore expose themselves to its possible hazards as well.

As noted, a number of independent research studies prove the use of meditation can be harmful. Dr. Heide and Dr. Borkovec indicate that 54 percent of anxiety-prone subjects tested experienced increased anxiety during the TM-like mantra meditation.[34] Dr. Arnold Lazarus showed that even serious psychiatric problems can ensue from the practice of TM.[35] Meditation researcher Dr. Leon Otis refers to a Stanford Research Institute study involving 574 subjects. It revealed that the longer a person practiced meditation the greater the number of adverse mental effects; indeed, 70 percent of subjects recorded mental disorders of one degree or another.[36]

The sad thing is that none of this is necessary if all we are seeking is stress reduction and relaxation. Five issues of *American Psychologist* (1984-1987) detailed an exhaustive TM research review and further controlled testing which demonstrated that TM procedures were no more beneficial for physical relaxation than merely sitting with your eyes closed.[37]

Self-Esteem

Dr. Susan Black is an education professor in the graduate program at Elmira College in New York and a professional consultant to a number of schools and industries. Perhaps more than anyone else Dr. Black has done extensive research on many of the pervasive self-esteem programs used in public schools around the country. In her *American School Board Journal* article "Self-Esteem: Sense and NonSense," Dr. Black explains why she became interested in this area:

> Most of the teachers and administrators I know assume raising students' self-esteem causes higher achievement and improved behavior. They believe programs designed to promote high self-esteem have desirable outcomes, such as reduced dropout rates, decline in teen pregnancies, less vandalism, and better test scores. . . . But, I wondered, is there any evidence these programs actually bring about

such outcomes? How are the relationships between self-esteem and achievement and self-esteem and behavior measured?[38]

After reviewing the relevant research on self-esteem in over 100 different publications from universities, independent researchers, school districts, and educational agencies, she realized that while schools can have a degree of influence upon a child's self-esteem, this influence is probably marginal. She concludes,

> Having reviewed the research, I now believe what I suspected before: many of the efforts initiated in our schools in the name of raising students' self-esteem missed the mark entirely. Indeed, self-esteem is so complex a concept and instructional time so precious a commodity that boards should be cautious about approving self-esteem initiatives. Such initiatives do not always deliver what they promise.... If the proposals aren't backed up by research, raise the red flag.[39]

Dr. Black further explains why self-esteem programs may be too late to do much good. She concludes by noting that true self-esteem is a product of effort and performance, not psychological coaxing, someone's inner fantasy life, or positive thinking. She gives the following advice to school boards:

> The research clearly shows schools can have some influence on a child's self-esteem but it also shows that self-esteem, whether high or low, is a rather fixed and stable psychological state, not too amenable to change. Generally, children's self-esteem is formed by the age of four or five and is derived largely from the student's home and family; schools have less impact....
>
> [Further] research consistently shows that improved self-esteem is an outcome rather than a cause of success and achievement. Study after study

emphasizes that students gain considerable self-esteem from putting forth effort to achieve.... Whatever you undertake in the name of self-esteem, it is important for us to review the research. That way your board can differentiate between what makes real sense and what doesn't.[40]

In addition, according to an article in *U.S. News & World Report*, there is "almost no research evidence that these [self-esteem] programs work."[41] Even the report of the famous California task force on self-esteem, *The Social Importance of Self-Esteem*, confesses that, "One of the disappointing aspects of every chapter in this volume is how low the associations between self-esteem and its consequences are in research to date."[42] *U.S. News & World Report* comments,

In fact, those correlations are as close to zero as you can get in the social sciences. This confirms the common-sense judgment that behavior is rarely changed by injections of positive thinking and psychic boosterism.... Fear of failure and parental hovering have much more to do with academic success than good feelings about self.[43]

The article points out that the basic problem with self-esteem programs is that they are counterproductive. If children are praised and told how special they are regardless of achievement, that they are perfect and lovable always, what motivation is there for children to strive to do better or change in the first place?

This is why the obsession with self-esteem ultimately undermines real education. When the self-esteem movement takes over a school, teachers are under pressure to accept every child as is. To keep children feeling good about themselves, you must avoid all criticism and almost any challenge that could conceivably end in failure. In practice, this means each child is treated like a fragile therapy consumer in constant need of an ego boost. Difficult work is out of the question, and standards get lowered in school after school. Even tests become problematic because someone might fail them.[44]

In its cover article of February 17, 1992, *Newsweek* also discussed the tremendous influence of self-esteem in the nation and the problems it has caused. It observed that "the concept of self-esteem has established itself in almost every area of society. . . . [But] nowhere has the concept taken root as firmly as education."[45]

As evidence that self-esteem is not the solution to children's learning problems, the *Newsweek* article pointed out that University of Michigan psychologist Harold Stevenson compared students in Japan, Taiwan, and China with those in America. In self-confidence about their abilities in math, American students ranked far ahead of the others; but in *actual performance* they fell far behind. In fact, in science and math a comparison of achievement by schoolchildren in 20 countries revealed that Americans ranked near the bottom.[46]

Newsweek revealed that a recent survey of self-esteem literature found that although some 10,000 scientific studies of self-esteem had been conducted, "there isn't even agreement on what it is."[47]

The article concluded that a lot of the self-esteem industry in the country was simply dealing in nonsense. Teachers, parents, and children who believe that emphasis on self-esteem will improve their performance are fooling themselves because self-esteem only follows, not precedes, true accomplishment. In the last decade, no other country in the world has even come close to flattering itself as much as America— yet just look at our decline in educational performance.

Indeed, in some ways the promotion of self-esteem apart from a logical basis for it is like the "mind-science" beliefs which attempt to convince people certain things are true which simply aren't. Self-esteem must be connected with the development of character, morals, and achievement if it is to have lasting value. What assists self-esteem is a combination of high standards and expectations, school discipline, and continual encouragement and reinforcement by communicating to the child to do the best he can.

No one denies that self-esteem is important, but it is also important not to waste great amounts of money and effort on programs that really don't work. Dr. Black points out that many schools adopt self-esteem programs based on the mere claim that "research says," without really evaluating the quality or legitimacy of such a claim.

For example, in the rewards and incentives approach of modern education (such as rewarding the child for doing homework), the first of the 14 points uncovered by Dr. Black's research was: "Students who do an activity, such as reading library books, without a reward believe that activity is worth doing; students who receive a reward for doing an activity believe it must not be worth doing without the reward."[48] Further, "Throughout my investigation, I wondered why schools persist in adopting new programs that reward students for achievement and behavior. How could the research I had found—which was so clear and abundant—be disregarded?"[49]

What Black found was that reward approach methods are characteristically counterproductive: "For most students, however, the research tells a compelling story: token reward systems are likely to produce the opposite of what is expected and desired."[50] Thus,

> Too many times, board members and others take statements like "research says" at face value without ever questioning the studies behind them. The result: Sometimes school leaders make important decisions based on little more than someone's gut feeling, misguided assumptions, or shoddy analysis.[51]

Dr. Black has suggested that school boards carefully and critically review research claims before adopting experimental programs. As the material below briefly documents, this is indeed a good idea. We begin with drug and alcohol prevention programs.

Psychologist Richard H. Blum and his Stanford University colleagues predicted in the early 1970s that a "process education that consisted of discussion groups, employing values clarification and decision-making" would help students refuse the offer of drugs. Two studies were conducted, one with 1586 students (grades 2–10) and another with 1413 sixth graders. To Blum's surprise, in both studies it was found that instead of the expectation, "quicker and wider use of alcohol, tobacco and cannabis [marijuana] resulted."[52]

Michael D. Klitzner, Ph.D., was commissioned by the U.S. Department of Education to produce an in-depth study which included an evaluation of the affective approach titled "Report to Congress on the Nature and Effectiveness of Federal, State and Local Prevention/Education Programs." He concludes, "The results of the studies are not encouraging. What effects were found, tended to be small or of short duration, and some of the programs may have stimulated rather than reduced substance use." Instead, Dr. Klitzner recommends a strongly reinforced abstinence-based approach.[53]

Dr. William Hansen of the Department of Preventive Medicine, Institute for Health Promotion and Disease Prevention Research, University of Southern California, reports on the results of his evaluation of the program known as Project SMART in "Affective and Social Influence Approaches to the Prevention of Multiple Substance Abuse Among Seventh Grade Students." He concluded,

> No preventive effect of the affective education program was observed. By the final post-test, classrooms that had received the affective program had significantly *more* drug use than the controls. . . . [This approach] may have *enhanced* [drug] experimentation.[54]

What about sex education? In "Schools and Sex Education: Does It Work?" published in *Pediatrics*, researchers examined five behavioral studies to determine whether evidence warrants support for conventional sex education. Most sex education was identified as being process-oriented (having decision-making and values clarification approaches). The results were as follows:

> The available evidence indicates that there is little or no effect from school-based sex education on sexual activity, contraception, or teenage pregnancy. . . . Individuals involved in these programs

must first provide evidence of effectiveness to justify the financial and emotional burden created by these programs.[55]

In *The Myth of Safe Sex* (Moody, 1993), Ankerberg and Weldon document both the failure and the tremendous consequences of modern sex education. In fact, a publication by the Alan Gutmacher Institute, a subsidiary of Planned Parenthood, reveals:

> Sex education is actually a cofactor for the initiation of sexual activity of girls ages 15-17. In one of the largest studies ever undertaken (based on a 1984 survey of 6000 young women) they found that 15-year-old girls who had sex education were 40 percent more likely to begin sex activity than girls who did not have such instruction. Further, 16-year-olds were 25 percent more likely to do so.[56]

What about DUSO and the Human Development Program? Dr. William Strein of the University of Maryland conducted 23 studies on the effectiveness of classroom-based elementary affective education programs. Two programs cited in the study were the Human Development Program (HDP) and Developing Understanding of Self and Others (DUSO). The research was reported in *Psychology in the Schools*. Dr. Strein points out the following:

> Despite the popularity of classroom based affective education programs, research on the effectiveness of such programs has been sparse and poorly disseminated. . . . This paper reviews the research on the effectiveness of elementary school affective education programs that are feasible for regular classroom use and examines the research results in terms of A. Methodological rigor of the study; B. Program type and outcome measures used; C. Grade Level; D. Length of program; E. Leader's profession.[57]

The results of Dr. Strein's research are compelling. He concludes:

> The available research evidence does not strongly support the effectiveness of affective education programs as defined in this study. This conclusion is strengthened by the finding that the *studies that were more rigorous tended to be less supportive of program effectiveness.* The almost complete lack of supportive evidence from programs that were compared against a placebo group is particularly damaging.[58]

What about DARE (*Drug Abuse Resistance Education*)—as we have seen, an extremely popular program used in schools throughout the country? A study from the Center for Prevention Research at the University of Kentucky suggests that Blum's and other research (cited on pp. 188-89) should be taken seriously.

The Kentucky researchers also found *increased* use of marijuana one year after DARE. They reported significantly fewer non-DARE than DARE children had tried marijuana within a year after taking the course. DARE, in other words, seemed to make participants more precocious in that they began experimenting with marijuana a year earlier than other children.[59]

All in all, the Research Council on Ethnopsychology observes the current situation in the schools as problematic at best. In its article "Experimental Mysticism, DARE, and the Hollywood Thirteen,"[60] the council points out that experimental mysticism has now been in the schools for over 15 years, "packaged for students and teachers of drugs and sex education under a wide variety of brand names."[61] Some of the more popular designations are "affective education," "humanistic education," "circle-based education," "process education," and "experiential education." The article defines "experimental mysticism" as a blend of "meditation, psychotherapy and encounter techniques."

The Research Council supplies a warning about this new wave of experimental mysticism, noting that the "long-term effects might be worse than the most concerned parent could ever imagine."[62] It observes that research to date indicates that such education tends to guide students toward early use of cigarettes, alcohol, and marijuana, and that it leads to public defiance, as well as a potential for violence and immorality.[63] For example, "Research suggests that drug education featuring lessons in self-esteem and the other usual fare of experimental mysticism [actually] leads to drug use."[64]

As noted, Professor W.P. Coulson was a colleague of psychologists Carl Rogers and Abraham Maslow. The educational establishment widely adopted the premises and methods of affective education developed by these psychologists even though these men have repudiated much of their former teachings and said that they must be considered harmful to children. Coulson warns,

> Carl Rogers died last year. He and I and our project teammates owe the nation's parents an apology. ...We experimented with classroom adaptations of humanistic therapeutic principles, active listening, eye messages, and unconditional acceptance and found them destructive of mind. Not only did intellectual learning not survive in a nondirective classroom atmosphere, a whole school system went under.[65]

Coulson also observed in a speech given on June 3, 1988, in Indiana that these techniques which tend to slow down brain waves may actually make students "more receptive to brainwashing" because their defenses are down. As a result, new concepts such as New Age philosophy may more easily have an impact.

Parents have repeatedly asked the educators who are using these programs to produce the scientific evidence justifying their use. To date, little or no such evidence has been forthcoming. To the contrary, the scientific research is indicating that these popular affective, nondirective decision-making programs intended to reduce drug and sex problems are in many cases producing just the opposite effect.

Chapter 10

OVERCOMING OBJECTIONS AND OTHER RESPONSES

Perhaps it is good to remember that controversy can be something positive. Intellectual growth and conflict resolution frequently occur when parties are stretched and challenged to consider something beyond what is normally safe and comfortable.

Unfortunately, it is equally true that becoming defensive and closed-minded can result from being challenged. In today's marketplace of competing ideas, individuals or groups committed to an agenda tend to resist a new direction or philosophy.

The result may be to erect barriers against a constructive outcome and produce misunderstandings, hurt feelings, polarization, or even unethical behavior.

The purpose of this chapter is to help minimize the barriers to constructive change in education. The range of objections we list (mostly on the part of educators) have been encountered through both experience and research in dealing with these issues.

Some of these objections are honest and sincere. But some are part of an organized and entrenched liberal segment of our society who have a calculated plan to impose their values on other people.

On the positive side, there have been some very encouraging articles in recent professional education journals. An entire issue of the journal *Phi Delta Kappan*, the professional fraternity in education, was recently devoted to improving education through parental involvement.

One article noted

> how California's policy on parent involvement enables districts and schools to develop *appropriate* programs that support the primary goal of improving student learning.... The policy on parent involvement was inspired and informed by an earlier initiative on curriculum reform.... Research on parent involvement *consistently shows* that parents can make a difference in the quality of their children's education if districts and schools enable them to become involved in education in a variety of ways.[1]

Even more important, Howard Kirschenbaum (codeveloper of Quest) published an article in the *Elementary School Guidance and Counseling Journal* which certainly justifies our concerns over these issues. Kirschenbaum outlines the rights and responsibilities of the school board. These include setting "*goals, objectives, policies* and *standards* for the school district ... [setting] *specific guidelines for adopting school curricula and reevaluating curricula* and due process for handling complaints or controversy from the community."[2]

He goes on to define the responsibilities of professional education, such as

> establishing ... curricula and teaching methods that are consistent with policies of the school district and *with the best professional knowledge available* to them ... to revise curricula and replace or change outdated materials and methods ... to have complaints or controversy dealt with in a professional manner.[3]

And finally he writes that students have a right to be exposed to "issues *appropriate to their age and readiness* ... [and] to maintain the right of privacy with regard to their personal views and private lives."[4] Such a perspective is extremely important to parents and families as their rights are challenged by certain parties inside and outside the educational establishment.

Below we list some common objections which may be encountered in seeking an establishment of policy to prevent children from being exposed to improper programs and curricula.

Response: This is not part of New Age religion. This approach may come in different forms such as "The New Age is not a religion" or "These techniques may be indirectly analogous to the methods of Eastern religions, but this is by coincidence, not design."

Answer: Many people have heard of the New Age Movement (NAM) but are really not knowledgeable about its beliefs, practices, agenda, or influence.

You may want to ask them to read chapter 2 of this book. If they still have questions, they may contact Spiritual Counterfeits Project, "The John Ankerberg Show," Watchman Fellowship, or related organizations[5] for additional documentation. Also, anyone who wishes may obtain books, magazines, and newspaper articles in the public library on this subject.

Next point out the Equal Employment Opportunities Commission (EEOC) regulation dealing with employee rights when being exposed to New Age training techniques. This is found on pages 25 and 171. Further explain that merely because a program does not use religious terminology does not mean it has no religious content. You might provide sample documentation from chapters 3 and 4, including the *Malnak* v. *Yogi* case (cf. pages 29, 171).

Finally, if there is continued confusion, explain that the burden of proof rests with the one making the claim. If it is appropriate for a person to make such a claim, it is appropriate he be able to defend and prove his allegation. Ask the person to explain what she/he understands about the NAM. For example, you might have the individual read the articles in the December 1979 *Elementary School Guidance and Counseling Journal* (see chapter 5, pp. 100ff.), as well as representative articles by leading transpersonal educators. Ask the person to explain his statements to you and to prove why we are not dealing with something religious. To deny the religious aspect of New

Age philosophy and practice after this review would not be a credible position to maintain.

Response: Don't you trust me? This objection may also take different forms. You might hear, "My Ph.D. was in education and I think I know the difference between learning facts and religious instruction," or "We are professionals, we know what we are doing," or "We wouldn't think of harming your children with unproven methods," or "But I am a Christian teacher!"

Answer: (Parents need to be very sensitive here, recognizing that a teacher's confession that New Age or psychotherapeutic methods were employed may call into question the person's judgment. This would be admitting he or she has used improper methods which may have harmed the children under the teacher's charge. Further, consciously or unconsciously, teachers who are using these programs may feel personally attacked.) So what can you do? Explain that New Age influences can be subtle and not easily discerned. You are not calling their integrity or motives into question. Further, no one is perfect nor can anyone know everything. An honest mistake is just that, and everyone makes them even with the best of motives. In fact, you are counting on their integrity and concern for children to cause them to make a careful evaluation of these issues. Let them know that even if you were leaving your children with a trusted babysitter or the child's grandparents, you would still leave instructions, being the one who knows your child the best. Together you can both resolve this problem.

Response: Are you against relaxation and use of the imagination?

Answer: Clearly state that you are not against either relaxation or use of the imagination. In some cases, not all, relaxation can enhance performance or cooperation, and imagination is a necessary and important part of human creativity.

But what we are talking about is more than relaxation and imagination. The sample policy statement of Watchman Fellowship (see appendix C) clearly defines the difference between the degree of relaxation as it relates to meditation/hypnosis, as well as the difference between things such as imagination and guided imagery. The programs we question may use relaxation to introduce children to altered states of consciousness via meditation/hypnosis in order to make the children more suggestible to program goals. Further, imagination may be used as part of a program of guided imagery which is other-directed and can be a powerful form of hypnosis/meditation, especially when used in conjunction with deep relaxation techniques (see the Glossary under "guided imagery").

Response: Children today need this program. This reply may be encouraged by parents who have told teachers that "this has helped my child so much."

Answer: There is ample documentation that many of these particular programs are flawed, ethically and empirically. That is the primary issue. Many things work which are less than healthy, such as drugs and car bombs. The issue is not utility but appropriateness. Some children have low self-esteem, and many do need to be instructed on the dangers of drugs or sexual behavior. But New Age hypnosis/meditation techniques and affective, nondirective decision-making processes not only tend to undermine parental authority and values, they can actually encourage the unhealthy behavior they are intended to prevent.

Certainly if particular children have problems, then the parents should be consulted and the best approach should be undertaken individually to help them. But a shotgun approach is not appropriate. If statistics tell us that only 5 percent of a class will have migraine headaches, why should anyone consider it appropriate to treat every child with powerful ergot derivatives and painkillers?

Response: But the children really love it.

Answer: A program should not be evaluated on the basis of the subjective reports of children. Children also love ice cream, parties, and the video arcade. Permitting children to do whatever they want, especially if it conflicts with their best interests, is counterproductive.

Response: We only use certain parts of these curricula; we don't use the relaxation techniques, guided imagery, etc.

Answer: We are heartened to hear that the most objectionable portions have been dropped. But what still needs assessment is the overall approach and goal of the program. Does it actually build self-esteem? Does it curtail wrong and harmful behavior? Does it undermine or conflict with traditional family values?

Further, without official school policy how can parents be assured that teachers won't change their mind? How do we know the current superintendent, principal, or teacher will be here next year?

Response: In an age of increased peer pressure for sex and drugs, it is essential that children learn how to make decisions internally, apart from harmful external influences.

Answer: This is true. In appropriate situations, encouraged through responsible programs, this is excellent advice when it is soundly based. This approach is valid for juniors and seniors in high school, as long as their choices are not illegal or harmful (drugs, alcohol, premarital sex). But when these programs offer situation ethics or are applied to primary and middle school students, we have a problem. Young children cannot go inside themselves to access their values. They are still in the process of learning values from outside influences: parents, church, laws, and teachers. To offer children a subjective, relative value system is to work contrary to responsible decision-making.

The question also revolves around who decides what is a positive or negative outside influence: developmental theorists, curriculum writers, teachers? Or do parents have the primary right?

This brings us to the last and most serious resistance parents may face. Unlike the other objections, which are usually honest misunderstandings, the following response is part of a larger, well-orchestrated effort to promote a liberal agenda on children. This objection will be expressed in various ways.

Response: These are religious extremists (fanatics, bigots) engaged in censorship; the far religious right is trying to take over education. Book burners are imperiling academic freedom and we simply cannot permit a vocal minority to dictate what the majority want for their own children.

Answer: This kind of response has convinced many people to reject those people who question controversial curricula. Consider the comments made by a state school superintendent when speaking to teachers about future potential problems in education. He said,

> Be on the lookout for religious fanatics. They are backed by the electronic media, have unlimited funds and seek to control the schools.... Censorship... is possibly the biggest threat to you and your children today.... We can't let a handful of narrow-minded fanatics dictate and limit what our children can and cannot learn.[6]

We find the same pattern in author Jill Anderson's and Timberline Press' material generated to respond to objections by parents to the Pumsy curriculum.

This is an old ploy. If you want to help get your own agenda adopted, try to see that those who oppose you are properly labeled as incompetent before other people hear their arguments. In effect, this is a form of censorship which tells the public that certain critics aren't worth listening to.

Another example of a censorship defense can be found in the books and lectures of Dr. Edward Jenkinson, professor of English history at the University of Indiana, senior fellow of Phi Delta Kappa. He is the author of books on censorship and a frequent witness at textbook trials.

His videotapes seem to have influenced many school boards and educators. He warns about the sharp escalation of censorship incidents which target ideas and teaching techniques, especially in the areas of "secular humanism, New Age, and globalism."[7]

Dr. Jenkinson also mentions that the focus of these attacks includes sex, drug, and alcohol education programs and values clarification. He derisively cites Mel Gabler, a leader in the reform movement, and he sarcastically caricatures conservative Christian parents and parental groups by using unfair and extreme examples.

Dr. Jenkinson did strongly recommend that school boards adopt a comprehensive material selection policy with procedures for handling challenges and objections. He even went on to advise that the educators become more informed about challenges, but then without comment he added, "And learn how to refute those challenges." Many parents who have seen this video have wondered if their concerns would be granted respect or just summarily dismissed. The materials of Dr. Jenkinson lead us to four issues raised by some educators.

1. *Are those who question these programs bigots and religious extremists?*

Whenever a person or group has a weak position in debate, they may resort to an *ad hominem* approach, shifting the subject away from real issues to attacks on character.

Someone once said that the definition of a fanatic is anyone who believes emphatically in something with which you strongly disagree. Simply and politely request such persons to deal with the issues involved.

2. *Do such persons violate academic freedom?*

Every freedom carries responsibility. Educators, for example, have a responsibility to school boards, parents, and taxpayers because they are public employees. Their primary responsibility is to the children they teach. How can raising the mercurial concept of "academic freedom" possibly mean that teachers are not accountable to anyone? Academic freedom cannot mean absolute freedom to teach anything, for then teachers could promote pornography and hatred in the classroom. If our freedoms are absolute, why are children *forced* to go to school?

True academic freedom operates within legal and moral boundaries, personal accountability, and community guidelines. The real issue is one of the legality, credibility, and appropriateness of these controversial methods that have been questioned by responsible citizens—not one of academic freedom.

3. *Is this censorship?*

The word *censorship* is properly applied when a national government officially prohibits the printing or distribution of a book or material. For example, Communist governments typically censor religious material, preventing the population from access to it. Censorship is quite different from a government agency (such as a public school) deciding what books it will select and purchase with taxpayers' money for use on a captive audience: our children.

For instance, when a textbook selection committee reviews 100 textbooks and selects 5, does that mean they censored the other 95? No. But what if, in fact, those five books are full of revisionist history and socialism? For example, most school texts today provide classic examples of the rewriting of American history in order to delete the crucial influence of Christianity on this nation. This is far closer to censorship than parents' questioning of inappropriate school curriculum. Parents are concerned with the welfare of their children. Are there not some established guidelines for determining an appropriate manner by which school materials can be screened? How can this logically be considered censorship?

4. Is this narrow-minded intolerance?

Intolerance can be either good or bad. Coauthor Craig Branch was recently on a popular talk show when a caller phoned in to accuse him of intolerance and narrow-mindedness. The host asked Mr. Branch, "What about that—are you being intolerant?" Mr. Branch replied,

> Yes, of course. So are you and so is the caller. I hope we all are intolerant of things such as shoddy educational standards, consumer fraud, unfair treatment of children, religious bigotry—not to mention such evils as rape, pornography, and murder.

Even public schools are intolerant and practice selection. For example, how many elementary schools have *Playboy* or *Playgirl* on their library shelves? Why don't they? Because the very idea that public schools should be allowed to expose minor children to such materials over the opposition of parents, common decency, and good sense is unacceptable even in a free society.

In a similar manner, when parents attempt to protect their children from school materials that are offensive to their religion or values and may actually harm their children, those who cry "intolerance" or "censorship" are asserting the right of the public school to *force* on children *contrary* values—what even they have confessed as "the widest diversity of views and expressions, including those which are unorthodox or unpopular with the majority."[8]

But who ever gave a curriculum dictator the right to select materials that undermine parental authority or children's religious values? Or don't the rest of us have First Amendment rights so that our children are *not* forced to participate in programs that are offensive or harmful?

We might even begin to wonder where the real censorship lies. Could it be among those who decry every absolute but one: the absolute truth that no absolute values exist? Or could it be among those who are zealous for the ideals of secular humanism and seek to remove every iota of religious principle from our culture? What about the individuals and groups who believe that they know with absolute certainty what is best for everyone else's children? Or those who will secure their personal agendas by any means necessary—even if it means prohibiting traditional American family and religious values from ever being expressed in schools?

Are there censors today? Believe it. Consider the following excerpt from *U.S. News & World Report* (Oct. 5, 1992, p. 33):

> In his new book, "Free Speech for Me—But Not for Thee," Nat Hentoff tells the story of a Pennsylvania high school pressuring two fundamentalist students to read "Working," a Studs Terkel book containing a chapter on prostitutes and a good deal of blasphemous language. Backed by their parents, the teenagers asked in conscience to opt out from reading it. The school, vengeful to the end, wanted to withhold the students' diplomas and settled for failing them in the course. Along the way, the school board said haughtily that "with all deference due the parents, their sensibilities are not the full measure of what is proper education."

That's a rather conventional attitude among educational bureaucrats: We are the professionals; parents are the nettlesome amateurs to be mollified or brushed aside. . . . These things have a way of happening without parental input, possibly because the sensibilities of parents, poor yahoos that they are, aren't as good as the sensibilities of enlightened bureaucrats in instructing the young. . . . Besides, you can get a lot more done if parents don't know what's going on. . . .

[Consider that] Washington, D. C. has just acted firmly to emancipate students from parental objections of condom distribution. . . . David Blankenhorn, president of the Institute for American Values, thinks parents are quite intentionally kept in the dark. Educational bureaucrats, he says, "accept the proposition that parents are kind of backward, repressed, held back by religion, and have to be handled." Look for more stealth programs in schools.

We have already stated that we are in a cultural conflict, a philosophical war over who determines the values of our culture that will shape our future. Underlying many critical responses to those who question New Age/secular humanistic education is a deep philosophical/social agenda that is hostile to Christian beliefs and traditional family values.

The better people understand the mind-set and tactics of such persons, the easier they can respond both constructively and responsibly. The following is a representative sampling of those groups in the educators' network.

American School Counselor Association (ASCA)

One illustration of the bias (and even arrogance) of some people in the educational establishment is revealed in a series of articles in the *Elementary School and Guidance Counseling Journal*. The following excerpts are representative:

New Right groups [are] linked by a web of money and associations [and] seek to influence uninformed parents through the use of emotionally charged buzzwords and phrases.... The New Right groups attempt to *play on* natural concerns and fears of parents. Claims that godless schools are undermining the religious teaching of the hearth and the pew quickly disturb parents....

The strange tactics of *extremism* have changed little over the years.... Where fundamentalist preachers were once limited to tents and small time radio stations, now they have millions of viewers through satellite relay. ... Putting themselves firmly outside the mainstream of America's heritage of religious freedom, these people of the church seek to put rigid state regulations on the personal conduct of others....

Targets of the *radical censors* include such essential guidance topics as... death and dying, drug education, affective awareness, decision making, and self-understanding. Technique counselors who share with teachers on ways to improve student self-esteem and self-confidence inevitably will be viewed with suspicion—if not ignored totally by teachers fearing *New Right reprisals*....

In addition to undermining confidence, *radical* right individuals and groups seek to limit and restrict materials from school programs. Some of the programs used in developmental guidance programs singled out by the New Right *censors* include: TA for Tots (transactional analysis), Human Development Program, Values Clarification, and Reality Therapy (Jenkinson, 1979).

Radical right propaganda... New Right propaganda.... *extremist* groups.... The call for action to combat this threat from *censorship* should be self-evident.... [We must oppose] their politics of *fear* and *resentment*.... Counselors must be prepared to counter this very real danger through a series of well-conceived and implemented actions....

The New Right *censors* seek to limit citizens' access to ideas they oppose and to *impose* their own ideology.... Counselors must develop procedures for handling *censorship* complaints.... Would-be *censors* are being spurred on to increasingly aggressive postures by the self-appointed guardians of the "American Way." ...

A formal policy to handle attempted *censorship* or complaints must be established. . . . If the goal of the would-be *censor* is something other than responsible criticism and the attack is escalating, counselors must consider going public. Often problems of attempted *censorship* can be handled through normal channels. But for those occasions when it cannot be, counselors under extreme censorship attack should consider the aid of professional organizations.[9]

The article lists a number of organizational resources to combat such "censorship" including the ACLU, the National Education Association (NEA), and American Library Association.

School authorities who insist on repeating false accusations like this have probably been influenced by these kinds of "anticensorship" materials.

In responding to this approach, remind the educator that the thrust of these comments assumes that only those in education could possibly be right. But should only "progressive" educators have the right to dictate educational philosophy, not to mention social values? In constantly ridiculing parents who strongly believe in their Christian beliefs, these detractors come to the ironic conclusion that "there are absolutely no absolutes."

This is not rational. For example, the American School Counselor Association (ASCA) issued a position statement in 1985 setting forth its belief that guidance counselors have an absolute right to teach a "diversity of viewpoints and ideas," all under the umbrella of "academic freedom."[10] (Fortunately, it does allow parents to press their point. The students are "to receive services *appropriate* to their needs" and there is to be the "advocacy of *appropriate* services.") Nevertheless, the policy implies arbitrary definitions of *student needs, appropriateness,* and *censorship.* In other words, *censorship* is any "denial of a student's basic rights to receive any of the commonly recognized guidance and counseling services offered by school counselors." That pretty much covers everything we are concerned about.

The ASCA also instructs its members "to provide open exploration of alternative views, and to foster freedom of thought in accordance with our democratic society." This is fine, but again, how far can this be pressed either in society or in the classroom? Does anyone need to argue today that freedom of thought and speech can be corrupted in a society that has rejected moral values? Can even a democracy survive without moral standards?

For millions of people, hasn't the term *democratic* come to mean doing whatever they want, including the use of things like child pornography and illegal drugs? If we don't expose our children to pornography in the schools, why *don't* we— and what does this tell us about the relationship between democracy, personal freedom, and social responsibility? What if, for some people, freedom of thought incorporates actively teaching children themes that are anti-Western, anti-American, anti-moral, anti-democratic, or anti-Christian? Just because something is possible doesn't mean it is in a child's best interest.

In a democratic society the majority rules. But what if the majority happens to be wrong because it has rejected the time-honored principles of morality and basic Christian values that made our nation great? What happens to society then? Perhaps this is why the founding fathers established America as a republic that was to be lived "under God" and based on *Christian* values.[11] They knew what we have apparently forgotten: This nation will not survive as a democracy if its Christian values are destroyed.

Although what people believe as adults is their business, the issue here is the teaching of schoolchildren, not adult freedoms.

The National Education Association (NEA)

Consider the response of the National Education Association to those who would place appropriate, responsible limits on curriculum development. We stress that there are many good teachers in the NEA, teachers who are concerned over the very issues we raise. Nevertheless, the July 1992 annual conference adopted several aggressive resolutions condemning "censorship" and "legislative interference." In addition, resolutions were passed restricting parental attempts to supervise what their children are taught.

For instance, resolution E-1 emphasizes,

> The NEA believes that teachers and librarians/
> media specialists have the right to select instruc-
> tional/library materials without censorship or leg-
> islative interference. The Association urges its
> affiliates to seek the removal of laws and regula-
> tions that restrict the selection of a diversity of
> instructional materials or that limit educators in the
> selection of such materials.

Resolution E-3 asserts, "The Association deplores pre-
publishing censorship, book burning crusades, and attempts
to ban books from the school library/media center and school
curriculum."[12]

In other words, the NEA wants unrestricted access to America's children and hopes to "censor" all the laws and policies
adopted to date with which they disagree. But whoever made
the NEA the guardian of our children—other than the NEA?
Recently the NEA created another network to respond to
"censorship attacks" called "NEA Human and Civil Rights."[13]

We think this is shifting the appropriate focus of education
from the issue of educational quality/reform to that of censorship. This is reminiscent of the tactics of the pro-choice camp
who, unable to win in the arena of fact, have instead focused
on a series of pseudo arguments such as defending women's
so-called "*reproductive* rights" against the innate right of an
unborn child to live.

The issues before us are *appropriate selection of materials*
(sound policy criteria) and how the state or local school district
is to spend taxpayers' money. In question is whether schools
can mandate the exposure to curricula, programs, techniques,
or ideas that are potentially harmful, religiously based, illegal,
or abhorrent to the parents' values. Again, we are not talking
about censorship—unless it is censorship of the fundamental
right of parents to guide the education of their own children
and to preserve the values of their family.

Are we to encourage young people to form their values
autonomously, independent of parental wishes, and call this
"enlightened decision making"? Or are we to impose a certain

set of religious or humanistic beliefs or attitudes on children and call it "education"? State-sponsored indoctrination in religion is as wrong as state-sponsored indoctrination in ethical neutrality. But in many places, this is where we are headed.

People for the American Way

Many educators and the national press frequently utilize publications or press releases from People for the American Way (PFAW). Concerning "censorship attempts," the PFAW observes, "In the past few years we have witnessed a vicious assault on free expression in all its forms."[14]

The PFAW annual report, *Attacks on the Freedom to Learn*, is replete with *ad hominem* propaganda which works to create prejudice rather than debate the issues. Instead of discussing facts, PFAW constantly refers to conservatives and/or Christians with pejorative descriptions such as "far right," "religious right," "extremists," and "censors."[15] PFAW also employs a technique of biased selection, listing extreme examples and generalizing them to include legitimate challenges from parents.

Ironically, the report complains that the "attackers" use "tactics" like letter-writing campaigns, the media, petitions, letters to the editor, and even paid advertising—all "devices intended more to generate controversy than to facilitate discussion about education choices."[16]

They also claim that one by-product of the efforts of the "censors" has been the "diminution of America's appreciation for and willingness to defend freedom of speech and expression."[17] Yet this attitude is from a group which has aggressively attempted to censor traditional values and to impose humanistic ones. For example, it has sought to suppress a textbook which objectively presents the scientific data on both evolution and creation: *Of Pandas and People*.[18]

Thus the double standard of the PFAW becomes evident as they seek to castigate other people who are indeed exercising their own freedom of speech. Presumably, even PFAW would agree that freedom of speech is a constitutional right. And perhaps even they might concede that such a freedom would serve as a legitimate vehicle to expose illegal, religious, harmful, unscientific, or inappropriate educational material in the schools.

The NEA has funded the production of a recent 196-page manual titled *What's Left After the Right*. Its stated goals are to provide information about the "Far Right movement" and to deal "with the tactics of educational censors."

The manual caricatures Christians and those believing in traditional values as "ultra-conservative, far right, religious right, righteous right, new right, and radical right." At least it admits we are right.

The manual lumps conservatism with a monolithic mold and presents conservatives as extremists without any justification to their charges. The manual claims that the large percentage of critics of public education are self-serving, power seeking, out for revenge, or seeking financial gain.

Representative leaders of the "extremist" groups are William Bennett, Ronald Reagan, Orin Hatch, James Dobson, Beverly LaHaye, Jerry Falwell, Pat Robertson, and Phyllis Schlafly.

This list along with the types of tactics listed in the manual to repel efforts by concerned parents demonstrates how far removed the NEA is from the American mainstream.

In conclusion, those people who oppose controversial curricula are not at all unwilling to frankly examine the issues. But it *is* their desire that discussion be kept to factual matters and in accordance with federal, state, and local law and community standards.

Chapter 11

WHAT ARE PARENTS AND EDUCATORS TO DO?

As we have seen, sometimes conflicts arise between parents and educators over what is best for children. This chapter will give some general suggestions for constructive involvement, and specific suggestions for the particular issues addressed in this handbook. There is a battle for the minds of our children, and parents need to be involved.

Being involved means to interact with your child's school. This involves occasionally going to the school to observe and communicate with teachers in ways to help your child so that the input received at school is compatible with your family's values. It means knowing the right questions to ask the teacher and reviewing problematic curricula.

Being involved means active participation in school parent-teacher organizations in a way that is truly meaningful. It means seeking leadership positions in areas of influence. This includes school boards, state and local curriculum and textbook review committees, and whatever local bodies are applicable.

It means going to school board meetings, and establishing rapport, understanding, and cooperation. Finally, it means electing board members who are responsible and believe in traditional values.

Responding to Problems

When a conflict occurs over educational curricula, how should a parent respond? We recommend the following:

1. *Understand your rights.* Tradition and the courts have consistently demonstrated that parents have *primary* rights and responsibilities in educating their children. By law, children should be educated, but parents have primacy in this.

2. *Be firm, but gracious.* Avoid a reactionary, emotive response. This creates a defensive atmosphere in which it is difficult to find constructive resolutions.

3. *Be informed.* Occasionally a parent will hear a rumor and go to the school with false accusations based on incomplete or inaccurate information. This reinforces certain stereotypes some educators have about Christians and other people with so-called "old-fashioned" values. It serves to discredit the parent and hinders not only personal respect but also the potential for communication.

It is very important to understand the school's perspective. Today schools encounter a wide variety of problems. There are children who come to school suffering from abuse, neglect, and dysfunctional homes. The school genuinely wants to be able to help these students. This is why schools are struggling for solutions. But unfortunately, conflict arises when the school initiates proactive programs, usually psychotherapeutic (developmental) in nature, which involves children in a way that may not be in their best interest and may conflict with parents' beliefs and values.

4. *Be active politically.* Be aware of legislation that may affect educational issues and work toward passing or defeating it as it relates to the needs of quality education.

5. *Go to the teacher.* Many school procedures recommend or require parents to first express their concerns to the teacher. This is appropriate in many situations. Using the first three suggestions, try to arrive at an agreeable solution. Remember, the parent has a legal right to inspect the instructional material required for their child.

6. *Go through channels.* Be aware of the school board's policy concerning complaints. Be sure to follow "reasonable" procedures. We say "reasonable" because it has been our experience that sometimes the procedures are, unfortunately, purposely obstructive. For example, some professional journals give advice to make the complainant go through bureaucratic procedural hoops, apparently to frustrate or weary the parents.

Discover if there is any local process of appeal. If there is none, push to install one. It is important, at least in the appeal process (if not in the regular review process), that parents as well as educators are involved in the decisions.

The above recommendations are standard suggestions for dealing with normal complaints over instructional method or materials. The issues raised in this handbook, however, are broader and therefore require a different direction.

Because current educational philosophy has produced a large volume of New Age or psychotherapeutic-oriented curricula, we are recommending that parents' focus should be with *setting policy, guidelines, or regulations,* and not with one particular curriculum, program, or instructional material.

Even though there may now be only one particular program used in a school or district, there are many others available on the market. Also, programs have been known to change names and emphasis. Therefore, it is the overall methodology and content that needs to pass appropriate guidelines, not just specific programs.

The best place for challenging and setting policy is with the local or state school board. Again, according to Howard Kirschenbaum, whose paper "Democratic Procedures for School-Community Relations" was excerpted for the *Elementary School Guidance and Counseling Journal,* the rights and responsibilities of the school board are

> to set goals, objectives, policies, and standards for the school district... *to set specific guidelines for adopting school curricula and reevaluating curricula* and due process procedures for handling complaints or controversy from the community.[1]

Thus, school boards need to consider issuing policies concerning religious and psychotherapeutic issues before disputes arise, not after finding themselves embroiled in controversy which generates mistrust, costly litigation, and emotional, educational, and even political consequences.

Opponents to family rights and traditional values will often attempt to counter with a cry of censorship. Simply remind them that this is not the issue. The purpose of the school board is to set guidelines in evaluating curricula. Further, on what logical basis can parents be prohibited from expressing legitimate concerns over curricula? Educators are implementing their ideas and methods on the children of other people. Don't parents have that fundamental right to question appropriateness? If this is truly censorship, then what is the appropriate term for what these educators are doing? Aren't they censoring the views of those people whose ideas they don't like? Further, aren't some of them even engaging in indoctrination? To cry "censorship" to other people while you yourself are engaged in indoctrination seems a bit too much. (See chapter 14.)

Nevertheless, in raising an issue with the school board, the first six steps should still be followed. An intelligent discussion with the teacher is helpful for at least an understanding and ongoing relationship.

But even though parents may have a legitimate complaint, there are, unfortunately, certain factions in the educational community (as well as political groups) who are causing resistance.

In light of this we recommend the following additional steps.

1. In the information-gathering stage, take advantage of the materials available and the resources of groups like Gateways to Better Education, Eagle Forum, Focus on the Family, Watchman Fellowship, "The John Ankerberg Show," Citizens for Excellence in Education, The Rutherford Institute, and others (see Resource List on page 319).

Be certain the information you are presenting is accurate for the program you are examining because even programs with the same name can vary in content.

2. Begin to draw in other parents to build a coalition. One parent can have an influence, but often the amount of attention given is proportionate to the number of parents expressing strong concern.

Reproduce materials, hold meetings, and get the information out. Some communities have effectively held large-scale informational meetings so that everyone hears both the information and recommendations at the same time. This helps to minimize uninformed and inappropriate emotional reactions which do more harm than good.

In some cases, organizing a nonprofit parents' rights group has also been appropriate and helpful.

3. Maintain a cooperative spirit. Always assume the best on the part of your child's teacher. Parents and educators should be reminded that they are working together. A cordial face-to-face meeting can do wonders. If an adversarial position is taken, let it be on the part of the educators and not the parents.

4. Make it clear that these instructional methods and their content raise a multiplicity of concerns—any one of which would require removing the harmful curricula and the setting of standards to screen out other problems. For example: a) the underlying religious philosophy of these materials; b) the use of inappropriate psychological methodologies; c) the lack of scientific verifiability, and d) their potential dangers.

5. Make sure documentation is available to school board members and all concerned parties (again, see Resource List on page 319).

6. Know the political landscape. Ideally, school boards are serving their constituents (the parents) and therefore will appropriately instruct the superintendents and teachers, but this is not always the case. Some school districts are actually run by the superintendents, who may be either elected or appointed. Determine the best approach to maximize passage of your policy recommendation.

Also keep in mind that a few dozen or a few hundred votes can radically change the makeup of a school board. Most school board elections have such a low turnout that the votes in a large Sunday school class can determine who is or isn't elected.

7. Recruit and select the most articulate and influential representative from the community of parents to meet individually and collectively with board members or superintendents.

8. If there is resistance, devise a well-organized plan to involve the media and to generate public support. But be circumspect about giving interviews to the news media (communication through press releases will lessen the chance of misrepresentation).

9. It is crucial to be aware of the arguments and tactics of certain professional educators' groups that actively seek to forward their own agenda and oppose those who disagree with them.

10. Obviously, a parent's own school district is of immediate concern, but we should not neglect policy enactment on a statewide level. We recommend parents or a coalition of parents' groups meet with each state school board member to formulate policy or regulations covering all state school districts (see sample policy statement in appendix C). Be aware that educators will acknowledge that a parent has the right to exercise domain over their own children, but not over other people's children. In other words, they believe the teacher or school has the right of greater influence over everyone else, and that an individual citizen or group of citizens don't have a right to influence other citizens through the democratic process.

11. Some parents have felt that a better route is to have legislation enacted.[2]

12. If all of these measures fail, then the last resort would be litigation. This is costly both in terms of money spent and community/school relations, but the issues involved and our children's futures are important enough to consider it.

13. Remember, parents have the legal right to remove their child from a program that conflicts with their values. However, this too can have liabilities. A teacher or other children can make the child feel ostracized. It is much better for a child to remain in the classroom and be assigned other activities

such as reading a book or doing homework. In fact, the other kids may actually be jealous of those who are excused from these programs since many of the kids don't even like them. In certain cases, older children are, with their parents' help, able to discern the issues and participate in these programs, using them to good advantage—asking questions of the teacher, seeking to point out program implications, weaknesses, or problems. Ideally, parents should only pull their child from a program when their child is forced to participate in something destructive or is so young the child will be swayed by the teaching. Make sure the procedure is done with kindness, respect, and discretion. But even if parents remove their children, they should continue to work for implementation of new policies.

All this underscores one important fact: The priorities here are upside down. The current approach is an "opt-out" philosophy where the burden is on parents to remove their child from a program that should, in all probability, never have been adopted in the first place. This has allowed educators to control education for their purposes without parental input. The school's approach should involve an "opt-in" philosophy. Here schools would be required to have parental permission before a curriculum is adopted, and it would have to involve full disclosure of what a program consists of philosophically and educationally. This would result in most controversial programs being rejected before implementation.

Be encouraged that there are many good educators who are not agenda-conscious and have introduced these programs innocently. When presented with appropriate documentation regarding a parent's concerns, they are usually reasonable and will comply.

But again there are segments in the educational establishment like the National Education Association, People for the American Way and others who may strongly resist family rights and traditional values.

We agree with Pearl Evans in *Hidden Danger in the Classroom*. She reminds us,

> You resist because you're working for the good of the child, sound principles and practices, excellence in education, the rights of parents and

citizens, and free access to information. . . . But be forewarned: If you don't put your whole heart and head into this effort, you'll lose this fierce and long term battle; it's not for cowards. You'll have to overcome and outlast. . . .

Even though it may not seem so at first, remember you [can] have the public on your side. One or two may have to work alone until others gain hope and courage. In the end, however, you'll find that parents of all backgrounds and beliefs care about the good of their children and will join you.[3]

In other words, "Fight the good fight of faith" and "let us not lose heart in doing good, for in due time we shall reap if we do not grow weary" (1 Timothy 6:12; Galatians 6:9, NASB).

PART

Important Articles

THREE

Chapter 12

EDUCATION: CAPTURING HEARTS AND MINDS FOR A NEW WORLD

BY *TAL BROOKE, M.DIV.*

It is 1990 and the kindergarten class sits eagerly on the floor. They are going through a visualization exercise created by the Science Research Associates. Lesson 10 is called "The Witches Ride." Bobo, the central figure in the story, wakes up and sees 12 witches in a hut across from his window. Each witch in turn mounts a broom crying, "Fly me faster than a fairy, without God, without Saint Mary" and soars "gracefully" off. Bobo goes over and imitates the 12 witches with the same chant using the remaining broomstick. As he chants "without God, without Saint Mary," he, too, soars gracefully off. Soon the object lesson comes: "But, alas he was not called a bobo for nothing. In his great glee he muddled the words, and said to the broomstick 'fly me faster than a fairy—Fly *with* God and *good* Saint Mary.' No sooner were these words out of his mouth than the broomstick began to fall."[1]

Bobo found both empowerment and enjoyment by rejecting God. He found impotence and fear by invoking God, *even accidentally*. There is no need to ask if there is a lesson here. The lesson is obvious, though it is never directly stated. Such negative conditioning about God (and other traditional symbols of good) will inevitably have a cumulative effect. Over

221

time, students will be introduced to the new, post-Christian agenda and drawn into the post-Christian spiritual arena.

Eight-year-olds down the hall sit in class attentively after returning from a field trip to a cemetery. They must think about death. Now they are asked, "If your town was about to come under nuclear attack and there was only room for three members of your immediate family in the bomb shelter, which ones would you leave out and why." A weighty decision for a formative mind. It is also one that delves into intimate family privacies as the kids explain why dad or mom should be left out to die in a nuclear attack. Deep feelings emerge. But that's okay. This course is based on the accumulated knowledge of decades of encounter sessions and T-groups at centers such as Esalen. The teacher's manual explains this fact with quiet authority. The teacher as therapist knows what to look for—that the kids will bond in the pain of disclosure and form a surrogate supra-family. They will learn that loyalty to "the group" is central in this new way of thinking. The teacher's manual explains that "the Group is Alpha" while parents, authority figures, even a divine creator, "are not Alpha." One can only gather that "Alpha" will be important in a future world.

Ninth graders down the street are having their environmental consciousness raised by watching a film of a beautiful landscape entitled *The Cry of the Marsh*. Suddenly they see a bulldozer with the label "American" clearly in sight. It wrecks the natural setting, cutting through it like a tank. One of its drivers pours gasoline around the outer area and lights it. Trees catch fire, and living creatures run for cover. Another worker drains the creek. Ducklings in the creek catch fire while the huge bulldozer plows bird nests into the ground. The kids barely get their breath before the follow-up exercise is thrown at them. It is called "Who Shall Populate the Planet?" The choices for populating the planet are a priest, a football player, a black minister, a microbiologist, a pregnant woman, and a teacher. Now they are told that only three will be allowed to live. Another life or death decision. One senses that the two Christians are the most expendable in making way for a new world.[2]

Captive Minds

The vulnerable young child sitting in the schoolroom who is just opening his eyes for the first time is a very captive audience. Trustworthy figures become automatic sources of truth in a child's quest to understand the world, and teachers are primary among such trustworthy figures. They carry natural authority not only because they are adults, but also because the adult world has appointed them to be dispensers of truth. Statements of "fact" from them sink deeply into the pupils' minds. The oracular role of educators in most cases continues right through college. Even cynical and disinterested older students manage to absorb the latest approved worldview—political correctness has just arrived while evolution and "Big Bang" cosmogeny are old hat and have long been accepted as undisputed fact.

New Age leader John Dunphy made a telling observation in *The Humanist* magazine (January/February 1983). In his award-winning essay entitled "A Religion for the New Age," Dunphy remarked:

> I am convinced that the battle for humankind's future must be waged and won in the public school classrooms by teachers who correctly perceive their role as proselytizers of a new faith: a religion of humanity that recognizes and respects the spark of what theologians call the Divinity in every human being. These teachers must embody the same selfless dedication as the most rabid fundamentalist preachers.
>
> The classroom must and will become an arena of conflict between the old and the new—the rotting corpse of Christianity, together with all its adjacent evils and misery, and the new faith. . . .

New Age bestselling author and leader Marilyn Ferguson also points out how the schoolroom is a critical arena for teachers, the powerful opinion-shapers of young minds under their care. In her bestseller, *The Aquarian Conspiracy*, Ferguson observed, "Even doctors, in their heyday as god-like paragons, have never wielded the authority of a single classroom teacher, who can purvey prizes, failure, love, humiliation and information to great numbers of relatively powerless, vulnerable young people."[3]

Ferguson's friend, Beverly Galyean, opened one of the earlier doorways for New Age penetration into the public school. Her program was called "Confluent Education." Galyean's beliefs were part of this classroom exercise. In 1981 she said:

> Once we begin to see that we are all God, that we all have the attributes of God, then I think the whole purpose of human life is to reown the God-likeness within us: the perfect love, the perfect wisdom, the perfect understanding, the perfect intelligence, and when we do that, we create back to that old, that essential oneness which is consciousness.[4]

Galyean's early prototype of classroom visualization involved first graders across the country lying on the floor of their classrooms and visualizing such "positive" things as the sun radiating within them. They would envision the light of the sun filling their entire being. Then the teacher would tell them: "You are inwardly perfect and contain all the wisdom of the universe within yourselves." First graders were introduced to spirit guides through the Galyean approach. Although, as she remarked at a plenary session at the conference entitled *Education in the 80's*, "Of course we don't call them that in the public schools. We call them imaginary guides."[5]

The Supreme Court bans prayer but has no laws against classroom "visualization," which is seen as a creative exercise of the imagination. Besides, positive affirmations such as, "You contain the wisdom of the universe," might elevate the pupil's self-esteem and relieve him of nagging fears that he might be an academic failure—even if he is. We did not arrive at this point in a simple swift *coup de academe*. There have been a series of steps, or waves, which have built on one another. Each wave has successively "softened up" the American psyche, and each in turn has prepared the way for the one to follow.

The First Wave

In the 1930s, the reality of influence in the schoolroom spurred John Dewey, the father of American progressive education, to write *My Pedagogic Creed*. In it, Dewey depicts public education as a massive behavior-shaping tool. Dewey knew that you could sway the beliefs of a whole generation in the classroom and thereby alter the course of a nation. While Roosevelt was introducing welfare programs, Dewey saw the public school system as an ideal platform to proselytize his radical socialistic views. Regardless of what the parents believed, it was only a matter of time before the successive generations took over. It was a quiet way to remake the world.

But John Dewey's ideas did not just come out of a vacuum. He was influenced by an insider group of intellectuals in England known as the Fabian Socialists. Dewey was an American ally of this clique. The Fabians had an agenda of gradualist global penetration by using education as a key tool of influence in this process.[6] Dewey, who remained close with Fabian leaders, had his own circle of academic disciples at Columbia University, especially Kilpatrick and Counts, who influenced textbooks and school curricula for decades. Through Dewey's influence, Harold Laski, right before becoming chairman of the British Fabian Society, lectured at Columbia Teacher's College for a semester in 1939 amidst John Dewey's best and brightest disciples.

What did all this mean for American public education? Columbia Teacher's College influenced other graduate schools and colleges of education. Before long, progressive education, the Dewey-designed tool for reshaping America, was a public school reality all across America.

Dewey knew that to penetrate the existing social order a united front of educators who embodied the new viewpoint needed to emerge from graduate schools. These teachers of teachers would then influence future teachers. Among the new views was a national self-criticism that spurned narrow patriotism for a broader globalism. At the same time traditional values, from parental authority to the validity of established religion, were to be questioned and ultimately dethroned.

Rather than equipping the child to handle the demanding academic and moral standards of the traditional order, with its McGuffey Reader and its implicit moral virtues, Dewey's progressive education considered behavior-shaping as its highest educational priority. "Socialization" was now defined as a type of learning at least equal to traditional learning. Now the old morals and ethics could be replaced by situational ethics or "values clarification." Reading, writing, and arithmetic took a backseat to an array of experimental programs such as "sensitivity training." The virtues of hard work were replaced by new permissive standards that would pass a failing child rather than harm his "self-esteem" by labeling him a "failure." Total equality was the new ideal; it would jealously guard against too much excellence in any child that might show others to be less endowed, thus implying that abilities were unevenly distributed.

What have these "learned" educators imparted in real terms? Certainly not education or academic competence. According to Kirby Anderson of Probe Ministries,

> Today's students do not possess the basic information necessary to survive in our culture. They do not know the basic facts of history, government, or geography. A recent survey of 17 year olds revealed that a majority could not place the Civil War in the correct fifty year span, could not locate the state of New York on a map, and did not know what event brought the U.S. into World War II.

After decades of "advanced programs" concocted by "experts," the students of the 1990s would be shamed intellectually by their own predecessors from any previous decade in this century. They are functionally, culturally, and morally illiterate. The "experts" have spent more money per student than in any country in the world. Yet the European programs have left us in the Dark Ages intellectually while American educators proceed with whole new schemes for further "advancement." They are creating students who cannot read the directions on the free condoms that they are given in school—they might choose instead to *"visualize"* nonfertility as they engage in "activities" sanctioned in sex education classes. Failing this, they can still resort to the next sex education option—abortion. What is interesting is that high school pregnancies have tripled in number since the start of sex education classes, the absolute reverse of the promised outcome.

The truth is that since Dewey's time, public school programs have been brazenly shaping children's beliefs without even pretending to impart useful skills or academic knowledge.

Two names keep appearing in this effort to change thoughts and feelings: Sidney Simon, the "expert" who introduced *values clarification,* and Lawrence Kohlberg, who introduced *moral reasoning.* Both programs annihilate traditional values. Again, the Fabian theme emerges: A handful of "experts," in this case psychologists, foist their views upon millions with impunity. They arrogantly become founts of wisdom—about the family, about sexuality, and about ultimate reality. In a sweep they can destroy the student's faith, beliefs, and moral system. Their ideas are omnipresent in today's classrooms—in stories, in class exercises, in discussions, from "Who will live?" to "Why can't Johnny marry Fred?"

Gender Bending

In 1984, the U.S. Department of Education conducted hearings to gauge public opinion and propose regulations regarding the implementation of "The Protection of Pupil Rights Amendment," otherwise known as the Hatch Amendment. Testimonials revealed a new agenda was well under way in countless schools. One witness displayed a blueprint for our educational future, produced with support from the National Institute of Education. It was entitled *Future Studies in the Kindergarten Through Twelve Curriculum* by John D. Haas, and it recommended that teachers subtly introduce such subjects as fertility control, abortion, family planning, women's liberation, euthanasia, New Age consciousness, mysticism, new religions, changing older religions, guaranteed income, and so on. These issues had become hot stuff in many classrooms anyway. Haas wanted to expedite the process of preparing children for the new order. Gender bending kept coming up.

There was a time when Johnny was happy to be a boy and Susan was happy to be a girl. Now the kids, with the help of the experts, believe in the new myth of androgyny. A case in point is the Title IX-funded Sex Equity Program, or the Women's Educational Equity Act Program tested in five counties across the United States. The plan is to change the thinking patterns of America's children, starting with the youth in these five counties who have acted as guinea pigs for the greater national experiment. What happens in classrooms under this program?

On March 13, 1984, in Seattle, Washington, at the official proceedings before the U.S. Department of Education, one observer described the Sex Equity field experiment in Lincoln County, Oregon:

> One of the demonstrations was in a 1st grade room. The students each had two naked paper dolls, one male, the other female. They were asked to dress the dolls in work clothing to show that both genders could work at any job. The thing I found interesting was there were no dresses. All clothing was male oriented. Then the teacher had the students sit in a circle while she pulled out objects from a sack, like a pancake turner or a tape measure. She asked, "Who uses this, mom or dad?"
>
> If the student did not answer the way she had wanted, she would say, "Well, who else uses this?" Finally, one little boy raised his hand and said, "I don't care. Men ought to be doctors, and ladies nurses."
>
> The teacher then asked how many students agreed with the little boy. By the tone of her voice, they knew no one should raise a hand, so no one did. The little boy was so humiliated by the peer pressure and class manipulation by the teacher that he started to cry. This is classic of the type of discrimination, bias, stereotyping, and harassment that this program has included.
>
> As I reviewed different manuals that teachers were using in the schools . . . questions on family values, self analysis, opposite role-playing, unisex ideas, discussion of family roles in students' homes, and sex-role values were discussed. One book said, "Students are no longer

to be called helpers, or boys and girls, or students, but WORKERS" (a part of the Socialist lexicon).

Another book showed *only* pictures of opposites to traditional roles, such as the father feeding baby, or mother holding a fire hose in her "fireperson" job. The children didn't realize they were being fed only one side of the picture.... Our school district received federal funds to teach "Sex Equity." ... The teaching is firmly intact in the system after five years of funding. Teachers are required to attend sex equity workshops sponsored by Northwest Regional Laboratory in Portland, which received federal funds. They provide resource material and teachers.

I discovered there was no set curriculum. Teachers chose what to teach from several manuals. They were to integrate the teaching into the entire day's classes. Women were really exalted in all the material I viewed, while male minorities were almost ignored. The goal of the Sex Equity program was to eliminate traditional roles of male and female.

Clearly this is a behavior-shaping program that uses the classroom as a laboratory under the cloak of education. Dr. Benjamin Bloom, the father of mastery learning, in his recent book, *All Our Children Learning*, agrees that "The purpose of education is to change the thoughts, feelings, and actions of students."

The San Francisco Chronicle on March 16, 1988, in an article by Adrian Peracchio described an outrage in Britain that may soon cross the Atlantic: "It began last year with parents' howls of outrage at the publication by local municipal councils of *Jenny Lives with Eric and Martin*, a graphically illustrated pamphlet showing a cherubic little girl smiling at her father, naked in bed with his live-in gay lover."

The *Chronicle* then reported: "The pamphlet, printed with British government funds, attempted to prove that young children brought up by homosexual couples could adjust and thrive just as well as those reared in more traditional households."

The above book appeared in local school libraries alongside *How to Be a Happy Homosexual* and *The Children's Playbook of Sex*, two other publicly financed pamphlets in which homosexual themes were explicitly treated. Britain clearly heads America in the official promotion of "alternative lifestyles." But we may be catching up.

On January 21, 1992, CNN headline news had a short feature on the latest breakthroughs in the public school classroom. Elementary school children were nervously trying to elude the camera. They looked ashamed. They had just seen a movie that would easily qualify as pornography. The teacher proudly barked her disclaimers into the camera. "No, this is not sex-ed, the kids are having their AIDS awareness heightened." These young kids had just seen a film of full-on genitalia with a condom being donned. What was illegal in the fifties in porno houses was now sanctioned in public elementary schools. And more is on the way.

Homosexual groups have been campaigning militantly to have "gay" sexuality graphically shown in this quest for "AIDS awareness." Perhaps in a few years elementary school kids will see movies of sodomy. NAMBLA, the North American Man/Boy Love Association, also appeared on CNN angrily picketing a major network for legitimate recognition and the legalization of pedophilia. Speechless mothers were protesting in shock that this was actually happening. Homosexual groups are pushing hard for homosexual teachers' quotas and "gay awareness."

Unfortunately, the values and morality barrier is only one of the barriers being broken in this broad onslaught.

The New Age Wave

In other testimonials before the U.S. Department of Education, which were compiled from across the country in 1984, there were numerous examples of New Age thought flooding classrooms. Common activities involved learning how to do horoscopes, conduct seances, cast the witch's circle, use a Ouija board, meditate, and role-play such characters as warlocks and spiritists which appeared in required readings. Wiccans (witches) and neopagans were invited on public school premises to speak about their alternate views (they do not use the word *religions*). Witches could now enter where ministers were forbidden to tread, a new milestone in America's "liberation." Children also partook in the visualization of invisible guides not just through the Galyean approach but through Silva Mind Control. They would lie on the floor and empty their minds, invoking the invisible presences within them. In Buffalo, New York, students were required to learn Silva Mind Control and reportedly contacted the spirits of various long-deceased historical figures—a new way to study George Washington and Abraham Lincoln. Why just read about historical figures when you can speak with them "live" (or rather, "dead").

The State of Connecticut represents a working model of how New Age curricula can enter the public school system. First of all, there is the federal grant. In Connecticut, several million dollars were granted to develop the Connecticut Teachers' Center for Humanistic Education. The opportunity was created by the Department of Health, Education and Welfare's allocation of 75 million dollars for the teaching of humanistic education nationwide (via the 1978 amendments to the Higher Education Act, Title V). Stratford, Connecticut's Board of Education initiated the first grant for one million dollars to have humanistic education taught in the Connecticut public school system, thus becoming the *legal* education agency and employer. This was how the door opened up.

Connecticut's Center for Humanistic Education then used such resources as The Institute for Wholistic Education in Amherst, Massachusetts. The Institute's codirectors, Jack Canfield and Paula Klimek, came and led workshops at various Connecticut Teacher's Center programs. Featured in a brochure entitled "Education in the New Age," Canfield and Klimek led workshops on "Meditation and Centering in the Classroom" and "Guided Imagery."

Canfield and Klimek had already written an article for *The New Age*, February 1978, entitled "Education in the New Age," which essentially spelled out the New Age agenda for penetrating and using the public school system across the United States. This article is a manifesto that deserves to be examined.

The New Age Journal stated, "They consult with schools, train teachers, and have coauthored numerous books such as, *The Inner Classroom: Teaching with Guided Fantasy*, and *Wholistic Education*." Not surprisingly, some Connecticut parents began to take note when their children returned home from school with new ideas. They were quietly moving into the new paradigms, beyond the obsolete mind-sets of their parents' generation. It was all happening with the invisible stealth of *Invasion of the Body Snatchers*.

A consortium of parents described what was happening in the classroom with these words: "In the name of discovering their 'life purpose,' children are encouraged into trance-like states of mind where they communicate with 'guardian spirits.' The use of Yoga exercises and mind control techniques are other examples of the format of this program."[7]

Jack Canfield had a proven track record. A Canadian paper, *The Editonion Journal*, on October 11, 1979, featured an article by Marilyn Moysa, entitled "Improving Images Seen as a Key to Help," about Jack Canfield and the high-powered educators and lawyers he was addressing. It reported:

> Imagine more than 800 of North America's top judges, lawyers, education professors, social workers and just plain parents chanting an Indian mantra.
>
> Even Meyer Horowitz, University of Alberta president, sang along in the guitar-accompanied chant. "What ever happened to the keynote address?" I kept asking myself. "Wasn't this supposed to be the big opening number of a national conference on children with learning disabilities?" What happened, quite simply, was Jack Canfield, Director of the Institute for Wholistic Education in Amherst, Mass. . . . Images, claims Dr. Canfield, can have power beyond the will of an individual when it comes to change.

The article then showed how Canfield took a learning disabled sixth-grade girl and had her go through guided imagery with a "wise old woman" up a stairway of light. Through this the girl discovered the "meaning of life." The 800 lawyers and educators applauded this profound experiment and its insight.

Canfield and Klimek's long feature article in *The New Age Journal* is packed with disclosures. New Age education has arrived and "more and more teachers are exposing children to ways of contacting their inner wisdom and higher selves."[8]

The coauthors diagnosed breakthroughs in the sixties when the educational system began to break down, saying:

> An influx of spiritual teachings from the East, combined with a new psychological perspective in the West, has resulted in a fresh look at the learning process. . . . People everywhere are looking for a new vision, a new approach, a new paradigm of life. . . . A new vision is beginning to manifest.[9]

Much of guided imagery begins with Roberto Assagioli's 1960s consciousness expanding exercise known as *psychosynthesis*. This is the creative root to reaching the all-knowing higher self within. Canfield and Klimek continue:

> Within the past five years we have also witnessed the birth of "transpersonal education," the acknowledgment of one's inner and spiritual dimensions, through working with such forms as dreams, meditation, guided imagery, biofeedback, centering, mandalas, and so forth. Now is the time to combine both of these focuses, for the New Age means integrating the soul and personality. . . . Holistic education . . . views the student as being engaged in an integral process of unfoldment under the direction of his/her higher self. This process is perceived as taking place in a universe that is also constantly evolving: each of us is seen as an important part of the larger planetary and universal evolution of consciousness.[10]

There were endless pointers:

Children of all ages love physical exercise and seem to be particularly fascinated with yoga: they move easily into all sorts of contortions.... There are numerous books on yoga for children. One of our favorites is *Be a Frog, a Bird, or a Tree*, by Rachel Carr (Doubleday, 1977).[11]

Intimacy games are described, as are sensory awareness games, in which children get over inhibitions against touching one another. "Centering" becomes the more acceptable word for meditation. "Relaxation and centering exercises are a fundamental process for New Age education, because they provide a space for listening to the voice within."[12]

Chanting is recommended to reach the transcendent within. One chanting method is called "seed planting" (in India we used to call them Bija mantras or "seed mantras") in order to plant the chants deep into the consciousness. It is a group event with one child sitting in the middle of the room. They take turns sitting in the middle.[13] Then there are meditation techniques that use media ideas. Canfield tosses out model questions:

"What's this thing called The Force in *Star Wars*? How does Luke communicate with it? How does it help him?" The next question is, "Well, would you like to have this kind of experience?"[14]

There are some telling insights regarding guided imagery in New Age schooling:

We believe that guided imagery is a key to finding out what is in the consciousness of New Age children.... Children are so close to spirit if we only allow room for their process to emerge.... Additional emphases in the transpersonal dimension are using nature as teacher, and aligning and communicating with the other kingdoms such as the elemental and *devic* realism (the term *Devic* is a Sanskrit word for the realm of the gods), ... working with children's psychic capacities (such as seeing auras); working with astrological charts.... The souls that are presently incarnating seem to be very special.[15]

Canfield and Klimek's "Education in the New Age"—a ground breaker in the late 1970s that paved the way into America's public school—ends with the admonition:

> We must not get caught in the trap of putting them into developmental models which will soon be irrelevant.... The only requirement is to provide a *space* and an *environment* where these beautiful young spirits can open up and allow their wisdom to be seen.[16]

And that "space," that "environment," has been expanding through the 1980s and into the 1990s.

The Next Wave

The educational "environment" has continued to explode with wild and audacious pilot programs. They are being closely monitored for effectiveness in the public arena as they push the envelope of radical change. Educators look closely to see which ones escape scrutiny and public outrage. These pilot programs blanket the nation with names like SOAR, QUEST, PAT, GLOBAL 2000, PAIDEIA, MEOLOGY, DECIDE, DARE, THE NEW MODEL ME, and so on. Looking at this scattergram of programs inductively, one can only conclude the educational elite are preparing future citizens for a very different world—economically, socially, and spiritually.

By all appearances American history is no longer required. Perhaps there will no longer be much of an America left to study. Multiculturalism appears to be very important in these programs, so we can only conclude that the experts can anticipate with great enthusiasm a racially and culturally amalgamated world. We gather it will be a tightly governed world with the capacity to observe its citizens quite closely, making privacy a luxury of the past. It will be a world with quota systems where "equality" is rigidly enforced. Knowledge and ability will be most rare indeed. More important in this future world will be one's attitude, the right kind of attitude.

The present generation of latchkey kids, whose parents are busy with careers, operates almost unsupervised in a permissive world. They are a lonely and captive audience ready to sponge up any new agenda. As former Yale professor Allan Bloom observes, each succeeding group entering college from public school comes less equipped to deal with the university world, an index of a tragic and costly experiment. Bloom likewise calls them "impoverished."

The new breed of students tends to be more passive and hedonistic than their predecessors as they live for the moment. They have few goals, a diminished concept of history, little discipline, and almost no sense of what is noble or good. Instead they specialize in taboo-breaking decadence and grin cynically at moral correctives. They have learned self-esteem by being affirmed through cheap and empty slogans. They have empty heads and hard hearts while the "self" that they have spent so much time affirming keeps changing like Proteus, forever being redefined by the "experts."

Students more and more are modeling clay in the hands of social engineers. These unlettered future citizens may be instructed by the planners to finally free themselves from the past. Perhaps it will be time for all the books of the past in all the vast libraries of the earth, "with racism, sexism and other thought crimes," to be tossed in the bonfire of history.

Perhaps UNESCO will declare it "freedom day" as bonfires light up the skylines of the world. Obedient world citizens here and there will struggle to read the words on the covers as they playfully toss the outdated works into the fire. A title or name will pass by. Those sounding out the titles and authors phonetically may feel the last traces of reading knowledge that is soon to be obsolete. *1984* appears with the name George. The second name sounds like "Oh Well." "George Oh-Well" whose book *1984* shows how out-of-date it is right on the cover. "Oh Well" is chanted around the bonfire as others see the outdated book eaten up by the flames. And America ends not with a bang but a whimper, after decades of "education," which made straight the path for a New World Order.

ABOUT THE AUTHOR

Tal Brooke spent two decades intently exploring the occult. His quest ultimately landed him in the heart of India where for two years he was the top Western disciple of India's miracle-working superguru, Sai Baba. A graduate of the University of Virginia and Princeton, and a frequent speaker at Oxford and Cambridge universities, Tal has written six books, including his recent popular sellers *Riders of the Cosmic Circuit* and *When the World Will Be As One*. Tal Brooke is president/chairman of the Berkeley-based Spiritual Counterfeits Project (SCP) Inc., a nationally known research think tank and magazine.

Chapter 13

A PSYCHIATRIST'S PERSPECTIVE

BY DR. GEORGE TWENTE

A report published by the National Center for Health Statistics based on a survey of more than 17,000 children shows that close to 20 percent of the children between the ages of 3 and 17 have or have had a developmental learning or behavior disorder. Thirteen percent were shown to have had significant emotional or behavioral problems. In relation to this report Dr. Lawrence Stone, Chairman of the American Psychiatric Association's Council on Children, Adolescents and Their Families, concluded that the burden caused by the breakdown of social values and norms falls heavily on children. He said that "we have lost a lot of structure based on families, neighborhoods, religion and ethnicity." He also says that "those changes cause a society to lose its predictability, which means that children do not have anticipatory responses to everyday situations. Without that, they lose confidence in themselves and in others."[1]

A heavy burden has been placed on our public school system to educate and often raise our children. We, as parents, must make sure that we are providing proper education about life, values, relationships, responsibility, and citizenship at home before we criticize our educational system for undermining the sanctity of the home and its values.

I believe in counseling children that have demonstrated

emotional or behavioral problems and am in favor of counseling offered through the school system. I have been a practicing psychiatrist since 1974, and primarily work with young people and their families who are having overwhelming problems. To adequately work with any disturbed child, you must first evaluate that child as to the type of problems he is having, the strengths and weaknesses of the child and the system he comes from, and then prescribe a program to realistically help the child within the family system. I am concerned that a number of programs being used in the public schools use techniques that are contrary to these ideals.

One area of concern is the issue of relative values, usually emphasized in training kindergarten through twelfth grade schoolchildren in the process of decision-making. Studies show that the majority of American children come from family systems that believe in the God of the Bible or absolute authority, such as the Ten Commandments or the Golden Rule. So when dealing with decision-making processes, the teacher/ guidance counselor should respect the absolute values that most family systems hold.

In particular, a 1992 study showed that 67.5 percent of adults in the United States or 125.6 million adults hold to traditional mainline Protestant, evangelical, or Roman Catholic values. This study was reported by John C. Green, a political scientist with the University of Akron in Ohio, who directed the study. The study was done on 4001 American adults that were weighted by region, race, and gender and was sponsored by the Ray C. Bliss Institute of Applied Politics at the University of Akron.[2]

Also, any decision-making process should be within the absolute values of constitutional, federal, state, and local laws or we are encouraging our children to follow group or hedonistic principles of right and wrong.

In addition, the moral growth issues should be in the context of accepted stages of moral development that children go through as they move toward adulthood. For example, well-respected Lawrence Kohlberg divides moral growth into preconventional, conventional, and post conventional or autonomous developmental stages.[3]

Children aged 4 to 10 years are usually in the preconventional stage in which "good behavior" results in rewards and misbehavior results in punishment. Hence good or bad is determined solely by physical consequences, a "child's morality."

The second level, a conventional level, is marked by the need to meet the expectations or to follow the rules of one's family, peer group, or nation. Maintaining the rules of the group is a value in itself. Early adolescents are usually in this stage of moral development.

The postconventional level consists of a major thrust toward autonomous moral principles that have validity apart from the authority of the group or individual who holds them, an "adult morality". This last level begins in middle to late adolescence.[4]

Accepting these overarching principles should be especially heeded when trying to educate children in the areas of drug and alcohol abuse, sexual activity, and becoming a good American citizen.

Another concern is the use of a shotgun approach to all children with the idea that this affective education program will help them avoid problems in the future. Consider the following excerpt:

Dr. David Shaffer said at the annual meeting of the American College of Psychiatrists, that standard school-based suicide programs do little good and may do harm; they should be abandoned in favor of interventions that target high-risk adolescents.

"In the absence of clear benefit, there is no justification for continued application of these programs," said Dr. Shaffer, the Irving Philips Professor of Child and Adolescent Psychiatry at New York Psychiatric Institute, New York. Primary prevention programs, which aid to reduce first incidence of pathology rather than prevent recurrences or complications, have high status in medicine: A good example is the success of vaccination against infectious illness. But in mental health, "the primary prevention approach is elusive and has never demonstrated efficacy," he said.

Cost effectiveness is low when prevention programs are applied to unselected populations. To reach 12 potential suicides, a program would have to serve 200,000 low-risk 16 to 18-year-olds, at a cost of $300,000. For $240,000, on the other hand, a targeted intervention could provide 2,400 therapy hours for 120 male suicide attempters, a high-risk group.

Interventions designed in ignorance of underlying factors may be risky. A study in Cambridge and Somerville, Massachusetts in the 1930's randomly assigned 506 average and high-psychiatric-risk boys, average age 10.5 years, to either a control group or a group that received 5 years of comprehensive therapy, including family counseling, tutoring and psychotherapy when indicated. The treated group also attended summer camp to improve social skills. At follow-up 30 years later, treated subjects were significantly more likely than were control subjects to have committed more than one crime. They were significantly less likely to be doing skilled, professional work, or to report high satisfaction with their work. The average age of those who had died was lower for members of the treated group.

Primary prevention programs in mental health have been largely educational, based on "the psychologically naive assumption that people harm themselves because they don't know any better," he said. Drug and sex education programs designed along these lines have been markedly unsuccessful, and some may have increased the behaviors they were supposed to prevent.[5]

I think that affective education programs are a waste of valuable schooltime for children who have demonstrated a lack of need for help. In particular, 87 percent are not in need of emotional help or behavioral help. I do believe that it is proper for teachers, along with guidance counselors, to identify children who do need help. One particular guidance counselor in our county went to different classes and handed out questionnaires that identified children at risk without the child having to expose certain issues to the group process, peer pressure, or ridicule. Thus, the high-risk student was identified. The child would then go to the counselor for individual and family evaluation and determination of what would be proper to help him/her, either within the school system or referred to proper professionals. This should be done with the cooperation and permission from the family or guardians of the child.

When a school system looks for means to enhance a child's self-esteem, I would recommend that they consult with Professor Susan Black and her studies on self-esteem and her forthcoming book on how to evaluate affective education programs.[6]

Another aspect which concerns me about some of the programs used in the public school system is they tend to imply that the answers to the child's problems are within him or herself. This approach is directed toward kindergarten and elementary school age children when it is well-known that developmentally, children of this age are normally dependent on external authority for guidance and security. I will specifically describe one program that is representative of a number of programs I have evaluated, as far as the techniques that are of grave concern to me and many others in the field of psychiatry.

First, I need to explain and encourage you to understand hypnosis. I suggest that you read *Encyclopedia Britannica*, the 1980 15th edition, which gives an excellent overview of what hypnosis is and how it is to be used in a reasonable way.[7] In general, hypnosis is described as creating an altered state of consciousness, a partial sleep. The person being hypnotized is responding to suggestions in an uncritical and automatic fashion.

These techniques that are used for induction are usually simple techniques that are acceptable to anyone. But, as the process continues, they increasingly demand attention that distorts perceptual reality and brings in a new reality that does not actually exist. For example, a person may be told to concentrate on his hand, his breathing, a visual image, or a tone. Then to continue the induction process, it is quite effective when the hypnotist paints a vivid word picture of concrete images that are easily imagined. Once this hypnotic state is achieved, then suggestions are given.

The problems with these suggestible altered states of consciousness is that the person being hypnotized may have distortions of recall, and believe that suggested fictitious events have actually occurred. The subject may not only remember them as true but may also elaborate on them. These subjective memories may be accompanied by very strong subjective convictions that would even be convincing to the interviewer and the person who has been hypnotized. This is one of the reasons that testimony is not allowed in court for people who have retrieved memory through hypnosis.

Another concern of the use of hypnosis is that appropriate hypnotic suggestions also can prompt the subject to embrace false beliefs or delusions; for example, a belief that they lived in a previous lifetime.

Hypnosis that is used for pain control can be quite effective but first the person must be evaluated to the source of the pain. It is well-known that young people, if under enough stress, such as abuse, may be able to disassociate emotionally and mentally to protect themselves in order to survive. This phenomenon is like a naturally occurring hypnotic state. This type of disassociation only occurs with a certain percentage of people under extreme stress.

It is a mistake to train children to learn to disassociate from reality when there is no stress. It may take years of therapy to help a person overcome the effects of disassociation. One example of extreme disassociation is multiple personality disorder.

Very little training is necessary to practice hypnosis. I myself learned hypnosis by watching my 16-year-old sister do it with her friends when I was 13. I just did what they did and it was effective with my peers. Induction of hypnosis requires little training and no particular skill, a tape recording often being sufficient. Even though little skill is needed to induce hypnosis, considerable training is needed to evaluate whether it is appropriate or not. When used in the treatment context, hypnosis should never be employed by individuals who do not have the competence and skill to treat such problems without the use of hypnosis. For this reason, hypnosis schools or institutes cannot provide the needed training for individuals lacking the more general scientific and technical qualification of the healing professions. Improperly used, hypnosis may add to the patient's psychiatric or medical difficulties. Thus, a sufferer of an undisclosed brain tumor may sacrifice his life in the hands of a practitioner who successfully relieves his headache by hypnotic suggestions, thereby delaying needed surgery. Broad diagnostic training and therapeutic skill are indispensable in avoiding the inappropriate and dangerous use of hypnosis.

Of particular concern to me is that children are told that they can feel the way they want to feel just by using self-suggestion or self-hypnosis.

Another concern that I see in a number of these programs used in elementary and kindergarten school levels is that they encourage the children to try to solve their problems all by themselves outside of any relationship with external authority. They also are not taught the discrimination needed to judge the information that comes from within themselves. It is well-known in psychotherapy that the most important part of therapy is the relationship with the therapist.

As an example, I will discuss one aspect of the "Pumsy in Pursuit of Excellence" program that is used from the first grade on through elementary school in approximately 18,000 public schools. In the program summary it says, "Pumsy decides to stop waiting for something good to happen to her and learn how she can feel good about herself all by herself."

Most of the Pumsy program is dependent on hypnotic trance induction and hypnotic suggestion. Most of the slogans that are used, such as, "I can choose how I feel," "I am me, I am enough," and "It's good to have a friend," are all introduced to the child in an altered state of consciousness or hypnotic state. I will give you an excerpt from Session 6 of the teacher's manual which is typical of hypnotic induction in all the sessions, but this one in particular has to do with manipulation of feelings.

Session 6

Discuss how we can use that power in whatever way we want. That is, we can choose to have positive thoughts or negative thoughts, and nobody can stop us. Nobody can make us feel bad, and nobody can stop us from feeling good—unless we let them. That is a lot of power!

Painting Mind Pictures (To Be Read Aloud Slowly):

Let's take a moment to paint a Mind Picture. Relax and get comfortable with both feet on the floor. Let your shoulders relax, and let your arms and hands rest in a comfortable way. Let your head relax. You can let it fall forward a little if that helps you relax. Let your whole body work like it was a slow motion. Close your eyes, but not tight. Take slow, deep breaths. When you let your breath out, you might feel like you could sink into your chair.

(When children are relaxed, continue with the Mind Picture as follows):

Imagine for a moment that you are outdoors sitting next to a stream of water slowly going by you. It is a beautiful day with the sun dancing and sparkling on the stream in front of you. It is quiet here except for some of the nice outdoor sounds that you enjoy so much—maybe the sound of the water as it trickles over rocks and into little pools. This is a good place where you may come when you want to feel good.

Imagine that a picnic basket is next to you on the ground. Can you see the basket? What color is it? How big is it? This is your picnic basket, and you always bring it with you when you come to visit this special place. Also next to you on the ground is a pile of little rocks just the size that you can pick up very easily and wrap your hand around. These rocks have words written on them that say how we might feel. Some of the rocks have words for a good feeling. Other rocks have words for a bad feeling.

You can pick up the rocks one at a time. The first rock you pick up has the word "happy" on it. Do you want to feel that way? If you want to feel happy, keep the rock and put it in your picnic basket. If you do not want to feel happy, throw the rock into the stream. Here is another rock. This one has the word "safe" on it. If you want to feel safe, keep the rock and put it in your basket. If you don't want to feel safe, you can throw the rock in the stream...(pause)...The next one you pick up is the word "awful." Decide what you want to do with that rock—if you want to feel awful, keep the rock. If you don't want to feel awful, throw it away.... Here is another one. This one says "wonderful." What will you do with this one?... And here is another rock. The word on this rock is "mad." Decide what you want to do with that rock, either put it in your basket or throw it in the stream. ... And now we have a rock that says "selfish." Decide what you want to do with that rock too.... Here is another rock and it says "friendly" on it....

There is one more rock left. But it doesn't have anything on it. You decide what feeling this rock will say. When you have decided what you want the feeling to be, decide if you will keep that feeling or not. You can choose any feeling you like and either keep it or throw it away. You may take a moment to think of the feeling for this last rock and what you will do with it... (allow about 10 seconds).

As you do whatever you are going to do with the last feeling, get ready to go because now it is time to leave your special place by the stream. If you like, you may take your picnic basket with you or you may leave it here. It is your picnic basket and the feelings in it are your feelings, so you can do whatever you wish with them.

When you are ready, you may start wiggling your fingers, and then when you are ready, you may begin to move your arms around a little bit. Next, you may begin to open your eyes and repeat aloud with me in a clear, strong voice... "I can choose how I feel.

"I can choose how I feel.

"I can choose how I feel."[8]

When you read this section from Session 6, after you have studied what hypnosis is, you will recognize this as standard hypnotic trance induction and suggestion.

One of the problems we have in our society today is that young people and adults seek instant gratification. To suggest to the children that they can feel any way they want to by mind manipulation encourages this problem.

Also, if this type of program were successful, the child could easily become a sociopath. In therapy, we try to help a person become aware and accept his feelings. Feelings act as a signal for what the problem may actually be. Many children who would try to do this exercise may become frustrated when they are not able to manipulate their feelings as some will be able to do. Part of this Session 6 states that by picking up a rock with "happy" on it, a child should be able to feel happy whenever he chooses to. This could encourage drug abuse by implanting the idea of instant gratification, especially by associating instant happiness with a "rock," the street term for crack. The abuse of this drug is destroying many communities in our country.

In closing, I would like to reiterate that I am not against counseling young people. I am against using a shotgun approach to all students with affective education programs. I am for identifying a child with problems and trying to get appropriate help within the framework of the system the child comes from. There are no psychotherapeutic techniques that are adequate for all problems, but specific ones can be used when they are compatible with a specific problem. In my opinion, the most important means of helping children feel better about themselves is to help them in their relationships and help them gain confidence in dealing with challenges they meet, not in withdrawing from reality by convincing themselves that they feel fine about themselves no matter what is going on in the external world.

Once you understand the general concept of hypnosis, I think you will recognize this technique in many other programs used in the public school system that emphasize some kind of immediate gratification. You will also see how it encourages children to look within themselves for answers without being given guidance as to what is healthy and what is not healthy. Turning them away from appropriate external authority to an internal authority is much like the blind leading the blind.

Considering "self-realization or self-actualization" techniques used in public school systems, such as yoga, meditation, guided imagery, etc., I respect the right of any person to make an educated decision to pursue such endeavors, but it is malpractice and/or illegal to impose these procedures on an uninformed captive audience of children. Abraham Maslow in his 1970 edition of *Motivation and Personality* said, "Self-actualization was a concept that was definitely applied only to older people."[9]

And finally, when decision-making processes are taught, they should be done within the framework of our Constitution, laws, and respect for the values of the majority of the people in our unique, cherished United States of America.

ABOUT THE AUTHOR

Dr. Twente graduated from Vanderbilt University in 1967 (BA); the University of Mississippi School of Medicine in 1971, and the University of Florida School of Medicine in 1974, after completing a psychiatric residency. He also spent 16 years involved in meditation, yoga practice, and "scientific mysticism," eventually becoming a nationally recognized leader in the field of "eidetic imagery" and other New Age techniques. He is a former vice president of the International Imagery Association and was on the editorial board of the *Journal of Mental Imagery*.

After his conversion to Christianity in 1988, he critically reevaluated his former worldview and now gives expert testimony about the consequences of New Age and questionable psychotherapeutic methods in the classroom. He is currently chief of psychiatry at Decatur General Hospital and medical director of the adolescent program.

Chapter 14

ABOLISHED MAN: FROM INSTRUCTION TO INDOCTRINATION IN THE NEW EDUCATION

BY *BROOKS ALEXANDER*

The difference betwen the old and the new education will be an important one. Where the old initiated, the new merely "conditions." The old dealt with its pupils as grown birds deal with young birds when they teach them to fly: the new deals with them more as the poultry-keeper deals with young birds—making them thus or thus for purposes of which the young birds know nothing. In a word, the old was a kind of propagation—men transmitting manhood to men: the new is merely propaganda.[1]

—C.S. Lewis

C.S. Lewis noticed destructive trends in education earlier and critiqued them more cogently than most. He did so specifically in his 1947 book, *The Abolition of Man*. Lewis chose that title because he recognized that the new educational trends were destructive to our humanity, since they redefined mankind in subhuman terms. Lewis himself believed that *The Abolition of Man* was his "most significant statement."[2]

Lewis chose an existing elementary textbook as his example and focus of concern; he referred to it as *The Green Book*. As Lewis described *The Green Book*, it seems to teach an early form of "value-free" learning that is radically humanistic. Lewis called it the "new education." According to Lewis, *The Green Book* undermined deity, truth, and value at their source by seeing them all as human creations. By syllogism, if we make them, we can change them. Since they come from man, they can be defined by man.

But by which men? No definition prevails without a struggle against its rivals. Thus, humanism "politicizes" everything. Ultimately, there is no "reality," there is only a contest of powers—which, in the long run, means a contest of wills.

Lewis understood that the new education deliberately disconnects its students from the things that define human nature—namely ultimates, absolutes, conscience, values, culture, and tradition. When we are disconnected, we become more subject to manipulation. The reason is simple: when we detach ourselves from the specifically human, we remain connected to the generically living—with all of its urges and desires. When we cast off the cultural and traditional things that define our "human nature," we remain captive to the biological and instinctual things that drive our "nonhuman" nature, i.e., our appetites and our primal emotions.

> When all that says "it is good" has been debunked, what says "I want" remains. It cannot be exploded or "seen through" because it never had any pretensions. The Conditioners, therefore, must come to be motivated simply by their own pleasure. . . . My point is that those who stand outside all judgments of value cannot have any ground for preferring one of their own impulses to another except the emotional strength of that impulse. . . . Their extreme rationalism, by "seeing through" all rational motives, leaves them creatures of wholly irrational behavior.[3]

If Lewis were alive today he would be saddened, but not surprised, by the way in which his predictions have been fulfilled. For over four decades, we have been subjected to a relentless debunking of our culture, our religion, and our values. We have responded appropriately—by turning ourselves into a nation of alienated, amoral, rootless, self-serving, ego-units.

Education and Popular Culture

Education is not the only culprit in that regard—entertainment and advertising are both subject to heavy indictment. And both, of course, are uniquely joined in the modern medium of TV. More than one observer has noted that the very nature of TV technology has an alienating effect, *regardless of the content being broadcast.* Culture-watcher Kenneth Myers summarizes the criticisms:

> Robert Hughes has noted that the "swift montage and juxtaposition" of images that characterizes TV viewing has had an effect on the modern consciousness. The effect has been, he maintains, "to insulate and estrange us from reality itself, turning everything into disposable spectacle: catastrophy, love, war, soap. Ours is the cult of the electronic fragment." . . . The fundamental assumption of the world of television, argues Neil Postman, is not coherence, but discontinuity. Choosing in a coherent world requires deliberation and thoughtfulness, but choosing in the midst of chaos becomes arbitrary, a sheer act of will.[4]

Those influences of popular culture reinforce destructive trends in education. The two work together in ways that complement one another. Entertainment, advertising, and television surround us with a disorganized clamor of yearning and alienation, while education systematically turns students into autonomous units of will and ego, of "empowerment" and "self-esteem."

That combined influence of education, popular culture, and television has already produced results in our society. One result is a large pool of people who respond readily to manipulation because they have been cut off from the knowledge (of

God, of culture, of right and wrong) that would enable them to sift their experience and evaluate it. Another result is a breed of young people who have learned to feel good about themselves while behaving in ways that are ruthlessly antisocial. The same influences create both the herd and the psychopath who cuts from the herd.

A decade after Lewis, Norman Mailer noticed a similar phenomenon, and hinted that in a fragmenting and anarchic society, the psychopath's lack of conscience gives him a certain competitive edge.

> The psychopath may indeed be the perverted and dangerous front-runner of a new kind of personality which could become the central expression of human nature before the twentieth century is over.[5]

Lewis analyzed the new education by going directly to its basic and most destructive assumptions. Those were: first, that all values are creations of man; and second, that man therefore owes no allegiance to any values but those that he makes or chooses for himself. In Lewis' view, that was a metaphysical statement, not an educational one. He pointed out that the new education was thus more than a new method of teaching, it was a new worldview, and a new definition of man.

Dangerous Results

And he understood the consequences that would flow from those ideas. Lewis foresaw two dangerous results of the new education. One was political, the other cultural.

The political danger, briefly put, is that such "education" really prepares the many to be controlled by the few.

> The man-moulders of the New Age will be armed with the powers of an omnicompetent state and an irresistible scientific technique; we shall at last get a race of conditioners who can really cut out posterity in whatever shape they please.

> For the power of Man to make himself what he
> pleases means, as we have seen, the power of some
> men to make other men what they please.[6]

Lewis warned that the debunking of values favors the rise of dictatorship. In his view, the new education was really a way of training people to be docile and responsive subjects of a power elite that controls public appetites (falsely called public "opinion") by controlling public information. By coincidence, Lewis published *The Abolition of Man* the same year that George Orwell was finishing *1984*.

Lewis also saw an even deeper danger. The new education not only redefines man, it also redefines human society. It is thus inherently subversive and hostile to the forms of society that already exist. Before the new can come, the old must go. Wherever the new education takes root, it begins automatically to work at cross-purposes with established society and social institutions by debunking their basis in shared values. Lewis spoke plainly in that regard: "The practical result of education in the spirit of (the new education) must be the destruction of the society which accepts it."[7]

By disconnecting individuals from shared beliefs and allegiances—from the social fabric—the new education disrupts the transmission of cultural values from one generation to the next. It is the cultural equivalent of nerve gas, which kills by interrupting the transmission of nervous impulses within the body.

There is a third danger in the new education that Lewis did not specifically foresee. It is the danger to the family. The new education's danger to the family comes in two stages. The first stage weakens the family by "atomizing" its members—an effect that is reinforced by popular culture. As the family flounders, the second stage capitalizes on its failures.

Because the family has been undermined, individual families become disabled—there are some functions they can no longer perform at all, and others they can't perform fully or well. At the personal level, families struggle, and often fail, against the forces that weaken and divide them. Problems increase in number and severity. At some point, state bureaucracies, typically led by education and social welfare, step in—

first to oversee, then to take over the functions that families are unable to exercise, *or are willing to abandon.*

When this process runs its course, the influence of the family will be mostly displaced by the influence of the collective, in the form of the bureaucracy, the schools, and the media. The natural, biological family in general, and parents in particular, will become appendages of the "omnicompetent state," watchfully regulated by state agencies. The family will be redefined to prevent it from becoming a focus for loyalties apart from the collective. If a form of the "family" survives at all, it will be as a convenient device for bureaucratic bookkeeping, and will be redefined in mostly economic terms.

At the time Lewis wrote, the "abolition" he described was still in its nascent stages. He saw the beginning of the process, not its completion. He viewed the "abolition" as a potential, not a fact. Today we are fast approaching the fact—the outcome of that process. Today our educational system works to produce "Abolished Man" in increasing numbers, with increasing efficiency.

Education as Propaganda

True to Lewis' prediction, modern secondary education (i.e., above sixth grade) is largely becoming an "attitude factory" that indoctrinates students with a political and social agenda.

That fact is becoming so flagrant that even advocates of the new education have ceased to claim that they "teach" or "educate" in the traditional sense of that term. Dr. Shirley McCune is director of a federally funded educational laboratory in Aurora, Colorado. Speaking at a national "educational summit," she recently acknowledged that "we are no longer teaching facts to children" because "none of us can guess what information they will need in the future." Schools, she said, should just teach students "how to process information." She said that teachers "should be worried about a class that is quiet" because the students "may just be learning facts, but not how to process the information."[8]

The modern version of Lewis' "new education" has two main thrusts. The first is a program of propaganda directed at students, with the purpose of invalidating mainstream culture, values, and institutions, including the family. The propaganda is organized at the level of the curriculum and carried out at the level of the classroom.

The second thrust is an active effort to remove the family from its place of preeminent influence and replace it with the schools, the media, and the state. This move to displace the family is conceived on a broader scale and is carried out at the level of bureaucratic networking. The educational bureaucracy is a central part of that network.

It is important to notice that, without being directly coordinated, the two thrusts work together—that is, the propaganda supports the validity of the collective and its displacement of the family, while the displacement in turn makes the propaganda more pervasive and more effective.

Three main themes of indoctrination are currently "hot topics" in curriculum design. They are: 1) Globalism, 2) Environmentalism, and 3) Political Correctness (also known as "diversity" and "anti-bias"). Curriculum packages that promote one or another of those themes began to appear in the late 1970s; today, versions of all three are in common use.

The environment is one of the hottest issues in politics, and it is one of the hottest topics in education. Today, some 317 U.S. colleges and universities offer majors in environmental science.[9] At the high school level, environmental courses are ubiquitous.

> Unlike previous attempts at issues-oriented education—such as peace studies—environmental education seems to be taking hold, thanks to the efforts of environmental groups and the Bush administration. The Environmental Protection Agency's new Office of Environmental Education . . . is working to "ensure that topical environmental issues are part of an environmental education curriculum.[10]

Government Sponsors, Media Allies

In fact, the government has long been active in raising the profile of the environmentalist agenda. Eco-consciousness went mainstream on April 22, 1970, when President Nixon, with the approval of Congress, formally declared the first "Earth Day"; later that same year, he established the Environmental Protection Agency (EPA).

But many think that the government's eco-boosting began in earnest almost a decade earlier. *Report from Iron Mountain* (1967) describes the deliberations of a government-sponsored think tank created in the early 1960s, under the Kennedy administration. The author of the report had taken part in those discussions. For publishing purposes, he called himself "John Doe," but he later identified himself as none other than the economist and establishment insider, John Kenneth Galbraith.

The entire group was sworn to secrecy about their deliberations and their recommendations to the government—in order to encourage a "more frank and open discussion." Galbraith decided to break his promise of silence and reveal the report because he believed that the group should be accountable for its opinions and conclusions.

The main task of the group was to consider the possibility that peace would actually break out, and that war as an organizing principle in society would have to be replaced by something else that would serve the same functions. Several options were considered, including the contrived threat of an extraterrestrial invasion. High on the list of *realistic* threats was an environmental crisis. The main drawback of the eco-threat scenario was that pollution would take at least 30 to 45 years to become threatening enough to demand self-sacrifice for the sake of the "common good." The Iron Mountain thinkers thought as follows:

> It may be, for instance, that gross pollution of the environment can eventually replace the possibility of mass destruction by nuclear weapons as the principal apparent threat to the survival of the species. Poisoning of the air, and of the principal sources of food and water supply, is already well advanced, and at first glance would seem promising in this respect; it constitutes a threat that can be dealt with only through social organization and political power.

> But from present indications it will be a generation
> to a generation and a half before environmental
> pollution, however severe, will be sufficiently men-
> acing, on a global scale, to offer a possible basis for a
> solution.[11]

If a "generation" equals 30 years (*Webster's New Twentieth Century Dictionary*), then *Report from Iron Mountain's* projected time frame would begin to apply right about . . . now.

The *Iron Mountain* thinkers did not specifically suggest that the concept of an eco-crisis be promoted through the schools— or in any other concrete way—they were thinking much too abstractly for that. But other, more practical men *have* made the obvious connection between schooling and public attitudes. And some have put forth specific suggestions of their own for bringing the eco-crisis/globalism agenda into the public schools.

Norman Lear's New Civil Religion

Norman Lear is one such practical man. Lear, a highly successful TV producer, is founder of People for the American Way (PFAW), an advocacy group that has attacked the presence of (Christian) religion in public life and public schools.

Nevertheless, in November 1989, Lear addressed the American Academy of Religion with an astonishing speech in which he urged educators to open their classrooms to pantheistic spirituality as a new kind of "civil religion." As Lear describes his concept, this ancient spirituality would be presented as the cutting edge in human thought; it would be a "spiritual reorientation, a fresh examination of what we regard as sacred in the universe, on earth, and in our daily lives."[12] Lear's astounding thesis is that the media and the schools should join forces to promote a generic, earth-centered morality and spirituality, for the sake of the common good.

> We need to popularize this sensibility—trumpet
> it in the media and in our schools—and demon-
> strate that respecting the natural dynamics of our
> planet is not just good science, it's a spiritual re-
> sponsibility and pleasure. An ecological morality

and spirituality to fill the gap between science and our religions may be just what we are seeking.[13]

If Lear ever sees his hope fulfilled, he will doubtless find curriculum planners ready to help him propagate his new civil religion. In fact, curriculum programs that teach essentially the same thing are already in use.

Ten years ago, one unit of a social-studies or science class or one chapter of a textbook might have been dedicated to ecology. Today, entire classes and textbooks focus on the environment and dozens of activist organizations are working to shape environmental curricula nationwide. Environmental education has become a growth industry.[14]

Earthkeepers: Mystery Cult

One example is the "Earthkeepers" curriculum, designed and offered by "The Institute for Earth Education" (IEE) in Warrenville, Illinois. The IEE describes itself as "the only organization of its kind dedicated to the development and dissemination of quality, focused environmental education programs."

Officials of the IEE readily acknowledge their own political, cultural, and spiritual bias. They also acknowledge that they are trying to pass that bias on to students by indoctrination. An IEE spokesman recently declared, "We consider Earth Education to be a part of the Educational arm of the deep ecology movement. And we do try to stress in all of our activities and programs a biocentric rather than an anthropocentric world view."[15]

The "Earthkeepers" program is aimed at sixth grade students. Its indoctrination process is structured like an initiatory mystery religion. It begins with the pseudo-scientific assertion that all things are interconnected, and ends with the mystic revelation that the Self is the center of all things. Along the way, several levels of secrecy are revealed and several levels of initiation are attained:

E.M. is the "Keeper of the KEYS" whose secret identity is revealed individually to the participants as they complete their Earthkeeper training and receive their fourth key. . . .

The secret meanings of E.M. are revealed in four stages. After receiving the "K" key on the first day at the Earthkeepers Training Centre, the participants open a locked "K" box and discover the secret meaning of E.M. for Knowledge—E.M. means *Energy and Materials*. After getting their "E" key later on in the program, they open a locked "E" box to discover the secret meaning of E.M. for experience—E.M. means *My Experience*.

The participants receive their "Y" key back at school after completing their personal lifestyle tasks and then open a locked "Y" box to discover the secret meaning of E.M. for Yourself—E.M. means *My Earth*. Finally, they share their knowledge and experience with others to earn their "S" key, and then open the locked "S" box which reveals that E.M. is really *ME*—"I am E.M., the Keeper of the KEYS!"[16]

It is clear that the main purpose of this curriculum is indoctrination. There is very little actual learning about the earth that takes place. What facts there are serve as support for the ideology that is the point of the exercise. "Earthkeepers" is an almost pure form of education as indoctrination (rather than instruction). What C.S. Lewis saw as a nightmare of the future now walks among us in the light of day.

Education and Activism

The politics of environmental crisis requires a certain sense of urgency. If the threat is not strong and immediate, "we will not be moved." Thus, at all grade levels, environmental education tends to speak from a political viewpoint, to speak from a sense of emergency, and to promote political activism as a response.

Many of those who shape environmental education believe that their purpose is not to weigh conflicting facts, values, and theories, but to instill a sense of crisis. "Understanding that the world is going to hell in a handbasket is half of environmental education," says Ed Clark, president of the Wildlife Center of Virginia, which tries to instill respect for animals through school assembly programs.[17]

This attempt to politically "activate" students is not restricted to the higher grades. Second graders at an elementary school in Queens, New York, founded the national KIDS Save the Ozone Project (S.T.O.P.) The S.T.O.P. starter kit for teachers and students "includes blank petitions, personal letters, pledges and a list of suggested projects."[18]

Those examples show why many parents are concerned about so-called education that is really an agenda in disguise. The fact is that children are being trained to take sides on an issue that their parents and elders have not been able to settle among themselves. They are being trained as change agents in ways that their parents probably don't understand, and would probably not agree with if they did. After all, how can second graders conceivably grasp the chlorofluorocarbon controversy? Its chemical, economic, and political components are, for them, beyond even a near approach to understanding. And the S.T.O.P. training will not change that fact—indeed, it is not designed to. Like most eco-education, the training is designed to leave the student with two things: 1) a collection of values and attitudes that are derived from an essentially pantheistic worldview, whether or not that worldview is made explicit; and 2) the belief that environmental problems are to be solved by stirring up an essentially confrontational political process. Both of the above are often integrated into an overall program of debunking that puts black hats on white males, makes bad guys of capitalism, and demonizes Western culture in general.

That process of debunking is carried to its greatest length in "anti-bias" (or "diversity," or "multicultural") education. Anti-bias curriculum design also includes a thorough form of "activism training." A good example is the *Anti-Bias Curriculum: Tools for Empowering Young Children*, published by the influential National Association for the Education of Young Children (NAEYC) of Washington, D.C.[19]

Anti-Bias Education

The Anti-Bias Curriculum (ABC) brings together several versions of politically correct indoctrination under one label. *More important, the ABC claims that its agenda sets the scale of values for the rest of education:*

> The point to remember is that an anti-bias approach is *integrated into* rather than *added onto* existing curriculum. Looking at curriculum through an anti-bias lens affects everything a teacher does. Much classroom work will continue; some activities will be modified, some eliminated, some new ones created. . . . After a while—six months, a year— it becomes impossible to teach without an anti-bias perspective.[20]

In the Middle Ages, Theology was known as the "Queen of Sciences." That title meant that Theology (as the study of God) stood behind and above all other studies to give them context, grounding, structure, and direction. Today, it seems, Political Correctness is making its bid to be the new "Queen of Sciences." Like medieval Theology, "anti-bias education" wants to give context and direction to subsidiary disciplines. Thus Political Correctness endeavors to become the new standard of understanding in all things.

But in that way, the ABC sets itself on a collision course with reality. Ideologies inevitably run into stubborn facts that won't line up the way they're "supposed to." The ABC approach to Halloween, for example, teaches a feminist-revisionist line on history that is demonstrably false.[21] Here, facts are mangled for the sake of ideology:

> Moreover, the mean, ugly, evil witch myth reflects a history of witch hunting and witch burning in Europe and North America—from the Middle Ages through the Salem witch hunts of the 17th Century directed against midwives and other independent women.[22]

The ABC recommends the following Halloween "activities," originally created for an after-school care program (children 4 to 6 years old). The teacher earnestly instructs the children:

> "What I know is that the real women we call witches weren't bad. They really helped people. These women lived a long time ago ... most of the women called witches healed people who were sick or hurt ... the healers were like doctors."
>
> To contrast the prevailing imagery of black and evil (witches, cats, darkness), Kay teaches the children an already existing Halloween chant:
>
> Stirring, stirring, stirring the pot;
> Bubbly, bubbly, bubbly hot
> Look to the moon, laugh like a loon,
> Throw something into the pot.
>
> (This chant is usually accompanied by hand movements. Kay, integrating another aspect of anti-bias curriculum, substitutes signing.)[23]

In general, the ABC promotes the ideological line that is known as "political correctness." That means, among other things, that it is opposed to the traditional culture, opposed to the traditional family, and opposed to traditional sex and gender roles. It also regards potential parental opposition as an inconvenience to be deflected, humored, or, in extreme cases, simply endured.

But the most controversial aspect of the ABC has been its endorsement of activism for children who can have no real concept of its purpose or meaning. The authors of the curriculum make it clear that one of their *central* purposes is to create miniature protesters who are trained to challenge and disrupt whatever system they are a part of in order to achieve whatever goals they can be persuaded are important:

> Children learning to take action against unfair behaviors that occur in their own lives is at the heart of anti-bias education.
>
> Without this component, the curriculum loses its vitality and power. For children to feel good and

confident about themselves, they need to be able to say "That's not fair," or "I don't like that," if they are the target of prejudice or discrimination.... If we teach children to recognize injustice, then we must also teach them that people can create positive change by working together.[24]

This is pernicious education. The fact is that high-schoolers can barely have a workable concept of "justice" and fourth graders can have almost none at all. Most fourth graders can't make a meaningful distinction between "I don't like that" and "that's not fair."

But fourth graders can and do have an exaggerated sense of their own wants, needs, and self-importance. The average primary pupil already has more "self-esteem" than he or she can integrate with the real world. In fact, what most students need is not tips on self-assertion, but ways to deal with the tasks of learning.

Like eco-education, anti-bias education is advanced propaganda, pretending to be schooling. The proportion of ideology to information in the ABC qualifies it as an almost pure form of indoctrination—i.e., of attitude construction. The process of educational deterioration that C.S. Lewis drew attention to at its beginning, seems to be nearing its completion. It seems likely that the results he warned of will follow soon as well.

ABOUT THE AUTHOR

Brooks Alexander, the research director and founder of Spiritual Counterfeits Project, is an expert in the field of New Age, mysticism, and the occult. His penetrating analysis and depth of understanding are widely respected by peers throughout the field of apologetics.

Chapter 15

SEX, DRUGS, AND SCHOOLCHILDREN: WHAT WENT WRONG?

BY DR. W.R. COULSON

In remarks at a conference promoting teenage abstinence from drugs and sex,[1] Pat Funderburk—African-American mother and director of the federal government's Office of Adolescent Pregnancy Prevention—reported on an observed effect of too much "openness" in school classrooms. Her teenage daughter, she said, had told her what happens:

> Momma, when the girls leave the room, we have to go in groups and protect each other. It's because of what they tell us in those classes. The boys get excited. When we walk out the door, Momma, they want to touch your behind. . . . I had to smack one guy.

What are "those classes," and what do they tell students?
They aren't just sex education classes. They include sessions called drug education, health education, family life education, and "death and dying." They tell the students about sex, yes, but they also tell them to pull their chairs into a circle and tell one another about sex, drug use, suicide, feelings, relationships—whatever comes up. The idea is to

practice "in-depth sharing."[2] The theory behind it is that, having opened up, students will be more nearly "self-actualized."

Psychologist A.H. Maslow popularized the concept of self-actualization, but he didn't appreciate the idea that it should be applied to children. Nor did he like the idea that schools should provide children with what he called "unearned applause." By unearned applause he meant various devices for artificially elevating self-esteem; they are often provided in guidebooks that tell teachers how to become "facilitators" and run their own in-depth sharing sessions.

In the sixties there was a lot of misunderstanding about Maslow's views on self-actualization, self-esteem, and children. He tried to straighten out these misunderstandings in the last major writing of his life. It was a revision to his classic text of 1954, *Motivation and Personality*. In 1970, in a lengthy new preface that he called a "critique of self-actualization" and "a marvelous catharsis and fighting-back for me," he wrote that "in [the new edition's] chapter 11 on self-actualization I have removed one source of confusion by confining the concept very definitely to older people. By the criteria I used, self-actualization does not occur in young people. In our culture at least, youngsters have not yet achieved identity, or autonomy...."

Maslow didn't believe children could simply be handed their autonomy. He didn't believe they could be parked in sharing circles, "opened up," allotted a measure of unearned applause, and subsequently could watch their "self-actualization" blossom. He believed instead that they had to earn their way. A hard worker himself, he believed in hard work for children. He thought there was no other way to get educated. In many ways, getting educated was better than getting actualized. His studies had been unable to convince him that more than 1 or 2 percent of the adult population was capable of self-actualization. It was not something for children to spend time on in a classroom.

Maslow listed a dozen reasons why self-actualization might even be dangerous to kids. The list included his observation that American children have not "learned enough about evil in themselves and others to become self-actualized... nor have they generally acquired enough courage to be unpopular, to be unashamed about being openly virtuous. . . ."[3]

He also had objections to the many misinterpretations of the research on self-esteem. Various "true believers" (as he sometimes called them) had taken his concept of "high self-esteem" to represent something entirely positive. But in chapter 14 of *Motivation and Personality* he reinforced some of the negatives that had turned up, not only in his own research but in that of others:

> Eisenberg's studies very strongly supported [my] conclusions. . . . For instance, the high scorers in my test of dominance-feeling or self-esteem were more apt to come late to appointments with the experimenter, to be less respectful, more casual, more forward, more condescending, less tense, anxious, and worried, more apt to accept an offered cigarette, much more apt to make themselves comfortable without bidding or invitation . . . much more apt to be pagan, permissive, and accepting in all sexual realms.[4]

Maslow looked long and hard—and with increasing dismay—at what had become of his theories along the "Eupsychian Network," his name for some 200 educational institutions and "growth centers" that had enthusiastically implemented his views and those of colleague Carl Rogers in the mid-1960s. But things were not going well along the network. He wrote that

> women and children get the short end of things here, as I remember discussing with X, who yearned for continuity, a home, and a child instead of [having sex with] some transient male every once in a while, which she didn't even enjoy. . . . My vague impression is that [random sexual coupling] is much more a male wish-fulfillment than female. The male fantasy of unlimited [sex] without responsibility of any kind to woman or child, a modern version of the older "stag" fantasy. . . .[5]

Maslow's words have returned us to the problem faced by Pat Funderburk's daughter and her female classmates. A certain freewheeling, psychological style of education has developed that seeks too much for openness among students, stirs up their impulses (especially among young men), and winds up putting women and children at risk.

Informal surveys indicate that no small number of adults got in trouble in the sixties and seventies by yielding to "openness inductions" of the sort that are now routinely offered to children as part of the "process" or "affective" approach to education in the lower schools. For example, one popular drug education curriculum offers a classroom "energizer" called Pretzel.

> It involves two teams of five to 15 people each. One person ("it") from each team leaves the room, and each group forms a circle, holding hands. Each group now takes a minute or so to form a "pretzel." This is done by continuing to hold hands and entwining themselves with each other... until they are a mass of bodies, still linked. The "its" are now invited back in. Their job is to untangle the opposing team.[6]

It's this idea that drug or sex education classes might include an "entwining... mass of bodies" that seems questionable, as the experience of students who have had to guard themselves after class—either their bodies or their impulses—also suggests.

Carl Rogers' Role

Process education is derived from the practice of group psychotherapy, especially from encounter groups which were called "therapy for normals" when they began to catch the American imagination in the sixties.[7] In encounter groups, emphasis was on the value of "dropping facades." Psychologist Carl Rogers had as much to do with popularizing this idea as anyone else. But he never meant it to be used against schoolgirls in hallways or on playgrounds after class (i.e., "Come on, baby, drop your facade").

Problems experienced by adult followers of Rogers in recent years can briefly illustrate outcomes increasingly likely to befall children in an era of more and more process-oriented education. At the end of the sixties, Rogers had written that the "intensive group experience" was well on its way to becoming "perhaps the most significant social inventor of this century."[8]

But shortly thereafter, troubling developments began to be recorded in the follow-up surveys of participants. As the planned 20-year follow-up of participants in his Educational Innovation Project of 1967 continued, Rogers gradually developed concerns about what could be called "moral fallout" or "the disappearance of ethics."[9] One version of the problem involved sexual misconduct among counselors who had identified themselves with Rogers' person-centered approach to life, a newer version of his client-centered approach to psychotherapy.[10]

If moral troubles of a sexual sort are rightly to be traced to the massive stimulation of psychological openness within adult encounter groups over the last 20 years, we can anticipate more troubles of the same sort now that children have been drawn into the group movement. In group therapy—any psychotherapy—the most important thing is to get people to talk openly. Much of the practical training to conduct therapy, therefore, focuses on methods for drawing out one's clients. The aim is for clients to learn to identify what their feelings really are. Rather than providing answers, successful group therapists devote themselves to insuring the thoroughness of the process of personal exploration. Successful group therapists never censor or correct.

Inner Experience

We must notice now what is unique about therapy: It is all about inner experience, the subjective realm.

But drug education (and sex education) ought to be about the objective realm, specifically about the objective dangers of using drugs. It ought not to be about remaking the personalities of students, for this cannot be done briefly, cannot be done by amateurs, and, in any case, should not be done in school. It doesn't really matter, then, what schoolchildren feel about drugs (any more than it matters what they feel about the alphabet). There is something to be learned, not something to "explore." What must be learned is that experimenting with drugs hazards their entire futures.

The difference between the subjective and the objective realms (and the related lesson that group therapy misfires if applied to the objective realm) is hard to convey at first to professional students of psychotherapy. They've become conditioned to think in terms of the technical problem—namely, how to bring a patient's inner world to the surface.

A few years back, my colleagues and I found an informal way to convey this difference with a line of dialogue lifted from the Harrison Ford movie *Witness*. Ford plays a government agent investigating a crime. Wounded, he is taken into the home of an Amish family. One day, rising from his sick bed, Ford catches the family's eight-year-old reaching for the agent's loaded pistol. What treatment is offered? The spontaneous voice of a commanding adult: "Samuel!" he shouts, "Never, ever play with a loaded gun!"

Samuel is not asked how he feels about what he's doing. Nor is an offer made to teach him a four-, or six-, or eight-step decision-making regimen. Getting him to make up his own mind about whether loaded guns are dangerous is not what the situation calls for. Instead, a knowledgeable adult leads him through an exercise in single-trial learning. And it is clear at the end of the subsequent conversation between them that the boy has learned. He is unlikely to forget what he must never, ever do.

A typical teacher's guide of a typical process education program takes a different tack. It directs teachers to accept virtually whatever vision of the world a student announces. This is how Quest, the most successful distributor of process education, puts it in the 1986 edition of the Skills for Adolescence Workshop Guidebook: "Don't advise, evaluate, or moralize."[11]

Here is what the problem has become: Process education is badly out-of-date. It reflects the premise of the 1960s and 1970s that everyone has a right to his or her own opinion. It reflects the epistemological conviction that (as it is sometimes said) "each of us has his own reality"—as if eight-year-old Samuel had responded to the "never ever" of the government agent with, "You have a right to your view of guns, but I have a right to mine."

For another drug-education example, the 1986 teacher's guide for Me-ology, a popular process education program, explicitly directs teachers to conduct discussions about drugs "free of right and wrong answers," and it emphasizes that "the instructor is never judgmental." Obviously these rules are offered to the end that everyone is unreserved and that everyone's opinion and feelings be heard in-depth. But what is the subject? Is it drugs or not? What if Johnny or Mary's opinion about drugs is wrong? In process education, this question seems to matter less than it should. The expression of judgment is minimized in favor of playing at being a nondirective, client-centered psychotherapist.

Often the only absolute such programs seem to recognize is that the rules of successful group therapy be honored. For the rest, especially on such subjects as drugs and sex, where young people so desperately need loving and authoritative guidance, students are to make up their own minds. Heavy leverage is applied to insure "group process," but that alone. Again Me-ology illustrates: Students who violate the rules of good group discussion are first required to confess and apologize to the group and, on second offense, to go to the corner.

In such programs, information provided to process learners about the dangers of drugs typically gets less space and emphasis than lessons about "interpersonal communications." Specialists in interpersonal communications tend to denigrate the value of exhortation or persuasion. The issue is sometimes put this way: "It won't work to tell children what to do." But the success of these same specialists in enforcing the rules of group therapy denies that claim. The child who is sent to the corner for being a poor listener and returns from the corner a better listener illustrates this.

For health educators to withhold authoritative teaching on anything more provincial than the rules of group therapy is to underestimate children's willingness to take instruction in matters of importance. It is also to disadvantage them in a market economy. From dealers of one kind and another—whether boys chasing them down the hallway after sex education or billboards advertising cigarettes—they receive memorable advice on undermining their own health; but from health educators they receive little of equivalent weight for preserving it. Consider the most extraordinarily successful advertising campaign in the history of commerce: "Come to where the flavor is." Salesmanship works exceedingly well. Far more children smoke Marlboro cigarettes, the most repetitively advertised brand, than any other.[12]

Concerning decision-making, which is a central component of all the process education methods, students of Meology, for example, are taught that a peer group's habit of forcing "quick decisions" is sufficient reason to resist peer pressure. It's right, of course, to teach children to resist negative peer pressure, but what's implied here is the belief that all will be well for children who make up their minds slowly. The error again lies in the commitment to work the subjective realm alone. In truth, decision-making about drugs ought to have an objective referent. In that sense, no decision about drugs is even necessary. The person must simply face reality.

Students are handicapped for being taught they must make decisions about what reality has already settled for them, as for everyone. To teach decision-making in such matters is to put them seriously at risk. It's understandable that the tobacco industry (or any other trade association marketing dangerous products about which adults have become wary) might want children and their parents and teachers to believe children can make up their own minds. But it's hardly right that society should cooperate in the scheme.

What then do students learn from the contrast between energetic, authoritative instruction offered in school on behalf of good group technique and the idea that, on issues of substance, they must make up their own minds and never ever be "judgmental"? What they learn is that drug educators will take a stand (even to banishing rule-breakers to the corner), but only on matters of importance. Doing the right thing about drugs does not seem to be one of them.

It must be said that the world is so constructed that children cannot prosper in it by their own lights. The vision that guides them will either be the vision of those who love them or the vision of those to whom they are a market. To be a child is to need and deserve guidance. But the only guidance many are getting is from salesmen. Such is the effect of construing children as "decision makers."

Of the caring adults in their lives, too many by now have tumbled to the "therapeutic" idea that the best way to show care is to be nonjudgmental, lest self-actualization be thwarted. But self-actualization was never meant for children, and non-judgmentalism, I have argued here, is a technical psycho-therapeutic principle, not a principle to be invoked in daily life. Children who get their education "free of right and wrong answers" become targets of exploitation. They become prone to experiment with drugs and sex, and thereby lose freedom.

ABOUT THE AUTHOR

A licensed psychologist, *W.R. Coulson* is director of the Research Council on Ethnopsychology and long-time consul-tant to Georgetown University Medical School in Washington, D.C. In the 1980s he served as a member of the Technical Advisory Panel on Drug Education Curricula for the U.S. Department of Education. He has served internships with the psychotherapy research group of the Wisconsin Psychiatric Institute and the neuropsychiatric service of the U.S. Veterans Administration Hospital in Phoenix. He has also served as consultant on ethnopsychology for the Federal Bureau of Prisons and the Office of Juvenile and Delinquency Preven-tion of the U.S. Department of Justice.

Holding doctorates in philosophy from the University of Notre Dame and counseling psychology from the University of Berkeley, in the 1960s Coulson was research associate to Carl R. Rogers and fellow humanistic psychologist, Abraham H. Maslow, at the Western Behavioral Sciences Institute in La Jolla, California. From 1968 to 1974, the two men coedited a series of 17 volumes on humanistic education for Charles E.

Merrill Publishing Company, a major educational textbook firm.

In 1972, Harper and Row published Coulson's preliminary examination of the destructive influence of encounter groups on American education: *Groups, Gimmicks and Instant Gurus.*

Appendixes
Glossary
Books & Resources
Bibliography
Notes
Index

Appendix A

ANTHROPOSOPHICAL EDUCATION: OCCULT REVELATION AND THE WALDORF SCHOOLS

We have had several devoted students of anthroposophy/anthroposophical education (and medicine) vehemently deny that its founder, Rudolf Steiner, ever encouraged any form of spiritism or occultism. But put bluntly, Steiner was a necromancer. He believed resolutely in contacting the dead and other spirits. However, the reader should understand that his use of words such as *spirit*, *spiritual*, and *supersensible* are euphemisms for occult realities. In other words, Steiner's "spiritual science" was occult science, not biblical theology; his "world of spirit" and "spiritual world" referred to the world of the occult. For example, when he referred to "supersensible cognition," he meant clairvoyant vision of the occult world where the spirits of the dead lived. Thus, whenever Steiner used terms like "spiritual world," one may substitute "spirit world," for, like Swedenborg, the beings living there were always predominant in his consciousness.

In simplified terms, Steiner stressed ritual initiation and various forms of meditation as the means to awaken cognition of the spirit realms and even to enter them. Steiner preferred the term "supersensible worlds" and "supersensible knowledge" to describe contact with or information he derived from the spirit world.

His meditational methods utilized mantras, concentration on or absorbing oneself in mental images, and other practices. Even the Bible became a vehicle for occult use (properly utilized in an occult fashion, biblical verses "become an exceedingly significant meditation").[1]

How did Steiner become so enamored with the spirit world? A look at his childhood explains this. Steiner was psychic from a young age and "endowed with innate clairvoyant faculties."[2] At seven he had clairvoyant perception of the astral world. Anthroposophical student McKnight comments that from that time, "He had in fact been conscious of impressions of the spiritual world by which he felt surrounded, but of which he could speak to no one."[3] It was only when he met the Theosophists years later that he found a group of people to whom he could relate. Noted religion professor Dr. Robert S. Ellwood of the University of Southern California affirms that "many stories were told of his clairvoyant and psychic powers. He performed psychic healing on members of the families of many highly placed persons in German Society" prior to World War I.[4]

In his autobiography Steiner discloses an incident when he "was very young indeed"—probably between five and seven. The event involved contact with the dead. A fully materialized apparition (presumably of a recent suicide, but indistinguishable from a normal person) had walked into his room and told him he was to assist the dead: "Try now, and later in life, to help me as much as you can." Steiner confesses the dramatic encounter produced a profound transformation within him, a metamorphosis bringing both animistic and necromantic cognition.[5]

From then on, his life was characteristically guided by unseen powers.[6] Like all committed occultists, he underwent spiritual testing, training, agonizing suffering, and other "preparation" for his future occult work.[7]

That necromantic contacts routinely occurred in Steiner's life and were endorsed by him is unquestionable. It is thus surprising to encounter anthroposophical students who deny this. Steiner taught that anyone who follows the proper "inner mediation" can contact the dead directly: "He makes himself capable of coming in contact with human beings dwelling in the world of spirit between death and a new birth."[8] Further, "The first spiritual beings we encounter will, as a rule, *be the dead with whom we are in some way karmically connected.*"[9]

Steiner maintained that "anthroposophical teaching will bridge the gulf between the so-called living and the so-called dead."[10] Because of his committment to necromancy, Steiner wrote on such topics as "We Can Help Our Dead" and "The Dead Are with Us."[11] In "The Relationship Between the Living and the Dead" he further encourages necromancy and claims, "Every one of us is in constant intercourse with the so-called dead."[12] Steiner also gave instructions for conduct at spiritistic table tapping.[13]

By contrast, the Bible warns:

> There shall not be found among you anyone who . . .
> uses divination, one who practices witchcraft, or one
> who interprets omens, or a sorcerer, or one who casts a
> spell, or a medium, or a spiritist, or one who calls up the
> dead. For whoever does these things is detestable to the
> Lord (Deuteronomy 18:10-12, NASB).

The reason the Bible warns against necromancy is because it is not the dead who are contacted but lying spirits who impersonate them for purposes of deception. For example, if the truly human dead can be indiscriminately contacted, then the unsaved are not in judgment as the Bible teaches (Hebrews 9:27; 2 Peter 2:9; Luke 16:19-31) and faith in Christ is not required for eternal salvation (John 3:16,36). Further, because people think these spirits are departed loved ones and not demons, they trust the spirits' teachings and advice, leading to further spiritual error. All this is why many former mediums have stressed that contact with so-called spirits of the dead is really contact with lying entities who impersonate them.[14] For example, this was Raphael Gasson's conclusion after many years as a professional medium.[15] Yet he confessed:

> As a former Spiritualist minister and active medium,
> it is possible for me to say that at the time of my partici-
> pation in the Movement, I actually believed that these
> spirits were the spirits of the departed dead and that it
> was my duty to preach this to all those with whom I came
> into contact day by day. *It was my earnest desire that mankind
> should accept this "glorious truth" and find joy in the knowledge
> that there was no death.*[16]

But he realized the spirits' true nature when his own control spirit "attempted to kill me when it became obvious I was out to denounce spiritualism."[17]

Nevertheless, Steiner was uncompromising in his attitudes: "The spreading of anthroposophical occult knowledge and the pointing of the way to occult development are vitally necessary. . . . Occult development is a step from semblance towards reality."[18] And, "Occult knowledge is necessary for the whole process of evolution."[19]

Not surprisingly, Steiner's devotion to occultism produced a paganized theology. In texts such as *Christianity As Mystical Fact*, *Christianity and Occult Mysteries of Antiquity*, and *Building Stones for an Understanding of the Mystery of Golgotha*, we discover a thoroughgoing occult reinterpretation of Christianity; every major historic biblical doctrine is repudiated and reinterpreted to teach Gnostic, occult principles.

But nevertheless, one of Rudolf Steiner's most pervasive influences has been in educational theory for teachers. *MD*, a medical news magazine, commented, "Perhaps the most famous of Steiner's courses are the ones in pedagogy, which to some degree have influenced modern educators the world over."[20]

Thus, besides his significant contribution to occultism, Steiner is perhaps most well-known for his development of the Waldorf schools. In 1907 he wrote *The Education of the Child in the Light of Anthroposophy*, which became the model for his occult educational method, "based on a totally new [anthroposophical] consideration of man and therefore of the growing child."[21] For example, his educational philosophy teaches that karma from a past life may lead supposed discarnate spirits to inhabit sick or deformed bodies. The special education of the Waldorf schools is designed in part to help these souls develop new strength for their next incarnation.[22] Reputedly, some 40,000 children in Europe and America (mostly Europe) attend Waldorf schools. For example, over 200 Waldorf schools exist in Germany alone.

In America, the *Elementary School Journal* observed that the Waldorf schools were the "second largest nondenominational private school system in the world." It also noted, "An important aspect of Waldorf education is Steiner's theory of human development and school readiness, which is based on an ancient but recently rediscovered concept of growth . . . [through] vital forces, or bioplasmic energy"— in essence occult energy. Thus,

> The curriculum of the Waldorf Schools is based on this theory of developing and transmuted growth energy. . . . The sustenance of these bioplasmic forces during the growing years permits the physical body and the bioplasmic forces to remain more pliable longer. Hence, the child has greater capacity for intellectual growth and creativeness.[23]

Journalist Stephen Davis points out that Steiner's anthroposophical program "was designed to illuminate the world with occult knowledge"[24] and that "the mystical system of anthroposophy . . . forms the [Waldorf] schools' philosophical underpinnings."[25]

As a result of this approach, "Ritual and ceremony are an important part of the lives of the younger children in many of the schools. In some, first graders form a 'morning circle' around lighted candles and recite chants and praise of the wonders of the natural world."[26] The Steiner system of education is intended to develop fully the "noncognitive faculties of children in the early grades" and has as its ultimate goal the attainment of "full consciousness on the part of both school and child."[27]

Nevertheless, Rudolf Steiner emphasized that Waldorf schools were not to become places to teach anthroposophy. For example, in his *Education As an Art*, he emphasized that Waldorf schools were least of all "concerned with introducing anthroposophical 'dogma'... into the school."[28]

When someone talks to Waldorf teachers they will also emphasize that their schools do not teach anthroposophy. But this is something of a half-truth. It is true that the entire occult/philosophical religion of anthroposophy is not taught in Waldorf schools. Nevertheless, the underlying philosophy of anthroposophy, including its view of the nature of man, the world, the cosmos, and everything else, undergirds Waldorf education to varying degrees. Given the fact that Rudolf Steiner was a committed occultist, who had received much or most of his philosophy on life from the spirit world, the philosophy of anthroposophy is to a large extent a philosophy revealed by the spirits. What this means is that children attending Waldorf schools are ultimately being educated in a system based to some degree upon teachings received from the spirit world.

Because the claim is widely made that Waldorf schools are really quite separate from anthroposophical belief, we wish to show that this is not exactly the case. Steiner himself confessed that Waldorf education "takes its own stand on the basis of modern educational thinking by deepening and broadening what has been done, by making use of what can be studied and discovered by anthroposophy."[29] He also concedes that "an anthropological foundation" underlies the Waldorf school.[30] Thus, he freely agrees that, "The aim at the Waldorf School is to teach and educate according to the findings of the science of spirit."[31] (For Steiner, the term "science of spirit" was another word for anthroposophy.)

Second, Steiner is clear that the Waldorf teacher, although not teaching anthroposophy directly, is to seek to integrate the findings of anthroposophy into the life of the child. For example,

> And above all he [the Waldorf teacher] needs a deeper knowledge of the human being than present day science can give him. On the basis of this deeper knowledge of the human being, that is, on the basis of what the science of spirit comes to know about the human being ... [the

teacher learns] to handle the child according to what the
human organism itself demands of the educator, the
teacher. . . . The Waldorf teacher holds the conviction that
what he meets in the child from week to week, from year
to year, is the expression of a divine spiritual being that
descends from purely spirit-soul existence and evolves
here in the physical-bodily existence between birth and
death, uniting the line of heredity which gives it its
physical-etheric nature from parents and ancestors.[32]

In other words, the Waldorf teacher is to view the children he/she
teaches as being incarnate spirits according to the larger anthroposophical cosmology. Thus because of the teacher's "knowledge of
anthroposophy . . . he can adapt and change his method according to
what the child needs."[33] For example, the anthroposophical teacher
is well aware that the child supposedly has both an etheric and astral
body and that these can be recognized through meditative or occultic
exercises. Even though these ideas are not introduced into the school
itself, "Those who are to teach and educate the child gain the possibility of looking at the evolving person in such a way that he can
approach the innermost being of the child through what he has
learned about man as a being of body, soul and spirit."[34]

Thus, occult anthroposophy itself, according to Steiner, becomes
for the teacher "a means of orientation" for his educational philosophy:[35]

In getting to know the human being by means of the
science of spirit we become able to distinguish the more
inward astral body and the more external etheric body.
. ... The science of spirit teaches me how I stimulate a
particular part of the soul that brings about a certain
relationship between the educator and the child, which
allows something to flow from the teacher directly to the
innermost feeling-life of the child's soul.[36]

Third, Steiner believed that Waldorf schools, or schools with similar
perspectives, should become the basis for a worldwide educational
movement. If children were "fostered spiritually in a world association of schools [this] would bring the peoples of the whole earth
together."[37] Thus, he wrote,

I am convinced that nothing is more important for the
social development of humanity than the foundation of

such a world association of schools which would then awaken a real sense for a free cultural and spiritual life in the widest circles of people.[38]

In essence, although some may claim that the Waldorf schools have nothing to do with anthroposophical philosophy, this is simply not so because anthroposophical premises underlie their educational method. Consider an article written by anthroposophical teacher Nora Vaughn Baditz, "The Needs of Young Children: A Guide for Parents and Teachers." Here we see how the assumption that the child is a reincarnated being guides the approach of the teacher to his/her students. She observes the following of the Waldorf student:

> The child comes down to earth from other [spirit] regions, and he has first to know and love the earth. Everything depends on this "way down to earth"—the strengthening of the child's functions, his soul's enjoyment of the earth, his spirit becoming able to carry out the decisions to incarnate fully—all depend on this.[39]

This is why Dr. Geoffrey Ahern points out the anthroposophical flavor of the Waldorf schools. In his scholarly treatment, *Sun at Midnight: The Rudolf Steiner Movement and the Western Esoteric Tradition* he observes the following:

> Anthroposophical "Waldorf" education . . . can only really be understood if integrated with Steiner's cosmology. . . . He believed that everything tangible in the solar system has condensed and "fallen" into matter from an original state of a [divine] spirit. The cosmos is (by no means smoothly) starting to respiritualize. . . . Its end is the heightening and extending of the consciousness of one's spiritual individuality. . . . The individual as a microcosism is part of this evolutionary spiritual progress. Through the path of knowledge, through Imagination, Inspiration and Intuition, the future respiritualization can be anticipated to some extent on earth now. Much of the Steiner adult education . . . is directly concerned with the transmutation of matter and cosmic respiritualization. . . .
> Steiner's revelation is not taught directly at primary or secondary levels. This, it is thought, would preclude later free choice as an individual. But, inevitably, the

social context, the ambiance is Anthroposophical. (Here the macrocosism is seen as being faithfully reflected to pupils.)

It seems, for example, that rebirth is not taught explicitly; but the soul may be compared to a butterfly that has developed from a chrysalis. Steiner believed that—reflecting the macrocosism—human beings develop in seven-year stages. At the birth of the physical body there is a spiritual nature (the "etheric") in an "envelope" around the baby assisting its growth, just as, before birth, the mother enveloped the fetus.... Anthroposophical education starts from the pre-natal preparation of the mother.[40]

In other words, it cannot be logically denied that anthroposophical ideas which were originally derived from the spirit world influenced Waldorf education. The question then becomes, who were the spirits that gave this information to Steiner? If they were lying spirits, then no child who is educated under anthroposophical premises can be expected to benefit from such an approach to education.

Let us consider one more example proving anthroposophical ideas undergird Waldorf education.

L. Francis Edmunds was chairman of the Rudolf Steiner Educational Association for 15 years and is vice president of the Steiner Schools Fellowship Limited, the official association of the Waldolf schools in Great Britain. He has pioneered several Waldorf schools in New York, Los Angeles, and Mexico City. In his *Rudolf Steiner Education: The Waldorf Schools*, he points out that although Waldorf schools do not teach anthroposophy directly, the Waldorf educational method is based on Steiner's philosophy:

One cannot be long acquainted with a Waldorf School without hearing of Rudolf Steiner and his teaching which he called Anthroposophy.... Anthroposophy offers disciplines whereby any one who has the will can develop ... [intuitive] faculties, possessed by all human beings in varying degree, into higher organs of perception.... The teacher admits his great indebtedness to Rudolf Steiner.... Do we teach Anthroposophy? No, we do not, but we try to teach in such a way that it may lead towards the fullness of an [inner mystical freedom]... that it may open ways, within the grasp of each one, to advance his inner life, and therefore also outer life, further. To help towards this is possible through education.[41]

Thus, another premise of Waldorf education is the concept of childhood enlightenment based on the belief in reincarnation:

> Rudolf Steiner, by the methods he describes, was able to arrive at quite special forces of insight into nature and human nature. Out of this insight he could then evolve a form of education addressed to the full measure of a human being. We, too, with his help, may arrive at a totally new conception of man: we may learn to recognize him as a being of body, soul and spirit, and so bring into practice an education which attends to all three. . . . Childhood assumes quite another importance for us if we learn to view it as an incarnating process which partly conforms to the laws of physical nature and partly transcends these laws. Indeed, the true nature of man lives in his *non-nature*, in the world beyond outer nature which declares itself in him. Thus each human life is the revelatin of an immortal spirit which was before birth and which will be after death. . . . The object of Rudolf Steiner education is to aid children so that as men and women they may bring their powers, their own innate and sacred human qualities, to greater fulfillment. It is an education which serves the [occult] *freedom of the human spirit.*[42]

Thus, anthroposophical education attempts to usher in a new level of human awareness and even a new humanity because:

> We find ourselves entangled in the decaying elements of an old world order with its traditional faiths and authorities . . . [while] the world awaits the birth of a new faith, a new vision, and a new conscience, a new awakening to the reality of man as a spiritual [occult] being. . . . It is out of a renewed knowledge of man, a knowledge imbued with wisdom (Anthropos-Sophia) that Waldorf education has been born. Waldorf education directs itself to the growing forces of the child.[43]

What all this means is that the Waldorf teacher is to be a sage of a particular type:

> A teacher needs to be an artist, he needs to practice *the art of education*. He needs to be of the order of the magi [an occultist], an interpreter of wisdom, a magician who can

conjure up reality in a thousand forms, a servant of truth drawn from a higher source of reason. This provides nourishment for growing. Lacking this we are poor indeed and our children must then needs be poverty-stricken.[44]

For example, in Waldorf education all religions are taught as coming from the same source and as being summed up in the same occult Christ of Steiner's philosophy:

The Christ Event in its dynamic and evolutionary aspect is looked upon as the fulcral centre of all that story, seen in its intimate connection with the advance to ego-consciousness typical of the whole human race. This is a view that transcends that of any particular religion, for it has room for all of them, yet paying due reverence and regard to each. Religion lessons are given in most of our schools.... Eurythmy... plays an important part in all our schools.[45]

Indeed, many Waldorf teachers—probably most—are committed disciples of anthroposophy, and nearly all admit their "great indebtedness to Rudolf Steiner."[46]

In conclusion, when Waldorf schools claim they do not teach anthroposophical dogma, technically this is true. But no one should assume that anthroposophical ideas have no influence in Waldorf education.

Appendix B

MONTESSORI EDUCATION

No one can deny the influence of modern Montessori education. As Montessori teacher Elizabeth G. Hainstock observes in *The Essential Montessori*,

> By the mid 1960's the Montessori Method was one of the fastest developing and most talked about phenomena on the American educational scene. Over the years it has been closely examined by and has found support from important leaders in the fields of education and child psychology. Its greatest application has been in the preschool and primary grades, and its influence has been great. There are now over 3,000 accredited Montessori schools in the United States, and Maria Montessori's philosophy and materials are used in numerous public school classrooms, in the field of special education, and in federally funded programs such as Headstart and day care centers. The method has proven itself adaptable to all social strata and specialties within the educational spectrum, serving the objectives of many situations and applications. . . . Her method has become a part of every teacher-training course, and there are several hundred such courses specifically concerned with providing the Montessori credentials.[1]

Maria Montessori was born in 1870. As one concerned with radical reform of "outdated" educational methods, she was deeply influenced by Jacques Rousseau (1712-1778), Johann Pestalozzi (a follower of Rousseau), and Friedrich Froebel—all of whom stressed the inner potential of the child and his ability, with proper guidance, to develop along his own natural lines.[2]

But Montessori was also influenced by Hindu philosophy. For example, in 1939 she arrived in India to establish an educational training center.

> She was warmly received in this country, where her method had been growing in popularity; her ideas had many parallels with the Theosophy of the Indians. Interned there during the war years as an Italian national, she became closely involved with the people and their culture. Her time in India strongly influenced her, introducing a mystical quality into her thoughts and writings, which was probably better suited to the ways of India than to more rationalist cultures abroad.[3]

Montessori's basic philosophy is given in her books such as *Education for a New World*, *To Educate the Human Potential*, and *The Montessori Method*. In *Education for a New World* she describes her basic educational philosophy as a significant restructuring of educational method and approach to children:

> If education were to continue along the old lines of mere transmission of knowledge, the problem [of humanity] would be insoluble and there would be no hope for the world. . . . We have before us in the child a psychic entity, a social group of immense size, a veritable world-power if rightly used. If salvation and help are to come, it is from the child, for the child is the constructor of man, and so of society. The child is endowed with an inner power which can guide us to a more luminous future. Education should no longer be mostly imparting of knowledge, but must take a new path, seeking the release of human potentialities.[4]

What are the "human potentialities" that Montessori wanted to unleash? In part, they deal with the inner powers of the child:

> Observation proves that small children are endowed with special psychic powers, and point to new ways of drawing them out—literally educating—by cooperating with nature. . . . So far is man from recognizing the riches that lie buried in the psychic world of the child, that from the beginning he has continued to repress those energies and grind them into the dust.[5]

Montessori's use of the word *psychic* was principally in a psychological sense, although the occult meaning was not at all to be ruled out. For example, she observes,

> The ancient art of palmistry is based on the recognition of the hand as a psychic organ; its practitioners claim that the whole history of the man is written on the palm of his hand. Therefore, the study of the psychic development of the child should be closely linked with the study of the development of the hand.[6]

Montessori opposed traditional education[7] and instead put forth her own plan. Thus, "An ordinary teacher cannot be transformed into a Montessori teacher, but must be created anew, having rid herself of pedagogical prejudices."[8]

Montessori held that imagination was essential for both teacher and student. The "secret of good teaching" is to encourage the child's intelligence and to so "touch his imagination as to enthuse him to his inmost core."[9]

Montessori saw her educational method as part of "the Cosmic Plan in which all, consciously or unconsciously, serves the great Purpose of Life":[10]

> This plan of cosmic education as a foundation stone of the Advanced Method was first explained in England in 1935, and it has already proved itself to be the only path on which our feet can firmly tread in further educational research. . . . It is received with joy by the child who has indirectly been prepared for it in the Montessori School.[11]

When Montessori refers to the newly-born child as "the secret of an infinite taking bounded form," she reveals her view of the divine potential of humanity because

> super-nature is now his background of potentiality. A wider, loftier life is his than ever before, and children have to be prepared for it, so the fundamental principal in education is correlation of all subjects, and their centralizations in the cosmic plan.[12]

Although the Montessori method is generally seen as a spiritual method, its spiritual applications vary from neutral to New Age. Montessori schools vary in their educational and philosophical approaches, and there are even approaches labeled "Montessori" that have little to do with the Montessori method per se.

The three primary principles most Montessori schools stress are 1) early childhood development, 2) the learning environment, and 3) the role of the teacher. While forming the foundation of Montessori education, they have blossomed into a variety of educational approaches. Montessori's *Cosmic Education* has the goal of developing the child as a total being, especially the child's inner creative potential. Thus, the spiritual aspect of Montessori education involves "a philosophy beyond all religion" and demonstrates the idea that "the infinite manifests in the finite" and then evolves back upward in consciousness.[13]

> Cosmic Education stimulates and encourages the individual to listen to and follow his inner intuitive promptings on the one hand, and provides him with the means and tools to apply them analytically and constructively on the other hand.... Therefore, Cosmic Education is truly an education for the development of the whole human being, body, mind and spirit.[14]

The Encyclopedia Britannica summarizes by noting that the Montessori system emphasizes "development of initiative and sense perception through physical freedom and self-help instructional materials ... [and the] early development of reading and writing skills." Further,

> A large measure of individual initiative and self-direction characterize the Montessori philosophy, and self-education was the keynote of the plan. The teacher provided and demonstrated a special "didactic apparatus" but remained in the background, leaving the child to handle it for himself. In the Montessori system biological and mental growth are linked. "Periods of sensitivity," corresponding to certain ages, exist when a child's interest and mental capacity are best suited to the acquisition of certain specialized knowledge.[15]

Montessori's theories were formulated in response to the intellectual climate of the day and, as a psychiatrist, some of her educational observations were astute. The Montessori method does have its critics, and we would refer readers to the literature pro and con for assessing the problems and merits of her educational philosophy.

We are not here concerned with discussing the Montessori philosophy or method in detail, but rather how that method can easily be used in New Age education. For example, Joyce McDavid directed the County Montessori School in San Antonio, Texas, for almost two decades. As an active member of the occult Theosophical Society, she has lectured widely on both theosophical occultism and the Montessori method of education. She has her master's degree in early childhood education and accepts the wisdom of the theosophical "masters" (spirit entities) that inspired Theosophical Society founder Helena P. Blavatsky. For example, in one article on education she cites the spirit known as "Master K.H." This spirit says the following,

> [With] true spiritual intuition . . . the world will have discovered that individuals *have it in their own power* to procreate Buddha-like children—or demons. When that knowledge comes, all dogmatic religions, and with these the demons, will die out.[16]

Thus, she observes,

> It is evident to students of occultism that man is a being with a complete identity, even when newborn. . . . The being which inhabits that body may be very old and wise, yet unable to express that wisdom because of the limitations of the new body. The soul must build for itself a proper human form. This is the work of the child. . . . The work of parents is to aid this procedure in a loving and truly enlightened way.[17]

James W. Peterson is a practicing theosophist, volunteer worker at the Berkeley Montessori School, and author of *The Secret Life of Kids: An Exploration into Their Psychic Senses*. He recalls,

> A thirteen-year-old boy . . . was meditating one day and suddenly had a vivid vision of the entire mystic scheme of creation. . . . He "saw" himself being reincarnated in human bodies countless times before beginning the journey back to the source of life—God—through various stages of expanding consciousness.[18]

Peterson also comments on

> the educational importance and implications of obtaining a clear understanding of these [psychic] perceptions

of children and [discussing] the ways in which these
faculties can be better explained to children, and possibly
more easily integrated into their mental life, for often
such faculties are a nuisance and a burden to the children
who possess them.[19]

Not surprisingly, the Montessori emphasis on educating the
"whole child" logically opens the doors to holistic or transpersonal
education. For example, at the Montessori Children's Center in Pasadena, California, children are actively taught yoga. According to
Mary Jo Lewis, founder and vice president of the Montessori Children's Center and coauthor of *Not Too Young for Yoga*, "It gives young
yoga students the experience of being engaged in a process of self-discovery"—in fact, yoga is encouraged for children as young as
three.[20]

Another example can be seen in the lecture notes of Ursula Thrush,
who teaches a course at the University of California at Berkeley
Education Extension called "The Montessori Method: A Holistic
Approach to Education."

Thrush is a teacher at the Maria Montessori School of the Golden
Gate in San Francisco, and her lecture notes have been published as
Cosmic Education According to Maria Montessori. She describes Montessori's mysticism in the following terms—to a degree reminiscent
of the philosophy of spiritists Sri Aurobindo and Rudolf Steiner:

Montessori felt that mankind has a double function to
perform: (1) to spiritualize matter and (2) to evolve the
cosmos. To spiritualize matter means to master and transcend it, to recognize it for what it really is. [To evolve the
cosmos] . . . she pointed to the redeeming potential of the
child whom she called the spiritual embryo, and the role
education may play in his life.[21]

In this role, consciousness plays an important function. Montessori's goal was to bring about an adult human being, truly independent,
who has adapted to his environment and found his proper place in
the cosmos, well able to fulfill his own higher potential.

To achieve this he first has to recognize his own potential. He has to dare to follow his inner promptings and to
act on them. . . . Consequently, this development has to
do with increasing self-awareness, that is consciousness
and its consequent independence.[22]

Further, according to Thrush:

> The spiritual embryo is pure spirit who comes into life manifesting the infinite in finite form, physically and psychologically. It is absolutely pure and constructs itself through interaction with the environment.

Thrush points out that the spiritual entity is aided by what is termed *horme*, which she equates to the occult concept of kundalini energy.[23] According to Thrush, Montessori referred to her psychological approach as the formation of man.

> What this entails is that originally consciousness involved and expressed itself in matter. Consciousness now evolves out of matter; that is what she sees as the function of mankind—to realize how matter came into being in the first place, how it evolved to mankind's present stage of consciousness, and to leave it up to the future where this evolving consciousness may take man who is evolving the cosmos. This progression may be seen as a macrocosism, and the pattern of development of every newborn child, of every individual life, can be seen as a microcosmic expression of the very same progression.[24]

In discussing the *spiritual* aspect of Montessori's approach (that which is beyond the physical and mental/emotional aspects), Thrush also describes it as "a philosophy beyond all religion," illustrating in Montessori's theory "that the infinite manifest in the finite."[25] Thus, as a Montessori teacher, Thrush believes, "Education should direct itself toward deeper consciousness of the self and toward greater freedom. It should direct itself against all the errors preventing the development of these two main characteristics."[26]

In conclusion, Montessori education seems to be offered on a spectrum of approaches, depending on the philosophy of the educational institution and teacher. On the one hand, Montessori was exposed to Hindu and theosophical concepts, incorporating some into her educational theory. The citations of her by some followers almost make her seem like an occultist. On the other hand, much of what Montessori writes is her own unique pedagogy and not anything New Age unless appropriated by New Agers who see parallels with their own worldview. Thus, readers should evaluate the Montessori system on the basis of 1) its educational theory as evaluated by reputable educators, 2) how her occult view of the child as an incarnation of the infinite may condition the Montessori teacher's approach to educational method, and 3) the eclectic nature of the Montessori method as it is found in the world today.

Appendix C

PROPOSED POLICY STATEMENT (SAMPLE)

[To be drafted in accordance with local, legal, and technical vocabulary and requirements.]

I. The First Amendment of the United States Constitution states that "Congress shall make no law respecting an establishment of religion. . . ."

However, the U.S. Supreme Court has stated "that education without the study of religion is incomplete and that such study is not prohibited by the First Amendment" (*Abington* v. *Schempp* and *Murray* v. *Curlett*).

Therefore, it is the policy of the [your state] State Board of Education that its schools may educate about religions but may not promote, conform, impose, or indoctrinate students with the beliefs or practices of a religion. The approach of public education to religion is to be academic, not promotional or devotional.

In most cases, religious subject matter is readily identifiable, but recently there have appeared many curricula and techniques, some of which may or may not appear to have only secular significance, but may have important religious connotations.

A significant trend in curricula and techniques is the utilization of practices adapted from Eastern religion's meditation and yoga under the rubrics of stress reduction, enhancement of creativity, guidance counseling, enhancement of self-esteem, alcohol and drug prevention, and decision-making/problem-solving skills.

In addition to the inappropriateness of promoting and instructing students in various techniques of Eastern mystical religions, there is the concern of students utilizing standard induction techniques of hypnosis, which are similar or analogous to Eastern meditation practices.

For example:

1. *Progressive relaxation*—This activity involves the serial relaxation of a person. The sequence utilized may include elements such as turning off the lights; closing the eyes; reclining; deep, measured breathing exercises; counting backward; listening to soothing music; focusing on and repeating a single word or phrase; a process of tensing and relaxing muscle groups; guided imagery; or visualization exercises.

Many of the elements in progressive relaxation are recognized induction techniques for Eastern meditation and/or hypnosis, and are briefly described as follows:

a. *Guided imagery or visualization*—This involves the use of images communicated to the listener while he or she is in a relaxed or altered state of consciousness.

b. *Hypnosis*—An induced trance wherein a person is made highly suggestible. While this may be used in adult counseling therapy, it is inappropriate for use in a school setting.

c. *Meditation*—The production of a passive mental state for physical, psychological, or religious purposes.

d. *Deep breathing*—Measured deep breaths (slow, long, and regular), sometimes holding the breath, sometimes utilizing alternate nostril breathing, for the purpose of inducing a deep or relaxed, dissociative state.

2. *Yoga*—A series of exercise postures and meditation designed to facilitate the development of body-mind-spirit. Its stated purpose is to align the body's alleged psychic centers (*chakras*) into union with universal energy to produce "enlightenment." Yoga typically underlies Eastern mystical religious practices.

It is the Board's policy decision that these techniques promote the beliefs and practice of religion and are therefore subject to the Board policy which prohibits the practice of religion in schools.

Therefore, students in [your state] public schools should not be requested, encouraged, instructed, or invited to participate in techniques such as progressive relaxation, guided imagery, sequential deep-breathing exercises, creative visualization, meditation, hypnosis, or yoga.

II. It is the policy of the State Board of Education that no illegal activities will be proposed to public school students of [your state] as acceptable behavior or as options for their consideration.

Consistent with federal law, [your state] schools will teach students that "the use of illicit drugs and the unlawful possession and use of alcohol is wrong and harmful" (Drug-Free Schools and Communities Act of 1986, as amended by Public Law 101-226, December 12, 1989, United States Code, Title 20, Section 3224a).

Any program of health education shall attempt to persuade students of the impermissibility of unhealthy personal conduct. Prime among these behaviors are drug use, suicide attempts, and premarital sex [insert your state's legal codes]. These activities may not be regarded as subject matters to which students are to apply subjective decision-making processes any more than for truancy. Rather, students of the public schools of this state will be taught to perceive these behaviors as health-threatening and impermissible.

III. It is the policy of the [your state] State Board of Education that any programs in [your state] schools which intend to influence students' attitudes, emotions, values, or behavior must be cognitive and directive programs which employ objective criteria to produce the intended result, and must be shown by reliable scientific evidence to produce such a result. Group counseling using psychological techniques shall not be done in the regular classrooms of this state. Where there is an identified need for help with emotional and/or behavioral problems, an individual plan shall be worked out by the school counselor upon receipt of fully informed, written parental consent. Thus, psychological counseling is to be done only after this need is identified, and not in a proactive way with entire classrooms.

Appendix D

State Senate Report Condemns Michigan Model

BY *K. Craig Branch*

A lawsuit filed by the Rutherford Institute representing parents against the Michigan State Board of Education prompted a large grassroots protest around that state.

The protests were directed toward the nationally famous *Michigan Model for Comprehensive School Health Education,* as the parents objected that the same issues detailed in this book were being imposed on their children by this curriculum. The objections focused on the 40 percent of the curriculum dealing with emotional and mental health.

The lawsuit and the objections centered on the fact that the Constitutional right to privacy, the parents' rights to govern their children, and the children's right to be free from psychological testing and treatment were being violated.

Because of the substantiative issues raised by its citizens, the Michigan Senate passed a resolution to set up a select committee to hold hearings. After 12 hearings held around the state with thousands of attendees and hundreds of witnesses including parents, teachers, and health educators, the committee issued a scathing report.

The report presented 30 findings concerning the curriculum and the way it was imposed on the families by the Michigan public school establishments, and made 30 recommendations.

The report states that when parents' concerns were brought before the educational establishment, they were ignored and in many cases ridiculed, which brought "parental frustration to a boiling point"

and thus "public confidence in public education was being threatened in a massive way."

Some of the findings of the committee were as follows:

— *The Michigan State Board of Education Was Too Far Removed from
Families to Make Effective Educational Policy.*

— *Parents Are Being Denied Choice About Michigan Model and
Nondirective Affective Education Classes.*

The stridency of local school district administrators toward
parents who have concerns about the Michigan Model or
any other curriculum needs to be dealt with. At best, many
administrators have exercised extreme arrogance in their
dealings with parents about the Michigan Model.

This is of enormous importance strategically because it exposes
the problem and the possible subversive action taken by some professional educators. It also demonstrates the negative political and
public relations consequences of not passing regulations prohibiting
transpersonal education.

— *Because of Mixed Messages About Premarital Sex, Michigan Model
Lessons Result in Increased Adolescent Sexual Promiscuity.*

— *The Michigan Departments of Education and Public Health Had
Organized a Campaign to Discredit Concerned Parents.*

The strategy of the Michigan Model Steering Committee
was simple. Any parent or teacher who got in the way of
implementing the Michigan Model at a local school district
was to be labeled a right wing, fundamentalist Christian
fanatic. The education establishment painted a picture of
that person that would qualify as slander in any court of law.
The opposition was to be squashed.

*Recommendation: The Michigan Attorney General and U.S.
Justice Department should investigate to determine if parental civil
rights were violated.*

— *Parents Are Being Denied Rights to Make Choices for Their Children.*

Many parents around the state were told either explicitly
or implicitly that they had no rights in deciding what their
children were being taught.

— *"Calm Breathing" Could Be Hazardous to Your Child's Health.*

When queried about the nature of calm breathing and the quieting reflex, the educational establishment expressed incredulity that "anybody could think three deep breaths would pose any danger to a student."

But what they failed to address was that many of the breathing exercises resemble the mystical elements of Eastern religions. There is not only a breach of church and state separation, but lack of acknowledgment that an altered state of consciousness can be induced through these breathing methods. Used by an inexperienced teacher, such exercises can produce hypnotic states in some children.

Recommendation: Warnings should be given to parents and research should be done about potential harmful effects.

— *Many in the Educational Community Treat Parents with Arrogance and Mistrust.*

They communicate to parents that they are the professionals and the parents are the unschooled amateurs. This anti-family attitude builds a wall of separation between the school and parents.

— *The Michigan Model Never Received Appropriate Evaluation to Determine Its Efficacy in the Classroom.*

— *School-Parent Communication Is in a State of Serious Disrepair.*

Many parents discovered that their children were receiving lessons on mental health, using nontraditional approaches after the fact.

Recommendation: We feel strongly that parents are the number one decision-makers for their children, and that public school employees, at whatever level, should be sensitive to this.

— *The Boundaries Between Church and State Were Violated with New Age Teachings.*

"It was a common refrain in much of the testimony we [the Senate committee] heard around the state. A large number of parents felt that many of the Michigan Model basics contained New Age teachings. At first blush, it's really hard to see how one can see Eastern mysticism, the occult, or the New Age in any of the lessons in the curriculum."

The committee started to see a troubling pattern emerge. The New Age is there in the Michigan Model. It's there under the guise of something else: relaxation techniques, calm breathing, problem-solving, values clarification, yoga, and meditation. [Even the senators failed to understand that yoga and meditation are clearly part of Eastern mysticism.]

Recommendation: Public schools should be vigilant and held accountable, so they do not endorse the religious teachings or practices of any religion.

The Senate Committee report also lists 18 of the main objectives from the hundreds of testifying parents and the committee response. Included in the objections were that the approach and techniques of the Michigan Model taught students to seek help from teachers and others before family; that students could decide for themselves what is right and wrong; that students were put in danger of being hypnotized; that classroom teachers became amateur psychotherapists with their children; that the model fostered techniques and teachings of the New Age Movement; that it promoted a form of transcendental meditation; and that it regularly resulted in invasions of family and student privacy.

The findings from the select committee agree with every issue raised by the Michigan parents. These are the same concerns being raised all over the country concerning the same approaches and techniques in various curricula and programs.

School board members need to be shown this information as it helps to validate the legitimacy of parental concerns. Full copies of the Senate Report can be obtained through Senator Gilbert DiNello's office, 26th District, P.O. Box 30036, Lansing, Michigan 48909-7536 (phone: 517-373-7315) or by contacting Watchman Fellowship (see Organization and Resource List, p. 319).

Appendix E

■

QUEST

The section on Quest (pp. 52-63) should be read on the basis of the following observations. First, according to Quest Senior Vice President Dave Miller, there are many Christians who accept this program, such as Bob Tiede with Josh McDowell Ministries in Dallas, Dr. Ted Ward of Trinity Seminary in Chicago, formerly a professor of education at Michigan State University, author Charlie Shedd, and Cliff Anderson, director of Young Adolescent Research with Young Life.

Second, the main concern of critics is Quest's lack of moral absolutes and its affective approach to education, wherein, e.g., children are taught to find values within themselves.

Third, Quest claims the affective approach to education was found only in the *Skills for Living* portions. Quest recently dropped its *Skills for Living* materials without an admission of controversy or noting concern over the affective approach to education.

Fourth, according to Quest, the *Skills for Adolescence* portion was revised in March of 1993, partly in response to criticism.

Our analysis concerns the 1982 version of *Skills for Living* critiqued in the 1987 Beeker paper. According to Citizens for Excellence in Education of Costa Mesa, California, to the best of their knowledge this material was basically accurate at the time of publication. Dave Miller, Senior Vice President of Quest, labeled Quest programs at this time as a "reflection of the best thinking for its time." Although this information is not currently distributed by Quest, it is still *used* in many school systems, hence its inclusion.

We also include this material to illustrate the problems involved in curriculum development, but not necessarily as a critique of the current Quest materials. Able critiques of current Quest materials may be found in the critical literature.

Fifth, there is currently conflicting information about Quest with claims and counterclaims being advanced. Critics of Quest, such as Dr. W.R. Coulson and Dr. William Kilpatrick, maintain that Quest remains an affective approach while Quest itself denies this. According to conversation with Dave Miller of Quest International, "the implication that we have turned kids against parents, onto drugs, and into a moral vacuum are accusations unsubstantiated by data. In fact, we have strong data showing and suggesting just the opposite." But Dr. Robert L. Simonds, president of Citizens for Excellence in Education, maintains, "Post Quest analysis studies show an increase in sexual, drug, and alcohol abuse . . ." (letter to Dr. Weldon, March 2, 1993).

Regardless, not everyone agrees that Quest is without problems. James C. Dobson, president of Focus on the Family, stated the following in the *Focus on the Family Citizen* (July 20, 1992):

> Speaking as an objective analyst, I wouldn't hesitate to point out that the *Quest* curriculum has a number of positive features. Several prominent Christian psychologists have had a hand in devising and developing it. The writings of reputable Christian authors are to be found among its recommended resource materials. Many of the morals it teaches (termed "values," or "social skills") are fully compatible with the Christian perspective. . . . In spite of this, however, I simply can't give *Quest* a blanket endorsement. Along with its good points, the program has what I feel are some serious problems. The authors of *Quest* have attempted in certain instances to incorporate the work of secular humanists into their curriculum. . . . In other contexts they have prescribed group exercises and techniques closely resembling those employed in psychotherapy—a risky practice in the absence of professionally trained leadership. Even on those points where the values promoted by the program are potentially compatible with Christian mores, interpretation and application are completely subject to the individual instructor's personal biases. This means that, in the hands of an atheistic or anti-Christian teacher, *Quest* could become a vehicle for communicating some distinctly un-Christian values. Since I can't possibly know about, much less sanction, the specific ways in which the program is used in thousands of classrooms across the country, I am uneasy about having my name attached to it or used as proof of the curriculum's appropriateness.

In response to the controversy over Quest, we asked Dr. W.R. Coulson to provide his analysis of the situation:

> Any claim of Quest that *Skills for Living* might be beyond criticism because the organization no longer sells it is, in my

opinion, disingenuous. A critic might conclude that the reason Quest no longer offers *Skills for Living* is that Quest apparently agrees that this product—which came from the hand of one of the founders of values clarification—is defective. But, in fact, Quest did not withdraw this program because it was flawed. Quest has made no admission to that effect.

An automobile manufacturer which produces a defective model, such as the Ford Pinto, is required by corporate ethics and by law to recall it. In 1984 *Skills for Living* author Howard Kirschenbaum boasted that the program was in the hands of 300,000 schoolchildren. Have their schools been notified that the product is defective? That Quest no longer distributes it simply does not take away Quest's responsibility for this program if, in fact, the schools have not been told of potential problems with the materials.

An affective approach to education is simply not in children's best interests. For example, Dr. William Hansen, Professor at Bowman-Grey School of Medicine and formerly with the USC School of Medicine, wrote in *Preventive Medicine* (Vol. 17, 1988), ". . . Evaluations of affective education programs have been few and generally of poor quality, providing no strong support for the effectiveness of these strategies. . . . One of the problems with the evaluated studies was a general lack of emphasis on behavioral outcomes. Furthermore, the few behavioral studies conducted do not suggest the general approach to be effective."

Hansen's article also distilled the essence of the common characteristics of affective education as involving 1) enhancement of self-esteem and self-image, 2) stress management, 3) values clarification, 4) decision-making, and 5) goal-setting. These are the topics which, in my opinion, concerned individuals need to be on guard for in any affective educational curricula because such topics have been influenced by an affective approach.

The problem with affective education is that it gives at least as much emphasis to feelings as facts—*at least*. Academic learning gets slighted. No longer can we afford a program like that— straight out of the '60s and '70s, which was a very bad era in American education. It was the era of TMP: Too Much Psychology.

Unfortunately, Quest programs keep TMP alive. Although it is no longer marketed, *Skills for Living* continues to influence the education of thousands of high school students. It offers them, for example, a list of 269 feelings to think about and practice. "Let's see all the angry people show their feeling at the same time." That's what the teacher is scripted to say at the end of one *Skills for Living* exercise (1982, p. 102).

Skills for Adolescence is even worse. To give middle school students "assistance in developing a vocabulary of feeling words" (1988, Unit 3, p. 11), Quest offers a sheet of *Mood Swing Buttons*—"Caution, Mood Swing in Progress"; "How 'Bout a Hug?"; "If You Yell at Me I'll Break"; "I Am Miserable!" (p. 34). Students in the Far East are learning math and science while American students are learning to say, "I am miserable!"

. . . Quest calls this package, with apparent pride, "in-depth sharing" and says that it helps children deal with "feeling alone and without hope" (cited in articles by Sprunger, Pellaux, and Gerler, circulated by Quest). But clearly feelings of alienation like that are not subject matter for classroom discussion; they're to be dealt with at home and by the church and, if necessary, in the clinic with fully qualified professional help. As a nation, we can't afford to turn classrooms into group therapy rooms. The children of the Far East and a reunited Germany are racing ahead of ours in academic and scientific attainment. We are becoming less and less competitive. It is indeed something to make us all feel "miserable."

Quest's response to criticism seems to be not to admit error or apologize but to do more of the same—now to reach into the lower grades for the feelings of students who are younger and more vulnerable. At the same time that *Skills for Living* was being quietly dropped, *Skills for Growing* was being pilot-tested for grades K–5. And it was described by Quest as "highly successful" (*Program Design* book, 1989, p. 29) before it was completely written, let alone tested.

You can't do that in science or scholarship. Unfortunately, feeling-centered education encourages it: If you *feel good enough* about yourself and have learned a dubious "decision-making regimen," then *whatever* you do is said to be good, just because you've decided to do it. . . .

Not all Americans are happy with this approach. When, as they sometimes will, students reveal that they are "really apprehensive about this class," the *Skills for Adolescence Workshop Guidebook* tells teachers to continue to "push their risk levels gently" (1986, p. 81); and if students still seem "scared of the new thoughts and feelings they are experiencing and afraid of owning up to them in front of their peers," the teacher is advised not to back down. . . .

Quest seems unaware that amateur psychology causes problems. But, in fact, all of its programs are rife with psychologically risky, feeling-oriented exercises. I have seen nothing in recent Quest materials which would cause me to change my opinion about this.

In March 1993, Craig Branch talked with Dr. Arlene Seal of CWD International. Seal has a Ph.D. in counseling and education and was an assistant dean at the University of Pittsburgh. Seal has communicated extensively with Quest, who asked her to revise *Skills for Adolescence*. Her response was that "the whole thing needs to be reframed," e.g., there was too much "open-ended decision making" and "many exercises that were totally inappropriate for children." To Quest's credit, they appeared to be very sensitive to her recommendations. (The day before this book went to press, she received a copy of the latest version of *Skills for Adolescence* which, hopefully, had incorporated her recommendations.)

In conclusion, when evaluating curricula, parents need to look at each program independently. They should realize that some curricula may be in the process of evolution. As shortcomings are pointed out, changes may (or may not) be made in subsequent versions.

We hope that Quest International will continue to revise its materials so that parents and educators who continue to have concerns with them will find those concerns addressed.

Glossary

Altered States of Consciousness—the deliberate cultivation of unique or abnormal states of consciousness, states not normally experienced apart from the specific technique or program to develop them. Proponents claim that altered states allegedly produce a "higher" state of knowing or "being," including dramatic revelations and positive restructuring of the individual's worldview.

The problem with developing altered states of consciousness in a New Age context is that they may induce 1) psychological problems, 2) spiritistic influence, including spirit possession, and 3) a radical restructuring of a person's worldview. Most contemporary cultural exploration of altered states is not truly participation in an alleged higher consciousness, let alone true spirituality. Instead it involves developing an abnormal, regressive state of consciousness conducive to spiritistic contact and manipulation. The worldview generated is characteristically occult and brings such consequences as encouraging occult practices or adopting occult philosophy (see chapter 7).

Affective Education—a psychological method intended to influence the emotional content of a child's learning process, usually internally and without outside influence. The goal is allegedly to lead a child to greater self-determination. The problem with this method is its emphasis on humanistic premises which demean absolute moral values. Thus its approach to ethical issues is entirely subjective. If children are personally comfortable with their decisions, this alone legitimizes them, whether or not they are right from the perspective of religious values or parental wishes. This approach may result in conflicts between what a child learns in school and what he learns from outside authorities in the home, church, or society (see *Values Clarification*).

Autogenic Training—a "mind/body" therapy developed by psychiatrist J.H. Schulz and his student Wolfgang Luth. In part, autogenic training is the result of Schulz's observation on the hypnosis research of brain physiologist Oskar Vogt, as well as Schulz's own studies into yoga, Zen, and hypnosis. Visualization and meditation may be employed in the attempt to place participants into an extremely deep state of relaxation.

Biofeedback—the use of special eletronic equipment plus mental exercises, such as visualization and meditation, to influence psychological responses and gain some degree of control of particular physical functions a person does not normally consciously regulate. Although biofeedback may be used scientifically, it may also be used irresponsibly or have unexpected consequences. It frequently has a New Age occult application, as in the developing of altered states and psychic powers. It offers only limited effectiveness for people who are highly motivated; indeed, those who are more adept at visualization or meditation seem to perform better (see note 1).

Bodywork Methods—the practice and goals of bodywork techniques vary widely. Typical examples include rolfing, functional integration, orgonomy, bioenergetics, and the Alexander method. Characteristically, the body is used as a tool to help enlighten or otherwise influence the mind and/or improve mind/body functioning along a predetermined path or perspective which is in harmony with the underlying philosophy and goals of the particular bodywork method. Yoga is perhaps the original bodywork method, viewing the body as a crude layer of mind. Thus, through proper manipulation of the body, these methods also seek to redirect the mind toward desired physical, religious, psychological, or even occult goals (see *Somatic Education*).

Centering—a term with various meanings. It can mean focused attention and concentration. But it is often used to label progressive relaxation techniques, which are the standard induction techniques for hypnosis or meditation.

Channeling—a New Age term for mediumism where a willing participant opens his mind and body to spirits to take control of him for their purposes. Channeling can be facilitated through a variety of means, including relaxation and guided imagery, meditation, visualization, hypnosis, and other altered states of consciousness, all of which may permit the spirits to enter a person, possess, and control him.

Dreamwork—attempts to engage students in the remembrance and use of their dreams for a variety of purposes, many of them New Age. Students will usually employ a dream journal, and may even attempt to manipulate their dreams (as in lucid dreaming) or to seek the wisdom and advice of "dream characters." In much modern dreamwork these methods become introductions to the occult.[2] Teacher Patricia Pirmantgen observes, "Educators who have tried dreamwork in the classroom know that there is no quicker way to capture the interest of a group of students."[3] (See next listing.)

Guided Imagery and Fantasy—terms often used for particular aspects of visualization. Eidetic imagery is a particularly potent form. So what could possibly be wrong with using guided imagery and fantasy in the classroom? This subject illustrates that even seemingly harmless methods may involve more than meets the eye.

Even if relevancy for education were established, the problem is not in the neutral use of these methods but when they are used by educators as a means of turning inward to achieve "spiritual awareness" in a New Age context. In her article on use of fantasy in the first grade, Claudia Binter comments, "If personal awareness is to be fully achieved by an individual, it should begin at an early age in order that the individual may function at a higher level by the time he reaches adulthood."[4] Transpersonal educators do have an agenda, and they may incorporate additional, more powerful methods along with fantasy and guided imagery.

Dr. Frances Vaughan Clark is a pioneer in the use of fantasy in the classroom and wrote her dissertation on "Approaching Transpersonal Consciousness Through Affective Imagery in Higher Education." She observes that,

> Fantasy is a tool for human growth and development which is effective and rewarding at any age. Its value has long been recognized in psychotherapy, but more recently techniques derived from Jung's active imagination, DeSoilles' guided daydream, and Assagioli's psychosynthesis have been introduced into education with very positive results.[5]

Thus the problem is certainly not with imagery or fantasy per se, but with structured methods of guided imagery and fantasy in the classroom based on utilizing powerful psychological methods. For example, Jung's technique of active imagination is conceded by even Jungian therapists as a very serious business and potentially as a dangerous method.[6] In a similar manner, Assagioli's occult psychosynthesis is simply not appropriate for classroom use. Further, dreamwork techniques frequently employ books such as *The Centering Book* by Hendricks and Wills. Unfortunately, these texts utilize the *Senoi* dreamwork methods which are pagan and, in their original form, attempt to use dreams as a means to contact the spirit world.[7] In pagan traditions, and now increasingly in America, the spirits have long had an interest in using dreams as a means to further their own goals.[8] For example, Seth (the spirit guide of the late medium Jane Roberts), dictated two books—*The Education of Oversoul 7* and *Seth, Dreams and Projection of Consciousness*—through her which attempt to employ dreams for occult purposes.

In using guided imagery and fantasy, active imagination, and dreamwork, are we ultimately preparing children to be more comfortable with explorations of the inner life and the world of the psychic and occult? As Robert Habes observes in his article on using fantasy in the elementary classroom, "Once started, it is amazing how eagerly children want to look inward and learn about themselves."[9]

Human Potential Movement—a belief system or worldview which holds that there are latent powers and abilities within man that can be unleashed to dramatically influence the quality of his life, or even his destiny. Meditation, altered states of consciousness, visualization, etc., are characteristically the means to uncover this alleged human potential.

Hypnosis—a deliberately induced condition of heightened suggestibility and trance, producing a highly flexible state of consciousness capable of dramatic manipulation. The exact process through which hypnosis works is unknown; however, it does produce a unique altered state of consciousness with dramatic occult potential, including psychic development, spirit contact, automatic writing, astral travel, and past-life/reincarnation regression.

Martial Arts (aikido, Tai Chi Chuan, Tae Kwon Do, karate, judo, ninjutsu, kenpo)—systems of physical discipline stressing the control of mind and body for self-defense, physical health, or spiritual enlightenment. The martial arts claim to work by unifying the mind/spirit and body through meditation, physical discipline, and other procedures. In Eastern forms this allegedly helps regulate the flow of mystical energy (*ki, chi*) and enables one to attain a state of mind/body oneness, both of which are important for effective performance of self-defense, physical conditioning, or spiritual enlightenment. The occult potential of the martial arts include occult forms of meditation, development of psychic powers, and even spirit contact. Although martial arts programs are not necessarily Eastern/occult, most are, and interested parties are urged to be cautious about the program they select.

Meditation—an attempt to control and regulate the mind for various physical, mental, or spiritual purposes or goals. Meditation claims to work by stilling or otherwise influencing the mind. By this process, the meditator allegedly is able to perceive reality as it truly is, as well as his own true nature. In New Age forms, the goal is usually to achieve some form of spiritual enlightenment where the person is able to recognize his own inner godhood. In the classroom, meditation may be used simply for relaxation or it may have New Age goals.

The problem with most forms of meditation is that they are characteristically Eastern or occult in nature and frequently induce altered states of consciousness, psychic powers, and even spiritistic contact or kundalini arousal. Unfortunately, regressive states of consciousness are falsely interpreted as higher or divine states; meditation-induced psychic powers are wrongly interpreted as evidence of a latent inner divinity. Hazards of practicing meditation include psychiatric disorders, physical damage, and spirit influence and/or possession (see chapter 7).

New Age Subliminal Programming—audiotapes that supposedly contain hidden messages to produce a dramatic influence on the subconscious mind. They may be employed with visualization and altered states of consciousness to allegedly contact someone's higher self or even the spirit world. This supposedly leads to self-understanding and realization of full human potential.

Progressive Relaxation—a method, often a series of mental and physical exercises, designed to reduce stress or other problems in a person's life, enabling him or her to cope with the difficulties of modern living. Another purpose is to help improve thinking skills, including critical evaluation, as well as accessing alleged powers within one's self.

Psychic Anatomies (astral bodies, meridians, auras, chakras)—alleged invisible, nonphysical bodily "structures" frequently associated with Eastern/occult religion and often said to be influenced by New Age methods.

Psychosynthesis—a psychological/occult method of personal enlightenment developed by psychiatrist and occultist Roberto Assagioli, a colleague of Freud and Jung. Assagioli studied Eastern and Western philosophy and the occult and was the Italian director of the occult movement founded by New Age leader Alice Bailey: the Arcana/Lucis Trust. Psychosynthesis advertises itself as "well suited to psychology, education and medicine, and also to religion, the social sciences, philosophy and all other aspects of society in which the consciousness of the individual human being plays a role."[10]

Self-Esteem Education—Many leaders in education today believe that one of the most effective ways for countering problems relating to sex, drugs, and alcohol is to increase students' self-esteem. This involves the idea that if you help a child feel good about himself, he will perform better and have greater ability to resist peer pressure. Unfortunately, research reveals self-esteem programs have limited effectiveness at best.

Self-Help Therapies—These are frequently New Age methods which involve a turning inward to seek the alleged wisdom of supposed inner guides, the higher self, sanctified imagination, or archetypes. Psychological concepts from Jungian psychotherapy are particularly common. Allegedly, every person has a divine inner core which may be contacted by the proper methods, such as meditation, visualization, altered states, or shamanistic practice. This inner core is a supposed reservoir of divine wisdom and information on any number of subjects. Unfortunately, these methods frequently become a guise under which psychic development and spiritistic influence are encountered.

Somatic Education—the use of particular bodywork methods to influence the consciousness. For example, Marilyn Howell, a high school teacher in Brookline, Massachusetts, writes in her article "Somatic Education in Public School":

> While my students were learning biological facts, they had little awareness of their own bodies or body/mind potential.... Introducing Somatic Education to the Brookline schools has been a gradual process.... Body/Mind Research meets four days a week for 50 minutes in a large wrestling room.... [Classes include] an introductory lesson in a discipline such as yoga, tai chi, or judo... lecture/discussions on current research in the brain sciences or body/mind system such as Bioenergetics, Biofeedback, Psychosynthesis, and Rolfing.[11]

Transpersonal Education—a recent educational theory which advocates that students must go beyond the realm of the five senses into the transpersonal realm which allegedly takes people to a higher source of knowledge, wisdom, and ability. What is the transpersonal realm? Despite its fancy title, an analysis of the literature reveals it is concerned with the phenomena, practices, and beliefs of Eastern religion and the occult. A sampling of the areas covered by transpersonal psychology includes altered states of consciousness, visualization, meditation, developing psychic ability, spirit contact, hypnotic phenomena, bodywork methods, psychic anatomies, dreamwork, energy channeling, divination, martial arts, parapsychology, psychic healing, shamanism, and yoga. Because so many of these areas are studied "scientifically" (parapsychologically), some educators feel confident that some of these methods may be brought into the classroom.

Transpersonal Psychology—a recent school of psychology which, in large measure, led to the development of its educational counterpart. It also seeks to transcend the normal parameters of mental functioning to explore the mystical and paranormal. *The Journal of Transpersonal Psychology* identifies its purpose as being concerned with altered states of consciousness, mystical experience, self-actualization, occult phenomena, and other subjects listed under Transpersonal Education.

Values Clarification—also known as a nondirective decision-making process in education. The purpose is to encourage students to subjectively develop their own set of values and standards that are right for them instead of being influenced to accept the standards of adults—whether parents, society, or church.

Values clarification methods are based on a situation ethics approach and used extensively throughout the nation in drug, sex, and self-esteem programs. Unfortunately, as this book demonstrated, they are fundamentally destructive to moral standards as well as to the welfare of the children they are attempting to help.

Visualization—New Age visualization is the use of mental concentration and directed imagery in the attempt to secure particular physical, emotional, educational, or spiritual goals. It claims to work in a variety of ways; for example, by using the mind to contact an alleged inner divinity or higher self. Practitioners claim that through visualization they can manipulate their personal realities to secure improved learning abilities and concentration, and optimum health.

Visualization is often used as a means to, or in conjunction with, altered states of consciousness, and is frequently accompanied by occult meditation or yoga. It may be used to help develop psychic abilities. It may also be found in forms of channeling to contact alleged inner advisors or spirit guides. One problem with New Age visualization is that it assigns the human mind a divine or almost-divine status which can distort both perception and reality (see chapter 7).

Yoga—characteristically, the occult use of breathing exercises, physical postures, and meditation for alleged improved mental functioning, health maintenance, and spiritual enlightenment. Because the body is viewed as a crude layer of mind, various manipulations of the body are alleged to affect the mind, bringing supposed spiritual enlightenment. The problems with yoga are its inherently religious nature; the difficulty of separating theory and practice; and potential physical, psychological, and spiritual hazards (see chapter 7).

Recommended Books
and Resource List

Ankerberg, John and Weldon, John, *The Facts on the New Age Movement*, Harvest House.

Bloom, Allan, *Closing of the American Mind*, Simon & Schuster.

Brooke, Tal, *When the World Will Be As One*, Harvest House.

Buehrer, Eric, *The New Age Masquerade*, Wolgemuth and Hyatt.

Chandler, Russell, *Understanding the New Age*, Word Publishing.

Cosgrove, Mark, *Psychology Gone Awry*, Zondervan.

Eakman, B.K., *Educating for the New World Order*, Halcyon House.

Evans, Pearl, *Hidden Danger in the Classroom*, Small Helm Press.

Gow, Kathleen, *Yes, Virginia, There Is Right and Wrong*, Tyndale House.

Kilpatrick, William, *Why Johnny Can't Tell Right from Wrong*, Simon & Schuster.

Michaelsen, Johanna, *Like Lambs to the Slaughter*, Harvest House.

Miller, Elliot, *A Crash Course on the New Age Movement*, Baker Books.

Nash, Ronald H., *The Closing of the American Heart*, Probe Books.

Schlafly, Phyllis, ed., *Child Abuse in the Classroom*, Crossway Books.

Organization Resource List

American Family Association, P.O. Box 2440, 107 Parkgate Dr., Tupelo, MS 38803 (601) 844-5036

Citizens for Excellence in Education, P.O. Box 3200, Costa Mesa, CA 92628 (714) 546-5931

Eagle Forum (Education Reporter), P.O. Box 618, Alton, IL 62002 (618) 462-8272

Focus on the Family, 420 N. Cascade Ave., Colorado Springs, CO 80903 (719) 531-3400

Gateway to Better Education, Eric Buehrer, P.O. Box 514, Lake Forest, CA 92630 (714) 486-5437

The John Ankerberg Show, P.O. Box 8977, Chattanooga, TN 37411 (615) 892-7722

Research Council on Ethnopsychology (Dr. William Coulson), P.O. Box 134, Comptche, CA 95427 (707) 937-3934

The Rutherford Institute (legal service), P.O. Box 7482, Charlottes-ville, VA 22906 (804) 978-3888

Spiritual Counterfeits Project, P.O. Box 4308, Berkeley, CA 94702 (510) 540-0300

Watchman Fellowship, P.O. Box 13251, Arlington, TX 76094 (817) 277-0023 (free monthly newspaper available)

Watchman Fellowship, P.O. Box 19416, Birmingham, AL 35219 (205) 942-4004 (free monthly newspaper available)

Select Bibliography

New Age/occultic and hypnosis books which help demonstrate that the presuppositions, objectives and methodology are the same *as are found in the objectionable school curricula*:

Benson, Herbert, M.D. *The Relaxation Response*. New York: Avon Books, Aug. 1976.

Bloomfield, Harold H., M.D.; Michael P. Cain; and Dennis T. Jaffe. *TM—Discovering Inner Energy and Overcoming Stress*. New York: DeLacorte Press, 1975.

Copeland, Rachel. *How to Hypnotize Yourself and Others*. New York: Harper & Row, 1981.

Crawford, Quantz. *Methods of Psychic Development*. York Beach, ME: Samuel Weiser, 1982.

Fezler, William, Ph.D. *Creative Imagery*. New York: Simon and Schuster, Inc., 1989.

Freese, Arthur S. *Hypnosis Can Help You*. New York: Popular Library, 1976.

Gawain, Shakti. *Creative Visualization*. Mill Valley, CA: Whatever Publishing, 1981.

Hewitt, William W. *Hypnosis*. St. Paul, MN: Llewellyn Publications, 1990.

Hittleman, Richard. *Yoga for Health*. New York: Ballantine Books, 1983.

Houston, Jean. *The Possible Human*. Los Angeles, CA: J.P. Tarcher, Inc., 1982.

LeCron, Leslie M. *The Complete Guide to Hypnosis*. Los Angeles: Nash Publishing, 1971.

Masters, Robert and Jean Houston. *Mind Games: The Guide to Inner Space*. New York: Delta, 1981.

Nehel, Andrew. *The Psychology of Transcendence*. Englewood Cliffs, NJ: Prentice-Hall, Inc., 1980.

Otis, Leon. *Meditation, Classic and Contemporary Perspectives*. Alden, 1984.

Petrie, Sidney. *Helping Yourself with Autogenics*. West Nyack, NY: Parker Publishing, 1983.

Randolph, George. *The Road Beyond Yoga, Vol. II*. New York: Lancer Books, 1973.

Robins, Alan and Jane A. Himber. *The TM Program and Enlightenment.* New York: Berkley Medallion Books, 1976.

Van Over, Raymond. *Total Meditation.* New York: Macmillan Publishing Co., 1978.

Christian Analysis of the New Age Movement:

Ankerberg, John and John Weldon. *The Facts on the New Age Movement.* Eugene, OR: Harvest House, 1988.

————. *The Facts on Spirit Guides.* Eugene, OR: Harvest House, 1988.

Hoyt, Karen, ed. *The New Age Rage.* Old Tappan, NJ: Fleming H. Revell Co., 1987.

Miller, Elliot. *A Crash Course on the New Age Movement.* Grand Rapids, MI: Baker Book House, 1989.

Sire, James W. *The Universe Next Door.* Downers Grove, IL: InterVarsity Press, 1988.

Books and Articles Analyzing Problem Issues in Education:

Buehrer, Eric. *The New Age Masquerade.* Brentwood, TN: Wolgemuth & Hyatt, 1990.

Burron, Arnold; John Eidsmoe; and Dean Turner. *Classrooms in Crisis.* Denver: Accent Books, 1986.

Colson, Charles. *Against the Night.* Ann Arbor, MI: Servant Publications, 1989.

Kjos, Berit. *Your Child and the New Age.* Wheaton, IL: Victor Books, 1990.

Michaelsen, Johanna. *Like Lambs to the Slaughter: Your Child and the Occult.* Eugene, OR: Harvest House Publishers, 1989.

Schlafly, Phyllis. *Child Abuse in the Classroom.* Westchester, IL: Crossway Books, 1985.

Whitehead, John W. *The Rights of Religious Persons in Public Education.* Wheaton, IL: Crossway Books, 1991.

Books and Articles Written by Transpersonal Educators and Others Demonstrating Their Application in Education:

Anastasiow, Nicholas. "Updating Intellectual Growth in Children and Bioplasmic Forces." *Phi Delta Kappan.* Apr. 1974.

Armstrong, Thomas. "Children as Healers." *Somatics*. Autumn/Winter 1984-85.

Assagioli, R. *The Education of Gifted and Super-gifted Children*. New York: Psychosynthesis Research Foundation, 1960. P.R.F. Issue No. 8.

Astor, Martin. "Learning Through Hypnosis." *Educational Forum*. May 1971.

Bailey, Alice. *Education in the New Age*. New York: Lucis Trust, 1954.

Canfield, Jack. *The Inner Classroom: Teaching with Guided Imagery*. Amhurst, MA: Institute for Wholistic Education, 1981.

Carlson, Jon (ed.). "Health, Wellness, and Transpersonal Approaches to Helping." *Elementary School Guidance and Counseling Journal*. Vol. 14, no. 2, Dec. 1979.

Clark, Barbara. *Growing Up Gifted: Developing the Potential of Children at Home and at School*. Columbus, OH: Merrill Publishing Company, 1988.

Crampton, Martha. *Some Applications of Psychosynthesis in the Educational Field*. New York: Psychosynthesis Research Foundation, 1972.

Davis, Stephen. "Waldorf Education: The Life and Times of Rudolf Steiner Parts 1 and 2." *New Age*. Mar. 1978.

Demille, Richard. *Put Your Mother on the Ceiling: Children's Imagination Games*. New York: Viking, 1973.

Ferguson, Marilyn. *The Aquarian Conspiracy: Personal and Social Transformation in the 1980's*. Los Angeles: J.P. Tarcher, Inc., 1980.

Hanna, Thomas. "Somatic Education: A Scenario of the Future." *Somatics*. Spring/Summer 1984.

Hendricks, Gay and Thomas B. Roberts. *The Second Centering Book: More Awareness Activities for Children*. New York: Prentice-Hall, 1977.

Howell, Marilyn. "Somatic Education in Public School." *Somatics*. Spring/Summer 1984.

Jampolsky, G. and M. Haight. "An Experience with Biofeedback in a Public High School." *Journal of Biofeedback*. Winter 1974.

Katz, Richard. "Education for Transcendence." *Preludes for Growth*. New York: Free Press, 1973.

Krippner, Stanley. "Creativity and Psychic Phenomena." *Gifted Child Quarterly*. Vol. 7, 1963.

————. "Parapsychology in Education." *Journal of Humanistic Psychology*. Fall 1973.

Krishnamurti, Jiddu. *Education and the Significance of Life*. New York: Harper & Row, 1953.

Lee, James L. and Charles J. Pulvino. "Counseling According to Don Juan." *Counseling and Values*. Feb. 1975.

Lewis, Mary Jo. "Not Too Young for Yoga." and "Yoga for the Special Child." *Yoga Journal*. Nov./Dec. 1984.

Linden, William. "The Relationship Between the Practice of Meditation by School Children and Their Levels of Field Dependence-Independence, Text Anxiety and Reading Achievement." *Journal of Consulting and Clinical Psychology*. Aug. 1973.

Murdock, Maureen. *Spinning Inward: Using Guided Imagery with Children for Learning, Creativity, & Relaxation*. Boston: Shambhala Publications, 1987.

Ogletree, Earl J. "Rudolf Steiner: Unknown Educator." *Elementary School Journal*. Mar. 1974.

Peerbolte, N. "Meditation for School Children." *Main Currents in Modern Thought*. Vol. 24, 1967.

Peterson, James W. "Extrasensory Abilities of Children: An Ignored Reality." *Learning: The Magazine for Creative Teaching*. Dec. 1975.

————. "Psychic and Philosophical Perception in the World of Children." *The American Theosophist*. Vol. 64, 1976.

Ramirez, Sylvia Z. "The Effects of Suggestopedia in Teaching English Vocabulary to Spanish-Dominant Chicano Third Graders." *The Elementary School Journal*. Jan. 1979.

Roberts, Thomas B. (ed.). *Four Psychologies Applied to Education*. New York: John Wiley, 1975.

————. "States of Consciousness: A New Intellectual Direction, A Teacher Education Direction." *Teacher Education*. Mar./Apr. 1985.

————. "Transpersonal: The New Educational Psychology." *Phi Delta Kappan*. Nov. 1974.

Rozman, Deborah. *Meditation for Children*. Boulder Creek, CA: University of the Trees Press, 1989.

Shapiro, Stewart B. and Louise F. Fitzgerald. "The Development of an Objective Scale to Measure a Transpersonal Orientation to Learning." *Educational and Psychological Measurement*. Vol. 49, 1989.

Steiner, Rudolf. "The Education of the Child in Light of Anthroposophy." London: Rudolf Steiner Press, 1965.

Sutphen, Dick. "Infiltrating the New Age into Society." *What Is*. Summer 1986.

Zaichkowsky, Linda B., et al. "Biofeedback-Assisted Relaxation Training in the Elementary Classroom." *Elementary School Guidance and Counseling Journal.* Apr. 1986.

Other Related Books, Research, and Periodicals:

Anderson, Ron F. "Using Guided Fantasy with Children." *Elementary School Guidance and Counseling Journal.* Oct. 1980.

Black, Susan. "Self-Esteem: Sense and NonSense." *American School Board Journal.* Jul. 1991.

Bloom, Richard, Dr. "Drug Education: Further Results and Recommendations." *Journal of Drug Issues.* Vol. 8, no. 4, Fall 1978.

Bundy, Michael and Thomas LaRue. "New Rights Censorship: An Awareness Action Plan for Counselors." *Elementary School and Guidance Counseling Journal.* Oct. 1982.

————. "Changing Social Structure Taking Toll on Children." *Clinical Psychiatry News.* Feb. 1991.

Clayton, Richard R. "Sensation Seeking As a Potential Mediating Variable for School-Based Prevention Intervention: A Two-Year Follow-up of DARE." *Journal of Health Communication.* Vol. 4, 1991.

Coulson, W.R. "Helping Youth Decide: 'When the fox preaches, beware the geese.'" *New York State Journal of Medicine.* Jul. 1985.

Day, Robert and Robert Griffin. "Children's Attitudes Toward the Magic Circle." *Elementary School Guidance and Development.* Dec. 1980.

"EEOC's Policy Statement on Training Programs Conflicting with Employees' Religious Beliefs." EEOC Notice N-915. Feb. 22, 1988.

Hanes, Charles W. and Thomas H. Hohenshil. "Elementary School Counselors, School Psychologists, School Social Workers: Who Does What?" *Elementary School Guidance and Counseling Journal.* Oct. 1987.

Hansen, Richard, et al. "Affective and Social Influence Approaches to the Prevention of Multiple Substance Abuse Among Seventh Grade Students—Results from Project SMART." *Preventive Medicine.* Vol. 17, 1988.

Heide, Frederick J. and T.D. Borkovec. *Behavioral Research Therapy Journal.* 1984.

————. *Consulting in Clinical Psychology.* 1983.

Heikkinen, Charles. "Reorientation from Altered States: Please Move Carefully." *Journal of Counseling and Development.* May 1989.

Kirschenbaum, Howard. "The Rights of the School Community." *Elementary School Guidance and Counseling Journal.* Oct. 1982.

Klitzner, Michael. "Report to Congress on the Nature and Effectiveness of Federal, State and Local Prevention/Education Programs." Prepared for the U.S. Department of Education by the Center for Advanced Health Studies.

Levine, Melvin D., M.D.; William B. Carey, M.D.; and Allen C. Crocker, M.D. *Developmental-Behavioral Pediatrics.* W.B. Saunders Company, second ed., 1992.

Lowry, Richard J. (ed.). "The Journals of A.H. Maslow." Monterey, CA: Brooks/Cole, 1979.

Malnak v. *Yogi.* 440F. SUPP. 1284, 1977.

Maslow, A.H. *Motivation and Personality.* New York: Harper & Row, 1970.

Maslow, Abraham. *Toward a Psychology of Being.* New York: Van Nostrand Reinhold, 1968.

The Research Council Ethnopsychology. La Jolla Program *Newsletter,* Aug. 1991.

Richard, Dinah. *Has Sex Education Failed Our Teenagers?* Pomona, CA: Focus on the Family Publishing, 1990.

"School-Based Suicide Prevention Programs Held Ineffective, Risky." *Clinical Psychiatry News.* Apr. 1991.

Sendor, Benjamin. "When It Comes to Teaching About Religion, Sound School Policy Should Be Your Bible." *American School Board Journal.* Aug. 1989.

Singer, Margaret and Richard Ofshe. "Thought Reform Programs and the Production of Psychiatric Casualties." *Psychiatric Annals.* Apr. 1990.

Strein, William. "Classroom-Based Elementary School Affective Education Programs: A Critical Review." *Psychology in the Schools.* Jul. 1988.

Notes

An Important Word to the Reader
1. *Parade* Magazine, Sep. 20, 1992.
2. William J. Bennett, "The Case for Religion in Schools," *Readers Digest*, Nov. 1992, pp. 79, 81.
3. Most of the above was excerpted from "The Facts on Your Child's Education: You Can Make a Difference" by Robert Gerow (Chattanooga, TN: Ankerberg Theological Research Institute, 1990).

An Introduction to the Issues
1. Watchman Fellowship in Birmingham, AL, has several examples on file.
2. Gordon Melton, *New Age Encyclopedia* (Detroit: Gale Research, 1990), pp. 512-24.
3. Brooks Alexander, as cited in *Foreword* magazine, Fall 1986, p. 14.
4. As discussed in "Are the Public Schools Teaching Our Children New Age Religious Views?" series one, program two, broadcast on "The John Ankerberg Show," Sep. 1992.

Chapter 1—What Is the New Age Movement?
1. Rosemary Ellen Guiley, *Harper's Encyclopedia of Mystical and Paranormal Experience* (San Francisco: Harper Collins Publisher, 1991), p. 404.
2. Robert Burrows, "New Age Movement: Self-Deification in a Secular Culture," *SCP Newsletter*, vol. 10, no. 5.
3. J. Gordon Melton, *New Age Encyclopedia* (Detroit: Gale Research, Inc., 1990), p. xv.
4. Ibid., p. xiv.
5. Sophia Tarila, "A Global Outreach," *Publisher's Weekly*, Dec. 7, 1990, pp. 33,34.
6. Paragraph 5105, Commerce Clearing House, EEOC Notice No. N-915, Feb. 22, 1988.
7. *The Oxford American Dictionary* (New York: Avon, 1982), p. 617.
8. *Webster's Third International Dictionary Unabridged* (1981), p. 1560.
9. "Occult," in *Encyclopedia Britannica*, Micropaedia, vol. 7, p. 469.
10. J. Gordon Melton, *Encyclopedic Handbook of Cults in America* (New York: Garland, 1986), p. 113.
11. Ibid., p. 16.
12. Guiley, *Harper's Encyclopedia*, p. 403.
13. Melton, *New Age Encyclopedia*, p. xvii; cf. p. 10.
14. Ibid., p. xvi.
15. Ibid., p. xiv; see e.g., Ankerberg and Weldom, *Can You Trust Your Doctor?* (Chattanooga, TN: The Ankerberg Theological Research Institute, 1991).
16. *Malnak* v. *Yogi* (440F. SUPP. 1284, 1977).
17. Barry K. Weinhold, "Transpersonal Communication in the Classroom" in James Hendricks and Gay Fadiman (eds.), *Transpersonal Education: A Curriculum for Feeling and Being* (Englewood Cliffs, NJ: Prentice-Hall, 1976), p. 123-24, emphasis added.
18. Ibid., p. 146.
19. Hendricks and Fadiman, *Transpersonal Education*, p. 151.
20. Ibid., pp. 153ff, 174ff.
21. Giyu Kennett, "The Education of the Buddhist Child," in ibid., p. 167.
22. Ibid., pp. 166-67.
23. Ibid., p. 166.
24. Ibid., pp. 168-69.
25. Barbara Clark, *Growing Up Gifted* (Columbus, OH: Merrill Publishing Co., 1990), pp. 582-83.
26. Ibid., p. 576.
27. Ankerberg and Weldon, *The Facts on Spirit Guides* (Eugene, OR: Harvest House, 1989), p. 7.
28. Eric Buehrer, "Are the Public Schools Teaching Our Children New Age Religious Views?" series one, program two on "The John Ankerberg Show," Sep. 1992. See his *The New Age Masquerade*, chapter 9, for a discussion.
29. Tal Brooke, "Education: Capturing Hearts and Minds for a New World," *SCP Newsletter*, vol. 16, no. 4, p. 16.
30. John Ankerberg and John Weldon, *The Facts on the New Age Movement* (Eugene, OR: Harvest House, 1988), pp. 18-20; cf., *The Facts on Spirit Guides*.
31. John Weldon, "Self-Help Therapies," "Imagination Spiritism," and "New Age Intuition," mss.

Chapter 2—New Age and Psychotherapeutic Influence
1. Phyllis Schlafly (ed.), *Child Abuse in the Classroom* (Westchester, MA: Crossway, 1988), pp. 138-42, 201-04, 235-36, 282, 365, 423.
2. 1988 Birmingham School Board of Education, Community School Course Listing, p. 14.
3. Telephone conversation between Craig Branch of Watchman Fellowship and community school director Sara Roseman in the Fall of 1988.
4. Russell Chandler, *Understanding the New Age* (Dallas: Word, 1988), p. 154.
5. Ibid.

328

6. Ibid., p. 156.
7. *New York Times Magazine*, May 1, 1988, p. 36.
8. Ibid., p. 42.
9. Letter on file with Watchman Fellowship, Birmingham, AL.
10. Bob Eberle, *Visual Thinking: A "Scamper" Tool for Useful Imaging* (Edwardsville, IL.: DOK Publishing, 1982), p. vii.
11. Ibid., pp. 18, 38, 42, 52.
12. National Research Council/National Academy of Sciences, *Enhancing Human Performance: Issues, Theories, and Techniques* (Washington, DC: National Academy Press, 1988), pp. 49-50; promotional material on "Mind Mapping."
13. Ibid., pp. 50, 58.
14. *Peace, Harmony, Awareness*, pp. 37, 47; among suggested background music is "Music for Zen Meditation" and among suggested readings are Hendricks and Roberts' *The Centering Book*, D. Rozman's *Meditating with Children*, Herbert Benson's *The Relaxation Response*, and books by New Age enthusiasts Adelaide Bry and Jack Canfield.
15. Center for Health, Prevention and Education, "Handling Stress," *Teenage Health Teaching Modules* (Newton, MA: Massachusetts Education Development Center, 1983), Activity no. 5, pp. 36-38.
16. Ibid., p. 51.
17. Ibid., "Protecting Oneself and Others," p. 31.
18. *Elements of Literature, Teacher's Edition* (New York: Holt, Rinehard, and Winston), pp. 183, 226, 535-618.
19. *Education Reporter*, Eagle Forum, Nov. 1991.
20. Ibid.
21. Ibid.
22. Ibid.; DAD's booklet, 3979 Prairie SW, Grandville, MI 49418.
23. Reported by Craig Branch, who was personally present.
24. *Education Reporter*, Eagle Forum, Jul. 1991.
25. *Community Schools Spring Bulletin*, Wake County, NC, Public School System, Spring 1990, p. 21.
26. Concerned Women of America newsletter, Oct. 1989.
27. See the *Watchman Expositor*, vol. 6, no. 12.
28. *Education Reporter*, Eagle Forum, Oct. 1991.
29. Ibid., Feb. 1988, p. 1.
30. *The Florida Forum*, Pro Family Forum, Oct.-Dec. 1989, p. 6.
31. Report on file with Watchman Fellowship, Birmingham, AL.
32. Ibid.
33. *Citizen Magazine*, Focus on the Family, Sep. 17, 1990.
34. *UAB Special Studies*, catalog, Fall 1989, p. 33.
35. *The Martial Arts of the Orient*, pp. 158-59.
36. Swami Radha, *Hatha Yoga* (Boston: Shambhala Publishing, 1987), p. xi.
37. Ibid., p. xvii.
38. Material on file with Watchman Fellowship in Birmingham, AL.
39. David Ellis, *Becoming a Master Student*, fifth ed. (Rapid City, SD: College Survival, Inc., 1985), pp. 78, 134, 233.
40. Parents reported by telephone to coauthor Craig Branch.
41. *The Decatur Daily*, "Hartselle pulls school material called New Age," Nov. 13, 1990, p. 12.
42. *Gazette Telegraph*, "School bans 'Pumsy' from class," Dec. 24, 1991, p. B1.
43. *The Florida Times Union*, "Self-esteem critters get the ax," Aug. 26, 1992, p. 1.
44. Parents' group reported by phone to coauthor Craig Branch.
45. Eric Buehrer in "Are the Public Schools Teaching Our Children New Age Religious Views?" series one, program one.
46. Henry Niemann, Judith Cooper, *Astrology of Psychology: The Reference Book for Astrologers* (Tempe, AZ: American Federation of Astrologers, 1986), p. iv.
47. Derek and Julia Parker, *The Compleat Astrologer* (New York: Bantam, 1978), p. 166.
48. Marc Edmund Jones, *The Sabian Manual: A Ritual for Living* (Boulder, CO: Sabian/Shambhala, 1976), rev., pp. 196-97; cf. John Ankerberg, John Weldon, *Astrology: Do the Heavens Rule Our Destiny?* (Eugene, OR: Harvest House, 1989), chapters 11, 14–15.
49. Gloria Star, *Optimum Child: Developing Your Child's Fullest Potential Through Astrology* (St. Paul, MN: Llewellyn Publications, 1987), pp. 228-29.
50. Ibid., pp. 220-21, 230.
51. Textbooks reviewed include *Health: A Wellness Approach* (Merrill), *Choosing Wellness* (Prentice-Hall), *Personal Fitness: Looking Good, Feeling Good* (Kendall/Hunt Publishers), *Health for Life* (Scott/Foresman Publishers), *Working Skills for a New Age* (Delmar), and *Contemporary Living* (Goodheart-Wilcox).
52. *Health: Choosing Wellness* (Needham, MA: Prentice-Hall, 1991), pp. 3, 21, 33, 46-48, 60-67, 235, 243, 267, 506.

Chapter 3—Quest, DUSO, Pumsy, and DARE
[Note: The authors express their gratitude to Gary and Janice Beeker for use of their "Quest: Review and

Analysis," a critique containing photocopied material of the Quest program (available from Citizens for Excellence in Education, State Board of Ohio, P.O. Box 27415, Columbus, OH 43227).]

1. People for the American Way, *Attacks on the Freedom to Learn* (Washington, DC: PFAW, 1991-92), p. 5.
2. For example, Quest is used in approximately 20 percent of American schools, Pumsy in over 40 percent (16,000 schools). (For Quest, see Internal Report of Professor Stephen Jurs, University of Toledo College of Education, contracted by Quest to research the effectiveness of the program, cited in *Questianity: Why We're Losing the War on Drugs*, pp. 34-36.)
3. *The Arkansas Citizen*, Apr. 1990, p. 1.
4. William Kilpatrick, *Why Johnny Can't Tell Right from Wrong* (New York: Simon & Schuster, 1992), p. 37.
5. William Coulson, Director of Research Council on Ethnopsychology, La Jolla, CA, personal conversation; cf., researchers at Heidelberg College in Ohio who found no positive impact of Quest students compared with a control group as reported in *Education Reporter*, Nov. 1991.
6. Gary and Janice Beeker, *Quest: Review and Analysis*, 1987, p. 1.
7. Beeker, *Quest*, p. 14, citing p. 384 of Quest program.
8. Ibid., p. 16, citing p. 386 of the Quest program.
9. Ibid., p. 11, citing p. 375 of the Quest program.
10. Ibid., p. 13, citing p. 383 of the Quest program.
11. Ibid., p. 21, citing Unit 2, Session 1 under "Procedure" of the Quest program, p. 61.
12. Ibid. p. 17, citing p. 394 of the Quest program.
13. Ibid., p. 20, citing Unit 2, Session 10 under "Procedure" of the Quest program, p. 86 (student contract).
14. Bill Cosby and Rich Little, et al., Charles W. Shedd (ed.), *You Are Somebody Special* (McGraw-Hill, 1992), p. 54.
15. Beeker, *Quest*, pp. 23-24, citing Unit 1, Session 3 under "Procedure" of the Quest program, pp. 37-38.
16. Ibid., p. 18, citing the Quest program, p. 395, Activities 5 and 6.
17. Ibid., pp. 26-27, citing the Quest program, Unit 7, Session 4, pp. 345-46.
18. Ibid., p. 27, citing the Quest program under "You Are Somebody Special" and "Unusual People," pp. 44-45.
19. Ibid., p. 5.
20. Ibid., p. 7, citing Quest National Center, "Getting the Word Out," *Quest Energizer*, Winter 1987, p. 4.
21. Ibid., p. 7, citing Howard Kirschenbaum, Barbara Glaser, *Skills for Living*, Quest National Center, 1982, p. 53.
22. Kathleen N. Gow, *Yes, Virginia, There Is Right and Wrong* (Wheaton, IL: Tyndale, 1985), p. 24.
23. Beeker, *Quest*, p. 10.
24. National Education Association, *Values, Concepts and Techniques* (NEA, 1976), p. 131.
25. Beeker, *Quest*, p. 11.
26. In Michael Ebert, "One Man's Bonfire Ignites Quest Debate," *Focus on the Family Citizen*, Jul. 20, 1992, pp. 12-13.
27. Ibid.
28. Letter on file with Watchman Fellowship, Birmingham, AL, from the state superintendent's office of the North Carolina Department of Public Education, Apr. 2, 1991.
29. Kilpatrick, *Why Johnny Can't Tell*, p. 47
30. Don C. Dinkmeyer and James J. Muro, *Counseling in the Elementary and Middle Schools: A Pragmatic Approach*, p. 241.
31. Ibid.
32. See chapter 9.
33. As reported in *The Education Reporter*, Feb. 1988.
34. Law enacted in Colorado, Jul. 1, 1990, cf. *Educator Reporter*, Dec. 1990, p. 1.
35. Copies on file, Watchman Fellowship, Birmingham, AL.
36. Milfred Minatrea, Director of Church and Community Ministries Division, Dallas Baptist Association, Dallas, TX.
37. *Physician*, Jul./Aug. 1992, p. 12.
38. Lorraine Plum, *Flights of Fantasy* (Carthage, IL: Good Apple, Inc., 1980), pp. 11-13 (school curriculum).
39. Hadley and Standacher, *Hypnosis for Change* (Oakland, CA: New Harbinger Publishers, 1985), p. 22.
40. Life Education Centre, "Let's Learn to Live" (Elmhurst, IL: Noffs & Association, 1988), Section 5-9 (school curriculum).
41. Richard Hittleman, *Yoga for Health* (New York: Ballantine Books, 1981), pp. 62-63.
42. Letter of Brian Newman to Dr. Gene Davenport of Allen, TX, Feb. 27, 1990, copy on file.
43. Copies may be secured from Family Counsel, 1300 W. Park Drive, 5B, Little Rock, AR 72204; 501-664-4566.
44. Reported in *The Arkansas Citizen*, Apr. 1992, p. 4.
45. *Physician*, Jul./Aug. 1992, p. 12.
46. WWBT-TV 12, Richmond, Va, four-part series on "What Did Your Child Learn in School Today?" Nov. 7-9, 1990. Video on file with Watchman Fellowship, Birmingham, AL.
47. Seven-page letter of Jill Anderson, author of *Pumsy in Pursuit of Excellence*, to a Mrs. Hearn.
48. Jill Anderson, cf., *Thinking, Changing, Rearranging* (Eugene, OR: Timberline Press, 1981), p. ix.

330

49. Foreword, "Bureau of Justice Assistance, U.S. Department of Justice Handbook," *Implementing Project DARE: Drug Abuse Resistance Education*, p. 1, cited in Albert James Dager, "Special Report: D.A.R.E.: Experimental Mysticism in the Classroom" (Redmond, WA: Media Spotlight, 1992), p. 6.
50. Dager, "Special Report," p. 5.
51. Richard A. Baer, Jr., "Parents, Schools and Values Clarification," *The Wall Street Journal*, Apr. 12, 1982.
52. National Monitor of Education, *Your Children and Harmful Drug Education*, cited in Rick Branch, "DARE to Look Deeper into Drug Education," *Watchman Expositor*, vol. 9, no. 8, 1992, p. 3.
53. A reference to Alabama Senate Bill SB72, Companion House Bill HB302 as reported in Branch, "DARE to Look," p. 11.
54. William R. Coulson, "Experimental Mysticism, DARE, and the Hollywood 13," *La Jolla Program Newsletter*, 1991 (available from Research Counsel on Ethnopsychology, P.O. Box 134, Comptche, CA 95427).
55. Cited in Branch, "DARE to Look," p. 12.
56. Evaluation and Training Institute, *DARE Evaluation Report for 1985-1989*, p. 3, cited in Dager, "Special Report," p. 4.
57. M. Amos Clifford in *California Prevention Network*, Fall 1989, p. 32.

Chapter 4—Transpersonal Education: The Hidden Agenda
1. Gay Hendricks and Thomas B. Roberts, *The Second Centering Book: More Awareness Activities for Children* (New York: Prentice-Hall, 1977), p. xix.
2. Maureen Murdock, *Spinning Inward: Using Guided Imagery with Children for Learning, Creativity, and Relaxation* (Boston, MA: Shambhala, 1987), p. 14.
3. Marilyn Ferguson, *The Aquarian Conspiracy: Personal and Social Transformation in the 1980s* (Los Angeles: J.P. Tarcher, Inc., 1980), p. 281, emphasis added.
4. Deborah Rozman, *Meditating with Children* (Denver: University of the Trees Press, 1988), p. 130.
5. Ibid., p. 130.
6. Barbara Clark, *Growing Up Gifted*, 3rd ed. (Columbus, OH: Merrill Publishing Co., 1988), p. 601.
7. Jack Canfield, "Education for the New Age," *New Age*, Feb. 1978, p. 36.
8. Annette Hollander, *How to Help Your Child Have a Spiritual Life: A Parent's Guide to Inner Development* (New York: A & W Publishers, 1980), p. 47, emphasis added.
9. Ibid., p. 63.
10. Ibid., p. 64.
11. Gay Hendricks and James Fadiman, *Transpersonal Education*, p. vii.
12. Ibid.
13. Ibid., p. viii.
14. John Dunphy, "A Religion for the New Age," *The Humanist*, Jan.–Feb. 1983.
15. Thomas Sowell, "Ideological Crusaders Battle for Our Kids' Hearts and Minds," *Rocky Mountain News*, Jun. 3, 1992.
16. Dick Sutphen, "Infiltrating the New Age into Society," *What Is*, Summer 1986, p. 14.

Chapter 5—Where Transpersonal Education Is Headed
1. Gay Hendricks and James Fadiman, *Transpersonal Education*, pp. 1-2.
2. Ibid., p. 4.
3. Ibid., p. 10.
4. Ibid.
5. Ibid., p. 12.
6. Ibid., p. 13.
7. Ibid., p. 15.
8. Ibid., p. 17.
9. John Weldon and Zola Levitt, *Psychic Healing: An Exposé of an Occult Phenomenon* (Dallas: Zola Levitt Ministries, 1991), chapters 5–7.
10. Hendricks and Fadiman, *Transpersonal Education*, p. 18.
11. Shapiro and Fitzgerald, "The Development of an Objective Scale to Measure a Transpersonal Orientation to Learning," *Educational and Psychological Measurement*, 1989, vol. 49, p. 375.
12. Phyllis Schlafly (ed.), *Child Abuse in the Classroom* (Westchester, MA: Crossway, 1988), pp. 138-41, 201-02, 235-36, 282, 423.
13. Jack Canfield, *Self-Esteem in the Classroom*, also cited in *Vision* (Pasadena: Christian Educator Association International, Fall 1991). See also *The Inner Classroom: Teaching with Guided Imagery*, 1981, p. 39, and Canfield's ms., "Psychosynthesis in Education: Theory and Application," 1980.
14. "Education in the New Age," *New Age Journal*, Feb. 1978, p. 38. Similar information is found in Note 5.
15. Jack Canfield, *The Inner Classroom: Teaching with Guided Imagery* (Amhurst, MA: Institute for Wholistic Education, 1981), p. 39.
16. Jack Canfield and P. Klimek, "Education for a New Age," *New Age* (Brookline, MA: New Age Communications, Feb. 1978), p. 27.
17. Alice A. Bailey, *The Unfinished Autobiography* (New York: Lucis, 1970), pp. 224-25.
18. All but 4, see Raymond B. Whorf, *The Tibetan's Teaching: An Analysis of the Books of the Tibetan Master Djwhal Khul as Written Down by Alice Bailey* (Ojai, CA: Meditation Groups, n.d.).

19. Canfield and Klimek, "Education," p. 8.
20. Ibid., p. 30.
21. Canfield, *The Inner Classroom*, p. 29.
22. Canfield and Klimek, "Education," p. 32.
23. Stewart Shapiro, "The Development of an Objective Scale to Measure a Transpersonal Orientation to Learning," *Educational and Psychological Measurement*, 1989, pp. 47, 375.
24. Ibid., p. 376.
25. Ibid.
26. Ibid., p. 381.
27. Ibid., p. 377.
28. Ibid., p. 383.
29. Ibid., p. 377.
30. List on file at Watchman Fellowship, received from Dr. Shapiro.
31. Gay Hendricks and Thomas B. Roberts, *The Second Centering Book: More Awareness Activities for Children* (New York: Prentice-Hall, 1977), p. xx.
32. Ibid., pp. xviii, xx.
33. Thomas B. Roberts, "States of Consciousness: A New Intellectual Direction, A New Teacher Education Direction," *Teacher Education*, Mar./Apr. 1985, p. 55.
34. Ibid., pp. 57-58.
35. Barbara Clark, *Growing Up Gifted: Developing the Potential of Children at Home and at School* (Columbus, OH: Merrill Co., 1988), pp. 592-93.
36. Ibid., p. 593.
37. Ibid., pp. 582-83.
38. Jane Roberts, *The Nature of Personal Reality* (a Seth book) (New York: Bantam, 1978), passim.
39. Clark, *Growing Up*, pp. 387-88.
40. Ibid.
41. Available from The Ankerberg Theological Research Institute, P.O. Box 8977, Chattanooga, TN 37411.
42. Clark, *Growing Up*, p. 583.
43. Ibid., pp. 387-410, 576-77, 596.
44. Telephone conversation with Craig Branch and Dr. Carol Schlichter, University of Alabama, Spring 1992.
45. Deborah Rozman, *Meditation for Children* (Boulder Creek, CA: Aslan Publishers, 1989), p. 149.
46. Deborah Rozman, *Meditating with Children: The Art of Concentration and Centering* (Boulder Creek, CA: Aslan Publishers, 1988), title page.
47. Ibid., p. 1.
48. Ibid., p. 130.
49. Ibid., p. 134.
50. Ibid., cf. John Weldon and Zola Levitt, *The Transcendental Explosion* (Dallas: Zola Levitt Ministries, 1991).
51. Rozman, *Meditating with Children*.
52. Ibid., p. 134.
53. Rozman, *Meditation for Children*, 1.
54. Ibid., p. 27.
55. Ibid.
56. Brochure for Jean Houston Workshop, Feb. 13-16, 1992, "The Hero and the Goddess," Holiday Inn, Vanderbilt, Nashville, TN.
57. Jean Houston, *The Possible Human* (Los Angeles: J.P. Tarcher, Inc., 1982), p. 135.
58. Ibid., p. xix.
59. Ibid., p. 200.
60. Ibid., pp. 26-29.
61. Robert Masters and Jean Houston, *Mind Games: The Guide to Inner Space* (New York: Delta, 1981), pp. 5, 13.
62. Ibid., p. 199.
63. Ibid., p. 202.
64. Ibid.
65. Bernie Siegel, *Love, Medicine and Miracles* (New York: Harper & Row, 1986), p. 147-54.
66. Ibid., pp. 18-20.
67. Ibid., pp. 148-50.
68. Ibid., pp. 220-23.
69. Maureen Murdock, *Spinning Inward: Using Guided Imagery with Children for Learning, Creativity and Relaxation* (Boston: Shambhala, 1987), p. 1.
70. Ibid., p. 5.
71. Ibid., p. 137.
72. John Carlson (ed.), "Health, Wellness, and Transpersonal Approaches to Helping," *Elementary School Guidance and Counseling Journal*, vol. 14, no. 2, Dec. 1979.
73. John Carlson, "Guest Editor's Introduction," *Elementary School Guidance and Counseling Journal*, vol. 14, no. 2, Dec. 1979, p. 84.

74. Ibid., pp. 88-90.
75. Ibid., p. 91.
76. Herbert Otto, "The Potential of People," *Elementary School Guidance and Counseling Journal*, vol. 14, no. 2, Dec. 1979, pp. 93-94.
77. Thomas B. Roberts, "Consciousness Counseling: New Roles and New Goals," *Elementary School Guidance and Counseling Journal*, vol. 14, no. 2, Dec. 1979, p. 103.
78. Ibid., p. 105.
79. Ibid., p. 107.
80. Don Dinkmeyer and Don Dinkmeyer, Jr., "Holistic approaches to health," *Elementary School Guidance and Counseling Journal*, vol. 14, no. 2, Dec. 1979, p. 108.
81. Ibid., pp. 109-10.
82. Ibid., p. 109.
83. Beverly Galyean, "Impersonal Approaches to Language Teaching," *Elementary School Guidance and Counseling Journal*, vol. 14, no. 2, Dec. 1979, p. 118.
84. James Fadiman, "Reframing Reality: A Transpersonal Approach," *Elementary School Guidance and Counseling Journal*, vol. 14, no. 2, Dec. 1979, p. 113.
85. Dr. Deane Shapiro, "Self-Control East and West: Duplications for Psychological Health and Personal Growth," *Elementary School Guidance and Counseling Journal*, vol. 14, no. 2, Dec. 1979, p. 125.
86. Ibid., p. 126.
87. Gay Hendricks, "The Transformation of the Frog: Using Centering and Affective Education Materials in Schools," *Elementary School Guidance and Counseling Journal*, vol. 14, no. 2, Dec. 1979, p. 130.
88. Ibid., pp. 131-33.
89. Jack Canfield, Paula Klimek, "Discovering Your Radiant Self: A Transpersonal Approach to Expressing Your Potential," *Elementary School Guidance and Counseling Journal*, vol. 14, no. 2, Dec. 1979, p. 135.
90. Ibid., pp. 136-37.
91. Marianne DeVoe, "Classroom Meetings: An Approach to Transpersonal Education," *Elementary School Guidance and Counseling Journal*, vol. 14, no. 2, Dec. 1979, p. 143.
92. *Enhancing Human Performance: Issues, Theories, and Techniques*, National Research Council, National Academy of Sciences (Washington, DC: National Academy Press, 1988), p. 122, emphasis added.
93. Herbert Benson, M.D., *The Relaxation Response* (New York: Avon Books, 1976), pp. 9, 175.
94. Ibid., pp. 81-86, 107-09, 112-35.
95. In Dionne Marx, "Education: N. [from Latin, *educere*] Drawing Forth That Which Is Within," *Yoga Journal*, Sept./Oct. 1979, p. 15.
96. Ibid., p. 14.
97. J. Krishnamurti, "From Education and the Significance of Life" in Hendricks and Fadiman (eds.), *Transpersonal Education*, p. 30.
98. Marx, "Education: N.," p. 16.
99. Ibid.
100. Ibid., p. 17.
101. Ibid.
102. Ibid.
103. Charles Thomas Cayce, "Aspects of Child Rearing and Education from the Edgar Cayce Readings," *The American Theosophist*, Fall Special Issue, 1976, p. 296.
104. Excerpt from Republican platform of 1992.
105. *Wisconsin* v. *Yoder*, 406 U.S. 205 (1972).
106. The Republican platform of 1992, "The Vision Shared" (Houston: Charles P. Young), p. 20.

Chapter 6—Affective Education and Psychotherapy in the Classroom

1. North Central Alabama, Alabama Mental Health Board, "Directions" (Decatur, AL: PALS: Substance Abuse Prevention Workbook), p. 23, emphasis added.
2. Ibid., p. 20.
3. Ibid., p. 12.
4. Life Education Centre, "Let's Learn to Live Manual" (Elmhurst, IL: Noffs & Association, 1988), p. 18, emphasis added.
5. Michael Schwartz, "Classroom Brainwashing and Other Ills," *Wall Street Journal* (February 12, 1993).
6. Thomas Sowell, Dr., "Indoctrinating the Children," *Forbes* (February 1, 1993), p. 65.
7. Jerry Adler, et al., "Hey, I'm Terrific!" *Newsweek* (February 17, 1992), pp. 47-48.
8. "Protecting Oneself and Others," Teenage Health Teaching Module, p. 33.
9. Ibid., p. 36.
10. Kathleen Gow, *Yes, Virginia, There Is Right and Wrong: What Values Are Our Children Being Taught in the Public Schools?* (Wheaton, IL: Tyndale, 1985), p. 27.
11. *Life Education Centre*, Section Two, p. 15, emphasis added.
12. Adler, et al., "Hey, I'm Terrific!" pp. 47-48.
13. John Leo, "The Trouble with Self Esteem," *U.S. News & World Report*, Apr. 2, 1990, p. 16.
14. Paul Kurtz (ed.), *Humanist Manifesto I & II* (Buffalo, NY: Prometheus Books, 1973), p. 3.
15. Beverly Eakman, *Educating for the New World Order* (Portland, OR: Halcyon House, 1991), p. 81.

16. Selma Wasserman, "Louis E. Raths' Theories of Empowerment," *Childhood Education*, Summer 1991, p. 235.
17. Ibid., p. 236.
18. Ibid.
19. Ibid., p. 238.
20. Abraham Maslow, *Toward a Psychology of Being* (New York: Van Nostrand Reinhold, 1968), pp. III-IV.
21. Marilyn Ferguson, *Aquarian Conspiracy: Personal and Social Transformation in the 1980s* (Los Angeles: J.P. Tarcher, Inc., 1980), p. 420.
22. C.S. Lewis, *Miracles* (New York: Macmillan, 1947), pp. 84-85.
23. Abraham Maslow, *Motivation and Personality*, second ed. (New York: Harper & Row, 1970), p. xx.
24. Chuck Colson, *Against the Night: Living in the New Dark Ages* (Ann Arbor, MI: Servant, 1989), p. 80.
25. Ibid., pp. 79-80, 84.

Chapter 7—Common Practices of Transpersonal Education

1. William Johnston, *Silent Music: The Science of Meditation* (New York: Harper & Row, 1975), p. 26.
2. Daniel Goleman, *The Varieties of the Meditative Experience* (New York: E.P. Dutton, 1977), p. 118.
3. Roger Walsh, Frances Vaughan (eds.), *Beyond Ego: Transpersonal Dimensions in Psychology* (Los Angeles: J.P. Tarcher, 1980), pp. 136-37.
4. Karlis Osis, et al., "Dimensions of the Meditative Experience," *The Journal of Transpersonal Psychology*, vol. 5, no. 2, 1973, p. 121.
5. E.g., see Da Free John, *The Garbage and the Goddess* (Lower Lake, CA: Dawn Horse Press, 1974), pp. 69-100.
6. Swami Rudrananda, *Spiritual Cannibalism* (New York: Quick Fox, 1973), p. 85.
7. Chogyam Trungpa, "An Approach to Meditation," *The Journal of Transpersonal Psychology*, vol. 5, no. 1, 1973, p. 74.
8. Free John, *The Garbage*, p. 76.
9. Gertrude Schmeidler, "The Psychic Personality," *Psychic*, Mar./Apr. 1974, p. 30.
10. Osis, et al., "Dimensions," p. 121.
11. Daniel Goleman, "The Buddha on Meditation and States of Consciousness," in Charles Tart (ed.), *Transpersonal Psychologies* (New York: Harper Colaphon Books, 1977), p. 218.
12. Cited by Stanley Krippner in *Song of the Siren* (San Francisco: Harper & Row, 1975), p. 110.
13. Douglas Shaw, *The Meditators* (Plainfield, NJ: Logos, 1975), p. 98.
14. Os Guiness, *The Dust of Death* (Downers Grove, IL: InterVarsity, 1973), p. 298.
15. Swami Muktananda, *Play of Consciousness* (New York: Harper & Row, 1978), p. 122.
16. Goleman, *Varieties of the Meditative Experience*, p. 106-18.
17. E.g., Jack Kornfield, "Intensive Insight Meditation: A Phenomenological Study," *The Journal of Transpersonal Psychology*, vol. 11, no. 1, 1979.
18. Erika Bourguigon (ed.), *Religion, Altered States of Consciousness and Social Change* (Columbus, OH: Ohio State University Press, 1973), pp. 16-17.
19. John Ferguson, *An Illustrated Encyclopedia of Mysticism and the Mystery Religions* (New York: Seabury Press, 1977), p. 148.
20. Bhagwan Shree Rajneesh, *The Discipline of Transcendence: Discourses on the Forty-Two Sutras of the Buddha*, vol. 2 (Puna, India: Rajneesh Foundation International, 1978), pp. 313-14. For a fuller discussion and documentation, see Tal Brooke, *Riders of the Cosmic Circuit* (Berkeley, CA: Spiritual Counterfeits Project, 1988), pp. 74-208.
21. Bourguignon (ed.), *Religion*, p. 3; cf., 5.
22. J.H. Brennan, *Astral Doorways* (New York: Samuel Wizer, 1972), p. 98.
23. H.V. Guenther, Chogyam Trungpa, *The Dawn of Tantra* (Boston: Shambhala, 1975), p. 49.
24. Alfred Stelter, *Psi-Healing* (New York: Bantam, 1976), p. 41.
25. Jane Roberts, *The Nature of Personal Reality: A Seth Book* (New York: Bantam, 1978), pp. 64-65, 76.
26. Mike Samuels and Hal Bennet, *Spirit Guides: Access to Inner Worlds* (New York: Random House, 1974), passim.
27. David Conway, *Magic: An Occult Primer* (New York: Bantam, 1973), pp. 130-31; cf. chapter 4, "Visualization and the Training of a Magician."
28. A.R.G. Owen in I.M. Owen and M. Sparrow, *Conjuring Up Philip* (New York: Harper & Row, 1976), p. xviii.
29. Robert Masters, Jean Houston, *Mind Games: The Guide to Inner Space* (New York: Dell, 1981), pp. 198, 203.
30. Gopi Krishna, "The True Aim of Yoga," *Psychic*, Jan.-Feb. 1973, p. 15.
31. Swami Ajaya, introduction in Swami Rama, *Lectures on Yoga* (Glenview, IL: Himalayan International Institute of Yoga Science and Philosophy, 1976), rev., p. vi.
32. Ibid., p. 7.
33. David Fetcho, "Yoga" (Berkeley, CA: Spiritual Counterfeits Project, 1978), p. 2.
34. George Feuerstein, Jeanine Miller, *Yoga and Beyond: Essays in Indian Philosophy* (New York: Shocken, 1972), pp. 27-28.
35. Sri Chinmoy, *Great Masters and the Cosmic Gods* (Jamaica, NY: Agni Press, 1977), p. 8.
36. Hans-Ulrich Reiker, *The Yoga of Light: Hatha Yoga Pradipika* (New York: Seabury, 1971), pp. 9, 134.

334

37. Ibid., p. 79.
38. Sri Krishna Prem, *The Yoga of the Bhagavat Gita* (Baltimore: Penguin, 1973), pp. xv, 46; Arthur Avalon, *The Serpent Power: The Secrets of Tantric and Shaktic Yoga* (New York: Dover, 1974), p. 12; Swami Prabhavananda, *Yoga and Mysticism* (Hollywood: Vedanta Press, 1972), pp. 18-19; Reiker, *The Yoga of Light*, pp. 30, 79, 96, 111-12.
39. Krishna, "The True Aim of Yoga," p. 14.
40. Haridas Chadhuri, "The Psychophysiology of Kundalini" in John White (ed.), *Kundalini, Evolution and Enlightenment* (Garden City, NY: Anchor, 1979), p. 62, emphasis added.
41. Krishna, "The True Aim of Yoga," p. 18; cf., Free John, *The Garbage*, pp. 69-100.
42. E.g., John White (ed.), *Kundalini*, pp. 41-44, 62-65, 72-76; and Swami Narayanananda, *The Primal Power in Man or the Kundalini Shakti*, passim; and Da Free John, *The Garbage*, passim.
43. Yogi Amrit Desai, "Kundalini Yoga Through Shaktipat" in White (ed.), *Kundalini*, p. 69.
44. Swami Vishnu Tirtha, "Signs of an Awakened Kundalini," in White (ed.), *Kundalini*, p. 95.
45. Muktananda, *Play of Consciousness*, p. 76.
46. Gerald Jampolsky, "Hypnosis/Active Imagination," in Leslie J. Kaslof, *Wholistic Dimensions in Healing: A Resource Guide* (Garden City, NY: Doubleday, 1978), p. 257.
47. Daniel Goleman, "Hypnosis Comes of Age," *Psychology Today*, Feb. 1977, p. 60.
48. Charles Tart, "Transpersonal Potentialities of Deep Hypnosis," *Journal of Transpersonal Psychology*, vol. 1, no. 2, 1976, p. 30.
49. Ibid., pp. 28-30.
50. Cf., John G. Watkins, Helen H. Watkins, "Hypnosis, Multiple Personality, and Ego States as Altered States of Consciousness" in Benjamine B. Wolman, Montague Ullman (eds.), *Handbook of States of Consciousness* (New York: Van Nostrand Reinhold, 1986), p. 134.
51. Tart, "Transpersonal Potentialities," pp. 34-37.
52. Simeon Edmunds, *Hypnosis: Key to Psychic Powers* (New York: Samuel Weiser, 1978), pp. 39-40.
53. In Robert A. Bradley, "The Need for the Academy of Parapsychology and Medicine," *The Varieties of Healing Experience* (Los Altos, CA: Academy of Parapsychology and Medicine, 1971), pp. 100-101; Jane Roberts, *The Nature of Personal Reality: A Seth Book* (New York: Bantam, 1978), p. 324.
54. As quoted in Margaret Gaddis, "Teachers of Delusion," in Martin Ebon, *The Satan Trap: Dangers of the Occult* (Garden City, NY: Doubleday, 1977), p. 60; cf., p. 59.
55. Nandor Fodor, *An Encyclopedia of Psychic Science* (Secacus, NJ: Citadel, 1974), p. 179.
56. Kurt Koch, *Occult ABC* (Grand Rapids, MI: Kregel, 1980), p. 95.
57. Ibid.

Chapter 8—Psychic Development and Spiritism Through Education

1. Edward Robinson, *The Original Vision: The Study of the Religious Experience of Childhood* (New York: Seabury Press, 1983), p. xiii.
2. Ibid.
3. Ibid.
4. Ibid., p. 6.
5. Ibid., p. 5.
6. Ibid.
7. Johanna Michaelsen, *Like Lambs to the Slaughter: Your Child and the Occult* (Eugene, OR: Harvest House, 1989), p. 12.
8. Marilyn Ferguson, *The Aquarian Conspiracy: Personal and Social Transformation in the 1980s* (Los Angeles: J.P. Tarcher, Inc., 1980), pp. 280-81.
9. Ibid., p. 288.
10. Ibid.
11. Rene Weber, "Compassion, Rootedness and Detachment: Their Role in Healing: A Conversation with Dora Kunz" in Dora Kunz, compiler, *Spiritual Aspects of the Healing Arts* (Wheaton, IL: Theosophical Publishing House, 1984), p. 289.
12. Dio Neff, "Taoist Esoteric Yoga with Mantak Chia," *Yoga Journal*, Mar./Apr. 1986, p. 42.
13. Thomas Armstrong, "Transpersonal Experience in Childhood," *The Journal of Transpersonal Psychology*, vol. 16, no. 2, 1984, p. 210; cf., the editors of *Psychic, Psychics: Indepth Interviews* (New York: Harper & Row, 1972), passim, and John Weldon, *Psychic Healing: An Exposé of an Occult Phenomenon* (Dallas: Zola Levitt Ministries, 1991).
14. Geoffrey Hodson, *The Miracle of Birth: A Clairvoyant Study of a Human Embryo* (Wheaton, IL: Theosophical Publishing House, 1981), p. 98.
15. Armstrong, "Transpersonal Experience in Childhood," p. 222.
16. Ibid.
17. Ibid., p. 225.
18. Stanley Krippner, "Creativity in Psychic Phenomena," *Gifted Child Quarterly*, vol. 7 (1963), p. 51-61; Stanley Krippner, R. Dreistadt, C.C. Hubbard, "The Creative Person and Non-Ordinary Reality," *Gifted Child Quarterly* (in press); cf., M.L. Anderson, "The Relations of PSI to Creativity," *Journal of Parapsychology*, vol. 26 (1962), pp. 277-92; G. Murphy, "Research and Creativeness: What Does It Tell Us About Extrasensory Perception?" *Journal of the American Society for Psychical Research*, vol. 60 (1966).
19. James W. Peterson, "Extrasensory Abilities of Children: An Ignored Reality?" *Learning: The Magazine for Creative Teaching*, Dec. 1975, p. 13.

20. Phyllis Gilbert, "Psychic Children," *Psychic*, Nov./Dec. 1975, p. 19.
21. Annette Hollander, *How to Help Your Child Have a Spiritual Life* (New York: A & W Publishers, 1980), p. 36.
22. Ibid., p. 37.
23. Joseph Chilton Pearce, *Magical Child: Rediscovering Nature's Plan for Our Children* (New York: Bantam, 1986), p. 217.
24. Laeh Maggie Garfield and Jack Grant, *Companions in Spirit: A Guide to Working with Your Spirit Helpers* (Berkeley, CA: Celestial Arts, 1984), p. 116.
25. Ibid., p. 98.
26. Ibid., p. 96.
27. Ibid., p. 52.
28. Ibid., p. 44-45.
29. Jean Porter, "Psychic Development" in Gay Hendricks and James Fadiman, *Transpersonal Education: A Curriculum for Feeling and Being* (Englewood Cliffs, NJ: Prentice-Hall, 1976), pp. 77-78.
30. Ibid., p. 81.
31. Ibid., p. 82.
32. Thomas Armstrong, "Children As Healers," *Somatics*, Autumn/Winter 1984-85, p. 16.
33. Ibid., p. 18.
34. Ibid.
35. Ibid., pp. 18-19.
36. For a critique of *A Course in Miracles* see Ankerberg and Weldon, *Can You Trust Your Doctor?* chapter 12.
37. Joseph Chilton Pearce, "Freeing the Mind of the Magical Child," *New Age*, Oct. 1976, pp. 23-25.
38. Jan Ehrenwald, "The Occult," *Today's Education*, Sep. 1991, pp. 28-30.
39. Sylvia Z. Ramirez, "The Effects of Suggestopedia in Teaching English Vocabulary to Spanish-Dominant Chicano Third Graders," *The Elementary School Journal*, Jan. 1986, p. 326.
40. Sheila Ostrander, Lynn Schroeder, Nancy Ostrander, "Super Learning: The Miraculous Mind-Body Approach," *New Age*, Sep. 1979, p. 28.
41. Ibid., pp. 29-30.
42. This is a conservative figure based on adult occult involvement; cf. Kurt Koch, *Occult Bondage and Deliverance* (Grand Rapids, MI: Kregel, 1972).
43. James W. Peterson, *The Secret Life of Kids: An Exploration into Their Psychic Senses* (Wheaton, IL: Quest, 1987), foreword, p. xi.
44. Ibid., p. 205.
45. Ibid., p. 207.
46. Ibid., pp. 211-12.
47. Ibid., p. 213.
48. Ibid., p. 214.
49. Ibid., p. 215.
50. Ibid.
51. Ibid., p. 216.
52. Ibid., p. 217ff.
53. Ibid., pp. 217-18.
54. Ibid., p. 220.
55. Frances Vaughan Clark, "Rediscovering Transpersonal Education," *The Journal of Transpersonal Psychology*, no. 1, 1974, pp. 1, 3-4, 7.
56. Ibid., p. 6.
57. Ibid., pp. 1, 4-5.
58. Hugh Redmond, "A Pioneer Program in Transpersonal Education," *The Journal of Transpersonal Psychology*, no. 1, 1974, p. 9.
59. Ibid.
60. Ibid., p. 10.
61. Ibid., p. 9.

Chapter 9—Legal Issues, Malpractice Options, and Scientific Evidence

1. John W. Whitehead, *The Rights of Religious Persons in Public Education* (Wheaton, IL: Crossway Books, 1991), p. 19.
2. Ibid.
3. Ibid., p. 147.
4. Ibid.
5. *Pierce* v. *Massachusetts*, 1944.
6. *Abington* v. *Schempp*, 1963.
7. *Wisconsin* v. *Yoder*, 1972.
8. *Stanley* v. *Illinois*, 1972.
9. *Mercer* v. *Michigan*, 1974.
10. In Benjamin Sendor, "When It Comes to Teaching About Religion, Sound Policy Should Be Your Bible," *American School Board Journal*, Aug. 1989, p. 8.
11. Ibid., p. 11.

336

12. *Roberts* v. *Madigan*, 921 R.2d 1047 (10th Cir. 1991) *cert. denied*, 60 U.S.L.W. 3876 (Jun. 29, 1992).
13. Sendor, "When It Comes," p. 11.
14. EEOC notice N—915, Feb. 22, 1988, "EEOC's Policy Statement on Training Programs Conflicting with Employees' Religious Beliefs."
15. See p. 29.
16. A copy of this is available from Watchman Fellowship, Birmingham, AL, emphasis added.
17. Ibid.
18. Ibid., emphasis added.
19. Phyllis Schlafly Report, Nov. 1990, pp. 2-3 (available from Box 618, Alton, IL 62002, used with permission).
20. For professional educators, refer to studies in one of their own professional journals, *Elementary School Guidance and Counseling Journal*, "Imagery in Counseling" (Oct. 1987, p. 5); "Imagery: Painting of the Mind" (Dec. 1986, p. 150); "Discipline: Can It Be Improved with Relaxation Training?" (Feb. 1986, p. 194); "The Effects of the Relaxation Response on Self-Concept and Acting Our Behaviors" (Apr. 1986, p. 255); "Relaxation Training with Intermediate Grade Students" (Apr. 1977, p. 259), and many more.
21. In "Meditation As an Access to Altered States of Consciousness," Patricia Carrington of Princeton University points out that while meditation and hypnosis have different characteristics, "It is possible that in the broadest sense of the term, meditation is a form of hypnosis" (in B.B. Wolman and M. Ullman, *Handbook of Altered States of Consciousness*, p. 496).
22. Martin Orne, "Hypnosis," *Encyclopedia Britannica*, vol. 9, pp. 133-40.
23. Martin Orne, on WWBT-TV12, "What Did Your Child Learn in School Today?" four-part video series (Richmond, VA: Nov. 7-9, 1990).
24. Charles W. Hanes, Thomas H. Hohenshil, "Elementary School Guidance and Counselors, School Psychologists, School Social Workers: Who Does What?" *Elementary School Guidance and Counseling Journal*, Oct. 1987, pp. 40-41.
25. Statement by Ross S. Olson, "Primary Learning Center," np. nd.
26. Ibid., statement in "Can Students Visualize Diseases Away?"
27. Ron F. Anderson, "Using Guided Fantasy with Children," *Elementary School Guidance and Counseling Journal*, Oct. 1980, p. 46.
28. Robert Day and Robert Griffin, "Children's Attitudes Toward the Magic Circle," *Elementary School Guidance and Counseling Journal*, Dec. 1980, pp. 137-45.
29. National Research Council, *Enhancing Human Performance: Issues, Theories and Techniques*, Committee on Techniques for the Enhancement of Human Performance (Washington, D.C.: National Academy Press, 1988), pp. 16-23; cf. *In the Mind's Eye: Enhancing Human Performance* (Part II), pp. 12-17.
30. Ibid.
31. Charles Heikkinen, "Reorientation from Altered States: Please Move Carefully," *Journal of Counseling and Development*, May 1989, pp. 520-21.
32. *TM-EX Bulletin*, a Partial Research Review, reprints available from TM-EX, P.O. Box 7565, Arlington, VA 22207 (202-728-7580).
33. Margaret Singer and Richard Ofshe, "Thought Reform Programs and the Production of Psychiatric Casualties," *Psychiatric Annals*, Apr. 1990, pp. 190, 193.
34. Heide and Borkovec, *Consulting in Clinical Psychology*, 1983, pp. 171-82; Heide and Borkovec, *Behavioral Research Therapy Journal*, 1984, pp. 1-12.
35. Arnold Lazarus, *Psychological Reports*, 1976, pp. 601-60.
36. Leon Otis, *Meditation, Classic and Contemporary Perspectives*, Alden, 1984, p. 204.
37. David Holmes, "Meditation and Somatic Arousal Reductions," *American Psychologist*, Jan. 1984, pp. 1-10, cf. Jun. 1985, pp. 717-31; Jun. 1986, pp. 712-13; Sep. 1986, pp. 1007-09; Sep. 1987, pp. 879-81.
38. Susan Black, "Self-Esteem: Sense and NonSense," *American School Board Journal*, Jul. 1991, pp. 27-29.
39. Ibid.
40. Ibid.
41. *U.S. News & World Report*, Apr. 1, 1990, p. 16.
42. Ibid.
43. Ibid.
44. Ibid.
45. *Newsweek*, cover article, Feb. 17, 1992, pp. 46-47.
46. Ibid., p. 48.
47. Ibid.
48. Susan Black, "Research says . . . ," *The American Schoolboard Journal*, Mar. 1992, pp. 26-28.
49. Ibid.
50. Ibid.
51. Ibid.; cf. Kathryn Koch, "Self-Esteem: 'Earned' Vs. 'New Age'—A Comparison," *Vision*, Spring and Fall 1991.
52. Richard Blum, "Drug Education: Further Results and Recommendations," *Journal of Drug Issues*, Fall 1978, pp. 379-80.

53. Michael Klitzner, "Report to Congress on the Nature and Effectiveness of Federal, State and Local Prevention/Education Programs," prepared for the U.S. Department of Education by the Center for Advanced Health Studies, p. 10.
54. William Hansen, et al., "Affective and Social Influence Approaches to the Prevention of Multiple Substance Abuse Among Seventh Grade Students—Results from Project SMART," *Preventive Medicine*, vol. 17, 1988, pp. 135, 151, emphasis added.
55. J. Stout, F. Rivara, "Schools and Sex Education: Does It Work?" *Pediatrics*, Mar. 1989, pp. 375, 378.
56. *Family Planning Perspectives*, Jul./Aug. 1986.
57. William Strein, "Classroom-Based Elementary School Affective Education Programs: A Critical Review," *Psychology in the Schools*, Jul. 1988, pp. 288, 294.
58. Ibid., emphasis added.
59. Richard R. Clayton, "Sensation Seeking As a Potential Mediating Variable for School-Based Prevention Intervention: A Two-Year Follow-up of DARE," *Journal of Health Communication*, vol. 4, 1991.
60. The Research Counsel on Ethnopsychology, *La Jolla Program Newsletter*, Aug. 1991.
61. Ibid.
62. Ibid., p. 2.
63. Ibid., pp. 2-3.
64. Ibid.
65. Statement from Research Counsel on Ethnopsychology, p. 204, Oriole St., San Diego, CA 92114 (619-262-5752).

Chapter 10—Overcoming Objections and Other Responses

1. *Phi Delta Kappan*, Jan. 1991, pp. 359-60, emphasis added.
2. Howard Kirschenbaum, *Elementary School Guidance and Counseling Journal*, Oct. 1982, p. 37.
3. Ibid., p. 38, emphasis added.
4. Ibid., emphasis added.
5. See Resource List, p. 319.
6. In the *Opelika—Auburn News*, "State Superintendent Warns Teachers of Future Battles," Mar. 2, 1982, p. 1.
7. Video on file with Watchman Fellowship.
8. Cited in "The Freedom to Read," *American Library Association*, Jan. 28, 1972, p. 3.
9. Michael Bundy and Thomas LaRue, "New Rights Censorship: An Awareness and Action Plan for Counselors," *Elementary School and Guidance Counseling Journal*, Oct. 1982, pp. 28-33, emphasis added.
10. American School Counselor Association position statement, "The School Counselor and Censorship," adopted 1985.
11. "Did the Founding Fathers Intend to Establish America as a Christian Nation?" "The John Ankerberg Show," series one and two (Chattanooga, TN: The Ankerberg Theological Research Institute, 1992).
12. National Education Association, Jul. 1991 and annual conference.
13. Melissa Etlin, *NEA Today*, Apr. 1992, p. 6.
14. Cited in *Birmingham Post Herald*, Aug. 28, 1991.
15. *Attacks on the Freedom to Learn*, People for the American Way (Washington DC, 1992).
16. Ibid., p. 9.
17. Ibid.
18. Phyllis Schlafly Report, Aug. 1990, p. 1

Chapter 11—What Are Parents and Educators to Do?

1. Howard Kirschenbaum, "The Rights of the School Community," *Elementary School Guidance and Counseling Journal*, Oct. 1982, p. 38.
2. Write Watchman Fellowship or Eagle Forum (see Resource List).
3. Pearl Evans, *Hidden Danger in the Classroom*, p. 77.

Chapter 12—"Education: Capturing Hearts and Minds"

1. Rick Branch, *Watchman Expositor*, vol. 8, no. 9, 1991, p. 11.
2. Eackman, *Educating for a New World Order* (Portland: Halcyon House, 1991), p. 12-13.
3. Marilyn Ferguson, *The Aquarian Conspiracy: Personal and Social Transformation in the 1980s* (Los Angeles: J.P. Tarcher, 1980), p. 283.
4. Francis Adeney, "Educators Look East," *SCP Journal*, vol. 5, no. 1, 1981, p. 29.
5. The Society for Accelerated Learning, "New Dimensions in Education—Confluent Learning," San Francisco, Apr. 25, 1980.
6. Connecticut Citizens for Constitutional Education, Jan. 22, 1980.
7. Jack Canfield and Paula Klimek, "Education in the New Age," *The New Age Journal*, Feb. 1978, p. 27.
8. Ibid., p. 27.
9. Ibid., p. 28.
10. Ibid., p. 28.
11. Ibid., p. 30.

338

12. Ibid., p. 36.
13. Ibid., p. 36.
14. Ibid., p. 39.
15. Ibid., p. 39.
16. Ibid.

Chapter 13—"A Psychiatrist's Perspective"
1. "Changing Social Structure Taking Toll on Children," *Clinical Psychiatry News*, Feb. 1991.
2. Associated Press by George W. Cornell, Aug. 29, 1992, cited in *Decatur Daily*.
3. Kohlberg and Gilligan, 1973.
4. Melvin D. Levine, M.D., William B. Carey, M.D., Allen C. Crocker, M.D., *Developmental-Behavioral Pediatrics* (W.B. Saunders Company, second edition, 1992), pp. 68-69.
5. "School-Based Suicide Prevention Programs Held Ineffective, Risky," *Clinical Psychiatry News*, Apr. 1991.
6. Susan Black, "Self-Esteem: Sense and NonSense," *American School Board Journal*, Jul. 1991.
7. *Encyclopedia Britannica*, 15th ed., 1980.
8. Teacher's Manual of "Pumsy: In Pursuit of Excellence."
9. Abraham Maslow, *Motivation and Personality* (New York: Harper & Row, 1970), p. xx.

Chapter 14—"Abolished Man"
1. C.S. Lewis, *The Abolition of Man* (New York: Macmillan, 1947), reprint ed.
2. James Houston, "Faith on the Line" interview, *SCP Journal*, 1988, vol. 8, no. 1, p. 13.
3. Lewis, *Abolition*, pp. 77-79.
4. Kenneth A. Myers, *All God's Children and Blue Suede Shoes: Christians and Popular Culture* (Westchester, IL: Crossway Books, 1989), p. 176.
5. Norman Mailer, "The White Negro: Superficial Reflections on the Hipster," *Advertisements for Myself* (New York: G.P. Putnam's Sons, 1959), p. 345.
6. Lewis, *Abolition*, pp. 72-73.
7. Ibid., p. 39.
8. *Education Reporter*, Feb. 1991.
9. Holly Brough, "Environmental Studies: Is It Academic?" *World Watch*, Jan./Feb. 1992, p. 26.
10. Thomas Harvey Holt, "Growing Up Green: The ABC's of Environmental Activism," *Reason*, Oct. 1991, vol. 23, no. 5, p. 37.
11. "John Doe" (aka John Kenneth Galbraith), *Report from Iron Mountain on the Possibility and Desirability of Peace* (New York: Dial Press, 1967), pp. 66-67.
12. Norman Lear, "Nurturing Spirituality and Religion in an Age of Science and Technology," *New Oxford Review*, Apr. 1990, p. 10.
13. Ibid., p. 17.
14. Holt, "Growing Up Green," p. 38.
15. Dave Wampler (admin. coord.), "The Institute for Earth Education," personal correspondence (letter on file), 1991.
16. *Earthkeepers Teacher Preparation Packet* (Warrenville, IL: Institute for Earth Education, 1987), pp. 2-3.
17. Holt, "Growing Up Green," p. 38.
18. Ibid., p. 39.
19. Louise Derman-Sparks and the A.B.C. Task Force, *Anti-Bias Curriculum: Tools for Empowering Young Children* (Washington, DC: National Association for the Education of Young People, 1989).
20. Ibid., p. 8.
21. *SCP Journal*, 1991, vol. 16, no. 3.
22. Derman-Sparks, *Anti-Bias Curriculum*, p. 90.
23. Ibid., pp. 90-91.
24. Ibid., p. 77.

Chapter 15—"Sex, Drugs, and Schoolchildren"
1. Apr. 30, 1991. Cassette tape available from R.B. Media, Inc., 154 Doral, Springfield, IL 62704. Quoted with permission of Pat Funderburk.
2. Ben Sprunger and Daniel Pellaux, "Skills for Adolescence: Experience with the International Lions-Quest Program," *Crisis* vol. 10, no. 1, 1989, pp. 88-104.
3. A.H. Maslow, *Motivation and Personality*, second ed. (New York: Harper & Row, 1970), p. ix.
4. Ibid., p. 237.
5. Richard J. Lowry (ed.), *The Journals of A.H. Maslow* (Monterey, CA: Brooks/Cole, 1979), p. 1195. For Maslow's belief that "fighting back" against misinterpretations of his theories had become necessary, see p. 1168. For his remarks on "unearned applause," see pp. 1056-1058. For a list of institutions that he judged belonged to the Eupsychian Network (originally his term for psychologically healthy environments, but later a cause of concern to him), see "Addendum: The Eupsychian Network," in A.H. Maslow, *Toward a Psychology of Being*, second ed. (Princeton, NJ: Van Nostrand, 1968), pp. 237-40.
6. From *Skills for Living* and *Skills for Adolescence* (Granville, OH: Quest International, 1982 and 1986).

7. "Carl Rogers on Encounter Groups" (New York: Harper & Row, 1970).
8. Carl R. Rogers, "Freedom from Isolation," editorial comment in *The Humanist*, Jan./Feb. 1969, p. 1.
9. For his (and this author's) anticipation of the problem of moral fallout, see Carl R. Rogers and W.R. Coulson, "Educational Innovation Project" (La Jolla, CA: Western Behavioral Sciences Institute, Apr. 1968).
10. There isn't space to go into cases here, but readers can catch a hint of what went wrong in comments made by Rogers in recapitulating a key case study in one of the last articles he wrote before his death. (Carl R. Rogers, "Comment on Shlien's Article 'A Countertheory of Transference,'" *Person-Centered Review*, vol. 2, no. 2), May 1987 [posthumous], pp. 182-88.) He republished the case from his *Client-Centered Therapy* (Boston: Houghton Mifflin, 1951) and added the note that "the therapist . . . states his unwillingness (on ethical grounds) to engage in sex . . ." (p. 187). What this reference to ethics means is that any claim by a therapist to have chosen to have sex in therapy—or for his client to have chosen it—must be rejected. The State of California agreed with Rogers and, two years after the publication of his article, passed a law making therapist-client sex a felony. An epidemic of sexual misconduct had broken out among California therapists in the mid-1980s, and the most prominent and scandalous case had involved a group of 13 self-identified client-centered therapists. See Carol Lynn Mithers, "When Therapists Drive Their Patients Crazy," *California* magazine, Aug. 1988, pp. 76-85, 135-36.
11. Granville, OH, Quest International, 1986, p. 21.
12. W.R. Coulson. "Helping Youth Decide: 'When the fox preaches, beware the geese,'" *New York State Journal of Medicine*, vol. 85, Jul. 1985, pp. 357-58.

Appendix A—Anthroposophical Education
1. Rudolf Steiner, *The Gospel of St. John* (Spring Valley, NY: The Anthroposophic Press, 1973), p. 177.
2. H. Barnes, J. Fell, and N. Aniston, "Anthroposophy," n.p., 1978.
3. Floyd McKnight, *Rudolf Steiner and Anthroposophy* (New York: Anthroposophical Society in America, 1977), p. 12.
4. Robert S. Elwood, *Religious and Spiritual Groups in Modern America* (Englewood Cliffs, NJ: Prentice-Hall, 1973), p. 107.
5. Paul M. Allen (ed.), *Rudolf Steiner: An Autobiography*, Rita Stebbing (trans.) (Blauvelt, NY: Rudolf Steiner Publications, 1977), p. 426.
6. Rudolf Steiner, *Building Stones for an Understanding of the Mystery of Golgotha* (London: Rudolf Steiner Press, 1972), p. 18.
7. Rudolf Steiner, *Christianity and Occult Mysteries of Antiquity* (Blauvelt, NY: Steinerbooks, 1977), p. 22.
8. Rudolf Steiner, *An Outline of Occult Science* (Spring Valley, NY: Anthroposophic Press, 1979), p. 380.
9. Steiner, *Building Stones*, pp. 232-33, emphasis added.
10. Rudolf Steiner, "Occult Science and Occult Development" and "Christ at the Time of the Mystery of Golgotha and Christ in the 20th Century" (two lectures) (London: Rudolf Steiner Press, 1972), p. 3.
11. Rudolf Steiner, "How We Can Help Our Dead," *The Christian Community Journal*, vol. 7, 1953, p. 48; Rudolf Steiner, lecture, "The Dead Are with Us," London, 1945.
12. Rudolf Steiner, "The Relationship Between the Living and the Dead," *Journal for Anthroposophy*, Autumn 1978, p. 35.
13. In Kurt Koch, *Satan's Devices* (Grand Rapids, MI: Kregel, 1980), p. 256.
14. Victor H. Ernest, *I Talked with Spirits* (Wheaton, IL: Tyndale, 1971); Raphael Gasson, *The Challenging Counterfeit* (Plainfield, NJ: Logos, 1970).
15. Gasson, *Challenging Counterfeit*, p. 125.
16. Ibid., p. 36.
17. Ibid., p. 83.
18. Steiner, "Occult Science" and "Christ at the Time," pp. 19-20.
19. Ibid., p. 8.
20. "Scientific Seer: Rudolf Steiner," *MD*, Feb. 1979, report., p. 250.
21. Francis Edmunds, *Rudolf Steiner Education: The Waldorf Schools* (London: Rudolf Steiner Press, 1979), p. 12.
22. Samuel Pfeifer, *Healing At Any Price?* (Milton Keynes, England: Word Limited, 1988), p. 119.
23. Earl J. Ogletree, "Rudolf Steiner: Unknown Educator," *Elementary School Journal*, Mar. 1974, pp. 344, 347, 350; cf., Rudolf Steiner, *The Essentials of Education*, *Practical Course for Teachers* and *Education and Modern Spiritual Life*.
24. Stephen Davis, "The Life and Times of Rudolf Steiner," *New Age*, Feb. 1978, p. 41.
25. Ibid., Part II, Mar. 1978, p. 56.
26. Ibid.
27. Ibid., pp. 56-57.
28. Rudolf Steiner, *Education As an Art*, p. 21.
29. Ibid.
30. Ibid.
31. Ibid., p. 61.
32. Ibid., p. 23.
33. Ibid., p. 24.

34. Ibid.
35. Ibid., p. 26.
36. Ibid., p. 27-28.
37. Ibid., p. 73.
38. Ibid., p. 74.
39. Nora Vaughan Baditz, "The Needs of Young Children: A Guide for Parents and Teachers," Ibid., p. 108.
40. Geoffrey Ahern, *Sun at Midnight: The Rudolf Steiner Movement and the Western Esoteric Tradition* (Wellingsborough, Northamptonshire: The Aquariam Press, 1984), pp. 62-63.
41. Edmunds, *Rudolf Steiner Education*, pp. 109-11.
42. Ibid., pp. 15-17; cf., pp. 75-76.
43. Ibid., p. 122.
44. Ibid., p. 32.
45. Ibid., p. 88.
46. Ibid., pp. 110, 123.

Appendix B—Montessori Education

1. Elizabeth G. Hainstock, *The Essential Montessori: An Introduction to the Woman, the Writings, the Method, and the Movement* (New York: New American Library, 1978), pp. 1-2.
2. Ibid., pp. 14-15.
3. Ibid., pp. 21-22; on the Hindu approach to education see K. Sankara Menon, "The Eternal Educational Concepts in the Light of Indian Thought and Culture," *The American Theosophist*, Fall special issue, 1976, pp. 309-12.
4. Maria Montessori, *Education for a New World* (Thiruvanmiyur Madras, India: Kalakshetra Publications, 1969), pp. 1-2.
5. Ibid., p. 2.
6. Ibid., pp. 52-53.
7. Maria Montessori, *To Educate the Human Potential* (Thiruvanmiyur Madras, India: Kalakshetra Publications, 1973), p. 12.
8. Montessori, *Education for a New World*, p. 86.
9. Montessori, *To Educate the Human Potential*, p. 15.
10. Ibid., p. 2.
11. Ibid., p. 10.
12. The first quote is by Montessori teacher Joyce McDavid, "The Emergence of Life," *The American Theosophist*, Nov. 1976, p. 307, citing Maria Montessori; the second quote is from Montessori, *To Educate the Human Potential*, p. 82.
13. Ursula Thrush (lecture notes), *Cosmic Education According to Maria Montessori*, course lecture notes distributed at the course *The Montessori Method: An Holistic Approach to Education*, x304.17, education extension, University of California-Berkeley, 1977, p. 105. Published by the Maria Montessori School of the Golden Gate, San Francisco, CA.
14. Ibid.
15. Maria Montessori, qv., *Encyclopedia Britannica Micropaedia*, vol. 6, p. 1020.
16. Joyce McDavid, "The Emergence of Life," *The American Theosophist*, Fall special issue, 1976, p. 305.
17. Ibid., p. 307.
18. James W. Peterson, "Psychic and Philosophical Perception in the World of Children," *The American Theosophist*, Fall special issue, 1976, p. 313.
19. Ibid., p. 312.
20. Mary Jo Lewis, "Not Too Young for Yoga," *Yoga Journal*, Nov./Dec. 1984, p. 32.
21. Thrush, *Cosmic Education*, p. 4.
22. Ibid., p. 5.
23. Ibid., p. 27.
24. Ibid., p. 27-28.
25. Ibid., p. 105.
26. Ibid., p. 143.

Glossary

1. The introduction to an article by biofeedback/consciousness researchers Kenneth Pelletier and Erik Peper notes that, "Biofeedback has been called the yoga of the West, because it combines Western hardware with Eastern techniques for altering states of consciousness. Pelletier and Peper . . . present an account of remarkable phenomena and point to ways in which children might be trained to be masters of their bodies" (Kenneth Pelletier and Erik Peper, "The *Chutzpah* Factor in the Psychopsysiology of Altered States of Consciousness," in Hendricks and Fadiman (eds.), *Transpersonal Education*, p. 86.

   The influence of biofeedback programs among children can be seen in the literature e.g., Linda B. Zaichkowski, et al., "Biofeedback-Assisted Relaxation Training in the Elementary Classroom," *Elementary School Guidance and Counseling Journal*, Apr. 1986; John P. Masterson, Jr., William B. Turley, "Biofeedback Training with Children, *American Journal of Clinical Biofeedback*, Fall/Winter 1980;

W.J. Hampstead, "The Effects of EMG-Assisted Relaxation Training with Hyperkenetic Children: A Behavioral Alternative," *Biofeedback and Self Regulation*, vol. 4, no. 2, 1979; cf. article references).

What's disconcerting is many biofeedback researchers' use of occultists and spiritists such as Swami Rama as examples of what anyone can do through the powers of the mind which become "self-regulated" by biofeedback. The fact remains that the kind of feats they discuss are only accomplished in states of consciousness long associated with pagan religion, occultism, and spiritism. It would appear then that biofeedback states of consciousness can make one receptive to the same spiritual phenomena experienced by occultists because it places one in a similar mental state. Thus, "In many ways research with these adepts changed our belief structure of what is possible in self-control and self-healing and has helped to extend the parameters and possibilities of biofeedback training" (Pelletier and Peper, "The *Chutzpah* Factor," p. 89).

2. John Weldon, *Dreamwork*, ms.
3. Patricia Pirmantgen, "What Would Happen to the American Psyche If, Along with Homerooms, Flag-Saluting and I.Q. Testing, Schools Had Daily Dream Sharing?" in Hendricks and Fadiman (eds.), *Transpersonal Education*, p. 49.
4. Richard Meznarich, Robert Habes, and Claudia Binter, "How Three Teachers Use Fantasy Journeys" in Hendricks and Fadiman, *Transpersonal Education*, p. 76.
5. Frances Vaughan Clark, "Learning Through Fantasy" in Hendricks and Fadiman (eds.), *Transpersonal Education*, p. 67.
6. Barbara Hannah, *Encounters with the Soul: Active Imagination as Developed by C.G. Jung* (Boston: Sigo Press, 1981), pp. 6-7, 11-12.
7. John Weldom, *Dreamwork*, ms.
8. Ibid.
9. Robert Habes, "How Three Teachers" in Hendricks and Fadiman (eds.)., *Transpersonal Education*, p. 76.
10. Promotional brochure.
11. Marilyn Howell, "Somatic Education in Public School," *Somatics*, Spring/Summer 1982, p. 35; cf. Thomas Hanna, "Somatic Education: A Scenario of the Future," *Somatics*, Spring/Summer 1984.

Select Index

ABOUT THE AUTHORS

John Ankerberg is host of the nationally televised, award-winning "The John Ankerberg Show." He speaks internationally and has master's degrees in divinity and the history of the church and Christian thought and the D.Min. degree from Luther Rice Seminary.

John Weldon has authored and co-authored numerous books on the cults and occult, and has master's degrees in divinity and Christian apologetics, and a doctorate in comparative religion.

Craig Branch is the southeast director of Watchman Fellowship, a nationally known and respected cult ministry. He speaks and writes extensively on the New Age Movement in education.

OTHER BOOKS BY
JOHN ANKERBERG AND
JOHN WELDON